Even Odds

Clear Lake Quartet Series Book 2

Miah Onsha

Book Cover: Zuchal Rosyidin from Kamaji Studio

Editing: Tracy Pope

Proofreading: Rachel Bunner (@rachels.top.edits)

ISBN: 979-8-9907088-1-5

ASIN: B0F55JK8RM

First Edition: October 2025

CONTENT WARNINGS

Your mental health is very important to me. Before reading Even Odds, please be aware of the warnings and topics. This book is considered 18+ for its explicit content. It contains graphic sexual content, emotional abuse and manipulation by a trusted authority figure (former agent, on page), sexism in the workplace (on page), anxiety and counseling (on page), baseball-related injuries and rehabilitation (on page).

Playlist

Beanie — Chezile

I Know What They're Thinking — Amahla

Talk To You — Ricky Montgomery

Love Me Like You Used To — Lord Huron

Cool Again — Shoffy

Feels Like We Only Go Backwards — Tame Impala

OUTTA MY MIND — Monsune

Just Stay For Once — Imani Graham

The Dress — Dijon

Trouble Sleeping — Corinne Bailey Rae

If You Were the Rain— Stephen Day

Take Me Where Your Heart Is — Q

Boys Don't Cry — Lily Agnes

I Think I Love You Again — Aaron Taylor

Kiss Her You Fool — Kids That Fly

Turning Page — Sleeping At Last

4EVER — Clairo

Stone — Alessia Cara

Ne Me Quitte Pas (Don't Leave Me) — Orion Sun

Sparks — Coldplay

Swimming in the Moonlight — Bad Suns

It Isn't Perfect But It Might Be — Olivia Dean

So My Darling — Rachel Chinouriri

Vienna — Billy Joel

Right Here — Becky Hill

Home — Bruno Major

You're Still The One — Teddy Swims

To those learning that you don't have to earn your place here—not by
fixing, pleasing, proving, or doing.
Just being is enough. It always will be.

CHAPTER ONE

Shay

I SHOULD HAVE SKIPPED graduation. Sure, you only get your MBA once, but this is my chance to prove myself.

A gust of the warm May breeze smacks my cheeks as I dart between luxury cars. My sensible two-inch heels don't snap as I sprint toward the stadium entrance, and I thank years of soccer for strong ankles.

Joyful screams of spectators pierce the night sky, which is my favorite part about the retractable roof being left open for home games at Pilot City Stadium.

"Hi," I rasp, draping the lavender badge around my neck. "Agent."

The burly guard in a navy uniform gives me a slow once-over. I probably look like I'm headed to a dance in my pink dress, the one I wore under my graduation gown as I walked across the stage an hour ago, but my name tag and the diploma in my passenger seat prove I'm meant to be here as an agent. Not as a girlfriend, a wife, or a fangirl.

Even if that surprises men.

After inspecting my badge for what feels like eons, he grins. "Little late, don't you think?"

It's not my fault the commencement speaker droned on or that Turner is near the end of the alphabet. Either way, being late is not professional, and my stress spikes at the reminder.

With a glare, I slip past him and jog down the hallway. Pilot City Stadium, home of the Carolina Pilots, is breathtaking. The walls are a gleaming white with navy and shiny gold accents, much like the uniforms they wear for home games. As much as I love the Pilots, and have for years, I'm not here to watch the home team.

I'm here for Garrett Blane, the Virginia Jackals' first baseman.

Garrett isn't a client a junior agent would usually be tasked with signing, but my supervisor approved my request. I mean, Trevor laughed when he heard my lofty goal, but I got a halfhearted thumbs-up, so here I am.

After sending thousands of cold emails and social media direct messages, the awkwardness and hesitancy faded. I learned to press send and forget about it, distracting myself with something else. Coming back from a bubble bath to an email from Garrett agreeing to meet me after tonight's game felt like a victory.

If tonight doesn't go my way, it'll be just another no I've gotten in my pursuit of being a sports agent. The first was when I told my undergraduate advisor about my career aspirations. He swore he didn't believe in gender roles but recommended something more "feminine" like public relations or marketing.

Yes, he used air quotes.

Then the reminders I wasn't one of them kept coming. Guys huffed when I entered the classroom with my pink pom-pen. Suggestive snickers fill the boardroom when I discuss my male clients. My supervisor drills into me that agents must be tough, fierce, and knowledgeable.

As if those are three things I can't be.

"Eight and a half innings complete," the announcer booms. "Jackals six. Pilots four. Dirk is the new pitcher for the Jackals. Let's hope the Pilots will take advantage of their last batting opportunity. Parker at bat, Hofmann on deck, and Owens in the hole. I'm expecting something good from the golden rookie."

I barely manage to keep my head down. It would be easy to search for the familiar face, but I'm not here to open old wounds that have long been stitched up.

I'm here to make a name for myself.

"No, I'm not a fan. I'm an agent, and I was told to meet Garrett Blane."

The security guard blocking the entrance barely glances at my badge before crossing thick arms over his chest. "He said he's meeting Turner. Your name isn't Turner."

I tap the hard plastic. "Shaylene *Turner*. I am Turner."

His ruddy forehead creases. "Let's call that luck, little lady."

"Sir." I'm tempted to show him my badge again, but it's clear reading comprehension isn't his thing. "Will you please tell Garrett I'm waiting for him?"

"No can do," he sings. "And yes, I see your badge, but I've stopped many creative schemes. One woman dressed as Cade Owens's grandmother: muumuu, gray wig, and a cane. The whole shebang. Come back with a better story next time, okay?"

Frustration rushes up my throat, but I choke it down. This isn't the first time I've been denied access to a player area, and I'm sure it won't be the last, but it always hurts. Still, I lift my chin and walk away.

There's nothing men hate more than women who show emotion.

"Turner! Hey!" A wave of relief floods me at the deep voice I've heard in countless postgame interviews. Over my shoulder, Garrett waves me down with a tired smile. "Sorry. Media took forever. You ready?"

I nod and give the guard my sweetest smile, but he refuses to meet my eye, like a coward.

A confident sway hits my hips as I follow Garrett into the packed room, right on his heels. An unusually optimistic part of me hopes I'll get a tour of the stadium tonight, but when he leads me to a round table, I swallow my disappointment.

Settling onto the cold stool, I extend my hand. "Thanks for meeting me tonight." As he shakes it, his eyes linger on my ring finger, proudly adorned with a gold Clear Lake University class ring.

His fingers fly to the gold chain around his neck with an identical ring on it. "My fiancée lets me travel with hers for good luck."

I'm glad I did my research. Step one: a solid connection. Check.

I twist my ring. "Have you visited campus?"

Garrett's mop of wet, blonde hair flops. "For her graduation a few years ago. Prettiest campus I've ever seen. Especially with the lake running through the middle."

"I was there today for my graduation and people were swimming in it."

"You graduated from college today?"

"For my MBA," I clarify. "I was a full-time junior agent *and* grad student up until today. Now I'm just an agent."

He lets out a quiet, appreciative whistle. "How in the hell did you manage that?"

"Oh, you know." I shrug. "All work, no play."

Which is another way to say I've done nothing but work to chase this dream.

"Well, I applaud you. Layla, my fiancée, has been thinking about going back to school, but adding that to a job seems tough." Blue eyes flit to his phone, and I steal a glance at his wallpaper. The blonde woman is gorgeous. "So, tell me about yourself, Turner."

Athletes usually prefer talking about their wants and needs, so why the hell are we talking about me?

I clear my throat. "I graduated early from CLU with a degree in sports management and a minor in communications. During my final semester, I secured an internship with Permian Sports Agency and accepted a full-time position a year and a half ago."

"That's nice." The unimpressed notch between his brows tells me it's not really that nice. "What do you do when you're not working?"

My hackles rise at the first hint of a red flag. "Would you ask a male agent that?"

Dusty pink colors his cheeks. "Honestly? Probably. I'm a nosy guy, but I'll admit that I'm curious about you. I'd like to know who *you* are. Outside of work."

His answer puts me at ease as I look down at the badge hanging around my neck. Me outside of work doesn't exist. These days, I am my job. Every moment is spent either working or thinking about work. I'm always on duty for my clients, which doesn't leave much time for anything else.

"To be honest, I'm married to the job. In the rare moments I'm not working, I'm with my best friends. We played soccer at CLU."

A pang of guilt radiates through me at the memory of leaving Mallory, Jo, and Adri in the parking lot after the graduation ceremony to hightail it here. Being the supportive friends they are, they understood, but work has come first for so long, they probably weren't surprised.

"Yeah, I saw that when I looked you up." He shrugs at my narrowed gaze. "What? Preparation is key. So tell me about you."

If I didn't want to work with him before, I definitely want to now. He's the perfect client, so I indulge his personal request.

"I grew up in an all-athlete family. My dad's a former basketball player turned sports broadcaster. My mom's a sports attorney in Portland with a successful track career behind her, a three-time Olympian. And my brother, Myles, is a point guard for the Seattle Surge. As my dad says, sports are practically in our DNA."

By the indifferent look on his face, this isn't new information either. Everyone knows the Turners are a sports family.

"You were an incredible defender." He props his chin onto his palm and smiles thoughtfully. "Nationally ranked. They called you the Angel Devil because you looked innocent but were an imminent threat to everyone's ankles. I was surprised to see you didn't go pro."

As if on autopilot, my fingers play with my soccer ball stud earrings. "Soccer was my first love, but I always wanted to be the person who guides players through their professional careers. As a forever sports fan, I have certifications in multiple sports. Baseball, soccer, and basketball are my sweet spots."

"Finally! Something I didn't see online." Garrett grins and slaps the table. "I understand basketball and soccer, but why baseball?"

I swallow over the lump of emotion lodged in my throat. "When I was nine, my dad and I watched a documentary about Jackie Robinson. By the time it ended, I had fallen in love with baseball the same way I loved soccer."

Soon after, my parents separated. A few months later, Dad moved to Philadelphia with Myles while I stayed in Portland with Mom.

Summers in Philly with Dad became my favorite things in the world. Every evening, we faced the heat and walked to the ballpark. Our nights were spent rooting for the home team and feasting on stale stadium nachos, as if we hadn't already eaten dinner. That was the summer he fell in love with baseball too.

I hope my smile isn't too sad. "Baseball is special to me."

For many reasons, and one of them is in this stadium right now.

"It really is special." Looking pleased, Garrett drums two fingers against the table. "I want to be honest. I'm talking to a few agents."

"As you should be." Telling him not to talk to other agents isn't a good look. "There are many talented people out there to choose from."

"So why should I choose you?"

Although this conversation isn't going the way I expected, my answer is immediate. "Because you are the only thing that matters to me. Not money or fame. Your well-being will always be more important than any deal, but that doesn't mean I won't fight like hell to make sure you get what you deserve. At the end of the day, it's my job to advocate for you. To support you. To make sure you're safe. If being close to your family is what you want, I'll fight for a great trade. If an endorsement is needed, I'll find one that aligns with your brand. My only goal is to get you where you want to be. In the sport. In life. Everywhere." I smile. "And I'll do whatever it takes to accomplish that."

The silence that follows is weighted. According to my colleagues, my pitch is too emotional and vulnerable. I should treat my clients like dollar signs and nothing more.

But Garrett's eyes tell me I've done well, crinkled at the edges and full of approval.

"I like you, Turner." He stands, and I follow his lead. "There won't be a decision immediately, but you'll hear from me soon. And congrats on your graduation!"

Excitement bubbles to the surface as he exits the room. The moment the door closes behind him, I fist pump the air with a silent whoop.

I'm going to break into the boys' club whether they like it or not.

CHAPTER TWO

EMBARRASSING MYSELF AT WORK sucks.

Especially when tens of thousands of people purchase tickets to watch me play well. But tonight, for nine innings, I sucked.

I step under the stream of scalding water and scrub away the grime, failure, and shame that's nestled in every pore. It would be nice if I could do the same to my brain.

The knob squeaks as I turn off the water and blindly reach for my towel. Wrapping it around my waist, I step out of the shower and almost slip when I spot a shadow in the corner.

"What the hell, Daws? Are you trying to make me fall?"

Dawson Huber, the Pilots' pitcher, straightens and holds out my wire-rimmed glasses. We both know I can't see more than a few feet in front of me.

"Hey, golden boy. Nice shower?"

Slipping my glasses on, I ignore the nickname. "How long have you been there?"

"Long enough to hear you sniffling."

False. I wouldn't dare show that type of emotion in public.

Still, I force myself to smile. "Yeah right. You wish."

Dawson honks a laugh. "Is it bad that I did hope you were in there crying?" He reaches up to pinch my cheek. "This constant smile is terrifying."

As we enter the clubhouse, which is essentially our own private area away from the crowd, it's eerily quiet. It seems that my teammates have already moved forward with their nights before we travel to New York in the morning, leaving the loss behind them. I've never been good at that.

"Hey, rookie," Dawson says, rummaging through his locker. "I know what you're thinking, but tonight's loss wasn't your fault." His patient tone is similar to the one he uses while talking to Luke, his adorable five-year-old son. "You can't pin the loss on yourself when everyone has a chance at bat. We all hit the ball here."

Try to hit the ball, I think. I couldn't hit a single one tonight.

After being traded from California to North Carolina before spring training, I was paired with a veteran to help me acclimate to my new team. I assumed Dawson got suckered into making the new guys feel at home, but I quickly realized I was the sucker who became the little brother he'd always wanted. Which is why I'm getting yet another pep talk.

"By the way," he continues, "Jon said to hurry. He looked pissed."

I suppress a groan. "It's just our postgame talk. No biggie."

Lie. Big lie. *Major* lie. But Dawson doesn't need to know that.

Tying the drawstring on my sweatpants, I watch my friend. White light illuminates his face as his fingers fly across his phone screen. He's usually one of the first guys to leave the stadium, which means he's likely sending a text to his wife, Rosie, promising to be home soon.

Dawson is happy, in love, and playing like a superstar.

I'm the exact opposite.

He drapes an arm around my shoulders and leads me to the exit. As we step out of the clubhouse, the fragile calm I've been trying to maintain shatters when I spot Jon pacing a few feet away. I need to get away from Dawson before he hears something he shouldn't. Jon hates having an audience.

Shrugging out of his grip, I wave. "Get home safely, Daws."

"You too!" Dawson orders, walking backward. "Team leaves at noon, but text me if you want to get breakfast!"

Once the door closes behind him, I feel my shoulders rise before I can stop them. With every step down the hallway toward my agent, I infuse myself with hope that this conversation will be different but it's pointless. Even on my best game days, these talks aren't easy.

Nothing with Jon is easy.

"Hey," I say, pasting my smile on. "Sorry, I was—"

"Hiding from me?" Jon thrusts a legal pad full of notes into my hands. "The Jackals wiped the floor with you tonight! Did you even watch film or read my notes?"

He knows the answer to both questions. I don't just watch film and study. I memorize everything. I know each subtle clue to expect. Hell, I could recite exactly how many pores are on every player's face after staring at the screen until my eyes are bleary.

"You know I did, Jon."

"Then explain that shit-show!" he erupts, anger filling the hallway.

"I know." I sigh. "It was rough."

"Rough? That's an understatement. We need to discuss a plan before you head to New York tomorrow. I don't leave for LA until the afternoon, so I'll meet you here at five in the morning."

Exhaustion seeps through me. If I could, I'd fall asleep right here on the hard floor. I wasn't expecting to get much rest tonight, because I never do, but I was hoping for at least few peaceful minutes before assessing everything I did wrong.

"Come on, Jon. It's already past eleven." My voice cracks on the last word, and for a moment, I forget I'm a major league baseball player, not a child being scolded by a domineering parent.

I shove my hand into my pocket and sigh when my fingers find the familiar shape. The dice roll around my palm, and the soft knock of plastic on plastic is a soothing relief to the burn this conversation ignited.

It wasn't always like this, but soon after being drafted, Jon went from my agent and friend to the shadow I couldn't run away from.

"Listen, the league loves the golden boy, and it's my job to make sure you don't fuck it up." His palm roughly pats my cheek. "You either live up to the name or lose it. And losing it means losing baseball. Give them a reason to doubt you, and they'll toss you aside. People are already questioning if the Pilots brought you up too early."

I tug on a loc until my scalp burns. "It's not fair that one bad game—"

"You think baseball cares about fair? One bad game can and will ruin it all for you. For *us*. You can't afford to not be the best, so act like it. Train like it. Don't let my hard work go to waste because you want to slack off and have a shitty night."

My jaw drops. "*Your* hard work?"

It's only now that I notice the pride settled deep into his frown lines. "I monitor your stats and metrics. I ensure the media is up to date on your life and status. Whose notes are you constantly reading to help you figure out where to improve?" Gray eyes dart to the legal pad in my hands. "I make sure you look good to the front office and keep your coaches happy, but after tonight, it's going to take a lot to get you back in their good graces. All those failed stops are the reason for tonight's loss. I know it. You know it. The team knows it."

In an instant, the sliver of hope Dawson gave me vanishes.

"But we'll fix it," Jon continues, squeezing my shoulder. "You're on the field, and I'm in your head. That's what makes us a great team."

Relaxing his jaw, he morphs back into the cool agent I signed two years ago before I was drafted to the California Hornets. Smothering me with reassurance after ripping me to shreds is the next step on his manipulative agenda, and I always cling to it. Then he'll promise that we're partners.

But after endless postgame talks like this, I've finally realized what we have isn't a partnership.

It's my own personal hell.

"You're fired?"

As the words slip from my mouth, I squeeze the dice for support.

Jon's eyebrows wiggle, reminding me of those terrifying fuzzy caterpillars. They match his equally bushy mustache, slanted by his signature smirk. "I'm confused," he says. "Are you asking me or telling me?"

"I don't know." I shrug. "I've never done this before."

Narrowing his eyes, Jon assesses me. At first, his attention was incredible. I had finished my junior season at Clear Lake University and made the decision to play professionally. Jon Sweeney represented big names with big contracts and even bigger careers. Athletes I admired were on his client list, and he wanted to work with me. I was honored. Grateful. Felt like the luckiest person in the world.

Until I wasn't.

"Let's go," he grits out. "We can talk at your place. And walk normally. You're limping."

My left hip pulses as I correct my gait. Hiding the ache is for the best. For my career. For my image. People call it grit, treating me like a superhero because I never miss games for injuries or sickness. But they don't know about Jon's constant reminders to prove myself. I make do with over-the-counter pain killers to mostly dull the pain.

Stale air swirls around me as we step outside. Jon heads toward his sleek Mercedes that's parked beside my reliable minivan. Without much thought, I start to follow him.

Then I stop. "No. You're fired, Jon. I can't do this anymore."

The skin beneath his eye twitches. "You're joking, right?"

Rubbing my temples does nothing to deter the building pressure. I assumed firing someone would be easy, based on television and movies, but this is hard.

"Don't do this," he continues, contorting his lips into a tight smile. "Everyone's expecting the golden boy to shine this season, and I'm the only person who can get you there."

Golden boy. My mom called me that as a kid. Still does. One day, it moved from being a family nickname to something my friends called me in passing, but somewhere along the way, it became my identity. At first, it felt like it was given with love.

Now, it's a straitjacket of expectations.

"No. We're done."

His eyes flash. "After all I did for you? What about—"

"I'll pay whatever I need to," I say. I don't care about the money.

The distance between us vanishes as he barrels forward and shoves his finger into my chest. "Do you have any idea where you'd be if it weren't for me? I'll tell you." He sneers, spittle flying between us. "You would've been signed by some incompetent agent who doesn't know jack shit about building real athletes. How to make you look perfect. Without me, you'd still be sitting in the minors. This"—his arm jerks toward Pilot City Stadium—"is because of me. You're here because of *me.*"

As if our heights have been reversed, I shrink at the power of his words.

"The Pilots didn't want some kid. They wanted the golden boy I built. You think they'd still want you if they knew you were ready to quit and run home after your first major injury? Nope. I'm the one who held you together, and we got through it without missing a single game. You need me, Cade, whether you like it or not."

I open my mouth to fight back, but nothing comes out. He's right. Without Jon, there's no telling where I'd be.

The simple fact is that his methods work. I haven't tasted failure like tonight in a long time. Watching too much film, obsessing over every critique he writes on these yellow legal pads, pushing myself, diving into my perfect image, and focusing on stats and metrics may not be great, but all of that got me here.

As I'm about to take it back, a heavy hand lands on my shoulder.

A freckled hand.

Shit.

"Not sure what's happening here, but get lost, Jon." My best friend Kenneth's usually gentle voice is harsh with irritation. "Now."

Jon looks up, likely trying to place the redheaded intruder. They met once while I interviewed agents. Jon was Kenneth's favorite choice at the time, but the grit in his voice shows that has changed.

Smoothing his suit jacket, Jon steps back. "I worked with Ted Daily, Heisman winner and three-time Super Bowl champion. Eli Jones won the goddamn gold twice with me by his side. And now I'm being fired by some kid? Yeah. Good luck, *golden boy*." And with those final crushing words, he storms away.

The moment his car door slams shut, worried green eyes shift to me. I knew Kenneth was coming to tonight's game, but this isn't a conversation I wanted to have. Looks like I have no choice.

"So, how much of that did you hear?"

"Not much," Kenneth mutters, dropping his scowl to the sidewalk.

If I didn't know my best friend of twenty-plus years so well, I might have missed the way he pushed his tongue into his cheek before answering. All through high school, when I asked him how things were with his father, his too-quick answers were always preceded by his tell.

"Liar."

"That's not fair. You can always spot my lies." His cheeks darken to match his scarlet waves. "Fine. I came around the corner when he said you needed him. That's when I started running."

My heart drops. He didn't hear a lot, but it was still too much.

I squeeze the pad of Jon's notes, desperate to suppress the guilt pulsing through my veins. Kenneth Gray has been my best friend since before we could speak coherent sentences, but I can't figure out how to tell him everything. It's impossible to explain the invisible weight I carry.

Intangible and inescapable.

Before Kenneth can speak again, I smile. This is how I keep the people I love from worrying. This is how I survive.

"Don't worry about me, Kent. I'm okay."

"You're always okay. That's *why* I worry, Cadey Boy." Arms made strong from years of swimming wrap me in a hug, and I feel more secure than I have in weeks. Then he adds, "But you're not rehiring him. You'll find a better agent. I'm sure of it."

At least someone's feeling hopeful.

CHAPTER THREE

I NEVER WANT TO read legal jargon again.

"You've got big brains, but give up." Marcus Winters, the Pilots catcher, snatches the contract from my hands and sinks into the ice bath beside me. "You might've been Mr. Smarty Pants in college, but sports law is a different ballgame."

His damp fingers ruin the paper, but it doesn't matter. The sports agency that gave it to me three days ago has already been crossed off my list. Along with the other failed agencies.

Dawson's teeth chatter in agreement. "Guess how many times he asked what salary arbitration means?"

Marcus coos, "Oh, rookie. That's not something you need to worry about anytime soon, but you'll need an agent before then because it's a monster."

It has been ten days since I fired Jon. After getting home that night, Kenneth stuck around for a bit but didn't pry, turning on *The Dark Knight* and ordering sushi from our favorite late-night spot in Clear Lake. But the moment he left, my relief faded.

"S-speaking of that. Why did you fire Jon?" Marcus stutters. "People are g-going to f-freak out when they find o-out."

I ignore Dawson's gaze lasering into my temple and submerge my shoulders under the bone-chilling water. "We had a difference in priorities and management styles." The almost-truth slips easily past my lips. It's the same one I've recited to multiple agencies, my mother and friends, and the Pilots coaching staff when questioned.

Dawson boos my dishonesty, giving me a double thumbs-down. "Political answer. Been working with the PR team?"

He knows I have. Media training was the first thing the Pilots put me through when I made the 40-man roster. The PR team says I'm the lowest risk when it comes to yelling at a reporter or cussing during interviews. Marcus, however, is on the opposite side of the spectrum, already fined twice this season.

"Are you having any luck finding a new agent?" Dawson asks.

The back of my head bumps the rim of the tub. "Considering I've spoken with seven agencies and I'm not moving forward with any of them, it's not going well."

"Too big?" Dawson probes.

"Too small?" Marcus pries.

"Too picky," a gruff voice adds. Rio Arden, the Pilots' general manager, is a mountain of a man with broad shoulders that bump both sides of the doorway. He's got his kindergarten teacher face on, patient but drained. "You have until the end of the week to find an agent, Owens, or I'll pick for you."

I tap two fingers to my forehead and salute. "On it. Meeting Caldwell in an hour."

With a single grunt of approval, he leaves the training room.

Marcus flicks my numb shoulder. "Aw. He loves you."

"True. Rio may look like he hates us, but he's a softie." Dawson chuckles as I pull myself out of the ice bath. "Best of luck, and please tell Ms. Owens I need to put in an order for Luke's birthday."

Marcus's tongue lolls out of his mouth. "Can she make those Oreo brownies again? I have a feeling that'll pull the stick out of Rio's ass."

Billie's Eats has been a hit since Mom opened over a year ago. She caters all over North Carolina, but her favorite gigs are for the Pilots players' personal events.

"Of course." I smile. "Text me what you want."

Taking advantage of the extra space, Marcus stretches his legs out in the tub. "Good luck with the new guy! You're going to need it to find a better agent than Jon freaking Sweeney."

Marcus doesn't mean any harm by his comment, but the reminder forces my mind to shift to the last legal pad Jon gave me before I fired him. One line has been playing on a constant loop in my brain since I read it.

Do you even want to be the golden boy anymore?

Jon's question plagues me as I get dressed and rush to my car.

"Mom, I don't have an architecture degree." I squint up at the four-story building full of sports agents. "Looks pretty sturdy to me," I dutifully report into my phone.

The chuckle that fills my ear is sweet, so much like her demeanor. "Good. I need proper descriptions since I wasn't invited to this meeting."

"It's not parent-teacher night," I joke, even though having her here would make this easier. Pots and pans clang against each other in the background, but it's my equivalent of white noise. "What event are you prepping for?"

"Fundraiser at the animal shelter." A smile stretches each word. "Biggest event so far."

Billie's Eats is my mother's pride and joy, and helping her start her dream was worth every penny. She sacrificed everything to take care of me and my little sister, Violet. Working extra shifts to buy me a new glove. Spending hours in the sun on her days off to watch my games. Raising a newborn without a single complaint after my father left. Her support and love carried me through my pursuit of baseball.

And when I fail, I feel like I'm wasting everything she poured into me.

"Wow, Ma. Sounds like a big night. Are you sure you don't need me to come by and help? I'll have some free time after my meeting. I could run and pick up those—"

"Cade Charles." Her tone is sharp but loving. "Thank you again for taking Vi to school and cleaning the kitchen this morning, but no. You can do nothing else for me today. If you try, I will lock you out of the house." The oven door screeches. "This is the eighth agency, right? Lucky number eight."

My phone chimes, and I put Mom on speaker to check the new message.

Jon Sweeney

It's been 10 days. Come to your senses already.

You can't do this without me.

Swiping them away, I try to slow my spiral, but I'm rapidly tumbling down the stairwell of maybes and what ifs. Maybe I was too quick to fire him. What if I made a mistake? Maybe I should apologize and take it back. What if I can't do this without him?

I sigh. "Nothing about this feels lucky."

For the middle of May, it's unreasonably warm. The clouds above threaten to release a torrent of rain as I cross the parking lot, which means the roof will be closed for tonight's game.

"Your number is eight." Mom chuckles. "Your jersey number. Your angel number. Your lucky number."

Billie Owens is a spiritual woman. At a young age, she taught me that the number eight stands for abundance, success, and achievement. Considering it's also my favorite number, she believes it's lucky too.

"I know. Love you, Ma."

Mom hums. "Everything will work out. Love you too, golden boy."

The nickname nips at my skin, but as spotless glass doors slide open and I step inside, I'm soothed by the luscious smell of champagne and success floating in the air.

"Welcome to Permian!" the receptionist chirps. A flash of recognition crosses his face when he looks up at me. "I'll let Caldwell know you're here. The waiting room is right over there."

After grabbing a water bottle, I drop onto a glass chair that's more stylish than comfortable. Tipping my head back, I spot a black puma stretched across the ceiling. It's such a shock that I laugh, relaxing as I dig into my pocket for my phone.

Me

This agency is *fancy* fancy

It's lab day for his PhD program, but Kenneth answers immediately.

Mr. Kenneth Edwards

Nice! Where are you?

I snap a photo of the puma and press send. Gray bubbles appear, but before his response comes through, a man in an impeccable navy suit bursts into the spacious room.

Standing, I extend my hand. "Hey, I'm—"

"The golden boy! I know who you are, trust me."

His handshake simultaneously crushes my hand and my spirits.

"Cade works too," I say, forcing a lightness into my voice. Being called by my real name is a rarity these days.

"Of course, but golden boy is *you*." With a quick scan of his ID badge, he leads me down a hallway that reminds me of something out of a spy movie rather than a sports agency. "I'm stoked you called to discuss new representation. Before we talk shop, let me show you around. We've been at this location for about a year and rebranded before we moved. You may remember Triple 8 Sports since you're from around here."

A flicker of familiarity surfaces. Mom loved the name because they were my angel numbers and happened to be a popular sports agency. She'd swear being here was a sign.

"Thanks for getting me out of that meeting," he whispers as we pass a boardroom full of suit-clad men. "So, where are you living now?"

"In Clear Lake." Bryan, my hometown, is thirty minutes from Clear Lake, but the college town became my favorite place in the three years I spent there.

"Really? Seems small for a big man like you. Don't you want to be closer to Charlotte?"

"Nope." I scan the gold-framed photos of Permian athletes covering an entire wall. "Clear Lake is closer to my family and friends. Plus, I don't mind the drive."

"My contacts in real estate will find you a place more apt for a professional baseball player." He winks. "Once we get a contract signed."

Red sirens appear around Caldwell's head as the elevator doors slide open, blaring a warning only I can hear. It's not until we make it to the fourth floor that I manage to mute them.

At the end of the hallway, T. Caldwell is carved into the nameplate in a gorgeous script. Inside the room, a deep mahogany desk glitters in the dim light. Everything from the lamp to the pen holders screams elegance.

He drops into the leather seat. "Forgive me, but I'm dying to know why you left ProPact. You fired your agent early in the season, your first in the majors, which means things soured between you. Am I right or am I right?"

My jaw nearly drops at his brazen tone, but I smile. "We just had a difference in priorities and management styles."

His face crumples slightly before he grins. "I see I've got to gain your trust first, but I'm a patient man. Do you have any questions for me before we get this contract signed?"

I sure do. They're the same ones I've asked every agent. "Did you attend law school?"

"No. Law school isn't necessary, but I have a Master's in Sports Management, my certification for baseball, and I've negotiated contracts for eight years."

Adding a mental check mark beside that question, I move on. He answers every question about fees, contracts, negotiations, and future career with ease. I see why he's one of the top agents at Permian Sports Agency, but something shady lingers beneath his pearly white smile.

The last question on the list is the most crucial of them all. "How do you view your role in an athlete's success?"

He gestures at the ego wall behind him. "Look at my track record. The players I work with win, and it's not a coincidence. They perform, and I make things happen. That's why I'd love to start your major league career on the right foot. Me and the golden boy?" His grin morphs, and all I see is Jon. "We'll make a great team."

My stomach churns as the sirens reappear.

"Mr. Caldwell—"

"Trevor."

"Yes. Trevor." I glance at the door and make a decision. "Where's the restroom?"

"Oh, uh—" he stutters, tapping a stack of paper on the desk in front of him. Thick enough to be a contract that I'm not ready to sign. "This place is a bit of a maze. Go past the elevator, all the way down, turn left, and it's on your right."

It takes a solid three minutes to find the bleach-scented room. The moment I'm inside, I click the lock shut, push my hand into my pocket, and rock the dice in my palm.

"What are the odds?" I whisper. "What are the odds signing with Trevor is a bad decision?"

The question reminds me of a different time in my life.

Of the person who played the game with me.

If I don't leave Permian with an agent, Rio will choose one. I'm not sure if his choice would be better or worse than the man waiting for me, but I can't take that risk.

When I predictably don't get an answer from my reflection, I adjust my contacts and enter the hallway. After looking both ways, I realize I have no clue how to get back to Trevor's office.

I turn left, because it seems the most logical, and unlock my phone that hasn't stopped vibrating since Trevor met me in the lobby.

Mr. Kenneth Edwards

No

You're at Permian?!?!?

LEAVE NOW!

Leave? Why should I leave?

But before I can text him back, I breathe in and everything changes. The floor shifts beneath my feet as I'm thrown back in time. Sweet jasmine and lavender invade my senses without waiting for an invitation, and the flurry of feelings I've been holding tightly to make their way to the surface.

This is the scent that lingered everywhere *she* was. My skin. My car. My bed.

More permanent places like my heart and brain.

I walk slowly toward the room I assumed was a janitorial closet, but it's not a room filled with cleaning supplies and extra chairs. My breath catches at the name carved into the brass nameplate, cool under my fingers.

It can't be.

An out-of-shape wheeze grabs my attention, and I turn as Trevor jogs around the corner with a light sheen across his forehead.

My hand falls to my side. "Sorry. This place really is a maze."

"Told ya." Beady eyes stay fixed on the door behind me. "We should get back to—"

"I want her to be my agent."

Trevor's mouth gapes like a fish. "How do you know Turner's a girl?"

A *girl*? She's a woman, and thanks to social media and our shared best friend, Mallory Edwards, I know she's a woman with two degrees under her belt and years of experience.

"We knew each other in college." Hiding my very real feelings and our short-lived relationship under a flimsy lie feels like a betrayal. She'll probably hate me for this, considering we haven't spoken in almost two years and it's my fault.

"I don't think that's a good idea. I'm her senior agent. With the way I can help your career grow, I'd be the perfect agent for you."

I don't take the bait. "Does she have the proper certifications to represent me?"

"Yes. She passed the baseball certification exam."

"Is she good at her job?"

A pause. "Yes," he bites out, and I can tell it is hard for him to admit. "But I think—"

Great, that's all I need to know.

"If I'm signing with Permian, it's going to be with her."

CHAPTER FOUR

 *Shay*

I'M NOT SURE WHO decided the workday should begin at eight, but they deserve jail time.

Okay, that's a bit harsh, but I hope their life is plagued by not-so-fun things. Like finding both sides of their pillow to be warm in the middle of the night. Or their socks are always damp. Or their favorite show gets canceled on a cliffhanger, and they spend the rest of their life with only theories.

Yeah. Those are more appropriate.

Normally, I love Fridays, but not this one. All because of the red exclamation mark that is mocking me, swollen and urgent beside the email. I'm rarely asleep before two in the morning, but last night, I managed to crawl into bed around midnight. Then my phone pinged with a meeting invitation from Trevor, and I dove back into work to prepare for whatever he threw at me.

Updated data on the basketball league's salary structures? Done.

Possible endorsement opportunities for his vegan footballer? Here are ten options.

Contract renewal dates for his clients? Already in his inbox.

Trevor even canceled our weekly babysitting meeting, coined by The Quartet, which includes Mallory, Adri, Jo, and myself, because he spends an hour treating me like a child.

Unsurprisingly, I'm the first person here, which is sad, considering the amount of effort it takes to get to work. Fifteen minutes to stop snoozing my alarm, ten minutes to drag myself out of bed, twenty minutes to get ready, and another thirty minutes to drive from Clear Lake to Charlotte.

And at the expense of my sanity, I'm the "secret angel" who brings donuts every Friday.

After dropping off the donuts in the break room, I burst into my office and slip off my heels. I still haven't decorated the glorified broom closet. The walnut desk takes up more than half of the room, leaving barely enough space for two chairs, a coat rack, and a mini fridge that's stocked with more caffeinated drinks than a girl could need.

With my protein shake and energy drink in hand, I review my pink sticky note to-do wall and navigate to my emails.

A toothpaste commercial opportunity awaits Brett Reynolds, a center for the NC Grizzlies. Considering he's missing three teeth, he'll be ecstatic. Lionel Stiller, a shooting guard also on Reynold's team, is in Cabo for a family wedding and sent his social media logins so I can manage the pages. Victoria Hall's hosting a book club to get to know her new teammates after being traded in March to the Carolina Rage soccer club as their new right winger. Fretful energy trembles through the screen as she begs me to choose the book and theme. Delilah Anderson, my only tennis client, sent photos from Paris, where she's training for the French Open.

An ongoing email with Holly Trent, a striker for the Carolina Rage, appears next.

Holly Trent: Stop emailing me at 12 a.m. You need sleep. Also, is a Mercedes too flashy?

I snort and reply, *Way too flashy. Connecting you with a financial advisor this afternoon.*

My favorite part of being an agent is the random hats I wear. On top of managing contracts and negotiations, I'm a financial guru, social media manager, personal stylist, assistant, gift consultant, grocery shopper, advice giver, and a shoulder to cry on—which has led to a few therapy referrals.

My laptop chimes, and if it weren't for the name at the top of the screen, I would ignore the video call like I do with all nonwork-related texts and calls during work hours.

"What did I say about SOS texts, Shaylene?" Mallory's cheek is pressed to the camera like an old lady who recently learned how to FaceTime. "Send context or I'll assume the worst. We thought you were dead!"

She may be whispering, but I know I'm being scolded. She's CLU's former soccer captain and The Quartet's mom friend for a reason.

Adri's half-asleep laugh rustles the speakers. "Nope. Only Cap thought you were dead."

"I kind of thought you were dead." Jo yawns, smoothing wild blonde tendrils.

I forgot about the panicked text I'd sent after receiving Trevor's meeting invitation. I check the flood of messages on my phone. Twelve are from Mallory in the GOAL GALS group chat. Adri's and Jo's responses are much tamer. There's also one from my mom, wishing me a productive day, and my dietitian asking if I ate breakfast.

Me

Does a protein shake and energy drink count?

I ignore Sarabeth because she won't like my answer, and I apologize to my friends.

"It's fine. Just don't do it again." Mallory props her phone on the kitchen counter to make her morning cup of hot chocolate. "What caused the freak out?"

The vanilla shake sours on my tongue. "Trevor scheduled a last-minute meeting for this morning."

A curse leaves her lips. "Do you know what it's about?"

"Nope. No details, but I stayed up all night preparing."

"If you had no information, how did you prepare?" Jo, our resident voice of reason, asks.

I drop the pink five-pound binder onto the desk, and all three women jump. Out of the thirty files inside, only five are mine. The rest are Trevor's. He brings in the big-name clients, and I do the majority of his work.

"I read every file and jammed each word into my brain."

"Don't fret." Throwing off her wine-red comforter, Adri appears. For someone who just woke up, she looks runway ready. "That's Trevor's modus operandi."

"His huh?" I ask.

"Ignore her." Jo rubs tired eyes. "She's binge-watching Criminal Minds. Again. Looks like we've got a possible FBI agent in the group."

"Lose the sarcasm, JoJo. When a serial killer comes, you'll wish I were Detective Morgan."

"Derek Morgan does nothing for me. Prentiss though? Now we're talking."

I check the clock. "Guys, I'm running out of time! Adri, continue your FBI talk."

Her grin is victorious. "Trevor has probably known about this meeting for weeks and wanted you to panic. Like the time he didn't invite you to the agency lunch until thirty minutes before. Making you sweat is his favorite pastime, so don't freak out. It's probably nothing."

The logic is solid, but I'm not entirely convinced. "Okay maybe, but what if I'm getting fired?"

Mallory pulls her coils into a bun at the top of her head and lifts her mug. "If you get fired, make sure you kick every man right where it hurts. In the dick."

I'd laugh if I didn't know how serious she is.

Jo loses the battle and smiles. "Aren't you supposed to be a pacifist?"

Laughing, Mallory licks the foamy whipped cream mustache from her upper lip. "I am, but that doesn't mean I don't enjoy watching karma get terrible men."

"Agreed, Cap! It's never too early for violence," Adri cheers.

Rolling her eyes, Jo redirects the conversation. "Did you do anything to get fired?"

I wrack my brain, but nothing comes to mind. I've done everything asked of me by not only Trevor but everyone here. All assignments are done perfectly. I attend babysitting meetings without complaint. I manage my clients, and his, to the best of my ability, create rock-solid contracts, and negotiate like my life depends on it.

"No," I admit. "But—"

"What if Trevor is getting fired?" Adri cuts in.

The idea thrills me. Maybe another client dropped him and they want me to witness his termination and escort him from the building.

God, I wish.

Catching a glimpse of the clock, I sigh. "I love you guys, but I gotta go. Thanks for distracting my brain."

Air kisses and a chorus of encouragement fill my office. It's been like this since we became teammates and friends four-plus years ago. Constant love that I'll never deserve and never let go of. Even when I'm radio silent for work, they always come when I need them.

"Kick them in the dick!" Mallory chants before I hang up. She may be group mom, but she's as chaotic as Adri.

I stand and inspect myself in the mirror on the wall. Box braids fall past my hips, curling at the ends. I re-tuck my blush blouse into black slacks and slip my heels on before entering the hallway.

Professionalism is my number one. As the only woman at Permian, I can't afford to give anyone even the slightest idea that I'm not up for this job and all it entails. I must be capable, competent, and knowledgeable at every turn, because one mistake could ruin everything I've worked so hard to build.

Mom taught me how to survive in a male-dominated field, making sure I was prepared for a lifetime of being on the outside. The lesson that stuck with me most was only spending time on things I can control, like my reputation and performance, the emotions I show, how I present myself, and my level of independence.

But the things I can't control—like love? No thanks. Love is unpredictable. I learned that firsthand when Mom and Dad split up.

There was a brief moment where I thought I could be different, though. That I could have the job *and* love, so I went for it.

See how well that worked out for me?

"You okay, Turner?"

I let out a tiny yelp and grip the banister along the wall. When my vision focuses on one of Trevor's minions, I force myself to recover and stand up straight.

"Yes, Andy. Everything is fine."

Andy Walker and I completed the Permian internship with eight other college seniors, but only we received job offers. His babysitting ended after six months, while mine will likely never end. He is recommended for special projects over me, every single time. Trevor's man club took to him immediately, leaving me on the outskirts and all alone.

The only way I'll earn their respect is by being the best agent here.

He lifts his hand to open the door to the boardroom but pauses. "Do you know what this is about? Trev just texted me and asked me to sit in on this meeting."

My fear reignites. I'm getting fired, and *he* is the witness.

How goddamn embarrassing.

Because I can't seem to form an answer that doesn't end with me screaming, I say nothing and open the door. Sour cologne and sugary donuts mix disgustingly in the air. Leaning against the table, Trevor stuffs three donut holes into his mouth and gives Andy a bro nod or whatever men do instead of speaking. Then he looks at me and rolls his eyes.

Pink is his least favorite color, which makes me love it even more.

"Whoever brings donuts every Friday deserves a raise," he grumbles to Andy. "Makes my days much more tolerable. Especially with the shit that's about to happen."

That grabs my attention. "What's about to happen? There were no details in the email."

Trevor's lip curls, and I genuinely believe he would growl at me if it wouldn't come off as weird. When someone enters the room behind me, his face transforms into the one that's sleek, kind, and professional.

Bullshit. Bullshit. Bullshit.

"Winston," Trevor says. "I didn't realize you'd be here for this."

"Wouldn't miss it!" Winston beams his perfect smile at us. "Good morning, Andy and Turner. Now we're just waiting on the guest of honor. He should be here soon."

I smile at the CEO of Permian Sports Agency. Winston actually likes me. If Trevor had any say, I would've been fired on my first day.

"Good morning," I repeat. "Guest of honor?"

Winston opens his mouth, but Trevor pulls him away before he can say more. The men move into a small huddle, shoving me aside. It stings, but it's expected, so I make my way to the window and look outside, focusing on the navy-and-gold flags flapping in the wind at Pilot City Stadium.

Deep breaths. Good thoughts.

The air grows thick with renewed excitement when the door creaks open again. The guest of honor has arrived.

"Welcome back, golden boy!" Trevor shouts. "Glad to see you again."

"Golden boy?" I murmur. I'm sorely unprepared for the way my heart falls to my stomach when I turn and see the man shaking Trevor's hand, towering over my colleagues.

Turning my back to the blast from my past, I slow my breathing. I'd like to believe I'm hallucinating, but it's him. That's *his* voice. Deep yet light enough to make me feel like I'm floating when he speaks. Euphoria wraps itself around every syllable that falls from his lips.

Lips I happen to know are very soft.

No, Shaylene.

Even without looking at him, I know he's doing what he does best—making people feel special. All his attention is on my colleagues, casting Trevor, Winston, and Andy under his spell, laughing as if they've known him for years.

The way I know him.

Knew him.

"Turner!" Winston bellows, and I whip around at the authority in his voice. "Join us."

Gorgeous eyes are already on me, and I flinch at the intensity. I almost forgot how warm his hazel gaze is, more green than brown in the early morning light. So familiar that I could create a color palette from memory.

Against my better judgement, I don't rush toward the door and sprint back to my office. Instead, I walk toward the men and extend my hand. We haven't shaken hands since the day we met freshman year in that little study room. It's as awkward as that first time, his callouses sliding against my palm as his hand engulfs mine completely. Warm and welcoming.

So much like the man I quietly fell in love with.

Of course I knew he was traded to the Pilots a few months ago. It's my job to know what's going on in the baseball world, but Cade Owens isn't my business.

Hasn't been since the day he didn't come home.

CHAPTER FIVE

BEING SURROUNDED BY THIS much testosterone for a prolonged amount of time must be a hazard.

There hasn't been a single work-related discussion in the forty-two minutes we've been gathered around the table. Winston and Cade bonded over having younger sisters, and Andy and Trevor gave him an in-depth review of every restaurant that opened since he left.

The worst part, however, is the man who keeps trying to catch my eye.

If it weren't for our best friends' inability to stay away from each other, Cade and I may have never spoken. Our paths didn't cross until Mallory asked me to mediate her and Kenneth's ultra-competitive spelling bee freshman year. I wasn't keen on becoming friends with her rival, Kenneth, or their friend Cade, the baseball player Mallory had bonded with on the first day of college. But when I walked into the study room, it was impossible to ignore Cade's magnetic presence.

I surveyed the giant man sitting on the carpeted floor, carefully flipping through pages of a dictionary in a way that seemed almost pornographic. Golden skin glittered under the fluorescent lights, striped with tan lines from countless hours in the sun.

But it was Cade's smile that drew me in, so raw and real.

Even as Mallory spelled *onomatopoeia* and Kenneth yelled random letters to mess her up, his grin never wavered. That's how Cade and I became gamekeepers for the Brain Bowl.

Our switch from friends to friends-with-benefits during junior year was natural, and not much of a surprise. When he was drafted by the California Hornets at the end of junior year, I assumed things would end. Sure, we got along well, and the benefits were life-altering and toe-curling, but I didn't expect anything more.

Then we agreed to try.

Sadly, only I tried. He didn't.

Stop thinking about that.

"Education major?" Trevor asks. "Really?"

Cade straightens in his chair. "I had a great teacher and mentor in high school, and I wanted to be like him. Maybe one day I'll go back to Clear Lake University and finish my degree."

Trevor guffaws. "For what? Baseball is your future, golden boy."

If I wasn't watching, I might've missed the way Cade's smile dimmed imperceptibly, as if a shadow crossed his face for only a moment before shining brightly again.

"Plus—"

"How do you like being back in North Carolina?" My voice cracks from being silent for so long, but I cut Trevor off.

Eight eyes slowly turn to me, but the room spins when I meet surprised hazels. I blame the sudden dizzy spell on the PCOS.

"It's been really nice." Cade's throat bobs. "Leaving the people I care about wasn't easy, so I'm happy to see them again. All of them."

I can barely contain my groan at his poorly hidden attempt to say he cared about me. If he actually cared, he would've come home. Or at least he would've talked to me and explained why he didn't come back.

"Speaking of CLU!" Winston points at me. "Turner finished her MBA last week and got another CLU diploma. We're so proud of her. Turner, tell Cade a little about what you do for Permian."

I'd rather not, but I've got this script memorized. "I'm a junior agent and manage everything from contracts and negotiations to marketing and endorsements for my five clients. I do support work for several other clients, and have certifications in soccer, basketball, and baseball. I also work with a tennis star."

"Real jack-of-all-trades," Winston beams.

Cade's smile splits wide. "Wow. That's amazing, Shay ba—" Those stupid, perfect lips roll, and he goes quiet, but it's too late. My cheeks are already lit with fire. He almost used my old nickname in front of my coworker, supervisor, and CEO.

"So, now that we're relaxed, let's talk about your contract," Winston jumps in, and I send him a silent thanks.

This is where I thrive. Work is safe. Something that not even Cade Owens can derail. Since he's Trevor's new client, I'll be his go-to person for day-to-day operations like I am for Trevor's other clients. The thought makes my neck itch, and I reach for my glass of water. I'll be forced to talk to the man who broke my heart. At least twice a week.

Could things be worse?

"And Turner will be your agent."

The cup slips out of my grip and clatters onto the table, sending a wave of water across the gleaming surface. Embarrassment burns the back of my eyes as I accept the box of tissues that Andy slides to me. As I mop up my mess, I try to wrap my head around that bombshell.

Tossing the tissues into a trash can, I clear my throat. "*Me?*"

The blood vessel I named Chad in Trevor's forehead throbs as he straightens in his seat. "Yes, you. He actually requested you personally, Turner. Says you two have *history*."

His accusatory tone makes me bristle, but I don't react. No one knows about our almost-relationship outside of our inner circle. Cade's mom and Cade's mentor from high school know too, but I trust them with the secret. Trevor knows nothing at all.

"We went to college together," is all I manage. Not the whole truth, but I won't give him the satisfaction of learning about my personal life. "But what about my exception for Garrett?"

Noticing Cade's confusion, Winston faces him. "Junior agents at Permian are only allowed to have five clients, but Shay's a bit of a superstar around here. She received an exception for a client she's hoping to sign."

"And Cade would make seven if Garrett says yes," I say, hoping Winston understands this would be a super exception. One that clearly makes Andy uncomfortable.

Out of the four junior agents—me, Andy, Kyle, and Jonah—Andy has the fewest clients with two. Kyle and Jonah each have three.

"I have no problem with you having seven clients if Garrett chooses you. And Cade requested you, so who am I to reject that?"

"Wait," Trevor says. "Their history isn't a problem?"

Winston opens the manila folder. "Nope. Now, let's sign a contr—" Chirping birds cut him off, and he pulls a phone from his suit jacket. "Hey, honey. I'm in a mee—" He stands. "Recess. Fifteen."

His exit prompts Trevor to stand next, mumbling about another donut and a break. Andy, ever the dutiful minion, follows. I squeeze my eyes shut as they shuffle toward the door and count down from ten.

Ten. Nine. Eight.

It's a bad dream. When I get to one, I'll wake up in my bed.

Seven. Six. Five.

I'll call Mallory, and she'll organize a girls' night.

Four. Three. Two.

Adri will set me up with guys while Jo denies them as a good match.

One.

The door clicks shut behind me, and I open my eyes. The feeling of safety doesn't last long when I spot the words *Cade Owens* scribbled on my notepad.

Not a dream. This is my worst nightmare.

I glance over my shoulder and search for shadows under the door. Andy and Trevor might be lurking and waiting to overhear some juicy gossip.

"They're gone," Cade assures me. "No shadows."

"Get out of my head," I snap. Bringing my thumb to my mouth, I chew the skin until it's raw. "You told Trevor we have history?"

He shakes his head, a firm and resounding no. "Absolutely not. I wouldn't do that to you."

"I have no clue what you would do to me, Cade," I volley back. "I don't know you anymore. I'm not sure if I ever did."

Regret leaches into me when his broad shoulders slump forward and his head falls, but I'm angry. Hurt I didn't know I still held sits heavily on my chest, and I can't stomp out the flames right now.

"You're right," he says. "I met Trevor, and he reminded me of—" Stopping abruptly, he looks up at me. "It doesn't matter why I did it. I shouldn't have said that to him. I'm sorry, Shay baby."

As if the heater turns on, warmth spreads through me at the nickname. Still, the ice around my heart remains frozen. No amount of nostalgia or reminders that he once was my favorite person can fix this.

I've done so much to be taken seriously here, and for what? For my former friend-with-benefits to waltz in and request to work with me? No wonder Trevor looked like he was going to keel over.

"They're going to think I got the job because I slept with you."

A slow grin tugs at his mouth. "You have slept with me more times than I can count, but that's not why I want you to be my agent."

"Cade," I warn him, desperate to get away from the topic of us in bed. And in the car. And on the couch. And kitchen counters. My anger burns hot, but the memories are still sweet. "Because I'm a woman and you're an attractive, talented athlete, that'll be the assumption."

"Well, that's stupid. *They* are stupid."

"Stupid or not, it's my reality."

I never got to tell him how angry I was when things ended. Maybe this is my chance. I'll have to whisper-scream, but that'll do.

"You're right." The tenderness in his voice makes all the fight leave my body. "I didn't think about that. I'm sorry."

Cade stands and rounds the table, closing the space between us in long steps. He's bigger than he was when he left Clear Lake. More solid, filling his six-foot-five frame divinely with hard muscle and a soft spirit. My nose catches a faint whiff of mint when he leans in.

"You still bite your fingers when you're stressed." Pressing his hand against the table in front of me, he smiles. "I missed that about you. I'm glad not everything has changed."

I start to speak, but he's already walking away.

My breath hitches when I spot three Hello Kitty Band-Aids in front of me. In college, he carried these everywhere for his little sister, and he became my personal first aid kit.

There isn't much time to figure out what I'm going to do. If I say no, they'll—Trevor—will assume we had a thing. If I say yes, I'll be on Trevor's shit list for the rest of time.

There's no winning this game for me.

"What are the odds?" he asks.

I rip open the bandage with my teeth. "What?"

"What are the odds you'll be my agent?"

The audacity of this man. An unprofessional part of me wants to play our game that bloomed sophomore year in the student-athlete dining hall. The nutrition team was discussing Vitamin C, and because every-one thinks of oranges, they wanted to be different. Cade returned to our table with twenty lemons stuffed in his pockets, claiming he would make freshly squeezed lemonade. Well, he asked Mallory to make it, and she agreed.

Out of nowhere, I straightened. "What are the odds you'll eat a lemon? Peel and all."

A challenge burned bright in his eyes. "One through ten?"

With a number in mind, I held my fist in the air. "On three."

One, two, three.

"Eight," we blurted at the same time. Looking back, it seems so silly, but everything changed between us when he shoved the lemon into his mouth and started chewing with that smile still on his face.

Things were so simple then, but it's not our game anymore.

There is no us.

"No," I finally say. "I can't play the game with you."

The weight of his sadness dulls his voice. "I understand. And don't worry. I'll sign with—"

"Me," I breathe. "You'll sign with me."

His eyes go wide. "Why?"

Forcing myself to look at him, I smile. "Because it's my job, and I always do my job."

I'm a professional. I'll take care of Cade like I do my other clients. Our past is in the past, and there will never be a second chance.

Before he can argue with me, Winston bursts back into the room with a wide smile. It's a stark contrast to Andy and Trevor, who look gray and miserable. But my attention is fixated on the contract in Winston's hands.

The thing that will bind me to the first man I loved.

The man I can never love again.

"Requesting me!" I cram a handful of frozen dark chocolate chips into my mouth, followed by a spoonful of strawberry ice cream. "Can you believe it?"

Mallory fingers the gold four-leaf clover pendant around her neck and drops onto the pink gingham comforter beside me. I confiscated her phone before explaining Cade's ambush this morning because she would've called him.

"Men suck," she asserts, tipping her carton of rocky road ice cream to mine in a salute.

It's been too long since we hung out at what used to be *our* home. After graduating from CLU, Mallory moved to Lake Anita with Kenneth. This place doesn't feel like home without her, but my platonic soulmate found her happily ever after, and I love that for her.

An affronted gasp fills the space, and Mallory peers over the edge of the bed. "Do you have something to say, Gray?"

Messy tufts of fire-engine red hair appear as Kenneth drags his body from the floor. "*All* men suck?"

She cradles his face in her hands. "All men suck *except* you. Happy?"

"Now I know you're lying, Eddie." The nickname—a short form of Edwards, her last name—used to irritate Mallory, but now it makes her giggle. "You definitely thought I sucked last night when I forgot to start the dishwasher." His freckles practically glow from being so close to her. It's sickeningly adorable.

"Okay, I get it. You're the cutest couple to ever exist. Now, can we get back to the issue at hand? You two are best friends with the man who almost ruined my career! He just strolls in with no explanation of what happened between us and declares I'm his agent!" I flop back and stare at the ceiling. "If Trevor finds out about us, I'm beyond screwed."

Mallory lies beside me and pulls me against her side like we used to after a bad day. "He won't," she soothes. "But are you sure you can work with Cade? It's a weird position to be in."

I scoff. "I don't have a choice."

"What about seeing him in a friendly, non-work-related environment?" Kenneth asks.

Pressing the pillow to my face, I sigh. "Once again, I don't think I have a choice. We practically share custody of you two, so unless I want to split my already limited time with you in half, I better get used to seeing him around."

Personally and professionally.

"Want to come to Lake Anita on Tuesday?" she asks. "I know work has been a lot lately, but we miss you. *I* miss you."

If anyone understands how important my job is to me, it's Mallory. It's why she hasn't brought up any of the girls' nights I've missed because I was too busy drowning in work. Still, I feel guilty.

I sigh. "I have a ton of work to do, but I'll be there."

Kenneth grabs my carton of ice cream and dips his spoon into it. "I remember when you and Cade were inseparable. You two were practically in lo—"

"Stop." I sit up. "Do you want to give my best friend little red-headed babies someday?"

Emerald eyes dart nervously between me and Mallory. "We actually haven't decided if we want to—"

"That's not what I'm asking you, Kenneth. I'm asking if you want to keep your dick attached to your body or not." I scan my bedroom for something sharp. Tweezers may take an eternity, but they'll get the job done.

"Very badly."

I smile. "Then don't finish that sentence."

He shivers. "It should be illegal to be sixty-four inches of pure terror."

Mallory wraps her arms around us both. "Quit it. Play nice you two."

Because I love them, I'll play nice with Cade too.

CHAPTER SIX

Cade

"C.C.! Let me go! This is your fault!"

"No!" I scream, holding a wiggling Violet in front of me.

Mom grabs a heaping handful of flour and stalks through the kitchen like a tiger following its prey. "Taking a hostage won't save you, Cade Charles! Even if it is my baby girl."

I hoped using Violet would shield me from Mom's wrath, but now we're all covered in flour.

"*Moooooom!*" Violet screeches. "Help me!"

"I'm sorry, baby! Your brother dragged you into his mess." Deep smile lines crease her face, but there's a stern look in her eyes. "I can't believe you went into that woman's job and requested her! Have I not taught you anything about respect?"

As if on cue, Violet shimmies out of my grasp, and I take a powdery shot to the face, inhaling the flour like smoke.

"Yeah, C.C.! Learn some respect!" Violet mimics, sprinting to the living room for safety.

"It's been four days! How much longer are you going to be mad?"

"Forever!" they shout.

If I had known every important woman in my life would be upset, I'd go back and sign with Trevor in a heartbeat. Mallory's reaction was ten times scarier than the blow-up I'd expected.

MalPal

> You must have a death wish. Or big balls. Either way, you're stupid

> You better be glad Kenneth loves you

> Idiot

> I love you too but I'm still mad

> Furious, actually

I lift my hands in surrender. "I swear I tried to give her a way out." That she refused.

Finally, Mom relents and drops the bag of flour onto the counter. "Fine, but you're on cleaning duty," she says, assessing the damage. Flour fights were a common occurrence in our house growing up. A puff of flour thrown in my face when I got home late. Swiping flour on her cheeks while she stressed over a recipe.

The heart of my childhood home is right here in the kitchen.

"Come on out, Vi!" I call. "I surrendered."

Plastic hair beads clack as she sprints around the corner and launches herself into my arms. Sticky hands grip my cheeks, forcing me to meet eyes that are identical to mine. "Mallory says when men do dumb things, they should be shamed publicly."

I mentally curse my best friend. "You're eight going on eighteen."

Placing her on the counter, I head to the pantry for the broom. The oven dings, and the smell of perfectly baked peaches makes my mouth water. Assisting Mom with catering orders at home is my favorite, but the dessert in the oven is specially made by me with a heap of regret and sprinkled apologies.

"How are you feeling? Nervous?" Mom asks, grabbing a towel to wipe down the counters. Even when she wins, she helps me clean.

The nerves are eating me alive, but I smile anyway. "Great."

Mom looks mildly suspicious. She knows about my history with Shay, and in an hour, I'll be at Lake Anita for her surprise graduation party.

It was stupid to think seeing Shay at Permian wouldn't hurt. Her favorite color clung to her fluid figure in a way I wish I still could. Seeing her in that dusky pink reminded me of late nights watching the sun go down with our legs tangled. Of her laugh muffled against my skin. Of all my favorite memories.

She held herself high, knowing exactly how much space she takes up and daring anyone to ask her to shrink. Braids fell in loose curls around full hips, with delicate strands free near her temples, so stubborn like her. Standing in front of me, she was dreamlike yet completely real.

But the moment her eyes met mine, I knew everything was different. She didn't smile. Didn't soften. Her gaze was cold and untrusting, as if trying to protect herself.

From me.

"It'll be wonderful," Mom declares, ever the optimist. "You were out there chasing your dreams. There's nothing wrong with that. Leaving to do what you love is not a crime."

She's right, but I lost the woman I love in the process.

"Don't worry about that, Ma. Worry about how I'm going to explain why I have flour in my hair and look like a Black, loc'd Santa Claus."

Taking the broom, she smiles. "Go shower. I'll take care of the mess. Love you."

I kiss her temple. "Love you."

"Hey, Cade," Jo calls from the kitchen. "Can you come here?"

Ignoring the pulsing ache in my hip, I drag my attention from the rippling water outside to the tattered couch I jumped on as a kid. Lake Anita was my second home growing up, owned by Kenneth's grandmother. Nan taught me how to swim in the lake when I was six. She and Kenneth chased baseballs I hit into the water, letting me practice for hours without complaint. I haven't been here since returning to North Carolina, but it still feels the same.

A pink bomb exploded inside the small house. Hot pink streamers hang from the ceiling. Pretzels are dipped in white icing with fuchsia sprinkles. Cupcakes and donuts are stacked on the dining table.

Ducking to avoid hitting my head on the doorframe, I step into the kitchen. "What's up?"

Jo looks up, mixing something in a bowl. "Kenneth was supposed to help me finish the cookies, but he's too busy making googly eyes at Mallory."

A laugh comes from the hallway bathroom. "I'm just a man!"

"A weak man," Jo mutters, grabbing what looks like a massive condom and cutting the tip off. "Can you help me?"

I dive into action, taking what she explains is a piping bag, and funnel pink icing into it. Jo's stress baking kept The Quartet alive in college, constantly rotating between delicious goodies to battle her pre-med stress.

"Where's Adrienne?" I ask. "Doesn't she have first dibs on licking the bowls and spoons?"

Chilly hands with sparkly gold rings on every finger cover my eyes. "My senses are tingling. I sure hope everything said about me was pleasant."

When I turn around, Adri's pink dress glitters under the pendant lights. Tonight's dress code is all shades of pink, and everyone is complying. Jo's bubblegum sweatsuit looks incredibly comfortable. Mallory's cardigan and Kenneth's flannel are the same shade. The rose-colored tee I found in my closet is slightly faded but passes for pink.

Jo pushes a beater toward me and hands Adri the icing-covered spatula. "I don't know anybody who can eat sweets like you two. Yet neither of you have ever had a cavity. It's unfair."

Rich chocolate melts on my tongue. Jo makes the treats, but she's a savory kind of girl.

"Hiya, Cade," Adri says. "Can't believe you didn't come to Jo's and my parties."

"You know I was in Boston or I would've been there." Stepping forward, I wrap them both in a quick hug before Jo can scurry away from the physical touch. "Congrats on graduating. You're CLU alumni."

Like I could have been, except I left before getting my diploma.

"Stop it. You almost sound like a big brother."

"I practically am. How many parties did I pick you up from? And what about the bad dates I bailed you out of? Remember that magician who—"

"Okay!" Adri shouts, tossing a kazoo at my face. "No need to air all my dirty laundry."

"We already know about it," Jo mumbles, pulling a tray of cookies from the freezer.

Tired of what she calls bullying, Adri stomps out of the kitchen but blows us a kiss before disappearing.

I take a moment to appreciate Jo's precise and steady hands as she pipes icing onto the cooled *S*-shaped cookies. That skill will come in handy when she becomes a world-renowned surgeon.

"So," I start, "is it just us tonight?" Mallory would've warned me if a guy were coming, but I didn't have the courage to ask. And Jo doesn't care as much about hurting my feelings. I like that about her.

A rare tenderness overtakes Jo's meticulous features. She knows what I'm asking, but we both know I don't have a right to.

Finally, she says, "Yup. Shay doesn't have much time for anything but work these days. Dating is definitely off the table."

The knot in my gut releases, but a wave of sadness hits me as high beams float in through the large windows and bathe the living room with light.

Bursting into action, Jo piles cookies onto a glass tray. Mallory sprints from the back with Adri close behind, their arms filled with pink gift bags and boxes. Tonight, Shay will be surrounded by her favorite color with her favorite foods and the people she loves.

And one person she probably hates.

"Take your positions!" Mallory orders, standing in the corner of the living room with a confetti cannon. Adri holds a pink shot glass, and Jo crouches by the light switch.

Then I remember that Shay hates surprise parties.

"Hello?" Shay opens the door. "Why are the lights off?"

With a primal scream, Mallory releases the confetti cannon.

"Surprise!" everyone shouts.

"Mother fu—" Shay chops wildly at the air, as if preparing for a fight. The terror that flickers in her wide eyes fizzles as they roll, exasperated. "You assholes! I said no surprise parties."

"Yeah, and I said no clowns." Adri grimaces. "And guess who showed up at *my* party."

"He was a balloon artist!" Mallory argues. "I didn't think he'd come dressed as a clown."

"His name was Bozo, Cap! What non-clown person is named that?" Adri kneels in front of Shay and holds out the shot glass. "Tequila for the graduate."

Thick lashes flutter as Shay takes it, and the room cheers as she swallows the clear liquid without wincing. Their laughter is louder than the cannon still ringing in my ears, but I wouldn't turn the volume down if I could.

Then she spots me, and her eyes narrow. She may have known I was coming, but she's not happy about my presence.

Hot pink denim is tight around her thighs but flows around her ankles, revealing pink high-top Converse. A cream tank top clings to her chest, accentuating toned arms and shoulders. Seeing her at work five days ago was painful, but seeing her here is downright brutal.

"Hi," I say, waving like an idiot.

Shay's jaw ticks as our friends filter out of the living room, leaving us alone. We might have been alone in the boardroom for a few minutes, but this feels different. She doesn't have to hide our history here. And she doesn't have to act as if she likes me.

I clear my throat. "Congrats."

She presses her lips together, clearly unimpressed by my shoddy conversational skills. "Thanks, Cade. I look forward to working with you professionally."

Lie, but I want to believe it's true.

She ran out of Permian's boardroom before the ink on my contract was dry and didn't look back.

"Mallory said no work talk, but let's meet next week during your homestand." My lips quirk at her use of the baseball term as she opens her phone's calendar app and swipes to the first game of our series in

Charlotte. "We can discuss your goals and what you want from this partnership."

I nod, but what I want isn't possible. All I want is for Shay to look at me like she used to. I want to hear her bubbly laugh until she cries. I want to pepper her cheeks with kisses until she dissolves into a mess on my lap. I want her to hold my hand when she's scared like she did the night we got our ears pierced together.

Gold hoops dangle from her earlobes, and I rub the small silver hoop in mine.

"I see you conquered your fear and got a few more."

Slim fingers fiddle with the two additions at the top of her ear. "They hurt way less than the first. I still can't believe I bled that much. It looked like I had survived a horror movie."

"We should've gone to the hospital the moment you started screaming."

Shay's determination to get her ears pierced, even though she was afraid of needles, was admirable. Earlier that night, she'd eaten a spoonful of cat food so I wasn't alone, which is why I got my ears pierced too.

Solidarity was always our thing.

The heavy fog of tension lessens slightly, but as Kenneth and Mallory round the corner, it returns in full force. Bare shoulders rise, calm features pinch, and Shay puts an extra step between us. No matter how clear it is that things have changed, it still hurts like hell.

Mallory's smile is weak. "Hey, sorry to interrupt. Dessert is ready."

Kenneth's eyes bore into me as Shay darts away from us. They're not accusatory or judgmental. Just sad, which is almost worse.

"Did something happen?" he asks.

I grin. *Keep smiling.* "No. Everything is fine. You don't need to worry about her."

"What if we're not only worried about her?" Mallory snaps. "Have you thought about that?"

Her tone is what almost undoes me, but keeping them from worrying is my main priority. If I start digging into everything that happened over the last two years with Jon and baseball and my crumbling mental health, they would try to move in with me.

Losing Shay was my fault, and instead of talking about it, I bottled it up with everything else and threw myself deeper into baseball and my image.

I wrap my arms around my two best friends and rest my chin in Mallory's coconut-scented twist out. "Don't worry about me, MalPal. You either, Kent. That's the last thing I want."

After convincing them I'm fine, I snag a seat at the dining table beside Adri. The steaming peach cobbler sits in a pink baking dish with a graduation hat poking out of the flaky, perfectly browned top. Dessert before dinner is a Quartet tradition—stopping for ice cream on their way to pick up Thai food or buying candy before their pizza feast.

"Joelly Bean!" Shay beams. "You made me a peach cobbler?"

Cloudy blue eyes meet mine in a panicked stare, but before Jo can respond, Adri giggles.

"Jo didn't make that. Cade did."

My cheeks flush. It was supposed to be a secret, but Adri wasn't around when we discussed.

Shay lifts a skeptical, perfectly shaped brow. "You? Made this?"

Her doubt is valid. After starting two kitchen fires at her and Mallory's house in college, I was banned from touching any appliances that weren't the fridge or water filter. I may not have inherited the cooking gene, but Mom has the best peach cobbler recipe and isn't afraid of me starting a little fire.

I laugh. "I've changed a lot since college."

"Yeah. I know." Hurt simmers beneath her composed tone. She must hear it too because she clears her throat. "Thank you, Cade."

Kenneth, my saving grace, claps and begins serving dessert. Over everyone's heads, he gives me a look. *I'm here for you,* it says. I hold my hands in a heart above my head. For the rest of the evening, he doesn't leave my side.

There are a lot of reasons to be happy, but being back with them is at the top of the list.

CHAPTER SEVEN

DID YOU KNOW PROCRASTINATION kills forty people a year?

I'm kidding. There's no definitive statistic, but I bet there's been at least one death a year, and it isn't going to be me. Which is why I'm sitting in my car twenty minutes before my first meeting with Cade.

When we stopped talking nearly two years ago, I assumed the worst thing that would happen would be walking down the aisle together when Mallory and Kenneth get married. I never thought I'd have to work with him and act like I didn't know personal things about him. Like how he's deathly afraid of caterpillars and butterflies. Or how his sister calls him C.C., even though it reminds him of his dad. Or how the stubble along his jaw felt against my neck, collarbones, and between my—

A robotic screech pulls me from memory lane. It's ear splitting, but the assigned ringtone was chosen because the person calling me is likely to be crying when I answer.

"Morning, Holly," I say. Grabbing the basket in my backseat, I start down the sidewalk.

Holly Trent, my adorably needy client, wails, "She didn't know about the letters! All this time, he thought she was ignoring him. Isn't that heartbreaking? I'd cut ties with my mother if she cockblocked me like that."

Ah. She watched *The Notebook*.

Holly's pre-game routine is unique. She's convinced that if she doesn't cry before a game, she'll be more vicious than usual. Even though I'm an agent who believes in stats and metrics, her theory has proven to be true. Earlier this season, she watched *The Last Song,* sure it would make her sob. It didn't, and she ended up with a red card. Following that debacle, I sent her my list of the saddest movies I could think of. I'm twelve for twelve on Holly's tears.

"You and your weird rituals. Remind me why I work with you?"

She tuts. "Because your office is full of dicks, literally and figuratively, but you listened."

Holly was my first client, signed a week after I became a full-time agent. After tearing her ACL in a pickup basketball game, Holly went from high-profile star to forgotten. She lost her agent, interested teams, and potential endorsement opportunities. When she walked into Permian, healed and ready for a second chance, my colleagues passed on her.

I had no clue how my life would change when I stumbled into the normally empty restroom near my office and found Holly crying at the sink. After thirty minutes of talking to—and begging—Winston and Trevor, she was mine.

"Any fun plans for today?" she asks. I don't know why she does this when she knows I'm working. I'm *always* working.

Before I can answer, the hostess appears. "Welcome to Velvet Yolk. Do you have a reservation?"

"Yes. Shaylene Turner."

The raven-haired woman glides around the podium and beckons me to follow.

"Velvet Yolk?" Holly groans. "I'm so jealous! I heard it takes weeks to get a reservation. *Please* tell me you're on a date."

She knows better. "I took you to The Marlowe when I signed you, which was fancy too."

"Oh crap. I forgot you signed a new client." Her laugh is bittersweet. "Love seeing you grow, but I miss being able to blow your phone up."

"Miss it? You've never stopped." Thanking the hostess, I take a seat at the table in the back corner and drag my finger along the buttery yellow tablecloth. It's more secluded than I would like, but it'll work. "Did you see my email about the podcast?"

Her lack of response makes me assume she's scrolling through hundreds of unread emails. I organize it weekly, but it's always full.

After a minute, she shrieks, "Holy shit. *Women in Sports* wants to talk to me?"

"Of course they do. You're Holly freaking Trent." My eyes flick over the menu. "They want an answer by next week."

"My answer is yes! Duh! Best agent ever." She exhales. "Have fun at brunch and tell me if the Velvet Eggs Benedict is good. I heard it's life changing, but I feel like that word is overused nowadays."

After wishing her good luck for tonight's game, I hang up and refocus. Today, I'm welcoming Cade to my team, even though I'd rather eat glass. Still, I'll be professional. Nothing comes before my job.

Heart be damned.

During my time as an agent, I've crossed paths with many gorgeous athletes. Shemar Moore-level sexy, and if I can say no to a man who looks like an old-school Denzel Washington, I can control myself around the man who broke my heart.

"Hi, Shay baby."

I jolt, banging my knee against the thick table as I take in the man standing in front of me. Cade looks at ease in a sleeveless black tank and dark denim. Damn him and his ability to be hotter than my celebrity crushes.

Empty tables surround us, so nobody heard his very unprofessional nickname for me. But I have to put an end to it. Now.

"Rule number one," I say. "Don't call me that."

A tiny dimple appears in his cheek. "Noted. How about Agent Shay?"

The server appears before I can reject the unimaginative nickname. "What can I get you to drink?"

"Diet Coke, please," I say.

"Unsweet tea for me," Cade says.

"Wonderful. Are you ready to order food or do you need more time?"

I already know what I want, and by the look on Cade's face, he does too. We always researched menus before arriving at the restaurant. It kept us from decision paralysis. I order the Velvet Eggs Benedict, and Cade orders the Lobster and Grits Amore. This place may be a little bit fancier than where I took Holly, but I need to show Cade I'm all business.

Once we're alone, I hand over the wicker basket. "This is a thank you from Permian. We're happy you've joined our team."

Cellophane crinkles as Cade digs into the gift. "Hmm. I didn't realize Permian knew my favorite flavor of Laffy Taffy is banana, or that, while most people know I like sour gummy candy, I prefer sour gummy bears."

My face flushes. "I made the basket, but it's from Permian."

"Well, give the agency my thanks. And thank you, *Agent Shay*."

The moment my Diet Coke touches the table, I place the straw between my lips. I could've gotten the luxury-gift option Trevor recommended, but that's not how I roll. Because Holly loves Queen, I found her a Freddie Mercury pin and vintage Queen record. Brett loves mac and cheese and outer space, so I got him boxes of planet-shaped noodles. When I found out Delilah likes silly posters for her apartment, I entered an online bidding war for Beyoncé and Brittney Spears *Got Milk?* posters and won. Victoria loves Oreos, so she got a multi-year Oreo subscription. Lionel is picky, so he got a gift card.

Since it's Cade, it feels personal, but it's not.

Then he pulls out the last part of his gift, and wary eyes find mine. "Pink sticky notes?"

Every client gets a package, but I wish I hadn't put them in there for him. It was one of our things. Sticking them to his car's windshield. Hiding them in his textbooks. BYOB nights. I probably wrote him hundreds of notes, but they're long gone now. Probably rotting away in landfills.

"Yeah." I shove the memories away and cough. "For reminders."

Artificial banana fills my nose as he opens a piece of candy. "You stuck one to my forehead sophomore year at the library. Do you remember what it said?"

"Stop talking," I say, fighting off the warmth of that day. Our thighs were pressed together because it was the only table I could find.

"Exactly!"

"No. I mean yes, but no. I'm telling you to stop talking. We need to set rules." Grabbing my personal stack of sticky notes from my purse, I scribble *Rules* at the top and underline it twice. "Rule number one: no talking about the past."

"I thought rule number one is that I can't call you Shay baby?"

I glare at his stupid smirk. "Fine. Number two is no talking about the past."

He pauses mid-chew. "Is there a reason we can't talk about it?"

"You're joking, right?" Forcing myself to swallow my irritation, I take a drink before answering, "We had over a year to talk and didn't. Now we're here. We can't be those people anymore, and as of today, we're work partners, which means talking about the past and what we used to be can't happen."

Sadness isn't an emotion Cade shows the world. But seeing his downturned lips and somber eyes? I suddenly feel sick.

Still, we can't go backward. The rules will keep me and my job safe.

After swallowing the candy, he nods. "Okay. No talking about the past."

Relief replaces my unease. People can't find out we were more than friends. Not Trevor. Not the press. No one. That would be yet another reason on men's lists to not take me seriously.

I can't take back what I wanted in college, but I can move forward.

My stomach grumbles in response to the decadent smell of food, and I'm thankful for a distraction as our meals arrive, popping the awkward bubble surrounding us.

I grin at my plate, but when I spot the pickle spear, my smile disappears. Stabbing it with my fork, I stretch my arm across the table and drop it onto his plate. Now I'm ready to dig in, but Cade's laugh distracts me.

"What?" I ask.

Perfect white teeth snap the pickle in half. "Thanks for the pickle. Just like old times."

As a certified pickle hater, Cade always ate mine without complaint. Getting rid of old habits is going to take serious work.

"It won't happen again," I assure him, but it's mostly for me.

"Hmm. What are the odds of that?"

"Don't." I point my fork at him. "Rule number three. No game."

He holds up the half-eaten pickle in surrender, and I almost laugh. It's impressive how good he is at pulling people into his orbit. Cade makes you feel seen, heard, and trust that he'll always be there.

But he wasn't for me.

One bite is enough to categorize this meal as life changing. Holly's going to flip when I tell her it's even better than she could imagine, rich and buttery with a hint of lemon.

He picks at the massive piece of lobster on his plate. "Are you coming to tonight's game?"

I shake my head. "Wasn't planning on it."

"Do you want to? Feels like that would be an agent thing to do."

He's got me there.

"Sure," I concede, but I won't go alone. Yes, it's work, but I need support.

I open The Quartet's shared calendar. Mallory's babysitting and Jo's studying for medical school since she leaves soon. Adri's all-day event makes me chuckle into my drink.

Invite me to something. I'm too sexy to be this bored.

Me

> Want to go to a baseball game tonight?

Adri's response appears immediately.

Menace to Society

> Hot guys in baseball pants and I get to watch you work with your ex? Sign me up

Me

> Not ex. Almost-ex

Menace to Society

> Whatever you tell yourself to feel better! See you soon!

When I put my phone down, I realize how awkward this situation is. We finish our meals in silence, never getting to the other topics I planned.

Chapter Eight

 *Shay*

Baseball is so sexy, and I'm not talking about the men.

Pure athleticism is what makes this sport so captivating. There's beauty in every position. The catcher's incredible mobility and strength. The pitcher, throwing baseballs faster than most highways allow cars to drive. Infielders with their quick reflexes. Outfielders, who can rocket the ball across the entire field.

"Man, I love this sport!" Adri cheers, whipping a Pilots towel in the air above her head. "Best asses ever!"

Snapping a photo of the field, I send it to my dad. "You need help, my friend."

When I told Trevor I was studying for the baseball certification exam, he decided it was his civic duty to tell me that baseball players are usually married or in long-term relationships, as if I was only taking the exam to find a man.

He couldn't have been more wrong.

I'm here for the way baseball makes me feel. The electricity that crackles along my spine every time the ball connects with the bat. The roar of blood that fills my ears when someone makes an amazing stop. The players' proud smiles that I can't help but mirror as they make their home run lap. The way each player wears their heart on their sleeve, beating so hard, I practically feel it in my own body.

My watch lights up with a text, and I grin.

Daddio

> I'm so jealous. Take me next time! Work or fun?

One of my many bullet points to discuss earlier with Cade went unanswered, but the biggest is what happened with Jon, and how we should announce his new representation. Thankfully, my family doesn't know about Cade's and my history. Dad and Myles might not care, but Mom would blow a gasket if she knew. My professionalism is her main priority.

An unintelligible garble of sound leaves my lips when Cade darts to the right, stopping a ball from rocketing into the outfield. "Yes!" I squeal, writing on my legal pad. *Incredible speed!*

"Your boy is doing well," Adri says, red lips slanted into a smirk.

I attempt to pinch her thigh, but she pulls down the white Pilots jersey she's wearing as a dress. "Adrienne," I hiss. "Someone might hear you."

Worries of being overheard disappear when I notice every agent is absorbed in their phones. Cade kindly offered to upgrade our seating, but as badly as I wanted the best seats in the house, I declined. I'm his agent, not his friend. Professional boundaries are important if this is going to work.

Adri fans herself with a scorecard. "I meant your athlete, of course. Nothing more."

I roll my eyes. "I should have let you die of boredom."

My notepad is filled with notes from the last four innings, questions for the Pilots' general manager, and praise for Cade's game. Maybe it's not the worst thing to already know what kind of player Cade is. Sitting in the stands between Mallory and Kenneth is how I spent my evenings during college baseball season.

"Remember when you got injured during soccer playoffs your freshman year?"

Adri nods, fingers ghosting over her hip. "Coach almost benched me during the championship game. Why?"

I follow Cade's movement as he jogs to the dugout with his arms extended like an airplane, the Pilots' celebratory dance. It's barely noticeable, but there's a slight dip in his gait as he crosses the field.

"No reason," I say. I don't like thinking my player is possibly injured, especially while he seems so okay, but Cade has always been like that. You think you know him, but then you realize he hides other parts of himself. It's always sunshine with him.

"*Daaaamn*," Adri whispers, scrunching her curls. "Hottie alert."

Although I'm on the clock, Adri calling someone hot is the real deal, so I sneak a peek over my shoulder and immediately wish I hadn't.

Smoothing my slacks, I straighten as Andy takes a seat behind me. "Hey, Turner."

Back when we were interns at Permian, Andy was my friend. After we signed our contracts, I confided in him about the way Trevor excluded me. The next day, Trevor told me if I had a problem with him, I should say it to his face. I went from being in hot water with my boss to being scalded every time I entered the office.

Even now, it's painful to walk into work.

Without turning around, I point at Adri. "This is Adri. Adri, this is Andy Walker."

The moment she hears his name, her eyes dart to me, and I can practically read her mind. *I am not shaking this asshole's hand. He's the snitch.*

My lips quirk up. *Just a quick shake.*

She scowls. *Fine. Only because I love you.*

"Hello." Andy's easy-going charm deepens his voice. "It's nice to meet you, Adri."

In true Adri fashion, she wipes her hand along her leg and looks him up and down. "I'd say the same, but that wouldn't be true."

I bite down on my lip to suppress a laugh and focus on the game. Adri doesn't care who she offends, and it gives me the boost I need to get through the next four innings.

A hard-fought Pilots win has the stadium buzzing. My hands are still tingling as Adri and I make our way down to the players' area with our arms looped. She knows I've been denied entry before, but having a witness to my shame might kill me.

My chest tightens when I spot the security guard. "I don't need to meet Cade tonight. I'll email him or—"

"Nuh-uh. Look at me," she orders, pulling us to a stop in the middle of the hallway. "You're gonna go in there and talk to your client. Do you hear me? You're the best agent in that room. Having a great set of tits doesn't negate that fact."

It's impossible not to smile at the compliment and her undying loyalty. My boobs are pretty great.

"You may be a menace, but you're my menace. Thank you."

Her hip bumps mine. "Any time."

At the door, the guard assesses my badge. "Turner?"

"Shaylene Turner," I say. "Yes."

After a brief pause, he opens the door. "Go on in. Cade told me to expect his agent."

I almost trip over myself as I walk into the restricted area. Being taken seriously fills me with triumph, and I have Cade to thank.

Adri presses her lips to my cheek. "You've got this. Find me when you're done."

The bustling room is saturated with stunning women and partners, adorable children, and proud family members. I find a small table in the corner and take a seat. My first postgame discussion with Cade has to go well. He's bigger, faster, and stronger than he was in college. My notepad is filled with praises I didn't want to forget.

I'm debating how to ask him about his hip, when mint invades my senses and I lift my head. Dejected hazel eyes clash with the celebration around us, frozen on the legal pad in my hands.

"Nice game," I say, standing quickly.

He blows out a slow breath. "Not really."

Ready to prove him wrong, I tap on a note about his height being an advantage and smile up at him. "In the third inning you—"

"Missed two grounders. Back to back. It was bad. There's a lot to work on between now and the next series, especially if I want to keep everyone happy. So, tell me everything I did wrong."

Defensiveness sharpens his tone. And if I'm right, fear too.

"Why would you think I'd do that?" I ask.

As if bracing for impact, his spine straightens. "That's your job, isn't it?"

My mouth falls open. Who is this man in front of me?

"Cade—"

A hand slices between us, and I jump back. Tattooed vines and flowers are inked into the thickest forearm I've ever seen, but nothing could prepare me to find one of my favorite pitchers grinning at me.

Holy shit.

Dawson Huber leans against Cade. "Wow, rookie. She's even prettier in person. This is your—"

"Agent." The word leaves my lips so quickly, I worry I should repeat it for good measure.

Dawson's smile should shrink, but it widens. "You're Shay, right?"

And here come the hives. "Yes. His agent."

It takes a beat for Dawson to recover from his moment of shock, but then he extends his hand. "It's nice to meet you, Shay. Don't see many female agents. Pretty badass if you ask me."

His normalcy relaxes me, but fear drums quietly beneath my skin. "Thank you."

As if sensing my unease, Dawson scampers toward his family.

"Please tell me I'm overreacting," I say, watching Dawson launch an adorable round-faced child into the air. "Does he know about me? Us?"

Cade bows his head. "Sort of. I told him there was someone that things never worked out with. But that's all, I swear."

"You clearly showed him a picture," I hiss. "He recognized me!"

For the first time tonight, his smile shifts from plastic to real. Like my Cade.

"Kind of hard not to brag when it comes to you, Agent Shay."

A blush blooms under my darkened cheeks, but I glare at him. "He can't say a word. People can't know about us, Cade. Losing my job would—"

"You won't lose anything," he promises. "Dawson won't say a word. I'll make sure of it."

His assurance doesn't completely alleviate my stress, but what other choice do I have?

"Hey, Cade!" someone shouts. "You coming out tonight?"

"Not tonight, Marc. Gonna head home." He drops his head to meet my eye. "Thanks for coming, Shay ba—" A tiny smile tilts. "Agent Shay."

My eyes dart around the room. Every player looks like they could sleep for twelve hours, but Cade's exhaustion seems different. It's one of the first things I noticed when he walked into Permian a week ago. Even when smiling, there is something hollow about the curved shape.

After college baseball games, we had BYOB—Bring Your Own Breakdown—nights. Together, we broke down every high and low in a way that kept his spirits up. By the end of the night, pink sticky notes were scattered all over the ground. When I headed home, the sting of the harder notes was nearly nonexistent.

It wasn't until junior year that I started staying the night after.

People saw Cade as the golden baseball player and nothing more, but I only saw him.

I need to tell him that even though we aren't together and things didn't end on the best terms, I'm still in his corner. I always will be.

By the time I look up to speak, Cade's gone.

CHAPTER NINE

Cade

WHO KNEW SOMETHING AS harmless as a legal pad could cause so much distress?

I pace across the hardwood floor, stepping over scattered pieces of yellow paper. Jon's loopy scrawl makes my stomach turn, but I need to prepare for the upcoming series in Florida. Reading his notes may seem stupid, but mixed into the barbwire comments are random pieces of information that could help me stay at a high level.

After last night's win, the media called me the current best shortstop in the league. Keeping up this momentum is important if I want to stay in North Carolina with my people.

With Shay.

A pang of regret hits my temples, paired nicely with the dull ache in my chest. The yellow legal pad in Shay's hands turned on both fight and flight mode last night. I couldn't read her tiny script, but I already know she documented every mistake and slip up, just like Jon.

At least once a week, I swear I'll get rid of Jon's notes, but I hide them under my bed instead.

I didn't want to snap at her. I tried to imagine our first postgame meeting could be like our BYOB nights from college. Shay managed to make picking apart baseball games fun. Even my mistakes. She was a breath of fresh air in a suffocating room.

But it's different now. Her only job is to make sure I'm at my best.

My fingers itch, and I know I shouldn't, but I swipe my phone from the coffee table and press the familiar name before I can stop myself. After one ring, a deep sigh fills my ear.

"Wow." I laugh, slipping off my glasses. "Is that how you answer the phone for all your clients?"

"Nope. Only you." Shay yawns. "Is everything okay?"

Not really. Last night's dinner sits untouched on the kitchen table. An explosion of clothes went off in front of the laundry room, scattered around my partially packed suitcase. The living room looks as if a tornado destroyed an office building.

My brain is as much of a mess as my house.

"Yeah." I cough. "I'm fine."

The disbelieving hum she releases hits me hard. Probably because I spouted off the same lie every time she tried to check in after I left for California.

"It's fine."

"Everything is fine."

"I'm fine, Shay baby. Tell me about your day."

Cade Owens. Caretaker and peacekeeper, even at my own expense.

"You're up early," I say, desperate to fill the silence.

"So are you. What time are you meeting the team at the private terminal?"

I almost forgot about the game. "Nine."

"Is there a reason you're calling me at six in the morning?"

Because I needed to hear your voice, I think.

Papers crunch beneath me as I sit on the leather couch. "I wanted to see if you had any feedback for me before this series."

A beat passes. "You want my advice?"

It's physically painful to nod, but I do. "Yes."

Another pause. "Well, my best advice is that even if you strike out, run to first base and act confident. Everyone will be too confused to stop you."

A surprised laugh slips from me as I lie down and prop my head up against the armrest. With her voice in my ear, my body relaxes for the first time in hours. "I might give that a shot."

"Don't blame me if you do," she says. "But in all seriousness, I don't think you need any words of wisdom from me. You're the best shortstop in the league—"

"Aw." I press my lips together. "You think I'm the best?"

"I was going to say *according to multiple articles*, but whatever." Although she doesn't laugh, her cadence is light. "Actually, I made a note last night that I did want to talk about." Every fuzzy feeling dissipates at the sound of rustling paper. "Here it is. Your height is a real advantage, and you use it well. Buck, Orlando's pitcher, is on the shorter side, so remember that when it comes to his release point."

"Oh." That wasn't what I expected. Instead of berating me, her words are insightful and helpful. But it's not just that. It's the way she says it. Non-judgmental and constructive.

"Oh?" Shay repeats. "I'm sorry. I didn't mean to overstep—"

"No!" I blurt. "You didn't." The way her face fell last night flashes across my brain. I wonder how many times I've been the reason for that frown. "And I want to apologize for last night. I'm sorry. I shouldn't have spoken to you that way."

She hums. "Don't worry about it. I'm used to people being rude to me. Female agent and all." The casual tone of her voice makes me want to shake every person who has ever made her feel like that. Including myself. "I need to take this call, but good luck tonight, Cade."

The call ends before I can respond. Almost immediately, my phone vibrates with a text.

Shay Baby

> If you want to sleep, I can give you a wake-up call before your flight

It's sad to see it's been almost two years since our last message. Changing her contact name hurts, but I would hate for someone to get the wrong idea if they saw it.

Me

> I won't be able to sleep, but feel free to call me anytime

> And I mean that

Her reply is immediate.

Agent Shay

> Rule number 4. No flirting

With a laugh, I stand and leave Jon's notes behind. It doesn't seem possible, but they don't sting as much. For the next few hours, I'm not going to think about my old agent. I'm going to think about my new agent. Like I have since the day I met her.

And clean my house.

"Are eggplants supposed to be this big? Because this is impressive."

Violet nudges my sore hip. "Grow up, C.C.!"

"Listen to your little sister," Mom adds, voice crackling through the phone. "And grab the biggest ones. Gotta stuff those bad boys to the brim for tomorrow's event."

I hand Violet a tote bag. "Make us proud, little."

She nods and searches through the bin of dark purple vegetables. Clear Lake's farmers market has the best produce. On my scheduled off days, I take Mom's grocery list, which is longer than baseball season, and do the shopping.

"We stopped by Loc & Key," I tell Mom, twirling the brown paper bags around my wrist. Emma, my loctician, recommended giving my hair extra love, so I bought every product.

"Did Violet talk you into getting more beads?"

"Five different colors." I check eggplants off the list when Violet gives me a thumbs-up. "Anything else you need me to get while I'm out?"

"No." She grunts. "Off days are meant for rest, Cade Charles. Not running my errands."

After three long days in Florida, rest would be nice, but my mother is the reason I'm able to play baseball. If grocery shopping, spending time with my little sister, and helping her cook means I don't rest, then so be it.

"I'm failing to see the problem. I like doing these things for you."

"Fine," Mom yields, her voice tender. "Just make sure you're taking care of yourself, okay?"

I smile. "Okay, Ma."

With a promise to be home in an hour, I hang up and take the tote from Violet's trembling arms. Then her eyes dart behind me, she lets out an excited squeal, and she's gone before I can grab her. Slipping the woman behind the counter a hundred-dollar bill, I dash after Violet, but I freeze when I spot the person hugging her.

Toned legs are wrapped in sleek, black fabric that outline pure strength. Whatever fancy workout top Shay has on crisscrosses in the back, ebony skin sparkling in the sunlight. Violet's joy is blinding as they spin in circles, and my agent looks down at her with a rare, toothy smile.

Shay has always been one to give smiles to those who deserve them. *Earn* them.

"I rode the biggest slide at the water park!" Violet cheers, adjusting her swimsuit strap. "And I wasn't even scared. C.C. took me!"

"C.C.?" Shay stiffens when she finds me, those pretty lips pressed into an unreadable line. "Cade."

I plop my hand onto Violet's head. "What have I told you about running away, Vi?"

Her eyes drop to the ground. "That it's not safe because weirdos are everywhere. But I know Shay, and she's nice! Not a weirdo."

"Correct." I ruffle her chlorine-soaked puffs. "Hi, Agent Shay. Whatcha doing in Clear Lake on a random Tuesday afternoon?"

Her brow cocks in a way that says it's none of my business, but when she remembers my little sister is here too, she relaxes her evil eye. "I was at physical therapy with someone."

She's likely being vague on purpose, but it still hurts. I have no claim over Shay, anything she does, or anyone she sees, but the idea of someone else being able to hold and kiss her almost sends me to my knees in the middle of this farmers market.

"Want to shop with us, Shay Shay?" Violet jumps in. "We can't find the collard greens."

Shay shoots me a wary look. One that begs me to please let Violet down nicely, but I'm a selfish man, so I don't give her an out.

"Yeah," I say. "Join us."

I try and fail to bite back a smile at the venomous stare she shoots me as Violet grips our hands and drags us down the aisle.

"You could've said no," Shay mutters, refusing to look at me.

"But then I wouldn't have gotten to see you."

"Rule. Four. Cade."

I hate our rules so much. "How's it possible that I flirted nonstop with you for years, and you never noticed, but now you can identify it easily?"

A ghost of a smile lifts her lips, but her attention is snatched away by baguettes, ciabatta, and focaccia. "Mmm. My dietitian is a foodie. I'd get her some, but she's too far away."

I chuckle as she snaps a photo and texts it. "You have a dietitian?"

"Yeah, one of Mallory's old classmates. I see her virtually for my PCOS."

Violet tugs on her arm. "What's POCS?"

Shay pats her own belly. "PCOS. It stands for polycystic ovary syndrome. I've got some problems with my hormones, and it affects my ovaries."

Nodding slowly, Violet moves her hands to her stomach. "Lisa says that's where babies come from. Her mom's pregnant *again*."

My eyes fly to Shay's, and I can't even care about my little sister's advanced knowledge of female anatomy because Shay is seconds from gracing me with the sound of her laugh.

Until someone jumps in front of us.

"Oh my gosh! Cade Owens! I was grabbing beets and wanted to stay hi! I've been *dying* to meet you." A slender hand is thrust at me. "I'm Summer Moore with the *Carolina Gazette*."

Talking to the media may be part of the job, but I despise it. While some reporters are kind and compassionate, others are deeply personal and intrusive. It's hard to decide which side of the spectrum Summer will fall on with her severe bun and wild eyes.

"Hi, Summer," I say, shaking her hand. "It's nice to meet you."

"How are you feeling about moving back to North Carolina? How have things been? Oh my gosh! Your sister is so cute. How old are you? Seven? Eight?" Curious eyes shift to Shay after squealing when Violet holds up eight fingers. "And who are you? Are you his girlfriend? All social media says Cade is single, but I believe privacy is so important."

As if she's my bodyguard, Shay steps slightly in front of me, and I'm hit by the heavenly scent of wildflowers.

The barrage of questions doesn't seem to affect her as she shifts into work mode. "Hello. I'm Shaylene Turner, Cade's agent with Permian Sports Agency."

Seeing her like this is kind of hot.

Okay. It's *super* hot.

Summer's pupils somehow dilate further. "Holy shit!"

Violet reaches up and taps the reporter's arm. "Language," she scolds.

"Sorry," Summer whispers, letting out a winded breath. "I'm sorry. Last I heard, you were being repped by Jon Sweeney. Is this a recent change?"

Shay nods. "Yes, we started working together a few weeks ago."

"Wow, Shaylene. Can I call you that? Or do you prefer Turner?"

"I prefer Shay or Shaylene, but most people call me Turner since it sounds a bit more—"

"Masculine." Summer sucks her teeth. "Screw them. I'm gonna call you Shay." The reporter pulls a notepad from her pocket and turns to me. "I'm happy to hear you've found new local representation, and I'm even happier that she's a *she*! What made you choose Shay over all the other agents who were desperate to work with you?"

When asked this question in the past about Jon, I could barely string together an answer. But my reply flows freely after only two weeks with Shay.

"It was an easy decision," I say. "She's knowledgeable, dedicated, and cares about her clients more than anyone I know. There's nobody I'd rather work with."

Pleased with my answer, Summer bounces on her toes. "The paper's going to love this! Can I get a photo of you guys for social media?"

I say yes automatically, but when I notice Shay's frozen expression, I pause. "One second, Summer." When she steps back to set up her camera, I face Shay. "What's wrong?"

Her fingers pick at her forehead. "I can't take a picture."

"Is it not professional to take one with me?"

I savor her annoyed exhale. "Agents and clients take photos for social media all the time." Hovering over her chin, she pulls at something I can't see. "My acne hasn't been kind to me lately. And my facial hair is much thicker than I'd like. I haven't shaved in a few days. I'm just not prepared for a photoshoot."

My hands twitch at my side, desperate to reach out and touch her face. She didn't need to prepare because she's absolutely perfect.

She looks away. "And physical therapy was with a client, but I'm in tights and a crop top! I can't be photographed like this."

Learning that she was at physical therapy for work and not with a love interest eases some of my fear, but only slightly. It still won't help me get her back.

"Nobody sane wears a pantsuit to physical therapy. Wall sits would be even worse." My joke lands, and she rewards me with a tiny snort of approval. "You look beautiful, Shay. You always do. And I'll make sure Summer knows you were coming from a work thing, okay?"

Our eyes meet, and after a moment, she nods. "Thanks, Cade."

Before I screw up and kiss her forehead, I turn back to Summer. "We're ready. Can Violet be in it too?"

"Of course! I *need* the cutest sister in the league." I lift Violet onto my hip and prop her in the gap Shay leaves between us. "Say cheese!" Summer cheers.

After posing and making sure Summer knows where Shay came from before this meeting, the Energizer Bunny rushes toward the parking lot.

"Oh shit," Shay mutters, rubbing her temples.

"Language," Violet and I say at the same time.

"Oh crap," she corrects, which makes Violet giggle. "That story will be everywhere in twenty-four hours. The *Carolina Gazette* is the biggest newspaper in North Carolina." With a tight smile, she finally meets my eye. "Well, it looks like I'm officially your agent."

Playing with the dice in my pocket, I force myself to smile. "Looks like I'm officially your client."

And nothing more.

Chapter Ten

There's nothing I hate more than being wrong. And I was wrong.

"You have nine thousand followers!" Brett hasn't stopped refreshing my social media page since he walked into my office an hour ago. "Some of these people have blue checkmarks."

"You have a blue checkmark, and that means nothing to me," I mutter.

He scoffs. "Pro athlete, Shay Shay. Many consider me a *big* deal."

In the basketball world, Brett Reynolds *is* a big deal. First-round draft pick, former college star, and everyone's go-to brunette when they need a Pinterest model, but I can't let his head get any bigger than it already is. This meeting should've been short, only to discuss the toothpaste endorsement and his goals for the upcoming season, but my moment of fame is way more exciting to him.

Within six hours of saying goodbye to Cade and Violet at the farmers market, the news of Cade's new representation hit the press. Adri shared the photo of us looking like a happy little family. Then my mother called with a quick congrats and a reminder to stay focused. Dad called next, his excitement bursting through the line. The next morning, Winston emailed the link to the entire agency to congratulate me on the announcement.

Five days later, and things are still insane.

Brett props his feet up on my desk, revealing tanned calves. "Did you read the article?"

I swipe his sneakers off and recoil. The headline made me nervous.

The Rise of Female Sports Agents? Finally!

Brett clears his throat dramatically before he reads, "Golden boy and shortstop for the Carolina Pilots, Cade Owens, has found representation in an unlikely but incredible place. Shaylene Turner, junior agent at Permian Sports Agency, is a rising star. Many know her as the elusive Angel Devil of Clear Lake University, with a sweet smile and deadly slide tackle. Her client list is stacked with stars like Brett Reynolds and Lionel Stiller of the NC Grizzlies. With a knack for negotiation and fighting for her clients, we look forward to watching Shay shine." He grins. "Sounds like this Summer woman adored you. Listed all your socials too."

I owe her for the boost. Athletes and sports teams started following me immediately, along with an influx of baseball fans.

Cracking open an energy drink, I let the caffeine bolster my confidence and open Instagram. My jaw unhinges when I see that Cade's number of followers has tripled since the article was released. His posts are scarce, dating back to college, and each one has new comments asking if his sister needs a sister-in-law.

Women are so funny.

Then I click on my profile and find some not-so-nice comments.

@gopilots629 a girl??????? ew

@baseballfanboy_ don't get why he wud leave Jon for her

@darkestpilots5 won't last long

Brett looks up and grows serious, which is not like him. "What's wrong?"

Waving away the feelings, I force an airiness into my voice. "I think I'm being judged."

He leans over my desk and snatches my phone. "No more social media. Don't let keyboard warriors who don't even know proper grammar get you down."

I knew I wouldn't get a lot of support as a female agent, considering I don't even get it from the men in my field, let alone my office, but I didn't expect my bubble of privacy to be popped in such a public way.

After nibbling the skin around my fingers, I reach into my desk for a Hello Kitty Band-Aid. "People are going to keep saying nasty things."

"Yeah, they will. Sadly, it's par for the course." Brett's laugh is sad. "But there isn't a single person who can take away what you've accomplished as an agent. You're the one who made sure the Grizzlies picked up my third-year option."

I squeeze the trophy-shaped stress ball Brett gave me before our meeting. "No, you did. It would have been a loss to the franchise if they'd traded you away."

"But who reminded them of that?" He points at me. "You built a buzz around me. You stayed in contact with the front office and got feedback that paid off. You had my back, and not only do you have mine, but you have all your clients' backs." He stares out the tiny window. "I heard you're going to physical therapy with Deshawn Miller."

My eyes fly to him. "How do you know that?"

"Athletes talk." To provoke me, he swings his legs back onto my desk. "People like you. Not that bastard Tr—" Brett's lips zip as my phone rings.

Giving him a sympathetic smile, I hold up my finger and answer. "This is Shay."

A grunt. "Five minutes, Turner." Then Trevor hangs up.

Our Friday babysitting meeting isn't for another twenty-five minutes, but duty calls.

Standing, I gather my laptop, all-client binder, and pom-pom pen. Brett walks to the elevator with me, and I wait for him to leave before starting my death march to Trevor's office.

The repugnant scent of his cologne suffocates me when I step inside.

"About time." He grunts. "You aren't getting paid to hang out with clients."

I leave the door cracked, hoping someone will walk by, hear the way he speaks to me, and stand up for me. The cold shoulder he gave me before has turned into a blizzard since I became Cade's agent.

Keeping my voice even, I take a seat. "Brett and I were discussing an endorsement opportunity, which is part of my job as his agent."

Trevor clears a minuscule space for my computer. "Tee time is in an hour, so make it quick. How's Miller?"

I flip through the three-ringed binder, searching for Deshawn Miller's tab. The power forward for the NC Grizzlies was one of Trevor's favorites, but after a torn meniscus during the offseason that required surgery, things changed.

"His procedure was last week. Physical therapy is slow but going. He has a great doctor—"

"Timeline of return?"

I flip to the next page. "Dr. Pope says there's no estimated time right now. Historically, it shouldn't take more than three to four months."

"Damn." Trevor runs an agitated hand through his hair. "I need him to be good for the season. Miller is a damn good paycheck."

"He's also a human," I bite back. Deshawn deserves a better agent than Trevor Caldwell, and I'll never let Trevor speak about him, or any of his clients, like they're nothing more than dollar signs.

He levels me with a fierce glare but doesn't fight back. "What about Garrett Blane?"

"He won't be deciding on an agent soon, but I think I have a chance."

"Yeah. Whatever you say." The gold watch on Trevor's wrist sparkles in the light as he checks the time. "Updates on your clients."

Ignoring the dig, I push forward. "Holly's speaking with a podcast next week to discuss her journey to the pros. Brett signed a toothpaste endorsement this morning. Lionel is home from vacation, and we're going over his game plan for the season soon. Victoria's acclimating well to the new team. Delilah is playing well, as always. And I'm meeting with Cade next week to discuss what he wants from this partnership."

Blond brows wiggle. "I can tell you what he wants out of your partnership, and it has nothing to do with baseball."

Sitting on my hands is the only way to stop myself from reaching over the desk and strangling him.

"By the way," he continues, "Levi's old position of intermediate agent is open, and Winston wants it to be filled internally. No interviews. Only a letter of intent and a good track record is needed. The committee is looking for someone to make Permian proud."

He stands and ends our meeting, but I can't move. This could be my chance to finally rise in the ranks and be the agent I've worked so hard to be. There are only four junior agents, and I have the most clients out of all of us.

I must smile because Trevor sneers. "Don't kid yourself, Turner. You're not ready."

My resolve snaps. I spent too many years listening to my mom discuss sports law, working for free in the CLU sports marketing department, and shadowing sports agents to be told I can't possibly dream of moving up. It's especially condescending since I do *his* work.

But instead of giving him a piece of my mind, I remind myself Trevor isn't worth it.

I'm halfway out the door when he speaks again.

"And control yourself around Cade. Don't embarrass Permian."

"Stupid."

Swing.

"Misogynistic."

Swing.

"Sexist."

Swing.

"Asshole."

The machine stops with a sad sputter. I toss the bat aside and gather the scattered baseballs, continuing to mentally rip Trevor into shreds.

Batting cages are my favorite way to release feminine rage.

"Late night, huh?"

The classical music blasting in my headphones has nothing on the southern drawl that cuts through the staccato notes.

"Jimmy! What are you doing here?"

"I was gonna ask you the same thing." The gap between his front teeth is on full display when he grins. "Giving you my spare key doesn't mean I can't come check on my favorite girl."

Jimmy Teaks owns Slim Jim Batting, the only batting cages in Clear Lake, along with teaching and coaching varsity baseball at Bryan High School in Cade and Kenneth's hometown. Hours spent under the sun during baseball season have deepened the rich sepia tone of his skin.

"Bad day?" he asks. "If your colorful language is a hint, I'd guess Trevor was a real pain in your derriere today."

I groan. "Understatement of the century."

When I stumbled upon Slim Jim Batting as a college freshman, I was running away from yet another dinner invitation from my randomly assigned roommate, and now best friend, Mallory. Thirty minutes after sneaking out of our dorm room to avoid her, I was swinging a bat with a man who was old enough to be my father.

"You think becoming friends with Mallory could be a distraction?" Jimmy had asked, feeding baseballs into the machine.

"Maybe. I don't know." I swung at a ball. "College is about soccer and setting myself up for a successful career. Friends aren't something I can control. What if she decides she doesn't want to be my friend someday? Then I'm hurt *and* unfocused."

Jimmy chuckled. "Don't you think that's a sad way to live?"

"Nope." I swung harder. "It's smart."

He turned off the machine, walked over, and ruffled my braids. "Give your roomie a shot. She may change your life."

It took some time to accept Mallory's friendship, but Jimmy was the reason for that. She thanks him every time they see each other.

He holds a sheet of paper against the cage. "You wouldn't believe my surprise when I opened the newspaper and found a photo of two people I never thought I'd see together again."

My eyes roll at the image of me, Cade, and Violet. "Nosy old man."

"Nope. Just an old man who still reads the newspaper." He chuckles. "When were you going to tell me you two were talking again?"

Running into Cade at Slim Jim Batting sophomore year was weird. The batting cages had become my solace, and it felt like watching an intruder in my home, acting as if he belonged there. Possessiveness took over as I watched him and Jimmy—my Jimmy—chatting.

Little did I know, Cade and Jimmy weren't strangers. Jimmy was his former coach and teacher turned mentor. I was the intruder, but they never made me feel that way.

"First of all, we're not talking. We're working together." Each word is emphasized so he realizes this isn't fun for me. "And I thought you knew."

"Nope," Jimmy says. "Haven't seen or talked to Cade since he left."

My chest tightens. "What? You haven't spoken to Cade in almost two years?"

A shadow crosses Jimmy's usually joyous face. "Pro ball is a different kind of monster. It can be a lot on the young ones, but he'll come around. I'm sure of it."

Sadness tears its way through me. For Jimmy. For Cade.

"Jim—"

"It's okay, dear. I know you aren't happy about it, but it's nice seeing you work together. If anyone can scare that monster away, it's you." Jimmy opens my cage. "Come on. It's time for you to get some sleep. Go get your stuff from the office."

I pick up my gym bag and jog to the office across from Jimmy's. The wooden desk is chipped, the room smells like mildew, and the floor's a little uneven, but I love working here and hitting balls in between.

Beats working at Permian or going home to an empty house.

Once we're outside, Jimmy ruffles my braids like always. "Don't let those men get you down, Shay. You're too good for that. Give 'em hell. You hear me?"

I nod. I'm going to give them hell, and that promotion will be mine.

CHAPTER ELEVEN

Cade

LOCKER ROOMS ALWAYS SMELL bad, but today's reason is in the fetal position on the ground.

"You can't expect me to *not* get queso at a Mexican restaurant," Marcus wails. "That would be a crime against humanity."

"It's a crime against my nostrils," Dawson mutters. The air freshener he keeps in his locker sort of helped. Now it smells like fresh linen *and* farts. "And you didn't have to drink it."

"Wasting food I paid for? No thanks. It's not fair that I love dairy, but it hates me."

Baja Breeze is the team's after-practice spot, hiding in its secluded upstairs area away from the public eye. I'm usually tasked with monitoring Marcus's cheese intake because he prefers to rawdog his poor stomach, but I skipped lunch to work in an extra lift and batting practice.

"You also had a smoothie from the recovery bar, which didn't help." I extend my hand to Marcus. "Get out of here. I have a meeting with my agent soon and the place smells like crap."

Finally, on shaky legs, he sways like a branch in the wind. "Give me five. Be right back."

"Hurry up!" Dawson yells at his back. "I want to see my family."

With a one-finger salute, Marcus slinks into the restroom.

Then I realize what I've done.

Deflection is my specialty, and Dawson has learned that firsthand. After finding out that Shay is my new agent, he has been relentless in his attempt to get answers. Cornering me at the airport or trying to room next to me during travel games. Every message about the topic goes unanswered, even the ones where he uses his son Luke as adorable bait. I've been so careful until now.

"Are we really not going to talk about it, Cade?"

I sigh. "I'd rather talk about the rumors that you're retiring after this season. That seems *way* more pressing."

"Nice try." His weight settles on the bench beside me. "You were supposed to sign with Caldwell. Not the one that got away."

The one I *pushed* away.

By the time I finish telling Dawson everything, leaving out the real reason I fired Jon, our final fight, the red flags from Trevor, and the weird way Trevor treated Shay in the meeting, he looks even more surprised than Mom was.

He rubs a hand over his buzzed head. "How angry was she?"

"Furious." I search for the dice in my pocket. "She spends every second reminding me I'm her client and nothing more, but she's damn good at her job, Daws."

The way she reacted when Summer approached still plays on a loop. Jon loved throwing me into the fire when it came to the media. I was required to answer any question with a smile, even if it was overly personal and painful. But Shay was ready to protect me.

Even if it was as her client, it felt good.

Faint clicking of heels catches my attention, and my eyes dart to the restroom. Marcus doesn't know about Shay yet, but I'm ninety-nine percent sure he won't say anything too crazy.

Dammit. It still stinks in here.

"Is everybody dressed? Shay asks, knocking on the clubhouse door.

As if he wasn't recently in a dairy-coma, Marcus stumbles back in. "Who's that?"

"My agent, so be cool," I whisper. "Yeah, come on in, Shay."

It's as if we don't exist when she glides into the clubhouse. Her eyes are on the walls, but I'm purely focused on her. A pink ribbon holds her braids together, and an ivory sleeveless top is tucked into pinstriped black pants. The pressed creases add to the no-nonsense look on her face.

Marcus must also be drinking her in because he's too quiet. But not for long.

"Holy shit. You're a woman."

Blazing eyes flick to Marcus before looking down to trace the curves of her own body. "Wow. I had no idea. Thanks for letting me know!"

I grin. There's that fire.

"Real smooth, Marc." Dawson hurls a sock at his head. "Nice to see you again, Shay."

"Hi, Dawson. And it's nice to meet you, Marcus. I'm Shay Turner." She turns to me, not giving Mr. Popular Marcus Winters another look. It's a relief to know she won't fawn over him like most women do. "You ready?"

I'm about to nod when I remember today's purpose. Player development meetings are necessary, but that doesn't keep the impending dread away. I need to stall.

"Would you like a tour first?" I ask.

A flicker of excitement shimmers beneath her composed professionalism. "Um, yeah! I'd love that. I'll go set up for our meeting in the guest lounge, Cade."

Turning away from us, she leaves the clubhouse.

The moment she's gone, Marcus steps in front of me. "You aren't messing with me? That's your agent? Her?"

"Yeah, *her*." Rage replaces the usual love I have for my friend at his incredulous tone. "Is there a problem with signing a woman as my agent?"

He lifts his hand and waves an imaginary white flag. "No way. I'm not a total asshole. It's fucking cool! Relax. You just caught me off guard because you were supposed to meet some dude named Caldwell." Cartoon hearts dance in his green eyes. "Mind if I ask her out sometime? She's pr—"

"Don't you dare touch her," I say. Actually, I hissed it through gritted teeth. Shay is many things. Gorgeous. Stunning. Smart. Driven. Perfect. Pretty, however, is an understatement. "You can have any woman in the world, but not her."

"Uh-oh." Sniffing my shoulder twice, Marcus smirks. "Is that possessiveness I smell? Cute, but suspicious if you ask me. And I can have any woman but her? Do you want a stepfather?"

Rolling my eyes, I shove him away. "I'll end you if you try to date my mother."

"Stop fighting, children." Dawson loves to lecture us, but he's enjoying the show. "Let's go, Marc. You can empty your bowels in the safety of your own home."

"Fine." Marcus grabs his duffel bag. "Can't believe you called dibs."

Little does he know that I called dibs on Shay the first time I saw her eating dinner in the student-athlete center. While my teammates were excited about every girl on campus, all I cared about was her. I was desperate to know the woman who sat alone, scribbling on pink sticky notes.

As they leave the stadium, I spot Shay chewing on the end of her pen, the tell-tale sign she's in the zone. But my smile wilts when I see the yellow legal pad on the table in front of her.

Jon's voice always finds his way into my head, his words from our last player development meeting echoing loudly in my ears.

"Don't you care? This isn't good enough for the golden boy."

"Hey." Shay stands, pushing aside the legal pad. "Ready for the tour?"

I nod, not trusting myself to talk.

Steering us toward the trophy room, I listen as she tells me about her meeting with Rio, our general manager. I slow our pace as we enter the exhibit area. Every piece of Pilots memorabilia, each trophy, and countless photos of historical moments from the team's past is in this room.

"This is the coolest thing I've ever seen," Shay says, eyes frozen on the Commissioner's Trophy from the World Series five seasons ago. Sterling silver with shimmering gold flags gleam bright in its protective case. It's the symbol of resilience for the Pilots. I'll never forget the night they won this trophy.

"We watched the game together. Remember?" I ask.

"Rule number two. No talking about the past," she reminds me curtly. Then she presses her fingertips to the glass. "But yes. It was a fun night."

For nine innings, her eyes never left the tiny television. That was the night I learned she attended the home games of as many sports as she could. Bundling up for hockey season, sweating under the hot sun at track meets, and sitting courtside at basketball games. But my favorite was when she came to baseball games.

Shay knows baseball. From history to stats to how to improve. BYOB nights taught me that. With every sticky note she wrote, she broke down each play with knowledge and grace.

"Want to go on the field?" I ask.

She chews on her full bottom lip. "Can I run around the bases too?"

Her excitement is contagious as I swing the door open to the dugout. "Anything you want, Agent Shay."

"This smoothie is like ninety-nine percent milk. No wonder the locker room smelled like ass."

I choke on my peanut butter smoothie, coughing over a laugh. "Poor Marcus. And the queso didn't help."

The tour has gone longer than either of us expected. Restricted areas like the recovery room, data and analytics office, clubhouses, and equipment storage aren't shown to everyone, but she deserves more than the usual fan tour.

"You've never come to a tour? The Pilots host them often for agents."

She tosses her empty cup into the trash. "I'm not usually invited to things like that."

The words are tossed out like nothing, as if it's okay and normal. But it's not, and I need her to know that.

"Well, as my agent, you have a forever pass to this stadium. Restricted areas and all." I nudge her shoulder. "And if anyone has a problem, point them my way. I'll take care of them."

Uncertainty swims in her dark eyes as we enter the guest lounge, but she gives me a small smile. I'm about to return it when a flash of yellow paper reminds me why we're here. Shay isn't running laps around the bases and reminiscing about the good times as my girlfriend. She's my agent, here to do her job.

Which is ripping me to shreds.

Once seated, she opens the thick binder and jumps right into it. "This isn't urgent, but I'm curious. Why don't you have any endorsements?"

I decide to go with a partial truth. "I haven't had time."

"Are you interested in one?"

I shrug.

"What if it was for your favorite hair care line?"

My interest piques. "Loc & Key?" She slides her iPad across the table. I read the whole email three times before I can speak. "How did you do this?"

"I didn't do anything." Leaning over the table, she taps the screen, pulls up the photo of us from the farmers market, and points at the brown bag hanging from my wrist. "Apparently, their sales jumped after their logo was plastered in the *Carolina Gazette*. They asked if you'd be willing to work with them. I think it would be good for you, and fun too. It'll require you to spend an afternoon in—"

I shake my head. "I can't."

"Can't what?"

"I can't miss practice. Baseball has to come first."

There it is. The other half of the truth.

It's clear how much those words cut into her. After being drafted, I spent our months apart choosing baseball over her every time.

But it's the truth. Who cares if I have an endorsement if I play like crap? Without baseball, there is no me, and that's been made clear at every turn. When I wanted to join the swim team with Kenneth in junior high, I received a resounding no. When I debated staying at CLU to finish my degree, Jon reminded me that baseball won't wait for me.

No baseball. No golden boy. No Cade.

Her retort dies on her lips as she locks the tablet with a quiet finality. "Alright. I'll let them know. Back to the player development agenda. I wanted to talk about a few things."

"A few?" I scoff, unable to hide my frustration. "That binder probably weighs as much as my sister."

She tuts. "It's not *your* binder, Cade. Every client I work with is in here. I lug it everywhere because I could get an urgent message that needs to be answered." Pink nails tap against the pages. "What is the purpose of a player development meeting?"

Usually I'd censor myself, but I don't. "To tell me everything I'm doing wrong."

My brain jumbles when a feathery touch lands on my forearm, light yet demanding. Then I forget how to breathe when she squeezes.

"I'm not sure where you got that idea, but I'm not here to rip into you, lecture you, or beat you while you're down, Cade. I'll never do that. You're the athlete. *My* athlete. Player development meetings are for discussing your career, on and off the field, and to check on your well-being. As your agent, my job is to support you. Can you tell me you understand that?"

Every part of me is desperate to cling to her words. Before I went pro, that's what I assumed these meetings were for, but Jon used them to dig into every mistake.

Giving her my best smile, I nod. "I'm trying. I promise."

Her usual level of disappointment in me seems to dwindle as she releases me and sits back on her stool. "I originally wanted to talk about your long-term career plans, but I don't think that's best today. I do have two questions though."

My shoulders loosen. "Shoot."

"Why haven't you told the media about what happened with Jon?"

I think of the messages Jon sent when Summer's article went live.

Jon Sweeney

> You're fucking kidding, right?

> Call me back. We need to talk.

Telling people about the hell I went through with Jon—that I'm still going through without him—would be too much. I'm not supposed to be the guy who makes people worry. Mom is supposed to have a dependable son who can make it through anything. Mallory and Kenneth need a friend who won't weigh them down with heavy feelings and emotions. The thoughts swirling around in my head aren't easy to deal with, but it's easier to hide than to explain.

"I don't have anything to say. It just didn't work out."

She scribbles something down. "Your silence looks bad for him, but people still love you."

"Then there should be no problem. If they're happy with the golden boy, that's all that matters." It physically hurts to say, but I choke out the truth.

The amber flecks in her dark eyes blaze to life. Pressing her palms against the table, she leans forward until our faces are only a foot apart. "Other people's happiness isn't what matters, Cade. *You* are what matters. You are the *only* thing that matters. So when you're ready to talk about whatever is going on, I'll be here." It's only when she sits back down and dives into the second question that I stop holding my breath. "What did you do this week for *you*?"

Forming sentences seems impossible with all that sadness looking back at me, so I keep it short. "Watched film. Studied scouting reports. Got in extra lifts and batting practices."

Pink fluff from her pen shakes in the air. "I asked what you did for *you*, so no baseball."

I shrug. The few things that were for me got canceled. Last night's dinner with Kenneth was rescheduled because I didn't get through scouting reports in time. I skipped today's team lunch to sneak in extra practice. Instead of joining Marcus for a drink tonight, I'm ditching to read Jon's notes.

"Sometimes," she continues, "stepping away from the job isn't a bad thing. It's okay to just be."

As if she sees right through me, I feel myself unravel.

Growing up, baseball was the love of my life. I enjoyed every second of it. Playing. Watching. Learning. Studying. Getting better. Before I knew it, baseball had evolved into something less fun. Instead of setting goals for myself, I started focusing on living up to the expectations of others. High school state trophies? Got it. College scholarship? Done. National championships for CLU? Did that too. Drafted professionally? Yup. Playing in the majors? I'm there.

Just being isn't something I can do, and I think we both know it.

But I smile anyway, ready for this meeting to end.

Chapter Twelve

"Men like me aren't meant to be flexible."

I look down at the elite athlete starfished on the ground. He blindly searches for his water bottle, chest heaving from our exercise. Sweat sparkles like glitter across his forehead, and I hold back a laugh as he struggles to catch his breath. The last round took it out of him.

Physical therapy is no joke.

"Men like you?" I chug half of my water bottle. "You mean seven-foot-tall basketball players?"

Deshawn Miller lifts his head off the turquoise yoga mat. "Exactly. We can't all be tiny agents in pink who have soccer-level flexibility and strength."

"I've done my fair share of physical therapy. When slide tackling is your favorite move, you become injury-prone and a danger."

"Angel Devil," he jokes, and our fists bump.

My thighs tremble as I grab two resistance bands for standing hamstring curls. Even though Deshawn isn't my client, Trevor designated me as his go-to person after his injury. He needs someone in his corner, and joining physical therapy is the least I can do.

Plus, since quitting the preprofessional soccer team, I need the workout.

I hand over a stretchy red band. "How does it feel today?"

His fingers trace the small incisions on his right knee, pale against his deep skin. "Better. Don't tell Doc, but I took the stairs this morning. The elevator was slow, and I'm tired of crutches."

"Good thing I've decided to clear you for unassisted walking today," Dr. Pope says, poking her head out of her office. Her silver-blonde bob sways with laughter. "It's been two weeks since your partial meniscectomy, and you're healing well. I'd like to get you in the pool next week if you're feeling up to it."

My cheeks tighten at the good news. "Flutter kicks?"

She nods. "Flutter kicks."

Deshawn smiles for the first time since starting physical therapy as his and Dr. Pope's hands collide for a high five. "Thanks for kicking my ass every day, Doc."

A slender finger points at me. "Thank your agent. She makes sure you don't cheat during wall sits."

"Agent adjacent," I correct her. Trevor would scream if he heard I was claiming his clients.

Deshawn flicks my ankle. "Regardless, thank you, Shay. Having you here helps. You're a great agent. Adjacent or not."

On the hard days when I feel unseen and disrespected, it's hard to remember why I do this job, but moments like these ground me. All I want is for my clients to feel cared for. As a former athlete, I know how difficult it is to be away from your sport. Players don't need extra flack from the person meant to support them.

Chiming bells interrupt our celebration, and Deshawn tries to slap my phone out of my hands. "I'd cry if my phone rang that much."

The moment I see the name scrolling across the top of the screen, I do feel like crying. With my finger hovering over the green button, I look up. "I'm sorry, but I need to take this."

"Take your time," Dr. Pope says. "Last exercise, Deshawn. Then we'll test mobility."

Once outside the training room, I choose a bench, take a deep breath, and answer the call. "Hello! I was starting to think I wasn't going to hear from you, Garrett."

The deep chuckle of the baseball player I'd like to represent fills my ear. "My apologies. It's been a little chaotic, but I'm happy to let you know you've passed the first test."

"The *first* test?"

I've overheard other agents discuss how athletes often complete vigorous testing before choosing: seeing if they will answer the phone at odd times, how long it takes them to pick up, and how long it takes them to return a call. But this has never happened to me.

"Yup. The first of many." Garrett clicks his tongue. "What was the score of the last Jackals game?"

I know the answer immediately. "Five to four. Jackals win."

"How many runs did I score?"

"One."

"What about Harrison Ryder?"

The Jackals designated hitter? "None," I say, sure of my answer but unsure where this is going. "Are you going to do this until you pick an agent?"

"Sure am. So, do you golf?"

My brows furrow. "Huh?"

"You can answer any random game stat, but that stumped you?" A gust of wind howls past his mic, mixing with his laugh. "Does the soccer star know how to swing a club?"

I bite my tongue. Golf is one of the many sports I watch, but I've never played. Deals are signed on the course, according to Trevor, which makes golf a vital business skill. Sadly, it's a business I've never been fully accepted into.

"Yeah," I cough out, hoping he can't hear my doubt. "I can golf."

Garrett hums, and I'm sure he sees right through my lie. "Perfect. Let's set something up when I'm back in Charlotte for the next series. I hope you answer next time too. See ya."

"Bye." The call ends, and I stare up at the ceiling.

This guy's making me work for this opportunity. I'm excited for the challenge.

Chapter Thirteen

"MEN ARE NOTORIOUSLY FICKLE creatures. They may think we're the unpredictable sex, but they're sorely incorrect. And Cade Owens, the sweet guy, is not an exception."

I watch a semi-truck whizz by. "I know one man who isn't fickle."

"Bullshit." Mallory rubs the continuous glucose monitor on the back of her arm. "Who?"

"Kenneth Gray," I announce, my voice rising like a game show host. "Boyfriend extraordinaire. The guy who spent three years waiting for you to pull your head out of your ass and love him too."

She tries to put up a brave fight against the lover-girl allegations, but one mention of his name has her melting into her seat. "He just knew a good thing when he saw it. Can you blame him?"

Soft rock flits through the speakers of her old Honda as we get closer to Charlotte. Mallory's meeting her graduate advisor, Dr. Martin, at an autoimmune disease conference to present her research on type 1 diabetes. Carpooling was one of my favorite parts of living together, so I jumped at the opportunity when she offered.

"But you didn't hear him, Mally. It wasn't like trying to decide which flavor of ice cream to order." I go silent, trying to find the right word to describe the hostility, fear, and exhaustion Cade revealed during our meeting last week.

I wasn't expecting him to change his mind about filming for Loc & Key. His email wasn't enthusiastic, but he agreed to miss today's optional practice.

Prying information about Cade from Mallory isn't something I do out of respect for our friendship. Especially because she's a locked vault when it comes to things I tell her in confidence. Still, I can't help myself.

"He hasn't talked to you about anything?" I ask.

Grimacing, she clicks on the blinker and moves into the left lane. "Honestly, not much. Kenneth might know more than I do, and we'll keep trying, but that's who Cade is: just smile, don't make people worry, and it'll all be okay. Which historically ends in flames. But today will be good for him. A day of pampering and baseball? That's exactly what he needs."

I try to believe her as she pulls into the studio's parking lot. Test calls from Garrett Blane don't make me as jittery as spending an afternoon with Cade.

"I'm nervous," I admit.

"I know, but you look cute. The sleek puff is peak professionalism."

Opening the vanity mirror, I smooth my edges. Hair loss is one of my many PCOS symptoms. It's exacerbated by stress, which isn't great because I'm constantly in a state of distress. With the long days, late nights, and occasional travel, keeping my hair braided is best for my lifestyle. Until I have a few hours to braid my hair this weekend, I'll be curly and free.

"How's the new medication?" she asks.

The bottle of Metformin rattles as I shake out a pill. It's the newest addition to my regimen to help with insulin resistance, whatever that means. Sarabeth, my dietitian, and Mallory, my best friend who happens to be a dietitian, have explained it many times. All I need to do is take it every morning and night, along with my Spironolactone every morning. That one is for decreasing testosterone levels, which is supposed to help my acne and facial hair.

I shrug. "So far so good."

She squeezes my knee with her free hand. "I know work's a lot, but are you making any progress on lowering your stress?"

I'm running on fumes and hardly sleeping, but I really am trying. Sarabeth recommended a few life changes that are doable, like drinking two cups of spearmint tea a day and walking after meals, so I've added that.

"I can't slow down, Mally. Getting this promotion would change everything, and I'm so close I can almost taste it."

Signing Garrett would be icing on the cake for the promotion.

"You're definitely going to get it." Pulling to a stop, she presses our foreheads together. Freshman year, I did this to help her through an anxiety attack, and now it's our thing. "Get in there and be the hottest, smartest, most capable agent the world has ever seen."

Buoyed by her encouragement, I grab the handle and blow her a kiss. "Love you big, and good luck today!"

"Love you bigger, and back at you!"

As she drives away, I feel a flicker of validation. Someone else sees it too. Something *is* going on with Cade.

My fingertips barely brush the doorknob when I hear a gasp that stops me in my tracks.

"Do my eyes deceive me?"

When I turn around, Cade's curiosity pins me like a spotlight. Crossed arms bulge, emphasizing the bulk of muscle that makes up his biceps. I bet they could hold me down—

Remember your rules, Shaylene.

Touching his arm at the player development meeting seemed harmless, but my hand tingled for the rest of the day. When I got home, I added new rules to our pink sticky note.

Number five: no touching him.

Number six: no time alone.

Number seven: no ogling him. Even if he looks devastating in his glasses.

I roll my eyes. "You've seen me without braids before, Cade."

"Sure, but that was years ago." Three confident steps close the space between us, and when he drops his head, those stupid glasses slide down his nose. "Just let me look at you for a moment. It's been too long."

Being the object of Cade's attention is equal parts thrilling and terrifying. He studies me closely, eyes sweeping over my face with intense focus. They linger just a beat too long on my lips, and he sighs, brushing my skin with a cool bite of mint.

Before I can create a new six-feet-apart rule, cherry-red locs tied into Bantu knots peek around the door.

"You're here! Hi! Cade! Ah! I'm Lula, the owner of Loc & Key. We're huge fans!" The skin-tight dress wrapped around her matches her hair. She's the epitome of an exclamation mark, limber, bold, and excitable. "And Shay! Thank you for setting this up!" She grabs my hand for what I assume is a handshake, but she yanks me inside and keeps my hand captive until we reach the lobby. "What can I get you two? Coffee? Coke? Tea? Mimosa?"

Cade grins. "Unsweet tea for me and Diet Coke for her, please." When Lula scampers away, he chuckles. "She's full of spirit."

Which reminds me, I need an energy drink.

After digging through my bag, I hand a sheet of paper to Cade. "I prepared questions for the interview today, but I need your input before

I give them to Lula. If there are any questions you don't approve of, I'll remove them."

Cade's eyes never leave mine. "You want my opinion?"

"Of course. You're the one answering them."

He blinks, and then blinks again. "Oh."

God, I hate that word. I never know if it's good or bad, and the weird look on his face makes me think it's a bad one.

"I've never been asked to screen questions before," he admits.

I pause. "Never?"

"Never."

My vision narrows, fading everything except the fury inside. What kind of agent doesn't let his client have autonomy over what they're asked?

"No question will ever be publicized without your approval. Your comfort and consent will always come first."

The crease between his brow eases. "Always?"

"Always," I promise, tempted to lift my pinky in the air. "We should find Lula—"

"I have a confession," tumbles out of his mouth before I can finish.

There's a ferocity in his eyes as they hold mine, and it's clear he's not going to shoot this promo until he gets it off his chest, so I follow him back to the front door.

Putting an extra step of space between us, I keep my eyes on the parking lot through the large windows. "What's going on?"

"This is going to sound weak, but bear with me." A hand drags over his face. "Missing practice scares me. I haven't skipped a practice ever. Optional or not. I've spent a lot of my life and pro career worrying about messing everything up. With baseball. With my friends and family." He doesn't say it, but I hear the *with you* in the pause. "And I can't afford to lose baseball."

It's as if a piece of the armor that he meticulously covers himself with has fallen off, giving me a glimpse into the mind of Cade Owens.

My hand itches to pat his shoulder, but I refer to rule five and play with a string on my blouse. "Thanks for being honest. You're safe with me, okay?" I don't expect him to respond, so I continue, "There's one more thing I need you to approve of before we start filming."

At that moment, my surprise opens the door behind Cade. Emma, Cade's longtime loctician, steps beside him and leans against his arm.

"Guess who gets to retwist your locs for Loc & Key?"

Pretty hazels dart to me. The moment he agreed to come, I called Lula and requested Cade's loctician to make him feel more comfortable. He's taking a day off, and I want to make sure today is worth the break.

"Surprise," I sing.

Cade's mouth gapes, but Lula reappears. "You guys ready?"

I look to my client. "Cade, are you all good with the questions?"

Handing the folded piece of paper to Lula, he nods. Without looking at them, he agreed to whatever I wrote. The realization makes my heart stutter, because it sort of feels like trust.

As we walk, Lula dives into the vision for the shoot. *Loc'd in. From the first inning to the last.* Cade's excitement grows as she talks, discussing the campaign's focus on strength, moisture retention, and shine. First, he'll get the full spa experience in the studio they transformed to look like a locker room. Emma will wash, retwist, and style his locs, and the day will end with an interview on top of the custom-built pitcher's mound.

And I have work to do, of course.

I catch Lula's eye and wave. "I'll be in the lobby. Let me know if you need anything."

"No!" she chirps, heels clicking as she sashays to me. "You're part of the spa experience too! I hired an extra hairdresser for you."

I shake my head in protest. "Today's for Cade, but thanks—"

"Oh, so I'm the only one who has to relax today?" Cade shouts, spinning in his salon chair. "That doesn't seem fair to me, Agent Shay."

My arms cross defiantly. "I have a job to do."

"Maybe, but I heard something important the other day. Someone I admire told me it's okay to step away from the job sometimes. I think she might need some help taking her own advice though." The grin across his face is equally smug and tender.

Somehow, using my own advice against me works.

"Fine, but I'm keeping my laptop."

Within seconds, a drink is pushed into my hands as Lula leads me to an empty chair. It's far enough away from Cade and the camera crew, but close enough for him to keep an eye on me.

"Ever had a client and agent spa day?" he asks.

Unlocking my computer, I take a swig of juice. "Can't say I have."

"So, this is a day of firsts, huh? First skipped practice. First spa day."

Instead of answering, I focus on the endless emails awaiting me, but it is a day of firsts.

Cade was honest with me.

Me

Cade's interview is almost over. Should be done in an hour

Mally?

I guess I'll hitchhike

"How long have you been using Lọc & Key products?" Lula asks, the final question on the list I provided.

Cade leans forward in his seat, and dark locs hang over his shoulders, perfected by Emma's hands. "Since I was eighteen. I started my loc journey right before college. I would've started sooner, but my mom was adamant I wait until I was an adult because locs are a long-term commitment."

Lula's rich laugh fills my ears. "Ain't that the truth."

Their conversation has flowed easily over the last half hour, but that's how it is with Cade. Everyone he meets walks away thinking they've made a new best friend.

"When you moved to California, did you see a different loctician?"

Cade's smile deepens when Emma shoots him a glare. "I did have to see someone else, but he was Emma-approved, and I'm thankful he squeezed me into his tight schedule. Now that I'm back, it's Emma or nobody."

"You've got that right!" Emma shouts, and a wild howl of laughter rips out of him.

This is the Cade I remember. The sunshine that lit up every room he walked into. People are often drawn to golden people. The ones who look like they don't have a single care in the world. The ones who shine bright, even if the world is crumbling around them. The ones who feel like they can't be themselves until everyone around them is happy. But as beautiful as the sun is, I've always preferred cloudy days. I spent so long hoping Cade's clouds would appear, saturated and heavy with all the things he kept pent up until they finally fell, released like a torrent of rain. Not because I wanted to see Cade sad, scared, or angry, but because I wanted to see the *real* Cade.

Like the one I saw earlier.

"This is my last question for the day." Lula tosses me an apologetic smile. "I'm sorry I didn't run this question by your team first, but I'm feeling snoopy."

Frustration sends me to my feet and my phone clatters to the ground, capturing Cade's attention. His head turns enough to meet my eyes, but when he nods, I sit back down.

He faces Lula. "You better be glad I like you."

She giggles like a schoolgirl. "Everyone wants to know if you're available. You haven't been publicly tied to anyone before, but is there a special someone in hiding? I'm dying to get a little more information about the golden boy."

I should be annoyed, but for some reason I want him to answer. I have no idea what Cade did after we split up, and I refused to ask Mallory for updates. Hearing he moved on would've wrecked me.

"Ah." A slow smile takes over his face. "There was someone very special to me. Still is, if I'm being honest, but that's something that'll stay between the two of us. And for those wondering, no, I'm not available or looking."

My breath hitches when his eyes dart to me for half a second.

Lula slaps her thigh. "A good man! Thank you for speaking with me today. I'm sure our partnership will be fruitful."

As the camera crew cuts, my phone vibrates against the plastic table, and I rush outside. I can't miss a Garrett Blane test, but when I check the caller ID, it isn't him.

"So, I have good news and bad news," Mallory whispers after I answer. "Which do you want first?"

I'm feeling oddly positive, so I say, "Good news."

"Dr. Darleen Johnson, diabetes research *queen*, invited me to get coffee and discuss post-grad opportunities! Should I be normal and get hot chocolate or be cool and get coffee?"

She's so cute when she's nervous. "Be yourself and get hot chocolate."

"That's why you're my best friend," She takes a deep breath. "The bad news is I can't take you home because I'm meeting her right now. I'm sorry."

I'm too excited to care. "Don't stress. I'll get a ride. Text me updates later."

"I will strangle you if you hitchhike, Shaylene!" she screams before clicking off.

Within thirty minutes, the studio is cleared out. After finalizing the shoot's details, thanking the millions of people on set, verifying the endorsement contract one last time with Lula, and ordering my ride home, I breathe in the crisp afternoon air.

"Hey."

I bristle at Cade's voice, surprised to see him leaning against the building. "Are you waiting for something?" I ask.

"Yes." He straightens. "You."

My glare is cutting. He walked out of the studio with Emma soon after recording finished, yet here he is.

We might as well review today's interview.

"Are there any questions you want removed from the final cut?"

Locs thump against his cheeks. "Nope. Lula can keep them all."

"Even the dating one?"

"Absolutely. I'm unavailable, and I'd like that to be publicly known."

A surprised cough bursts out of my chest, sharp and way too loud. "Got it," I choke out. "Well, enjoy your afternoon. I'm waiting for my ride."

"A ride?" Cade's jaw clicks. "Why didn't you ask me to take you back to Clear Lake?"

"Why would I?"

The good energy between us dissipates as he marches away, leaving me alone on the sidewalk. His steps are agitated, but I don't call for him. It's better this way. Today was nice as agent and client. There's no need to ruin it with a silent and awkward thirty-minute drive home.

My rideshare app chimes, alerting me that Teela's silver Subaru is five minutes away. Then I'll be home and safe from Cade and his random confessions.

"Get in the car."

Red fills my vision, a mix of rage and the red minivan beside me. "Excuse me?"

Cade pushes his elbow out of the open window. "You're not being driven home by some stranger, so get in the car."

"In your dreams." I flick my hand, shooing him away. "Go home, Cade. I'm fine."

Naturally, like the stubborn man he is, he does the exact opposite. The ancient minivan groans as he pushes it into park. "What are the odds you let me drive you home?"

"Rule three!"

"Fine." The door creaks open, and he swings his legs out. "Shaylene Joy Turner, you have three options." My blood drops at the use of my full name. "One," he continues, "you break the rules and play our game. Two, you be the angel I know you can be and get in my car. Or three, I'll *put* you in my car. The only downside to option three is that I'll make a big scene. And I'd hate to ruin that beautiful hair of yours."

"You wouldn't dare." My hands fly up to shield my perfectly puffed afro.

He cocks his head and smiles. "Try me."

CHAPTER FOURTEEN

I SHOULDN'T BE THIS happy, considering Shay is huffing, puffing, and ignoring the hell out of me, but I can't help but laugh at the situation.

"If I were in better shoes, I would've outrun you," she mutters, and I barely manage to avoid a high heel to the head when she tosses the dangerous weapons into the back seat.

"I'm glad we're in agreement," I say. "If it weren't for that crack in the sidewalk, you would've run all the way back to Clear Lake."

"Or hitchhiked."

My head whips to the side. "Absolutely not. If I find out you're hitchhiking, I'll—"

"Chase me down a sidewalk in broad daylight? Throw me over your shoulder like a disobedient toddler? Toss me into the car and buckle me in while I nurse my poor ankle? Yeah. Trust me. I know you will."

Suppressing another laugh, I click on the windshield wipers. Raindrops tap the windshield in a steady rhythm. The moment it starts raining, people act as if they've never driven in their lives.

To prove my point, I gesture at the BMW weaving through bumper-to-bumper traffic. "See how crazy people are driving? With the storm coming, there's no way you were catching a ride with some stranger who probably texts while they drive."

"Teela had four-point-eight stars and great reviews!" she argues. "But canceling last minute will ruin my perfect rider average."

"Well, I have five stars and zero complaints, so try to relax. I'll have you home soon. Plus, I'll give you five stars for being a great passenger."

"Sucks, because I'll be leaving you a one-star review."

Even though things are tense, this feels right. If I closed my eyes, I could probably pretend we're back in college, when having Shay in my passenger seat was normal. Driving her home from the student-athlete center, picking her and Mallory up for parties, eating dinner outside Slim Jim Batting.

Our first kiss was right here too. I remember it like it was yesterday. The earthy scent of sunscreen and grass from our practice clothes. The want that burned in her eyes as I leaned over the center console. The heavenly taste of strawberry ice cream on her tongue. The feel of her everywhere was electrifying and overwhelming, and the moment she pulled back, I already wanted to kiss her again.

I wonder if she's thinking about that night like I am.

Lightning cracks in the sky, illuminating the dark gray with dull yellow. A roar of thunder fills the car, drowning the yelp that leaves Shay's lips.

"Maybe we should pull over and wait out the storm?" she asks, gripping the handle above the door.

I shouldn't joke, but I want her to stay calm. "I thought you wanted to get home?"

Her lips twitch, not quite into a smile, but close. "Shut up, Cade."

It's a straight shot to Clear Lake from here, but she's right. Plus, more time with Shay is something I'll never complain about.

Turning on my blinker, I take the next exit and move onto the feeder road at a crawl. It's deserted, which gives me time to scan the run-down buildings.

When I spot a diner, I head straight for it. The parking lot is flooded and vacant, so I park in front of the entrance and turn to find the jacket and pair of slides I keep in my backseat. Handing them over, I say, "Put these on."

She gawks at the size-thirteen slides. "We're going inside?"

"Yup." When she doesn't move, I unbuckle, bend down, and slip them onto her bare feet. "In there is food, coffee, and a heater. We'll leave the second it stops raining, okay?"

Shay bites down on her lip. "Hanging out in public? I don't think—"

"We're not hanging out," I say, even though it stings. "I'm giving you a ride as your client. That's all, okay? We can be professional, Shay. And I *really* want a waffle right now."

Groaning, she finally slips into my jacket and zips it. "Let's go."

It takes less than a second for the rain to soak through my T-shirt, but I rush around the car, open her door, and hold out my hand. My whole body sighs in relief when our fingers lace, and I use my free hand to pull the hood over her head as we sprint through the puddles.

Once inside, I peel the soggy jacket off her and hang it on the lopsided coat rack.

Giving Shay a quick once-over, I try not to linger too long. After getting her hair done, it's no longer wrangled at the base of her neck. Thick, dark curls hang above her shoulders, sprouting around her face like the petals of a flower.

She's gorgeous, even when damp from rain and irritated with me.

"They better have good waffles," she mutters, marching toward an empty booth.

Bulbs flicker above, and paired with the cracked red vinyl booths, I feel as if we've stepped into a seventies comic book. Photos of vintage cars and newspaper clippings cover every inch of red paint. If I had to guess, these will probably be some of the best waffles ever.

"If they suck, I'll give you my mom's secret recipe to make up for it."

"Deal. I'm gonna run to the restroom. Order for me, please."

Every step toward the opposite side of the room oozes with a wet squelch. My slides are massive on her, but I'm positive they're more comfortable than those death traps she calls shoes.

"Hi, love. I'm Darcy, and I'll be takin' care of y'all today." She sets down two glasses of water and straws. A notepad appears out of thin air. "What can I get you and your pretty friend?"

"Hi, Darcy." I scan the menu. "Coffee for me and Diet Coke for her. Light ice, please. Can we get two waffle meals? And extra whipped cream on her plate."

With a nod, Darcy disappears into the kitchen.

It's only quiet for a second before Shay reappears and slaps the table. "Guess what I found?"

"The toilet?"

"Yes," she says, unbothered by my sarcasm. "Then I found the pawnshop connected to the diner. Do you know what pawnshops sell?"

Nostalgia grips me by the throat. "Baseball cards."

Most people don't think of pawnshops for baseball cards, but Shay's different. Three years ago, when shopping for Kenneth's birthday present, Shay and I were distracted by the pieces of cardstock. I spotted the Jackie Robinson card first, but when she looked up at me, my want for the card vanished. I had always thought her eyes were like ink, dark, steady, and impossible to read, but that day, I was proven wrong. Molasses is all I could think of, rich, warm, and syrupy. The smooth color held a quiet gravity that pulled me in, anchored by flecks of amber that kept me from drifting away.

Kept me hers.

Then she hip-checked me into the wall when the manager asked who wanted the card.

Darcy reappears with our drinks. "Feel free to look around while your food is cookin'. I'll give you a holler when it's ready."

A dusty brown curtain separates the diner and pawnshop. Large television screens are mounted on every wall, and glass cases are filled with gold watches, glittering jewelry, and every item you could possibly want for a good price.

And as I hoped, thick binders are stacked along a rickety bookshelf.

"Just don't hip-check me today." I laugh. "I'm getting old and can't handle that anymore."

Mainly because my hip isn't getting better.

She sticks her tongue out at me and reaches up onto her tiptoes to grab a book of cards. Before I can join her, something catches my eye. I reach into the wicker basket and grab the wrist lanyard. Pink and orange beads with tiny hearts and flowers adorn the string.

Perfect for the woman always on her phone.

"I'll be right back," I whisper, then make a quick escape.

Up at the front, I put it on the counter. The man at the cash register isn't a talker, which works because I don't want Shay to overhear us. After paying, I tuck the tiny gift right beside the dice in my pocket.

I freeze mid-step when Darcy pulls back the curtain. In her palm is a tray with our meals.

That was too quick. I'm not ready for this moment to end.

A quick peek at Shay reveals that she's completely absorbed by the baseball cards, slowly flipping through the pages with a smile on her face.

"Can you give us ten more minutes?" I ask.

As if sensing my desperation, Darcy winks. "Sure can! Get back over there to your girl. I'll keep it warm for y'all, Sugar."

Returning to Shay, I slide into the space beside her, warmed by the heater at my feet and the tiny point of contact between our arms. I'd say it feels like the old days, but I'm coming to terms with the fact that those days are gone. It's different. *We're* different.

Maybe it's not such a bad thing.

"I'm not sharing custody of a baseball card with you. I'm cool with being divorced parents of Mal and Ken, but for a card? No way."

I park in front of Shay's little red house. The storm didn't pass until four hours after arriving at the diner, which gave us time to buy baseball cards, eat, and work.

Well, Shay worked. I watched her work.

Reaching into the backseat, I grab her heels. "Why not? Might as well continue our shared custody agreement since we're able to be civil. I don't know many almost-exes who can."

She grunts but doesn't argue with that.

I'm glad I told Shay that Jon never made sure I was comfortable when speaking to the media. To him, it was my job to make *them* comfortable. But today, I got my locs retwisted, met the owner of my favorite haircare brand, answered questions that didn't make me feel sick to my stomach, and spent the day with Shay.

Even if she hated every second, I had the time of my life.

"Thanks for today," I breathe. "I needed that."

She doesn't reach for the handle. "What are the odds?"

I blink hard. Those words didn't come out of my mouth. "What did you just say, Shay?"

Covering her face, she lets out a dry laugh. "I know I'm breaking rule three, but I need to. What are the odds you'll tell me something honest and real?"

Pressure gathers in my chest at the thought. My shadows have never had a safe place. I'm expected to be comforting, not complicated. Steady, not struggling. Caring, not worrisome. That's why I'm always fine and happy. But if I play our game, I have to be honest.

I must be quiet for too long because she speaks again. "Never mind. It was a dumb idea—"

"I'll play." I hold up my fist. "If you win, I'll tell you something."

"With no deflecting." The corners of her mouth twitch, and a surge of pride fills me at being able to do that.

"On three." I count on my fingers. *One, two, three.*

"Two!" we scream, and I don't hate the idea of opening up to her.

"Ask away," I say. "What do you want to know?"

I hope she asks if I regret not coming home, because the answer is yes. Every single day.

"You pick," is what she says instead. "Big or small. Serious or silly. Tell me something I don't know. All I want is something real."

It's not that I don't trust my friends and family with what goes on in my head. The golden boy isn't a mask I wear for a morale boost. I loved the title and all its assigned traits until it became an expectation rather than a choice. An identity rather than a personality, and the moment I admit it aloud, it will become real and not something I want to believe is all in my head. It has always been easier to hide than explain the invisible heaviness that drowns me.

But Shay sees it. I think she always has. I worried what would happen if she realized I wasn't as golden as my image portrays, so I ran away from her, shouldering the weight alone like I thought I had to. Yet here she is. Listening. Waiting. With me.

So tonight, I want to start with a small step.

"I hate yellow legal pads."

The interior of the car goes silent, only the sound of the hazard lights clicking rhythmically filling the space. As silly as it sounds, it's the realest thing I can say, and I hope she sees that I'm trying.

She sits up in the seat. "Is that why you were upset after the game? You saw my notepad?"

I nod solemnly. "I'm sorry again."

It's clear she wants to ask more questions, but she respects the game enough not to. "Don't be. I'll never use them again." Digging through her bag, she doesn't break eye contact. "Thank you for being honest with me twice today."

Our elbows brush as I lean onto the console. "Thank you for listening to me twice today."

The only response that comes is the melodic scratch of pen to paper. It's a calming sound, especially when paired with her slightly off-tune rendition of "Love On Top."

The pen clicks, and she slides it behind her ear. "If I do or say something that bothers you, tell me. I don't want to hurt you." The interior lights flicker on as she swings the car door open and presses two pink sticky notes to the glove box. "Goodnight, Cade."

Once she makes it inside the house, I reach for her notes.

Rules are important. Stop breaking them

I grin, but my heart stutters when I read the next one.

Screw yellow legal pads. Pink is better. Thanks for being honest

Tucking them into my pocket, I glance at the front door and wish I could follow the woman who made me feel like me again.

"Good night, Shay baby."

CHAPTER FIFTEEN

 *Shay*

Golf is hard.

From under her visor, Jo shoots me a sympathetic look. It's been almost an hour since we made it to the nine-hole golf course in Clear Lake, and I keep whiffing it.

According to Adri, that means I suck.

"It's not too late to ask him to meet you on the soccer field," Jo offers. "That'll show Garrett how cutthroat you are. He'll immediately sign you as his agent."

"Can't." I stab a tee into the manicured grass. "Golf equals success as an agent. If I don't master it today, I'm screwed." I'm aware I sound delusional, considering professional golfers dedicate their lives to reaching the highest level.

Being invited to golf with Garrett felt like being invited to the cool kids' table after eating alone in the library. I even let Adri convince me to wear a cute skirt today, hopeful it would give me magical golfing powers.

It isn't working.

"I think you want it too much." Adri swirls the pretty blue drink in her hand. "The ball can smell your desperation."

Mallory hums. "She might be onto something. Empty your head and swing."

"Yeah!" Adri claps. "Go ahead and give us nothing!"

Jo, the only one with golf experience, shrugs. "Why not? Doesn't hurt to try."

Emptying my brain, I step up to the tee and follow Jo's instructions. Cover the red pieces of guiding tape? Check. Legs shoulder-length apart? Done. Bend the knees and push my hips back? Got it. Glare at the ball? Easy. Hitting it is the hard part.

"No thoughts," I whisper and pull my arms back. A warm ray of sun hits my skin, and I think the golfing gods are finally shining down on me and lighting a path for the little ball to fly down the green.

Squinting, I search for the ball. "Where'd it go?"

Wheezing laughter answers my question, so ear-splitting that the silver-haired golfers around us stare, but that doesn't deter my friends.

"Oh, sweet girl." Adri chokes on a gasp. "It never moved."

A scream rushes up my throat, muffled by my fist as I look down. The ball is still sitting on the damn tee.

"Maybe you should sign up for a class," Mallory offers. "You're heading toward Shayzilla, and although I love your feisty side, snapping a golf club over your knee may scare Garrett away."

Shayzilla is my alter ego. She's summoned when the words *calm down* leave a man's lips or "Hips Don't Lie" starts playing, but she's also awakened by failure.

And I'm failing right now. Hard.

I thrust my club at them. "If it's so easy, why don't you do it?"

It's a mistake, of course. Challenging Mallory is never a good idea. With a saccharine grin, she snatches a club. Everything about her movement is flawless, from the simplicity in her stance to the swing of her hips. The biggest difference between our attempts is that hers comes with that satisfying click, the sound of success. My failure intensifies when Adri hits the ball too.

I'm the only one here who sucks at golf.

As if she can sense my frustration, Mallory's competitive spirit shifts into concern as she hands us each a water bottle. "Let's try again at the first hole."

I send a silent thanks her way as we head to the gleaming white golf cart. Jo hops into the driver's seat with Mallory beside her, leaving Adri and I thigh to thigh in the backseat with the clubs. The other girls aren't height-challenged like I am, so they're sharing Jo's golf clubs, and I'm renting.

Jo's eyes meet mine in the rear-view mirror as she seamlessly maneuvers around other carts. "How are things going with Cade?"

Holding the claw clip in my teeth, I take my time roping my braids into a bun to think of an appropriate answer.

"Who cares about that, JoJo!" Adri cuts in. "I want to know how you can work so closely with a guy you used to sleep with and sorta date. You literally know what his dick looks like."

"And tastes like," Jo adds unhelpfully.

Mallory gags. "Jeez. That's my non-biological brother you're talking about."

"Not sorry. I'm expressing my respect for Shay, that's all." Adri beams like a proud mother. "I'm in awe of your ability to not fall back into bed with him."

I shrug. "It's easy. I refuse to let one man take my career down for a fun night."

I've successfully kept my head down and heart on lock for nearly two years. That isn't going to change because things are somewhat decent between us.

"According to college Shaylene, he's one well-endowed man." Adri lifts my chin to close my mouth when I glare at her. "Don't be mad at me for having a good memory."

"*Well-endowed*?" Mallory screams. "Did we transport back to the fifteenth century?"

TMI has never been a thing for The Quartet, and my stomach is in stitches when Jo pulls to a stop near the tee box. Mallory and Adri stay seated, but I follow Jo. From here, I can barely make out the red flag that signifies the hole. It'll take at least thirty attempts to get there.

"I want to try something. Let's treat this like baseball." The club Jo hands me looks like a high-tech sledgehammer, but she calls it a driver and grabs her own. "I wouldn't say they're necessarily similar, but humor me. Baseball's swing plane is horizontal, but golf's is vertical, like on a tilted circle. Got it?" I nod, and she continues. "Rotate your hips and keep your eyes on the ball. You don't need to be a pro to impress Garrett. You just need to make contact."

As she demonstrates the swing in slow motion, things start to click. It's different from baseball, yes, but maybe I can hit this damn ball. Even if it's only a few feet.

"You're a good coach, Jo. Thanks for taking a study break for me."

Blue eyes roll in that endearing way. "Anytime. I've missed your face."

When she steps back, an imaginary tilted circle appears around me. The practice swing is shaky, but I mostly stay on the surrounding lines. Aligning myself with the ball, I pull my arms back and bring them around quickly. My weight shifts to my front leg, and when I hear the sweet *click*, I leap into the air.

"I told you I could do—" I start, but when I turn around, I choke on my pride. It's hard to be a turd when my three best friends are celebrating my first successful stroke. I don't even care how far it went.

I'm just happy to be here with them.

Nine holes of golf shouldn't take four hours, but four chaotic women and one golf cart was enough to disturb an entire community.

Soothed by an Epsom salt bath and a bowl of dark chocolate chips, I fall onto the sectional. The thought of driving to Slim Jim Batting is too much, so I'll work from home tonight.

I grab my phone.

Me

Waiting on Chinese food. You alive?

A bubble appears as I curl into the multicolored quilt.

Marshmallory

Barely. Caught a charley horse so Kenneth is rubbing my calves. How are you?

Not great. The silence of the house is too loud. As a kid, I bounced between Mom's and Dad's. It wasn't until I moved into this house with Mallory that I understood what a real home should feel like. Four walls don't make a place home, but what she brought into the space did. Clanging dishes at the crack of dawn. Vibrant pieces of art she found at thrift shops on every wall. Oldies blasting from her room at all hours. Lively plants in every corner. With her gone, I haven't been able to make it mine. I haven't wanted to.

Before I can respond, another text comes in.

Marshmallory

I miss you. Sleepover next weekend?

I grin. She has always been able to read my mind.

My laugh falls short when I open my email and see hundreds of unread, urgent messages. It may be Saturday, but I never get a day off. A few of Trevor's requests—demands—are simple enough, but the rest are him passing off his work to me.

The most recent email is from Andy. We may be colleagues, but I can't remember the last time he emailed me separately.

Andy Walker: Not sure what happened. Doesn't seem good

I click the link he added, expecting bad news, but it's worse than I could imagine.

Carolina Pilots shortstop and golden boy, Cade Owens, stormed out of media.

My elbow connects with the coffee table as I roll off the couch, but I'm too preoccupied with opening my contacts and scrolling down to the C's. It took six months to lose the itch to call him every night, but in thirty seconds, the desperation to talk to him returns.

Then the doorbell rings, and I can't even be happy about dinner because my phone starts vibrating.

Chapter Sixteen

Cade

Calling my agent when things go wrong is part of her job description, right?

Getting under my skin isn't easy. I've had years of practice keeping my smile on through tough times. Like when my dad jumped ship and left me to take care of my mother and newborn sister. Or when I moved across the country, leaving behind my friends, family, and the woman I loved. Or every time Jon spoke to me as if I were a child.

I'm too aware of the familiar squeak her front door lets out, and I wilt into the hotel's comforter as her voice fills the room. Did I disrupt something important? A date?

Please don't let her have been on a date.

"Sorry," she breathes, returning to the phone.

"No, I'm sorry for interrupting whatever you're doing. I shouldn't have called. I'm sorry for bothering—"

"Stop it, Cade. You can call anytime you need me." The words are simple, but they hit me like a punch, forcing the air out of my lungs. "Where are you?"

"The hotel." After rushing out of media, I battled Seattle's windstorm and walked back before Rio could stop me. Marcus, Dawson, and a few others have knocked on my door, but I couldn't answer. I've been too busy reading every headline about me.

Golden boy can't take the heat? Maybe he should get out of the kitchen.

This can't be the same golden boy who never loses his cool.

Golden boy Owens isn't looking so golden.

"Cade?" Shay's voice is cautious, as if she's worried I might break into a million pieces. "What happened during media?"

A dry laugh slips out as I open another article. "Didn't you see the stories? The video?"

"No. That's perfectly constructed bullshit. I want you to tell me what happened."

"Video call?" I ask, fully expecting her to say no. But the chime in my ear surprises me, and I wait for the woman of my dreams to fill the screen.

There's no word to describe how seeing Shay makes me feel, but if I had to choose one, it's calming. Braids cascade down her shoulders, face brightened by what I assume is her laptop screen, but it's the puke-green color of her shirt that brings me out of my daze.

I choke on a laugh. "Why does your shirt say Go Boogers?"

Espresso eyes shine. "Because my teammates are silly. It's the team's secondary name. The one the preprofessional soccer league doesn't know about."

The smile slips off my face. "I didn't know you were still playing."

"I'm not." Pain dances across her tight features. "Not anymore."

Our words once flowed freely. Now, it's like pulling teeth to learn things about her.

"Is it okay if I ask why you stopped?"

"No, but honesty strengthens partnerships." She sighs. "When I started working full-time for Permian, I had to. I didn't play for long, but it was nice to be back on the field for a little bit. More than anything,

I loved supporting my teammates on their journeys to the pro league." Her laugh is sad. "I miss it, but it was for the best."

"You've always been good with athletes. Especially ones with a lot of emotions who don't know how to express them properly."

Her half smile tilts. "Guess I picked the right job then, huh?"

"Sure did." My skin buzzes from the ease between us. "Do you think you'll play again?"

The smile vanishes. "No. Like baseball is your life, being an agent is mine. There are things we have to sacrifice in order to have everything we dreamed of, you know? It's hard but I'll survive. *We* will survive."

I don't think survival is the way I want to live anymore. I'm tired of treading water and barely being able to keep my head up. I might not know what *just being* is yet, but I want to learn.

"I know you're a pro when it comes to deflecting, but I'm not giving you a pass tonight," Shay says. It's harsh but true, and her honesty is appreciated. "What happened tonight?"

I'm met with silence as she waits for me to speak. She has always given me space, waiting for me to open up and tell her what's going through my head. The problem was that I didn't hold up my side of the bargain.

I've been replaying the moment I walked away from the microphone since I stormed out. After a tough loss, they only wanted answers about Jon. I gritted my teeth as the reporters refused to take no for an answer, listing every accolade I'd accomplished with Jon by my side.

Then Scott Asshole, or whatever his name is, asked that question.

"He said something about you."

Shay's eyes widen. "Me?"

"You should watch the video. I'd rather not repeat it."

It's circulating on every sports app right now, considering this is my first public blow up. Hearing Shay's name come out of his mouth in that sour tone sent me into a frenzy.

"Do you think having a female agent is making you less focused on the game? Turner's definitely a looker. I'm sure I'd be distracted if she were my agent, and I'm curious if you believe she's helping or harming your game."

"Cade." Shay finally says when the video ends. "You didn't."

I rub my temple with my free hand. "I did."

She closes her laptop and stares at me. "You told Scott Butts"—I knew it was close to asshole—"the top sports journalist for the *Carolina Sidelines*, that he was, and I quote, 'a misogynistic prick who needs to learn some respect'? And instead of saying 'go fuck yourself', you told him to—"

"Suck my big toe. Just in case Violet saw it." I sigh, suddenly full of shame. "I know that was wrong but—"

A laugh, a real Shay laugh cuts me off. I watch in awe as she throws her head back, giving me a perfect view of her slender neck. It's been so long since the boisterous sound was aimed at me. More precious than any jewel or gem, and I want to bottle it and keep it with me wherever I go. I wish there weren't thousands of miles separating us so I could revel in this type of joy face to face.

I may have to pay a hefty fine and lose my golden boy reputation, but I couldn't care less.

"Oh god. I'm so sorry." She wipes her eyes. "As your agent, I know that shouldn't be funny, but I've never seen this side of you."

I want to laugh with her, but I'm still seething. "If you were a guy, he never would've asked that question. Treating you like you're less capable and more distracting because you're a woman? Commenting on your looks and not your talents?"

Something shifts behind her eyes. "It's part of life, Cade. My life. It's—"

An ugly noise rolls out of me. "If you say it's okay for men to deem you as below them because you don't have a dick, I'm going to get on a plane, come home, and force you to listen to me until you understand nothing about that is okay. It's not okay for anyone to treat you like that because you're a woman in sports. And I better not hear you apologize for being in this space. If anyone was meant to be here, it's you."

Pretty lips part as she stares at me. The Wi-Fi must've disconnected. I roll to the opposite side of the bed in hopes the signal will get better and lie against the stack of fancy hotel pillows.

"Thank you," she eventually whispers. "For standing up for me."

I hold my pinky in front of the camera. "Nobody is going to treat you like you're less than because you're a woman. You're a damn good agent. My agent."

My Shay baby.

She doesn't lift her pinky, but I get a real smile. "Sorry about the loss. You played well."

I did play well, but something was missing tonight. I'm starting to think it has been for a while now. Baseball used to be fun. Knocking balls into the lake as Kenneth and Nan swam after them. Learning from Jimmy, my former coach and mentor. Hanging out at the batting cages with Shay for hours, swinging until our arms were limp.

Now, I'm at the mercy of coaches, staff, and fans who always expect my best.

"You look like you haven't slept in days," she says, snapping me out of my funk. "Was it the hotel bed?"

"No, I just didn't sleep well last night." I yawn. "These days, I rarely sleep well."

In college, sleep always came so easily, especially when I knew I'd wake up beside Shay. After the draft, my nights were filled with Jon's endless notes, watching film, and preparing, as if sleep wasn't part of the athlete recovery regimen.

"That's new." As if she senses we're close to talking about the past, she clears her throat. "Now that we've gotten that out of the way, how are you feeling? I know being in the spotlight for something negative hasn't happened before." I open my mouth, but before I can answer, she holds up a hand. "And before you give me some bullshit answer that you're fine, and I don't need to worry, I need you to hear me, Cade. Sunshine doesn't have to be the only thing you exude. Not being okay doesn't make you weak or less than. It makes you human. So, I'll ask again. How are you?"

My immediate answer was that I'm fine. For years, I've lied to myself and everyone else by answering that way.

But today I'm done lying to her.

"I hate being the golden boy." I close my eyes for a moment. "I don't want to *be* him anymore, but I don't know who I am without him."

Then my eyes refuse to open, and I lose the battle.

"Ugh. Honesty is so damn attractive." Shay's laugh follows me all the way to my dreams. "Good night, Cade."

The last thing I see and hear is her, and I know this'll be the best sleep I've had in years.

Being summoned by the team manager feels like being sent to the principal's office. Except Rio Arden is the man who chooses the line up, speaks to the front office, negotiates contracts, and makes key decisions.

I'm out of a job if I can't keep him happy, and his cryptic text tells me he isn't happy.

Marcus lets out a low whistle as we exit the clubhouse. "Didn't know you had it in you, rookie. Seeing you yell at Scott was like seeing a tiger outside the zoo. Terrifying, but also fucking cool."

Dawson laughs but shoots me a wary glance. Since checking out of the hotel this morning, he hasn't left my side. On the plane ride home, he decided keeping an eye on me was more important than emptying his very small bladder.

"What did Shay say?" he asks.

A lot, and my chest tightens. I don't care that I admitted I hate being the golden boy because it's time I told her the truth. All that matters is that dozens of articles about Shay came out this morning, and I read them all. No wonder she thinks it's normal for people—men—to talk so callously about her as an agent. They were practically think pieces about her physical attributes, completely ignoring the hard work she has put into her career.

"She spoke with Rio this morning, which I guess is why he wants to talk." I stop in front of the coaches' area. "You guys didn't have to walk me here. I'll be fine."

A look passes between them before Dawson takes the lead. "Rio never takes meetings after we get back. The guy is obsessed with his wife and runs home to her after trips."

Marcus nods. "Him calling you in is a big deal."

I swallow hard. "Like getting demoted big deal?"

For the last month, I've worked my ass off to keep my spot in the majors. Studying Jon's notes in every free moment. Staying up all night to prepare for upcoming games. Smiling as if everything is golden in my world.

I'm not ready to leave the Pilots, but I'd do it all again if it meant standing up for Shay.

Rio's office door swings open, and he somehow looks even more annoyed than usual. "Go home, you two," he barks, and my friends blow him a kiss before heading for the exit.

He retreats to his desk, and I step inside. His office is as tidy and clean as the first time I sat here before spring training with Jon, who gushed about how great I would be for the Pilots' organization.

"He never causes problems. Does whatever you need because that's Cade."

That's what makes Jon's texts this morning so ironic.

Jon Sweeney

See. You can't do this without me.

I'm tired of these games. Call me back.

Instead of freaking out like I did the first few times, I deleted those without hesitation.

My butt isn't fully seated before Rio turns the television-sized monitor toward me. Scott Butts's cheeks are red with what I hope is shame, while I stand behind the podium, giving him an earful. It's odd to witness an emotion on my face that isn't happiness or contentment. I look furious, and it's nice to see and feel something else.

Something *real*.

"I'm not going to apologize," I say quickly. "Not to Scott."

I didn't say anything last night that wasn't true. Shay doesn't deserve disrespect, and I'll personally make sure she never has to hear that shit again. If that means I get demoted, then so be it.

Rio's brows lift. "And why is that?"

"Is it not obvious?" I jab an angry finger at the screen. "That's my agent. When have you heard of reporters bringing up how attractive male agents are and letting that trump professional conversations? Nobody has asked me if a man I work with distracts me from my job, so why was it okay for him to say that about her?"

Rio clasps his hands together. "It's not okay. I actually don't have an issue with anything you said or did last night."

Now I'm stumped. "You don't?"

"Nope. PR isn't happy, so you'll be hearing from Amber soon, but I'm proud." He turns the monitor back toward him. "I like Shaylene. She's smart. Before your player development meeting, she walked in with a list of questions for me. It was refreshing to see an agent who worried about your physical *and* mental health. It's clear she has your best interest in mind."

A brief smile touches my lips. Even with our history, she keeps proving that she's always on my side.

"And this morning," he continues, "she emailed me an article by Summer Moore with the *Carolina Gazette* that got me thinking."

The Energizer Bunny from the farmers market. "What did it say?"

"So much." Rio chuckles. "But my favorite part is when Summer tore Scott Butts a new asshole for his comment about Shay. Then she listed off every great thing Shay has done for her clients. It's impressive."

"She's impressive as hell, and I'm glad everyone will finally see her like I do." I stand. Dawson and Marcus will be happy to know I didn't need to stress about this meeting. "Thanks, Rio. See you tomorrow."

"Oh no, rookie. Sit your ass down," he orders, bending over to rummage through a drawer. "Do you know the average amount of time a player spends in the league?"

I'm confused by the switch in discussion. "No, sir?"

"Me either, but I know it's short. Wanna guess why?"

I shrug. "My first guess is injuries. Especially for pitchers. The body isn't meant for this high-impact lifestyle."

Rio nods. "What about the mental side of baseball? Do you think that could have any sway?"

"I don't know," I say, but it's a lie. I'm sure it is. I've spent many nights wondering if quitting would free me.

Ink fills my nose as I take the yellowed and worn newspaper Rio hands me. It almost looks like it could be from the nineties until I see my face looking back at me. Fifteen-year-old Cade had no idea what this headline would do.

Golden Boy Leads Bryan High to a State Championship!

That was the year I became the golden boy to the world. The reporter overheard my teammates chanting it lovingly and ran with it.

"You appeared on my radar after this," Rio says, sorting through the newspapers. "Little freshman on varsity. Not only were you the tallest on the field, but you were the star."

Of course he loved the golden look. Everyone does.

"Why are you showing me this?" I ask.

He taps the page. "Because I don't see this kid. I know you were fifteen when the photo was taken, but it's more than normal aging. I know what it looks like when a player who once bled baseball is going through the motions."

Damp palms rub against my sweatpants. "Rio—" I start, but he waves me away.

"You aren't being fined for last night's outburst. Well, you are, but you're not paying for it. If someone had said that about any woman I know, I would've reacted the same way." Clearing his throat, he stands. "One day, you're going to explode, Cade. Be honest with yourself. Take a break. Find someone to confide in. This shit gets heavy sometimes."

I watch him as he rounds the desk. "You sound like someone with personal experience."

His lips quirk slightly as he pulls me out of my chair and basically pushes me into the hallway. "Now get out of here. I want to go home and see my wife."

Home is calling my name too, but Shay's text from earlier means home will have to wait.

Agent Shay

Meet me here at 6

Current Location

CHAPTER SEVENTEEN

Bringing Cade to Slim Jim Batting will either be the best or worst decision I've ever made as an agent. Not because I'm worried about some big emotional pull that'll drag us back together once we're in our place.

It's the fact that I didn't tell Jimmy or Cade about my plan.

A flash of red darts past the window of my pseudo-office, and I watch as Cade parks and gets out of his car. Even with a multimillion-dollar signing bonus and a pro baseball salary, he still drives the minivan he got when he was sixteen.

From my desk, I lean forward to peer across the hallway into Jimmy's office, where he's reorganizing his desk drawers. His uneasy energy has been bouncing off the walls all afternoon. He scrubbed baseballs, mopped the concession areas twice, and hung new flyers in the neighborhood. If I had to guess, the article about Cade screaming at Scott Butts in his morning newspaper set him off.

"Hey, Jimmy," I call out. "Can you grab something from the front door for me?"

Tired eyes roll. "We're the same distance from the door, Shaylene. Why don't you get it?"

"I could, but it's a special delivery for you."

He leaps out of his seat. "A chocolate-covered-pineapple kind of special delivery?"

I grin. "Better."

A disbelieving snort leaves his crooked nose, but the ring of keys attached to his belt jingles all the way to the front door. It's not until I hear a gasp and the heavy thuds of what I expect to be an overly aggressive hug that I make my way into the hallway. Jimmy's arms are wrapped tightly around Cade like a snake.

Still, Cade looks comfortable in his embrace.

Then without warning, Jimmy flips him around and puts him in a headlock. "Dammit, Owens! You almost gave an old man a heart attack."

The lack of oxygen reddens Cade's cheeks. "Blame her," he gasps, pointing a finger at me until Jimmy releases him. Returning to full height, he rubs his neck. "She set us up."

When both of their eyes land on me, I take a bow. "Now that wasn't so hard, was it? All it took was one smart woman and two men incapable of communicating. I think I deserve to hear two magic words."

"Thank you," Cade sings, while Jimmy says, "Smart ass."

It feels so good to be back together. After Cade left for California, my time with Jimmy was special, but with Cade here, it feels whole again.

"I can't believe you still haven't found anyone to lease out the spare office." Just like the old days, Cade draws a smiley face in the dusty sign hanging in the window. "You've been looking for a tenant for years."

"Must be the constant yelling from the batting cages keeping people away."

"Customers?"

"Nope." Jimmy ruffles my braids. "I've got a sports agent who comes in at all hours of the day and takes her anger out on the balls. Plus"—he gestures at my office—"she made herself comfortable. Can barely get her to go home these days."

"I'll return my key," I threaten, but we both know I won't. Jimmy will have to pry this key from my cold, dead hands.

"Don't you dare." Misty eyes fall to the pink binder tucked under my arm. "I'm guessing y'all are about to have a work meeting?"

I nod. "Yes, if that's okay. I'll lock up when we're done."

"Of course. This place is just as much y'all's as it's mine." Jimmy turns to Cade and bows his head. "Don't be a stranger. Okay?"

A mix of emotions flits over Cade's face as he wraps Jimmy in one last hug before his old coach heads home. The professional part of me knows being alone with Cade is dumb because we'll always be two people with history, but the personal part of me knows we need to be here at our place.

"Hi, Agent Shay."

Our eyes meet. Although I see none of the sadness from last night, there's no hiding it anymore. I know it exists now.

"Is that your substitute for Shay baby? It's so not creative."

"Sure is, unless you're giving me permission to—"

"Nope," I say quickly. "What did I say about calling me that?"

His lips slant into a smirk. "That I should feel lucky I'm able to speak your name at all."

A grin breaks through my nerves. "I never said that."

"Doesn't mean it's not true."

Brushing off the mild flirting, I gesture for him to follow me into the building. Slim Jim Batting got a makeover last summer, so Cade hasn't seen any of the changes. There's new turf in every cage with clay batting mats. A paint job spruced up the walls from mildew-gray to charcoal. The rubber flooring is crack free with no bubbles. Jimmy splurged on machines with adjustable pitching styles controlled by the tablet in each cage. We even have a softball machine now.

Cade gently caresses the painted version of himself on the wall. "He always said he wanted a mural of his favorite baseball players." Continuing his perusal of the place, he chuckles. "Is this considered a work meeting if we're playing baseball?"

I step into my favorite cage and tap the tablet. "We *are* here for work, Cade." Regret floods me when he flinches. "No, I mean I'm here for work, but I'm also—"

His laugh is forgiving. "It's okay. I get it."

"No," I sputter. "You're my client, so I have a contractual obligation to work with you, and it's hard to explain caring about my job versus caring about you, because I care about both." Jeez, could I sound more unprofessional? "But I'm here for *you*. Nothing else."

I tried to stop caring about Cade years ago. I now know it's impossible.

"You've always been there for me." He looks toward Jimmy's office. "Even when I didn't let you."

I have no intention of diving into our past tonight, so I pull my helmet on and press start. Spreading my legs, I settle into my stance. With every click, I swing, knocking the ball into the net. They chuck out in the same, steady rhythm as always, but it's different today. It could be the heavy gaze on my back or the simple fact that he's here for the first time in years.

After the final ball, Cade claps until I turn around. "It's like I never left."

But you did, I think.

"Your turn."

Cade stares down at the bat in his hands. "Why'd you bring me here?"

I don't answer. "Do you really hate being the golden boy?"

His shoulders tense, and my mind starts playing whatever deflection he is preparing. *Last night, I overreacted. I was tired. No need to worry about me. Okay?*

Instead, he surprises me. "I really do. It wasn't supposed to be like this. Being on the field made me feel like nothing else in the world. I looked forward to every practice and game, even if it ended in a loss. I was happy."

Was.

"How long have you been unhappy?"

The veins in his hand pop as he grips the bat. "I don't know exactly. I woke up one day and didn't feel like me anymore. Most people don't even call me Cade now. I'm the golden boy or nothing to them." He digs his toe into the turf. "But I also don't know how to move away from it. I don't know how to—"

"Just be," I finish for him, repeating my sentiment from the player development meeting.

"Just be."

"Seeing all those headlines must be tough." I wince. "Do you regret what you said to Scott?"

There's a crazed look in his eyes when they meet mine. "Not one bit," he says, emphasizing each word. "For the first time in years, I didn't care about the fact that I could end up on the bad side of the media, and I didn't care about being the golden boy. You were the only thing that mattered. Not my image or baseball. *You.*"

"Me?" My heart leaps into my throat. I can't wrap my head around this. "Cade—"

"I know I'm breaking rule number two, but I have to say this. *Please* let me say this." His stare is unyielding, and because he let me break rule three after filming, I allow it. "I had you, Shay, and it was easily the best thing to happen to me. I'm sorry for so many things. For not coming home and making you mine. For not talking to you, even though you gave me every opportunity to. For forcing you to be my agent. Working with you for the last month has been the lightest I've felt in years. Possibly ever. But I was scared to tell you the truth. So I ran."

Part of me hoped to never learn why he didn't choose me. But now I can't help but ask.

"Why were you scared?"

Propping his bat against the gate, he steps closer. "Because it's a privilege to play baseball and be loved by all. I didn't want you to see me unhappy about something people would give anything for. That's not who I'm supposed to be. I'm supposed to be golden. Not struggling."

If there weren't a gate between us, I'm sure I'd break rule number five and touch him, but I can't, for a multitude of reasons.

I take the next best option and press my hand against the cool gate. The faint clang from my class ring gets his attention. Slowly, he lifts his hand to meet mine. Even with the metal between us, his warmth can be felt. It's a loophole, but I ignore that.

"All I wanted was for you to be you."

"I know," he breathes, mint sharpening my senses. "You saw me for Cade. Not the golden boy or whoever people wanted me to be. And I think I've always known that, but at that time, I was too lost to see what was right in front of me."

The end of us truly was that simple. Each problem was like a raindrop. One on its own wasn't a big deal, easily brushed away. Something he likely assumed he could push through. But when the storm came day after day, the harmless drops became an overwhelming flood.

And eventually, the dam broke.

"You fought harder than I deserved," he continues. "I pushed you away until you had no choice but to give up, and that's never been your fault. But you were never far away."

Before I can ask for clarification, he pulls something from his pocket with his free hand.

In his palm sit two dice. *My* dice.

When my parents divorced, I was hurt. When my dad accepted a job in Philadelphia, I was gutted. The two of us were connected at the hip, and he was moving across the country. Our last night in his apartment was spent eating pizza out of old Frisbees. It was then that he pulled out his lucky dice and placed them in my palm.

"No matter where we go, look at these, and we'll always be together."

Cade knew that when I slipped them into his pocket the night he left for California.

"You kept them?"

"Of course I did." He traces the edges of the smooth plastic. "They go everywhere with me. Every game, meeting, practice, trip. I'm not sure I would've survived without them." Our gazes lock. "Without you."

The thought of Cade carrying my dice after we split shocks me to my core. He didn't just keep them.

He kept *me*.

"I don't know what to say, Cade. Professionally speaking—"

"I know," he stops me. "You don't have to say a word. I just wanted to tell you the truth. Now, diagnose me with your special agent powers and tell me how to fix my whole life."

A brittle laugh escapes me as I drop my hand. "Can't promise you that, but I have two questions." I step away from the gate. "Number one. What do you want from life?"

His nose scrunches adorably. "Life?"

"Yeah." I nod. "Screw what everyone else wants. What do *you* want?"

He thinks for a moment. "I just want to be Cade."

"Does that include baseball?"

A pause. "I don't know."

"And that's okay," I say. "Question two. What's something you want to do for yourself?"

This answer is immediate. "Finish my degree," he says, and I smile. That's something I can help with. "Wait," he continues. "You don't care that I'm not sure about baseball? Shouldn't you tell me how much of a mistake quitting would be, and how I'll ruin my image?"

"I don't care about your image, Cade. I care about *you*." Swinging my bat over my shoulder, I shrug. "Your career is yours, and I'm here to support whatever decisions you make. Because I knew you, I do want you remember why you loved baseball. That spark in your eyes is special, and I'd hate to see you lose it forever."

Cade loved baseball, and not because he was good. At one point, it made him happy.

After a moment, he grabs the bat. "Okay. What's step one?"

"This." I wave my hands around. "Doing things that make you happy, like being here and hitting balls."

Clear, intentional eyes meet mine, and his lips tilt. "Maybe I was happy here because I got to be with you. Did you ever think about that?"

I press four fingers against the gate. "Rule four, Cade. No flirting."

His laugh breaks out, sharp and unguarded, filling the cages with a joy so familiar, it aches. I still know that sound better than my own heartbeat, and I love it just as much.

"Whatever you say, Agent Shay." Pointing his bat at me, he taps the cage—aimed right at my heart. "You don't have to say it, but I think deep down, you know you're happy with me too."

My lips stay sealed, but he's right.

And his laugh says he knows it.

CHAPTER EIGHTEEN

My nosy best friend is rubbing off on me.

Most days while walking around Permian, I overhear my coworkers talking about me. Their favorite topics revolve around my flowery perfume that's too distracting, my pink and overly professional outfits, and my off-putting intensity. Their words have never affected me, but the conversation happening in Trevor's office hooked me like a fish to bait.

"Garrett Blane won't choose *her*," Trevor bites out. "But she thinks she's special because she's taking him to the golf course today."

A grating wheeze from Jonah, a fellow junior agent, slips into the hallway. "Everyone has been to the golf course with a client except her."

"It's a waste of time," Kyle adds. "Just tell her no."

"I would, but I don't need shit from Winston today. He's already upset because another client didn't re-sign with me last week, which wasn't my fault." Trevor pauses for validation from his fanboys. "And for some reason, he likes Turner."

"We all know why," Jonah says, and it's easy to imagine the suggestive raise of his brows as they all burst into laughter at the implication of me sleeping with the CEO.

As if that's the only reason Winston isn't a dick to me.

Pressing my back against the wall, I cover my mouth. I've covered for Jonah and Kyle more times than I can count—stepping in for Jonah's clients when he took two weeks off for his grandmother's funeral, and handling Kyle's workload when he went away for his sister's wedding. I do half of Trevor's job because I'm the only junior agent he trusts.

All I do is try so hard to earn their respect. And for what?

As I creep away, the door opens.

Shit. Shit. Shit.

"Turner?" Andy's eyes dart between me and Trevor's office. I should've known he was in there. He's one of them too. "It's not what you—"

I barrel down the hallway without waiting for him to finish his sentence. Once safe in my office, I close the door, and press the heels of my palms against my eyes.

No. You will not let these assholes make you cry.

But it's too late. Warm tears slide down my cheeks as I grab my phone and open the calendar. Garrett's in town for the three-game series against the Pilots, and I'm meeting him at the golf course in an hour.

Does Garrett see this as a joke? A big waste of time?

The knock at the door makes my phone slip from my fingers.

Fixing my mascara, I bend down to pick up my phone. "Come in."

Frankenstein entering my office would be less surprising than seeing Andy standing in the doorway, looking like a sad puppy.

His shifty gaze lands on me for half a second. "You ran off before I could say anything."

I cross my arms over my chest. "Wasn't in the mood to hear anymore lies about myself. It's not fun listening to people joke about me sleeping with the boss. Now, if you'll excuse me, I need to prepare to waste Garrett's time."

Andy winces at my sarcasm. "Turner, please. Can we talk?"

"There's nothing to say. I heard everything."

"But that was Trevor, Kyle, and Jonah. I didn't say anything."

My laugh is harsh. "Which is almost worse."

Cade was the first person to speak up for me as a female agent when someone railed against me. Is it fair that my hard work wasn't enough, but Cade's words were?

No, but I'm thankful for him.

Andy's jaw twitches and he turns around, but instead of leaving, he closes the door and locks himself inside. In the crappy light, he almost looks familiar. More like the person who studied negotiations with me over mozzarella sticks in the break room. The only person who didn't laugh when I told him about my dreams as an agent. He treated me like an equal. An adversary.

"You're right, and I'm sorry." Andy drops his voice to a whisper. "You deserve to know the truth. Trevor's pissed because he reached out to Garrett and got ignored, but you didn't."

I blink hard at his unexpected confession. "*What*?"

"Right after you talked to him about throwing your hat in the ring, he tried to schedule a meeting with Garrett before you could."

My knees buckle, and I collapse into the chair. Trevor tried to steal Garrett from me.

"Why are you telling me this?" I ask, refusing to let my guard down. "You're one of Trevor's guys."

"Because I fucking hate being one of them! And I hate the way I've treated you. You knew more than every intern, and instead of being smug, you were kind enough to tutor me. You were my friend, but the moment we got our contracts, I saw you as a threat. Trevor didn't help that fear, but I can't blame him. I've had plenty of chances to speak up."

I peer at the door, waiting for the camera crew to burst in. "Am I being punked?"

"Nope. I'm just an idiot trying to make amends." He falls into the seat across from me and shakes his head. "I'm done watching Trevor treat you like shit. And I'm sorry for everything, Turner. Henrietta was pissed when I told her the real reason we stopped talking."

Andy's long-time girlfriend's name makes me pause. "You told her?"

"Every bit of the truth," he says. "Slept in the guest room for a month."

It feels good to laugh, but it fades quickly. "I don't know what to say, Andy, but thanks for telling me the truth."

"I don't deserve your gratitude." Patting my desk, he stands. "Now go golfing and get Garrett on a sweet contract."

I eye the golf clubs in the corner of the room. "Golf is hard."

"It is, but you can do it. I'm here if you need anything, okay?" Then, without waiting for a reply, he leaves my office.

My head spins from the whiplash of that conversation, but I don't have time to waste. I've got forty-five minutes to pull myself together and get to the golf course. The gold polo shirt and black golf pants match the Permian brand, but the pink bow earrings Cade picked out the day we got our ears pierced are in the first hole. I touch the cool metal, feeling a bit more like me.

When my phone chimes, I expect it to be Garrett, but a smile takes over my face before I can stop it.

Cade

Good luck today, Agent Shay.

"If I were a betting man, I'd be dirt poor right now."

My lips curve into a sly smile as I sink a ball into the fifth hole. "I'm full of surprises."

"I see that." Garrett flips his hat backward. "You were so spooked when I asked if you golfed, so I was expecting to whoop you."

I send Jo a silent thanks. It's not great, but I'm better than him.

The man who could alter the projection of my career walks up to his ball. Concentration tightens itself between his brows as he draws an imaginary ten-foot line with his eyes from the ball to the hole. Pulling back his putter, he sinks the ball.

"Nice," I say, holding my fist out.

He bumps my knuckles. "Sure, but you're still five strokes ahead."

Shayzilla didn't come to play; she came to win. After almost letting one group of men beat me today, I won't let this one get close. Even if he is nice.

"Only a few holes left. Then you can hide in shame at the stadium this evening."

A boisterous howl escapes him as he hikes the golf bag over his shoulder and leads us to the sixth hole. "This is why I like you, Turner. You've got that athlete spirit inside you."

"It's hard to let go of," I admit. It's why I loved playing in the preprofessional soccer league. Even if there were no stakes, I loved every second of competition.

I miss it every day, but my job is number one. It has to be.

"My fiancée loves golfing with me." Garrett's strong features melt at the thought of her. "She's got crazy luck with a club in her hand."

"That's adorable," I say. "How is Layla doing?"

He gawks at me. "You remember the name of my fiancée from a month and a half ago?"

Has it really been that long since I pitched myself to Garrett in the lounge at Pilot City Stadium? It seems as if time is flying by.

Readjusting my bag, I smile. "She's important to you, and I told you that those important to you are important to me."

"Yeah, but everyone says that." The proud crinkle around his eyes tells me I've gained another point in the running. "She's in town for the series and is dying to meet you. Will you be at any of the games?" He beams when I nod. "Great, and congrats. I saw you started working with Cade Owens."

My cheeks warm, and I can't blame it on the weather because it's perfect out. The clouds and slight breeze have kept me from nervously sweating through my shirt.

"Thank you. It's going well."

"Would you feel comfortable juggling multiple baseball clients?"

"Definitely." Fishing a tee from my pocket, I hand it to him. "I work with multiple basketball and soccer clients too. As someone who values quality, I'll always make sure every client gets their own unique partnership with me."

He sticks the tee into the ground and places a yellow ball on top. "Do you practice these answers in the mirror?"

"Sometimes, yes. But today you're getting answers straight from my brain."

Garrett hums his approval but keeps his eyes on the ball. It gets lost in a forest of trees, and he laughs. I love that he doesn't let it get him down. "Well, that brain of yours is definitely helping my decision. Now hit the ball. I need to figure out a way to beat you by the end of the ninth hole."

Shayzilla roars from deep inside me. "We'll see about that."

CHAPTER NINETEEN

Shay

THE PILOTS ARE ON fire, and it's not their special gold uniforms.

Still, the Pilots and Jackals are neck-in-neck. The last game of a series is my favorite because with two phenomenal teams like this, it's a fight to the finish.

"These are some nice seats," Brett says, stuffing a handful of popcorn into his mouth.

"I've already thanked you like ten times." I nudge his arm off my arm rest. "I get it. You're popular."

Thanks to my basketball client's star status, we got the best seats in the house. Well, to me. Most people would give their left lung to sit behind home plate, but my happy place is between home plate and the first-base dugout. The harmonious sound of cracking bats and snapping gloves is best from here.

Brett leaps to his feet when Dawson strikes out another Jackal, hollering for the man on the pitcher's mound. He's got the lungs of a toddler who had sugar for lunch.

A smug smile pulls at my lips. "I'm starting to question your lifelong hatred for baseball."

Affronted eyes cut in my direction. "I never said I hated it. I said I didn't get the hype."

Maybe not, but he does now. After two seasons with the NC Grizzlies, it's about time Brett dipped his toe into other professional sports in Charlotte. Halfway through the third inning, he promised to attend a Carolina Rage soccer match. Holly and Victoria will be thrilled.

"So, how'd it go with the future Mrs. Blane?" he asks, never taking his eyes off the field.

Layla was even sweeter than she looked, with adorable dimples and ringlet curls that shone like molten gold under the stadium lights. I expected her to be like Adri, but the moment she sat down, she was like Jo in that quiet way I love.

I shrug. "It went well."

"Do you think she'll give you a glowing endorsement?"

Again, I shrug. Making a good impression on family members and partners is important because they can sway recommendations, but I want Garrett to work with me because he thinks I'm the best agent for his career. Still, I hope she liked me.

Brett stuffs another handful of popcorn into his mouth. "How much longer until you get an answer from him? You've been courting him forever. He can't keep stringing you along."

"He isn't, Brett," I explain. "Garrett is exploring his options and figuring out who best fits his needs, which is normal. I probably won't know for another few months."

Courtships often require a slow-burn strategy. I must prove my value to him over time, not with one flashy pitch. It's part power play, part chess game.

Lucky for me, I love a good slow burn.

"Well, I picked you after one phone call—what the hell? That was a strike!" Brett leaps to his feet and waves down the plate umpire. Thankfully, the man ignores my passionate client. When he finally sits down, he grins. "Why didn't I know baseball was cool like this?"

The crowd cheers as the Pilots make the third out, bringing us into the bottom of the ninth inning. As Cade jogs to the dugout, stopping to pat Dawson's butt, I notice his gait is smooth with no limp. I'm still upset with myself for not bringing it up earlier.

Brett shivers, rubbing his arms. "That was weird."

"What was?" I ask.

"You know that feeling of being watched?" I nod, and his eyes shift to the home-team dugout. "I've been feeling that way all night and couldn't put my finger on why. Then your newest client ran by, and I felt like I was stabbed by a million daggers."

It wasn't until I sat down in our seats that I realized the colossal issue. I've got front-row seats to Cade and all the things that make him my favorite baseball player. The way he rocks forward on his toes between pitches, ready and twitching with energy. The crease in his jersey from bending forward to catch his breath. The double pat to his thigh when deep in thought. The beads of sweat running down his cheek that he never wipes away, refusing to be distracted for even a second during a play.

I clocked the moment he saw me. Then I watched his jaw tick when Brett sat beside me.

Going for a nonchalant professional and not a woman whose body is on fire, I wave Brett's concerns away. "We're in a big section. He could be looking at anyone. Don't think too far into it."

Brett opens his mouth to respond but stops when Cade makes his way to the batter's box.

The announcer whistles into the mic. "I don't know about y'all, but I feel like the golden boy is in his own league."

My lips twist at an odd angle, loving the praise for Cade while stewing at the nickname. "His name is Cade," I mutter. "Not golden boy."

Brett smiles. "Protective Shay. Me likey."

"Shut up." I laugh but grow serious when the Jackals pitcher winds up and releases a fastball. I would cry if a ball came at me like that, but Cade doesn't flinch.

"Ball!" the umpire shouts.

The next ball is a fastball too, and Cade swings. The umpire throws his clenched fist out to the side and the crowd lets out a collective groan.

Brett sucks in a sharp breath. "I changed my mind. I hate baseball. How is he not crying right now? I'd be in tears if I were him."

All I can do is nod, keeping my eyes on the man in front of me.

The third pitch cuts through the air, and I almost scream. Strike two.

I cover my eyes and peek through the gaps in my fingers. Even with a slightly distorted view, it's clear that Cade is unaffected. He's calm and cool in the batter's box with a simple tilt to his lips.

Some people are made to save lives. Some are meant to teach.

Cade is meant to play baseball.

The pitcher winds up, and the moment the ball leaves his fingertips, I'm on my feet. The roar of the crowd is deafening, but nothing can stifle the victorious crack of wood, signifying the perfect hit as the ball disappears into the upper deck.

"Clear skies! Fly high!" fills the air as Cade taps two fingers to his temples, a silent reply to the crowd's cheers. When the scoreboard flashes WALK-OFF, Cade tosses his bat aside and begins the home run trot.

But instead of focusing on the field, his attention lands on me, and one hazel eye flutters shut. It's so fast that I don't think anyone caught the wink, but I felt it.

And it's oddly nice to be the one he's looking at again.

"I have work in the morning," I whine, using my go-to excuse.

"You have work *every* morning." Adri tosses her sandals aside. "And I don't want to leave! I miss you and this house."

Her words aren't meant to be a barb, but they prick my skin anyway. The red brick house on the corner was our spot for years. Even when Mallory moved in with Kenneth, we still tried to hang out here. After I canceled three times for work, hangouts moved to their place at Lake Anita.

"We all do," Mallory butts in, pausing to glare at Adri. "But if you need us to go, we will."

It's not that I don't want them here, but the state of my house is embarrassing. Only Mallory has been here recently and has never commented on the bare space that used to be our solace. She's not one to bite her tongue, but she tries for me.

"No," I finally say. "We can watch a movie."

After saying goodbye to Brett at the stadium, I let Mallory, Jo, and Adri convince me to hang out for a bit. Being here reminds me of simpler days when Mallory lived down the hall and Jo and Adri would barge in at all hours. We would stretch across the couch after a hard practice or stay up all night for post-date recaps as we divulged private information. But ever since I started at Permian, I've lost those nights.

Putting my job first may be for the best, but I'm lonely.

Slipping on a tattered CLU sweatshirt, I ask, "Where's Kenneth?"

Mallory rolls a vial of insulin between her hands, warming it for her injection. "He took Nan and Titus home. Knowing them, they're finishing a puzzle, but he should be here soon."

"I missed our grandparents?" I groan. Nan and Titus, her man-friend—because boyfriend is apparently too juvenile—practically adopted us after Kenneth and Mallory started dating two years ago.

Jo drops a stack of flashcards onto the plastic dining table. "Nan said if she doesn't see you soon, she'll drag you out of the office by your bows."

I laugh. She would.

The doorbell rings, and I rush to it like a dutiful host. I'm expecting a head of red hair and freckled cheeks, but bronze skin and broad shoulders fill my vision. It should be illegal to wear thin T-shirts out in the world when you look like this. The fabric is literally bursting at the seams, and I almost want it to.

He's your client. Pull yourself together.

Cade Owens is on my doorstep. At prime booty-call hour.

What if one of my elderly neighbors is watching us right now as he looms over me? Him looking sinfully sexy with tired eyes and slutty little glasses. And me in my . . . Oh my god.

The CLU baseball sweatshirt he gave me before he left for California swallows my torso, hanging down to mid-thigh. The teal color is almost gray from being worn and washed so often. I tried to trash it once but chickened out. It was too comfortable to sacrifice.

"Nice outfit." He grins. "Looks familiar."

I refuse to smile back. "What are you doing here?"

"Movie night. Am I wrong?"

He's not, but the risk is too high. According to my contract, being linked to a client isn't a fireable offense. It's how Winston met his wife of twenty years. But me? Because I'm a woman, I'd be torched and judged for the rest of my career. It would be assumed I couldn't control my emotions or all I wanted out of this job is an athlete boyfriend. No agent would respect me, no player would want to work with me, and no player's significant other would trust me.

My worst nightmare.

Delicate taps to my temple pull me from my spiraling panic. "Don't worry. I'll go," he whispers. "Sometimes I forget that we're not still us. I can't just show up at your home. Please tell everyone I said—"

"Come inside, Cade." I push open the door. "It's fine. Your friends are here too."

He casts me a doubtful glance but holds his pinky up. "There will be no funny business. I'll be on my best behavior."

"You better," I mutter as we step into the house.

A stab of embarrassment nicks my skin as he takes in the foyer, so different from the last time he was here. Walking into a house that Mallory built was like being wrapped in a warm hug. Now the pale blue walls that were once covered with photos and vinyl albums are bare and sad.

"It's different," he finally says.

That's one way to put it. It feels and looks as if nobody lives here. I barely do.

"I'll be back," I say before sprinting to a spot Cade is not allowed. My bedroom.

I'm about to burst inside when the door swings open, and I run smack-dab into Mallory.

"I disappear for two seconds to find a Sharpie and you're freaking out." She grips my shoulders. "Where's the fire?"

Pressing my finger to her lips, I turn around and point at Cade as he disappears into the kitchen. "Isn't it obvious? I can't be alone with him."

"And why is that?"

"He's my client, Mally! It's unprofessional for him to be in my house, but I wasn't going to make him leave when all his friends are here. I'm not heartless."

"Are you planning on doing anything unprofessional with him?" When I glare at her, she pulls me into her chest. "Then get in there and talk to your client like he's an old friend you never had sex with. Okay? Jo and I need to study for a little bit. I'd ask you to quiz us, but Adri already offered. Keep it professional. Baseball talk only."

I can do that. Yeah. I love baseball.

"Hey, MalPal!" Cade appears and gives her a quick hug. "Studying?"

"Always, Cader Tot," she says, pushing us toward the living room by our shoulders. "Kenneth will be here soon. You guys should pick the movie."

Perching myself in my favorite corner of the sectional, I relax when Cade takes a seat on the opposite side of the couch and grabs the remote. Focusing on my phone, I navigate to the voting website for the All-Star Game in a few weeks, and lock in my votes since today's the final day for round two.

Cade clicks through the genres. "Do you think *Saw* could be classified as a romance?"

"You will not bring the spirit of that evil puppet into my house. Only Jo picks horror movies, and it's not her night to choose."

Though I missed her last movie night for work, so I don't know what she chose.

Cade finally stops scrolling through the terrifying thumbnails and navigates to the romance section. This isn't so bad. We're talking about movies and nothing even remotely personal has—

"Who was the guy you were with at the game tonight?"

Oh my god.

I cross my arms. "Maybe it's time for a new rule because that's a personal matter."

"So he's a *personal* friend." His lips curl as if he doesn't know if he wants to smile because he's teasing me or grimace at the idea of me having a "personal friend."

But it shouldn't matter to him.

Still, I ask, "Do you watch basketball?"

"Not often."

Locking my phone, I toss it aside. "I represent Brett Reynolds, the—"

"Center for the Grizzlies! I thought he looked sorta familiar." When I nod, his smile splits wide, all signs of jealousy vanishing. "Atta-girl. I always knew you'd be the best agent."

I hate the way my praise kink purrs at his words, so I focus on voting. Four pink sticky notes I wrote during his game sit on the coffee table, and he leans forward to grab them. Ever since learning about his aversion to yellow legal pads, I haven't used mine. By the look on his face, I think he appreciates that.

When he's done reading through them, I sit up. "What did you do for you this week?"

"Is this going to be a weekly question?" Hazel eyes roll, but he obliges me anyway. "You'll be happy to know I took a nap."

My butt glides across the couch. "That's a big self-care activity! How did you feel after?"

He shrugs. "A bit guilty, honestly."

I rest my hand on his shoulder. "I'm proud of you, Cade."

It should be illegal for men to have such long eyelashes, especially when they surround the prettiest eyes. Carefully carved orbs of moss and honey move from my hand on his shoulder and down my arm to meet my gaze. It's then I realize the lack of space between us.

Rule five has been broken. *Back up.*

His hand around my wrist stops me. It's gentle enough to slip out of if I tried, but I don't think I want to.

"We don't have to be ten feet apart to have a conversation, Shay." Releasing me, he moves back until there's a cushion between us. "You're clearly great at your job. You care more than any agent I know."

I'd curtsy if I weren't sitting down. "Thank you."

"So why are you working for a guy like Trevor?"

A surprised cough chokes me. This is the third time a client has said something negative about my supervisor. I assumed I was the only one who saw through his fake persona. Still, I don't answer. My professional line cannot fall.

"I'm not asking you to talk poorly about him."

My head snaps up. "Stop reading my mind."

"Can't help it." He laughs. "But seriously. Why?"

Flashes of the last year and a half play in my head. After Cade didn't come home, I reevaluated the things within my control. My job and success are controlled by me. Being the first one in the office, staying up late, and working my ass off are things I can do to ensure my success. But love? Relationships? No way. I learned my lesson.

"At Permian, I'll be successful. It's the best path for the life I want."

A life of work, work, and more work.

Cade sighs. "If you're happy, that's all that matters."

Happiness and success are the same thing to me. I guess in my own way, I am happy. Happy enough, at least.

"Plus," he continues, "if you weren't at Permian, who knows if we would be speaking right now. I'm glad I requested you as my agent."

"Why is that?"

"Because now you can officially say you've met your favorite client." He leans against the couch with a sly smile. "Me."

I toss a blanket at his head. "You're at the very bottom of the list."

"Yeah yeah. Keep telling yourself that, Agent Shay."

I've missed these moments. I lost a lot the day we ended things, but maybe it doesn't have to be gone for good. Even if it's not in the way I once wanted.

Who knows where we would be if things hadn't ended. Maybe I'd be his girlfriend *and* a successful sports agent, but now we're here. And I'm surrounded by constant reminders that there is no other future for us.

Not if I want to be the agent I've fought so hard to be.

CHAPTER TWENTY

 *Cade*

"Come on guys. Start shuttin' up."

The clubhouse goes silent at Rio's command, but our excitement doesn't wane. The Pilots are on a hot streak, racking up seven wins in a row. A slight curl is visible on even Rio's perpetually downturned lips. His pleased expression is a good omen.

"You're glowing, RiRi!" Morrison Davis, our second baseman, yells from behind me.

"Shut up, Davis." Rio throws him a glare but still isn't scowling. "I'm not big on speeches but tonight's win against the Raiders deserves one. I'm sorely proud of the baseball you all played today. You guys might be big pains in my ass, but if you keep playing like that, we'll bring home some hardware in October." Tapping his temple twice, he surprises us with a full smile, lips split wide and showing off bright white teeth. "Clear skies. Fly high."

The clubhouse explodes.

Hysterical howls fill the air.

There's a nonstop *vroom*, mimicking airplanes as we hold our arms out like airplane wings.

Rio's laugh bellows as he tries to act like he doesn't love us.

"Okay, okay. Simmer down." It takes too long to regain control, but when he does, Rio has reverted back to his normal self. "We leave for Texas tomorrow, so eat a hearty dinner and get some sleep. Be here at ten, and not a minute late." His attention shifts away. "Before you head home, Huber is gonna say a few words."

Everybody claps as Dawson makes his way to the front of the room. We don't have a formal captain position, but if we did, it would be him. The man who embodies the spirit of the Pilots.

Dawson rubs a hand over his smooth head, cheeks still red from celebrating. "The last seven seasons here in Charlotte have been nothing short of a dream. Everyone keeps asking when I'm retiring, and I want to set the record straight. You guys know how hard it is being on the road constantly. The season is long, and those with kids know it isn't easy to leave them behind."

A blast of warm air tickles my ear. "He better not be doing what I think he's doing," Marcus whispers, and I hold my breath. Giving Dawson crap about retiring is fun, but he wouldn't actually do it. Right?

"Me and Rosie have had a lot of long conversations about what is best, and I wanted you guys to hear it from me first." He pauses for a moment before sticking his tongue out like a petulant child. "You losers aren't getting rid of me yet, so stop listening to the rumors!"

"Jesus," Otis, an outfielder, shouts. "You can't play like that!"

"Yeah, not cool, asshole!" Marcus blubbers into my shirt.

Rio claps Dawson's shoulder. "That's not what he was supposed to say, but I'm glad we all have an answer. Now give them the real news."

"Sorry, I had to. I'm tired of being called Grandpa." The flush on Dawson's cheeks rushes to the top of his head. "As we all know, the All-Star Game is in one week, and the full roster will be announced tonight. We've already got one Pilot heading to Atlanta." Marcus shimmies beside me as our teammates cheer. He won the fan ballot for starting catcher. "And I'm happy to say we have another Pilot headed to the game."

A steady drumroll breaks out as I look around for the lucky player, but Dawson is staring at me. He's in full dad mode too, with watery eyes and a trembling smile.

"Our little rookie, Cade Owens, was chosen as the shortstop reserve."

Huh?

"Me?" I cough out. "I'm going to Atlanta?"

"Yes, rookie." Dawson throws his head back and howls at the ceiling. "You're going to the All-Star Game."

His announcement doesn't make sense. Not even as the bulking weight of Marcus tackles me to the ground, and I'm dogpiled by the rest of the team. The love from the men who have become my brothers is enough to distract me for a little while though.

"No twenty-four-year-old should have a landline. You know that, right?"

The frayed cord loops around my finger. "They're part of history, Mom. In an emergency, you'll be jealous that I can contact the world when cell phones don't have service."

She smacks her lips. "Son, I grew up in the age of landlines. Hush up."

I laugh until the reminder of why I'm using it sobers me.

It's ancient, with tan plastic and a spiral cord that I've stretched out over the years. Mom makes jokes about my favorite mode of communication, but it's the easiest way for me to shut the world out while being able to reach the people who matter. This is the first time since leaving the stadium that I've been able to breathe. No texts or calls to congratulate me on the All-Star roster announcement. No passive aggressive texts from Jon saying it's all because of his hard work.

Just me and my landline, hiding out.

"You don't sound like someone who got life-changing news tonight," Mom says when the silence stretches too long. "What's wrong, golden boy?"

I flinch at the name, even though it can't harm me.

Physically at least.

"I'm happy, Ma. I really am." I just don't know how to explain that the biggest moment of my career feels off. Groaning, I shove the box of Jon's notes away and lean against the couch. "Hey. Why did you start calling me golden boy?"

"Simple." Her laugh titters through the line. "You're golden."

The answer seems straightforward, but I don't understand. "Would I still be golden if I hadn't started playing baseball?"

My identity has always been rooted in the sport. Everyone encouraged me to forgo school to play baseball. When people around me were asked about their goals and dreams, I was passed over because they assumed I would go on to play professionally. There wasn't anything I could do about it either because I loved baseball with every piece of me. Instead of fighting back, I buckled in and started on a road trip filled with other people's hopes and dreams rather than mine. I don't regret my decision to play, but damn. I'd kill for a little bit of autonomy.

No laugh comes this time. "Oh, Cade," she whispers. "You're my golden boy because it's the best way to describe my favorite things about you in two words."

I immediately try to backtrack when I hear the wobble in her voice. "Ma, I'm sorry. Forget I said—"

"No. You need to hear this." She takes a deep breath. "When you were born, I felt like I had won the son lottery. As you got older, I only felt more validated in that belief. And it had nothing to do with your athletic abilities. You've always had an unbridled joy that shines brightly. Your kind heart makes you a friend to all. Your thoughtfulness had parents constantly asking me how I got so lucky with you and how their child could be more like you. You were my golden boy long before you ever picked up a bat, and you will be until the end of time."

My fingers reach for the piece of yellow paper with Jon's rules for the golden boy, which are so different from everything Mom is describing.

One, smile at anybody who approaches you.

Two, answer all questions. No matter what.

Three, never say no.

Four, emotions aren't for the public.

Five, if you feel like quitting, smile through it.

"Even if I didn't play?"

Her words hum with a smile I can't see. "Even then."

Quiet takes over as a rush of calm flows through me, but not for long. Muffled shouts send me to my feet, followed by impatient pounding on the front door. I go to check the doorbell camera, but my phone is still off. This maniac is going to wake up the entire neighborhood.

"Someone's at the door, Ma. I'll call you back."

"At this hour?" Worry laces her voice. "Let them be."

"Can't. The neighbors will riot, but thank you for talking to me."

"Anytime, golden boy."

The nickname doesn't hurt this time as she hangs up. I slip the yellow piece of paper into my pocket and pull myself off the ground, ignoring my throbbing hip. I hobble out of the living room and through the foyer, hoping I don't look as tired as I feel. By the time I peer through the peephole, the person on the other side has given up, taking the porch steps slowly.

Then I spot pink fluffy slippers.

I swing the door open. "Shay?"

She trips, barely catching herself before spinning to face me. "What the hell, Cade? I've been trying to get in touch with you for over an hour! I called like thirty times!"

Holding up my phone, I point at it. "It's off. What's going on?"

Without waiting for an answer, she marches past me and enters my home, headed straight for the living room. For someone who was so nervous about me being at her house last week, she looks comfortable—and stunning—storming into mine.

I chase after her and thank my lucky stars I stuffed Jon's notes back into the box, but it's sitting on the couch right beside her.

Taking a seat on the opposite side of the leather couch, I grab the box and slide it under the coffee table. "Is there a reason you almost beat my door down at midnight?"

"Yes. I have great news." Her nose wrinkles. "Well, bad, depending on who you ask. Carlos Medina got injured tonight. Something about a wrist injury. I didn't get specifics, but people in the crowd said they could hear the snap of bone."

Rambling Shay is my favorite. Her mouth moves so quickly that she stumbles over words, struggling to string them together without having to restart each sentence. The only thing I'm struggling with is trying not to look at her lips, full and glossed. Every few seconds, her tongue darts across them and I find myself even more distracted.

"So, he can't start anymore, which is why I'm here."

After a beat, my eyes lift to meet hers. "Who can't start?"

She cocks her head at me. "Did you hear anything I said?"

With a sheepish smile, I shake my head. "Kind of zoned out." I omit the reason being that she's in my house, looking like this, and I can't touch her without breaking a rule.

"Cade." She crosses her legs beneath her. "Carlos Medina isn't starting at the All-Star Game anymore."

My brain short-circuits, but I remember something she said. "Yeah. Neck injury."

"Wrist," she corrects. "Do you know what that means?"

I freeze. Now I understand her ferocity.

"I'm starting."

She nods. "You're the starting shortstop at the All-Star Game."

There's a familiar thickness in her voice. It's the same tremble I heard when CLU won the College World Series and when I was drafted to the California Hornets. The same voice that congratulated me over the phone after my first home run in the minors.

God, I've missed her so much.

My head falls into my hands as the confusion from earlier comes back in a rush. If I was with anyone else, I'd hide it with a smile. But Shay has already made it clear that she doesn't expect that of me.

She only wants Cade.

"What are the odds you'll tell me something honest right now?"

A quiet laugh escapes. "So, it's okay to break the rules when *you* want answers, Agent Shay?"

Her smile is weak. "Some things are worth breaking the rules for."

I wish that kissing her, hugging her, and holding her close were worth breaking the rules for, but anything I get with Shaylene Turner is enough for me.

"On three," I say, lifting my fist. *One, two, three.*

"Four!" I say at the same time she blurts "Six!"

Winning doesn't feel as nice tonight. Maybe it's because the thought of holding something back from her doesn't seem like a victory. Telling her everything is all I want to do.

"I thought it would feel better when I finally made it," I whisper.

The couch dips as she moves closer. "Talk me through your feelings. There's no judgement here."

It's crazy how I believe those words when she says them. There's no fear that she will twist my confession and eventually use it against me.

Not like Jon.

"I've worked my whole life for this moment. I moved across the country, forfeited finishing my degree, and gave up so much to get to this point." A dry laugh slips out. "When Dawson said my name, I was confused, but I also felt validated. For leaving and pushing and hiding and dealing with everything."

Shay nods for me to continue. "Then . . ."

"Then I got home and felt empty. Getting to this point was supposed to be the moment where everything clicked. I'd feel whole. Relieved. Proud. Brighter." My head bumps against the back of the couch. "I thought I'd finally feel like the person I'm supposed to be, but I feel more lost than ever. If I'm not ecstatic after getting this massive opportunity, what does that say about me?"

She almost touches me. Almost. But then she pulls back and sits on her hands. "It means you're human. You've spent your life working for this opportunity, literally chasing greatness. But now you're looking for the meaning. And sometimes, meaning doesn't hit all at once."

"Human? No." I swallow hard. "I don't get to be human. It's either play the part of the happy golden boy or lose it all. There's no other choice."

"That's not true." The argument is gentle yet unshakeable. "There's always a choice. It's usually just not fun to make. You can either keep living as the golden boy, or you can just be Cade. Embrace mess-ups and imperfections. And screw what everyone else wants."

I laugh. "Sounds easy when you put it like that."

She laughs too. "We both know it's not, but we'll figure it out. To-gether."

Shay's presence and support soothes me, and before I can stop it, my real fear slips out. "And what if baseball is all I am?"

"That's impossible, Cade. You're a dedicated son and brother. The best friend to two people I love very much, and Adri and Jo's de facto big brother. The first person I loved. And none of that is because you play baseball." As her finger lands over my heart, it finds my heartbeat, and time seems to hold its breath with me. "It's because of *you* and this amazing heart you have."

Everything she said makes my chest ache in the best way, but one part outshines the rest.

"You loved me?" I choke out.

Her lips part just enough to betray the laugh she's holding in. "I should've known that would be the only thing you heard."

It would be so easy to pull her against me right now. The Shay-sized hole in my heart has been waiting for her to crawl back into my arms so I can do it right this time and never let go. This is the perfect time to tell her she's the only woman I've ever loved.

Who I still love.

There's only a foot between us now. The smell of chocolate on her breath hits me, probably from her nightly snack of frozen dark chocolate chips. If she opened my freezer, she'd find the bag I eat from when I miss her.

Which, I'm not embarrassed to admit, is every day.

"Cade," she whispers, but it's weak, like how I am for her.

"I missed you, Shay ba—"

A shrill ring slices through my words, and Shay scrambles to the other end of the couch. I already know it's Mom. She's likely checking in after I rushed off the phone.

Shay grabs her bag and stands. "I should go."

"Wait." I ignore the landline and stand too. "Please don't go."

"I have to, Cade. We can't do this." She takes a step back, as if putting distance between us will make this any easier. "We've got no wiggle room for regrets."

My fists ball up. Not out of anger, but to keep from reaching out for her. "I wouldn't regret a thing that happened between us. Ever."

Her frame falters, swaying slightly as she shakes off my honesty. "Take the call. And congrats. You deserve it more than anybody."

The landline goes quiet as she turns to go. The twist of pain in my gut sharpens as the door clicks shut, but I spot a delicate piece of pink on the ground. I make my way to the door and grab the sticky note.

I'm so proud of you. Big things are coming

I clutch the piece of paper to my chest and stare at the door.

Wanting my agent is dumb, but I couldn't stop if I tried.

CHAPTER TWENTY-ONE

 *Shay*

"Shay and Cade sitting in a tree. K. I. S. S—"

I slam the volume button on my phone down, cutting off my best friend's childish song. Having Mallory on speaker is always a risk, but it's even riskier when I'm at work. Thankfully, my office is sequestered from everyone else's.

"Mallory Ella Edwards," I hiss, shifting the phone to my ear. "If I wanted to be teased, I would've called Adri. And we didn't kiss!"

Had it not been for that terrifying landline that broke the spell, I don't know if I could've stopped myself from letting it happen.

No matter how hard I tried, kissing Cade isn't something I've been able to purge from my memory. It's etched into my brain so deeply that only a lobotomy might dislodge it. The way his hands would alternate between holding my face so gently, then gripping my sides, like he couldn't decide whether to worship me or consume me. He kissed the way he plays baseball: intense, calculated, and full of passion.

One kiss might have killed me.

"Are you okay?" she asks, all traces of humor gone.

I sigh. "I don't know."

"Want to talk about it?"

She's already heard all about it. Mallory stood beside me when Cade didn't come home, letting me rant and cry for as long as I needed to. She never rushed my sadness, and for that, I'm thankful.

Still, my next meeting isn't for an hour and a half.

"Right before we leaned in, I accidentally let it slip that I loved him back when we were together, even though we never said the words. I think that's what charged the moment up."

"Ouch," she hisses. "What was the context?"

It's not my place to tell her about what Cade's going through. I know they're best friends, but I'll honor our client-agent confidentiality with my life.

"Not important. All that matters is that we aren't allowed to hang out by ourselves. Public outings and group hangouts only from here on out, because I apparently lack self-control."

She scoffs. "You're being dramatic."

"That's rich coming from you," I joke, nibbling on my bloody finger.

"True, but if *I'm* telling you you're overreacting, you're probably overreacting. Hold on, Shay." Children's voices fill the line, which is to be expected, since Mallory's at the diabetes camp she co-manages every summer. Once free of the chaos, she yawns. "Is there a chance you want to be with Cade again?"

I flop into my chair. "It doesn't matter, Mally. My job is the only thing that actually does. I'll never be able to control a heart or if a relationship works out, but I can control what I do to move up and earn the respect of my colleagues."

"Shay." Her voice hits that sweet spot between careful concern and fierce protectiveness. "I love that you love your job, but careers are just as out of your control as a heart is. You've done everything you can to be the best agent, and they still treat you like shit." As if she can see me wince, she softens her tone. "I'm sorry, but it pisses me off every time you get ignored by those assholes. You're constantly giving the job your everything, making sure your clients are happy, taken care of, and feel safe and cared for. And that's not even getting into your actual job duties. The meetings, the calls, the late nights, the early mornings. Your contracts are rock solid, and I'd be scared to negotiate with you. As your best friend, my number one job is to make sure you know how valuable you are. So, I won't stop telling you that you deserve better from them. And I also won't stop reminding you that you deserve happiness too. *Outside* of work."

I may not completely agree, but I can't help but smile.

People swear they have the world's best friend, but I'd die on the hill that mine's the best.

"You're too blunt for your own good. I love you big, Mally."

"I love you bigger." A smile stretches her voice. "I'm tired of talking about your cruddy coworkers and need a distraction before these kids pelt me with water balloons. Don't think about the job or the fact that you can't control it. Do you like Cade again?"

I've rehearsed this answer many times. Because I'm a professional, the two-letter word should be easy to say, but my mouth won't move.

Instead, a three-letter word rears its ugly head.

We weren't right before. He kept too much in. But now, he's letting me see parts of him I never had access to. And I don't know what to do with that except admit that I see the changes. And maybe, that part of me still wants him.

Even though I shouldn't.

After a beat, I nod, but she can't see me. "I do, but—"

"Turner!" My supervisor pushes my office door open. The smile on his face is faker than the motivational posters in the HR department.

I whisper, "Gotta go," before hanging up and standing. "Trevor! What can I do for you?"

Judgmental eyes take in the small space, likely because his office dwarfs mine. "Can't I come and see my junior agent?"

My eyes dart to the open door. "You haven't before?"

"You've never had an athlete going to the All-Star Game before. Speaking of, how's the star doing?"

No clue. Since rushing out of his house four nights ago with none of my dignity, we've barely spoken.

"Over the moon," I squeeze out, taking a seat.

"As he should be. Atlanta is nice this time of year. Gah, he doesn't know what's coming. The number of women that'll be throwing themselves at him is gonna be legendary. It'll be the best week of his damn life."

I swallow bile. "The best."

Cade may have made it clear he isn't available, but that doesn't mean women aren't completely obsessed with him. You'd be crazy not to be. He's a professional athlete who looks the way he does and has a heart of gold.

"And you're going to make sure of it," Trevor says. "Since the game is on Tuesday, you'll need to be there by Monday."

The papers in my hand fall to the ground. "You want me to go to the All-Star Game in Atlanta?"

His weighted pause tells me he'd prefer if I quit, but he recovers. "Winston damn near demanded it when he heard the news." Without waiting for me, he yells, "Ernie! Get in here!"

The rumpled man rushes inside. Based on the crease in his pants, he's been sitting outside the entire time. "What can I do for you?"

"Reserve a hotel room at The Prescott for Turner. Checking in on Monday and checking out on Wednesday. Book her flight, first class, and send us both the confirmation when done."

My office feels more cramped than a sardine can when Ernie takes a seat on the ground and opens his laptop. Nobody but my clients, except for Andy that one time, has been inside my office. Now, I've got my supervisor, who hates me, and the receptionist taking up all the space.

"After the game, take him to the swankiest bar in town and show him the time of his life. Invite anybody he wants to celebrate with. On Tuesday night, you're going to make the golden boy feel like a star."

I bite my tongue. He's more than the golden boy.

Then my nerves flare up. Taking players out to celebrate after a big game or win is normal. I did it with Holly after the Carolina Rage won the Cup and Lionel when he won player of the year. But this is Cade we're talking about. The man I almost broke the biggest professional boundary with.

And now I have to take him out for a night on the town.

"Was it a smile like this or like this?"

Andy leans back against the orange vinyl seat and curls his lips up like the Cheshire cat before turning into the Grinch. They're both terrifying, but they have nothing on Trevor's creepy grin.

"Worse," I pop open a pill bottle. In the rush of this morning, I forgot to take my Metformin. Adding that to the fact I haven't slept, my stress is eating me alive, and the PCOS monster in my ovaries is feasting on my stress, I'm in a weird freaking mood.

Andy shivers but flashes me a conspiratorial smile.

Friends isn't what I would call us, but it's impossible not to see that he's trying. Every morning since our heart-to-heart, Andy has made it his mission to stop by my office to say hello. I thought it was for appearances, but he proved me wrong during yesterday's staff meeting. When asked about ideas for the annual Permian BBQ, I offered to set up a cornhole tournament. Even though it's every man's favorite game, everyone quieted when I spoke. Then Andy raised his hand and offered to help. Trevor glared at him the entire time, but Andy didn't back down.

It's nice to have something like an ally.

"I'll go order—"

"Nope. Lunch is on me to celebrate your first All-Star Game." He nudges my purse off the table until it tumbles into my lap. "I'm basically eating with a celebrity."

Based on how much my name has been circling the media, I feel like one.

I wave my hand in the air. "You don't have to buy me lunch. I already told you, I'm over what happened between us."

His shrug is identical to the one he has given me every day for the last week after dropping a bowl of tortilla soup onto my desk. "I'm glad you're over it, but I'm not. Buying you lunch is the least I can do."

On the rare occasion I have time for lunch, Baja Breeze is my favorite spot. They have the best tortilla soup and dark chocolate chip cookies in the world.

Maybe some sugar will pull me out of this funk. My mind is jumbled from the conversation with Mallory. Not only did I admit that my feelings for Cade are less professional than they should be, but her comment about my job stuck with me.

"Can I ask you a question about work?"

Andy nods, his eyes on the menu in his hands. "Sure. What's up?"

"Do you think we're in control of our careers?"

"Like, in terms of what?"

"Getting clients and moving up in the company. Do you feel that you're in charge of those decisions and steps?"

Tapping his chin, he hums. "Not really. Getting clients is a two-person dance. We do all we can to sign an athlete, but it could all be moot if they decide to go with someone else. Same with moving up. Winston and our supervisors make those decisions. So, no. I wouldn't say we're in charge or have control."

My lips part. I hadn't thought about it that way before.

I lean forward. "Would you say that careers are as dicey as romantic relationships when it comes to the risks involved?"

Putting the menu down, Andy smiles, but he looks as confused as I feel. "This is too deep of a conversation to have on an empty stomach. I'll order our food, and when I get back, we can really get into it."

As he walks away, I mentally facepalm. Andy might not understand what I'm really asking. Gender roles play a huge part in the way women approach their careers and love lives. Men often feel more secure taking risks, but I don't have that luxury. I live every day in fear that I'll say or do something that boots me all the way to the bottom and I'll never recover.

I may not be able to control my career, but I can control what I put into it. If I keep working my ass off, one day, it'll be enough.

My phone buzzes.

Cade

You look beautiful. Enjoy your lunch

A quick scan of the room doesn't reveal the six-foot-five shortstop. The only people here are adorable families with salsa-covered children and employees in teal polos darting between tables.

I have half a mind to tell Cade to stop flirting and to mind his business, but sugar and caramelized butter steal my frustration away when Andy drops a wrapped cookie the size of my head onto the table.

"Holy shit these smell good. Chocolate chip for me. Oatmeal raisin for Hen. Dark chocolate chip for you."

My eyes narrow. "I never told you my favorite cookie."

As if it's no big deal, he says, "Cade told me." One bite in, Andy moans, loud and indecently. The family beside us halts mid-chew to stare at him. "Apparently, the Pilots come here after practice. As they were leaving, he said you'd like that one and bought our lunch."

Cheeks warm and feeling giddy, I replace my snarky message with something nicer.

Me

Thank you for the cookie

After a moment, his name appears.

Cade

Thank you for being you

CHAPTER TWENTY-TWO

Cade

ACCORDING TO GOOGLE, I'M either having an identity crisis or low blood sugar. Jury's still out.

I haven't had a moment of peace since arriving in Atlanta on Sunday. Every second has been stuffed with practice, interviews, media coverage, and preparing for the biggest game I've ever played in.

And I need to play like my career depends on it. Because it does.

"Cade?" Mom peers into the bathroom. "Is everything okay?"

I loosen the purple tie around my neck and toss it into the sink. "All good, Ma."

With a disbelieving lift to her brow, her eyes drop to my discarded tie. "I agree. No tie needed. You look red-carpet ready."

The lavender linen jacket blazes against my skin, lush and impossible to ignore. After a few days of no luck with outfits, Shay added me to a group message with the most fashionable person we know. Within an hour, Adri was at my house with color swatches, fabric samples, mood boards, and reference photos. In five days, she created my dream suit.

The tie was my idea, but Adri was right. It doesn't work with my T-shirt.

Reaching up, Mom adjusts my jacket's collar. "Are you ready?"

"As ready as I can be." I press a kiss to her cheek. "Sorry for hogging the bathroom."

"Never apologize for hanging out with me. It's like the old days. I'm going to get dressed. Vi's watching cartoons."

Back in the living room, I drop onto the couch and grab my phone. A blurry photo of Mallory, Adri, Jo, Kenneth, and Nan crammed into my minivan lessens the tightness in my shoulders. I offered to fly them to Atlanta, but a road trip was too cool to pass up. By the looks of it, Mallory is acting as chauffeur, which is why Kenneth has been blowing up my phone.

Mr. Kenneth Edwards

If we get stopped for speeding, blame Eddie

She's worried we're going to be late

90 in a 75. Send help

I'm so proud of you

The switch from fear to sentimental is jarring but appreciated.

Me

What for? I haven't even stepped onto the field yet

Mr. Kenneth Edwards

I'd be proud even if you never did. See you tonight

"What time is the red carpet?" The tulle on Violet's lilac dress rustles as she hops onto the couch beside me.

The crumpled agenda sits on the bedside table. I've already checked off breakfast at the hotel, uniform pick-up, morning media, practice, and lunch with the team.

"Two thirty," I say. "Are you ready?"

Violet shakes her head. "Mom said there are gonna to be lots of cameras. Are you allowed to hold my hand while we walk?"

I can't help but smile as I pull her against my side. More often than not, Violet seems so much older than eight years old, but right now, she's the little sister I held tight to as we waited for Mom to get home from work.

"Of course, but I'm scared too. Promise you won't let go?"

Her fear wanes, replaced with a smile. "I'll protect you, and you protect me, C.C."

"Wait, I'm feeling left out! Who's going to protect me when I get scared?" Standing by the door, Mom looks like royalty. The plum jumpsuit flows around her ankles, bringing out the flecks of green in her eyes.

"Wow, Ma. You look great." My head shakes as I take in our outfits. "Are we all matching by accident or was it fate?"

"Very planned." She pats my cheek. "Thank your agent for that."

My agent. The same woman who admitted she loved me. Past tense, sure, but even then, those were never words we shared.

They're words I wish I would've said long before I left for California. Words I felt before I even knew I'd be leaving. Words that still ring true and are very much present for me.

And as much as I want to bring it up and tell her I felt—feel—the same, I know the meeting she wants to have in a few minutes is not about that.

I kneel down to lace up my sneakers, white with lavender soles.

"I'll be back soon," I say, hugging them both. "Going to meet Shay."

As the elevator doors slide open, I find her in the crowd instantly. Amid the bedazzled gowns and sharp suits, her pink pantsuit blazes like a beacon. It pulls me by an invisible string across the room, unseen but unstoppable, until I'm standing right in front of her.

"It's unfair for you to look this good and not walk down the red carpet with me. Is there a chance you'll change your mind, Agent Shay? I'd love to have you beside me."

"In your dreams." Slender fingers drift toward my shirt, and the cotton sighs beneath her touch. "You look good too. Lavender is your color."

"Thank my seamstress. She did all the hard work." I follow her lead and take a seat on the cushy bench. "What did you want to talk about?"

She pulls three sticky notes out, and I smile. No yellow. Everything is pink. Exactly how I like it.

Shay holds up the first one. "The red carpet should be easy. As planned, you'll walk down with your mom and Violet. Fans will be lined up behind the barriers. They'll probably have baseballs to sign, so here's a Sharpie and a backup." She tucks them into the pocket of my suit jacket. "Selfies are okay, but only if you're feeling up to it." She taps her nail against a line, and I laugh.

Don't do anything you don't want to do

I nod. "I'll try my best."

"Good. Second note, I coordinated with the communication team. When they announce your name on the red carpet and at the game, they'll say Cade Owens. No nicknames. No titles."

The room stills. "You told them not to call me the golden boy?"

Her head bobs. "The crowd may be screaming it, and I can't make any promises with reporters, but yes. If the emcee even thinks about muttering golden boy, there'll be hell to pay."

For the guy who has been struggling to figure out who he is, having one event with my real name being called instead of the one assigned to me makes me more excited about tonight.

"Why did you do that?"

Finally, she meets my eye. There's an unreadable twinkle in the deep color. "Because boundaries are important, and today is for you."

We both look down at the final sticky note between her fingers, but she's cut off mid-read when my name is called. It takes a moment to locate the voice, but then I see the scruffy brunette charging toward us.

"Cade! It's really you!" Reed Jessen pulls me into a bear hug and lifts me like I weigh nothing. "I knew you were playing tonight, but I didn't think I'd get to see you before heading back to Arizona! Have you gotten taller?"

"Nope, but you may be getting shorter. And I'm sorry I missed the All-Star Futures Game. I would've loved to see you play out there." Placing my hand on Shay's upper back, I push her forward. "Reed, this is my agent, Shaylene Turner."

I don't need to explain who Reed is. The glimmer of admiration in her gaze tells me she's reciting his stats in her head.

"It's great to meet you, Reed." After folding the third sticky note, she hands it to me. "You two should catch up. I'll see you at the red carpet. Good luck out there, Cade."

As she disappears into the sea of people, Reed's hulking figure steps into my eyeline. I haven't seen my old friend in two years.

We hadn't been friends before the draft, but in the days leading up to the best day of our lives, a bond was formed. Between orientation with the staff, fittings for jerseys, and interviews, we were glued to each other's sides. Then, after being announced as the first draft pick, Reed was wheeled out of the ballpark and rushed to the hospital.

My chest aches. "I'm sorry I didn't reach out sooner. I should've—"

A squeeze to my shoulder stops me. "I could've called you too, C. Don't apologize. For that, or for what happened at the draft. To be honest, I'm surprised I didn't have a panic attack sooner. It was just bad luck that it happened on stage."

I shake away the mental image of him collapsing and try to smile. "Have things been better?"

The elastic band around his wrist snaps. Once. And then again. "Honestly? Yeah. Dad isn't pleased that I'm still in the minors, but oh well." A bony elbow jams itself into my side. "But enough about me. I see they're still calling you the golden boy. I hoped we would both be free of our weight by now."

Reed was the closest thing I had to a kindred spirit in baseball. High expectations shaped us both, but he is major league royalty.

"Free?" I blow a raspberry. "Impossible. Are you free?"

"I think so, yeah." His easy smile stiffens at the edges. "When we first met, we were the same. We ate, breathed, and shit baseball, trapped by the pressure to excel and succeed."

"Exactly." I point at the laugh lines around his eyes. At one point, getting him to smile felt like pulling teeth. "And now you look better."

Reed leans in. "What if I told you the secret is therapy and meds?"

Shoving him away, I laugh. "Honestly, I'd probably believe you. But seriously. How'd you do it?"

A hotel lobby isn't the place for a serious talk, but I need to know.

"You might not like the answer, but here's the truth." His eyes pierce right through me. "My life got easier the moment I stopped giving a shit about what was expected of me and started doing what I wanted. When I did, baseball became fun again. Hell, life became more fun. People were forced to see me for me and not the person they expected me to be. It was the hardest thing I've ever done, but I'd do it all over again if I had to."

Then, as if he didn't rewire my brain, he stands and pulls me into a hug. "I've got to catch my flight, but message me. Let's get dinner!"

As I watch him go, his words play on repeat. People's expectations didn't stop; he stopped holding on to them so tightly.

It sounds impossible, but as I reach into my pocket as unfold Shay's note, my heart skips a beat at the words. Reading them, I feel like I could do anything.

Just be Cade. That's all that matters

There's no space for negative energy at Peach Pit Stadium.

Coach Baxter's pre-game speech was about having fun, and my teammates are doing just that. Garrett Blane is laughing it up at first base with the opposing team's runner. Randy Alba did cartwheels after hitting an out-of-the-park home run. Even Marcus, who is eerily serious for games, is chatting with fans from his crouched position behind home plate.

I'm likely the only person in the stadium frowning.

Groans fill the air as a ground ball slips past me and heads to the outfield, thankfully picked up by an outfielder.

If Jon were still my agent, he'd document that mistake and spend the rest of the game thinking about how if I were better and faster, I wouldn't have let it get past me. Our postgame meeting would revolve around planning extra practices and conditioning sessions until he was confident I wouldn't make that mistake again.

But Shay's my agent, and she smiles at me from behind the dugout.

Good or bad, rain or shine, there's no scowl, no snarling anger, and no yellow notepad. Just an unwavering support I never want to lose.

"*Breathe*," she mouths. "*Just be.*"

I close my eyes. Fun and baseball haven't been used in the same sentence since I was in high school. That's when the game moved from something I loved and enjoyed to something that defined who I am.

But I set a goal to *just be*, so I'm going to try my hardest.

A crisp crack of the bat sends a wave of gasps through the stands. Little do they know that this time, I'm ready. My cleats dig into the dirt as I shift to the left, glove low and knees bent. Muscle memory kicks in before doubt has a chance to whisper in my ear and tell me I'm too slow.

Leather meets the ball with a snap, and I flip it to Marco at second base, who rifles it to Garrett at first base. The double play draws a chorus of screams, but for the first time, I'm not reveling in everybody else's excitement.

I'm reveling in mine.

CHAPTER TWENTY-THREE

"SHE CAN'T KEEP THIS up. Her hip is bound to give out soon."

I nudge Kenneth's shoulder. "Don't be so sure about that. Nan will probably outlive us."

The All-Star Game after-party isn't like any party I've been to. Star athletes mingle with rookies, agents dance with PR reps, and more people are starting to join Nan on the dance floor. There are no velvet ropes or VIP sections. Just good music, sweaty bodies, expensive drinks, and the kind of electric joy that makes you forget it's way past bedtime.

The DJ is playing all of Nan's favorites, from Abba to the Bee Gees. Her red hair hasn't dulled with age, the fiery color shimmering under the lights as she spins Mallory to "Boogie Wonderland."

Perched thirty floors above the city, the Whittaker Hotel's rooftop bar pulses with an electric energy I haven't felt since college. Dimmed yellow bulbs crisscross like constellations above us. Glass railings offer an uninterrupted view of the skyline, where the lights below flicker like champagne bubbles.

"At least she'll sleep well tonight," I say, waving the bartender down for another glass of water. "You'll probably have to carry her to the car though."

"Mallory or Nan?" he asks.

I spot the two women forming a conga line. "Both."

Kenneth's sigh straddles the line between a laugh and a yawn, but he doesn't sit down. After the fourth player slid behind Mallory, he has refused to take his eyes off the dance floor, ready to physically remove the next sucker who tries to make a move.

It must be exhausting having a hot, perfect girlfriend.

At least she can fight.

"Today was really nice. I'm glad we were all here today." The bar creaks under his heavy weight when he leans against it. "And thanks for taking care of Cade."

I pick at my nail. "It's my job. No need to thank me."

"Duh, short stuff. I know it's your job to be his agent, but instead of punishing him for what happened between you two, you're helping him in ways only you can." His attention finally strays from the dance floor to the corner of the bar. "Everyone knew Cade was going to be a star. People tried to take advantage of his light and his kindness, clinging to him in hopes they'd get something from him. Old friends. Jon." His jaw works angrily, and I wonder how much he knows. "But you? You don't want anything from Cade. You never have."

I look up at the man who stole my best friend's heart two years ago. Even before he and I became friends, I knew his love for the people in his life burned bright.

He's the best partner for Mallory and the best friend for Cade.

My head falls against his boulder shoulder. "I'm glad you're my best-friend-in-law."

"I'm glad you're mine too."

After a quick hug, Kenneth rushes to the dance floor to join Mallory, Nan, Jo, and Adri, but since I'm in work mode, I stay put and sip my water.

Against my better judgement, I let my eyes roam, and they find Cade almost instantly. He has always been the center of attention, and not because he goes looking for it; it finds him. In the tailored lavender pants and fitted white T-shirt, it's hard not to notice him. Which explains the women swarming him like bugs searching for light. The number seems to multiply every time I look.

That's why I swore to stop checking in on him an hour ago.

But our eyes meet as I lift the glass to my lips.

A second passes. Then two. After three, he winks.

And at this moment, I hate every single one of my rules.

"Shaylene Turner?"

I whip around at the slow cadence, and when my eyes find the owner of the voice, I pause. Pro athletes knowing my name will never get old.

"Yes," I choke out. "That's me."

"Hey, I'm Simon Godfrey. Second baseman for the Cleveland Dukes."

Simon was not only a first-round pick, but he was called up to the majors during his first season. It's nearly impossible to make it to the majors that quickly, but he did and was voted the starting second baseman for the All-Star Game.

"So, this is going to sound a little forward but"—*Oh no. Please don't hit on me*—"I've been watching how you move for a while, and I'd love to talk."

My brows lift. "About?"

"About having you as my agent. I'm looking for someone who matches the way I play. Smart, aggressive, and always three steps ahead. And everything I've heard about you shows me you're that person. Garrett Blane was singing your praises today."

A silent scream catches in my throat as I pull a business card from my pocket. "Then it sounds like we may be aligned. I'd love to have the opportunity to represent you."

After exchanging contact information, he walks back to his friends, and I grip the edges of the sticky bar. If I get the intermediate agent position, I can add more clients to my roster. It feels crazy to have this much hope, but I think all my dreams are about to come true.

"Did I overhear a potential client conversation, Agent Shay? Looks like you're getting a lot of attention tonight."

Hazel eyes are sewed to my skin when I turn around, his chest only inches from mine. Too close, considering I'm technically on the clock and he's my client, but his presence steadies me.

"Me?" I scoff. "I haven't seen you without a woman trying to cling onto you all night. It doubles every time I look."

Disgust spreads across his features. "No thanks. Attention from them means nothing to me."

I lift my chin in the direction of the woman in gold with sun-bleached waves. She was Cade's number one fan tonight, constantly trying to weasel her way into his orbit. "Why not her? She's pretty."

"Is she? Didn't notice," he murmurs, eyes locked on mine.

"Well, you should," I say.

"I'd rather not. I like this view *so* much more."

The stupid butterflies in my belly come to life. I try to remind them what's at stake, but the honesty radiating from Cade is enough to make me desperate to abandon my rules.

"By the way"—he steps back and I exhale—"Kenneth declared it was bedtime and corralled everyone into the minivan. They're probably halfway to their hotel by now."

Sadness washes over me. I know tonight was for work, but I wish I could've had a little more time with my friends.

Work always comes first, and tonight, I kind of hate it.

Recovering, I reach for my wallet. "Looks like my job is done for the night. Your people tapped out, which means I need to call a car—"

"Alone?"

I glare at him. "If this is your way of asking me if I'm going home with someone, you should be more subtle."

"There's nothing subtle about the way I feel about you, Shay." He pulls his phone out of his back pocket and opens the rideshare app. "I'll catch a ride with you. You're staying at The Prescott on Arlington Avenue, right? Good, so am I."

Sometimes I hate sharing a best friend.

I sigh. "Fine. Let me close the tab first."

"Don't worry." Our hands brush. "I'm not going anywhere."

For some reason, it sounds like a much deeper promise.

"What floor are you staying on?"

My vision clears at his question. Somehow, the ten-minute drive to the Prescott Hotel is already over, I crawled out of the Nissan, and now I'm standing in front of the elevator.

"Doesn't matter. You're not walking me to my room."

Cade repeatedly jabs his finger into the already lit button. "What kind of man would I be if I didn't make sure you get there safely?"

"A *client*." I put an extra foot of space between us. "How much did you drink tonight?"

Fingers formed into a circle, he holds up his hand. "None."

"You didn't have a single drink tonight? Not even the celebratory champagne?"

"Nope," he says, popping the P. "I'm stone-cold sober."

And then, god help me, he decides to prove it. Holding his arms out like he's about to take flight, he walks to the other side of the hall without swaying.

Heel. Toe. Heel. Toe. Heel. Toe.

"And look. I can say the alphabet backward. Z, y, x, w, v, u, t, s, r, q. Then it's my least favorite. P on MLK. J, i, h, g, f, e, d…"

I look around, thankful we're alone. "How are you doing this?"

"C. B. A!" He twists around with his hands still in the air. "Done!"

After he has bowed multiple times, I hold up my hands. "Fine, I believe you're sober, but our rules must mean nothing to you if you're flirting with me in public."

His hand disappears into his pocket. The hopeful part of me wonders if my dice are clacking around in there.

"They are important, but I'm struggling tonight, if you can't tell."

Tonight isn't easy for me either. I also didn't have a single drink, which means I can't blame alcohol for why I feel so pulled to him in this moment.

If I'm being honest, in every moment for the last few weeks.

As the doors slide open, I tear my eyes from him to look at the elevator.

"Going back up?" I ask when no one steps out.

"Yeah," a woman in a Wheezer shirt answers. "Pressed the wrong button for the pool. Y'all coming?"

Squeezing into an elevator with what looks like a family reunion isn't my vibe, so I shake my head. "All good. I'll catch the next—" I start, but I'm yanked forward by my front belt loop.

"Nonsense!" Cade laughs, walking backward. "Who knows when the next one will come. We need to get you to bed."

"I will strangle you," I hiss, but I let him pull me inside.

Cramped as it is, we both manage to fit, pushing through until we're in the very back. Years ago, if we had been caught in this predicament, this closeness would've been greatly appreciated. Cade's hand would have been spread across my stomach to keep me close, with his lips tracing my collarbones.

That can't happen though. It's not allowed.

"Seventeenth floor, please," I rasp out, thankful someone hears me and clicks the button.

On the third floor, the doors slide open, but nobody exits. Instead, my ass is jammed even harder against the solid body behind me as more people pile in. This has to be a safety hazard, but I can't seem to care when Cade's heart is beating erratically against my back and I'm touching the man I set a rule to not touch.

"*Fuck*," he mutters, stretching the word into two distinct syllables.

His finger grazes a sliver of bare skin on my lower back, and a jolt of electricity runs down my spine. He's barely touching me, yet I feel more than I have in years.

At the tenth floor, the rambunctious family reunion steps out and heads for the pool. It's such a relief when the woman in front of me removes her backpack from my chest, but I still can't breathe. Not with Cade behind me.

Halfheartedly, I step away, but fingers ghost over my wrist.

"Please." His voice is barely above a whisper, even though we're alone. "It's been too long since I've been this close to you. Stay."

There's no way I can move after that, so I don't. I return to the spot that feels made for me, and he does exactly what I need. Strong arms wrap around my waist before a hand covers my belly, his face buried deep in my neck.

I need this too, so I sink into his warmth.

The ding is intrusive when it happens, and my eyes find the bright red one and seven. Letting me go, he murmurs a quiet thank you.

My heels sink into plush maroon carpet as we make our way to my room at the end of the hall. The silence is loud, charged with words I'm scared to speak and words I'm even more afraid to hear.

"A penny for your thoughts?" he finally asks.

Telling him about the turmoil in my head and heart would be too much, so I pick a topic that's always safe between us. Work.

"I think I may have a chance with Simon Godfrey. I would need to ask for another exception, but I think it's possible."

"You're so good at your job, Shay." Cade grins like it's the best news he's heard all day, but his tone grows cold as we pass the ice machine. "I noticed how weirdly Trevor treated you at that first meeting. I hated sitting there and watching him glare at you. You're the best agent there."

I almost nudge his arm but decide against it. "You don't mean that."

"I absolutely do. I have no idea where I'd be without you." Sincerity coats his words. "Jon always said I'd be lost and a nobody without him, and I believed him. I believed a lot of things he said."

Rage boils inside me. Every piece of information I learn about Jon gets filed away in my mental evidence box.

I slow my pace. "You'd still be here without me because your hard work got you here, Cade. Nothing else."

"No," he argues, shaking his head. "I was, am still, a mess. Confused too, but you've kept me afloat for the last two months." A chuckle leaves his lips. "You should have seen my face when I saw your name at Permian. It was like seeing a ghost, but I had no doubts about choosing you. Regardless of our history, I knew you'd be the best agent for me."

I freeze because we've made it to my door, but mostly because I'm stunned. Cade being open and honest is still so new. Every day, I wake up and wait for the moment he decides to shut me out again.

I'm starting to wonder if that'll never come.

"You're the best thing to happen to me, Shay. And I'm an idiot for ever making you feel like you weren't the most important thing to exist."

My keycard clatters to the ground with a muted thump, but that could also be my heart trying to burst out of my chest. He can't say these words out loud. Everything will get complicated.

More complicated.

"Cade. Don't."

"I have to," he says, bending down to pick up my room key. "Screw the win and the biggest game of my career. All I want is to end my night kissing you." Leaning in, his voice drops dangerously low. "Can I please kiss you, baby?"

The professional answer gets stuck in my throat. Kissing Cade doesn't just break a rule. It shatters the rule, obliterating the control I have over this situation. There's no loophole that can make this okay for even a second. But there's a nagging reminder in the back of my head, screaming that it has been too long since I kissed him. Two years ago, he was drafted to the California Hornets, and I kissed him goodbye to chase his dreams. If I don't do it tonight, I'm not sure I ever will again.

Fuck it.

"Once to get it out of our system and never again?" I ask.

After a beat, he chuckles. "I swear I'll try my best."

An arm wraps around my waist and pulls me against him in one swift movement. It's me and Cade, hiding in the corner at a fancy hotel in Atlanta, and I know it'll never be like this again.

I'm already dreading the moment it will end.

My back hits the door, and the lock beeps when he presses the key to the scanner. Navigating us inside, I'm equal parts relieved and saddened when he enters the room only enough to close the door behind us.

"What are the odds this ruins everything?" I ask as the door clicks.

His fingers find my chin and lift it to meet his eyes.

"Even odds, Shay baby. But it'll be worth every ounce of pain."

And right then, I feel everything I had forgotten how to want.

Full lips consume me in a kiss that's not rushed or wild, but quiet and worth waiting for. The kind that says I missed you, even if the words aren't spoken. Our tongues tangle in that familiar dance I still know by heart, and when his hand cups my jaw and my fingers fist in his shirt, it feels like home.

This isn't a spark. It's a rekindling.

A homecoming.

It's desperate and needy and better than I remember. He still smells incredible, like him. He tastes the same too, with a hint of mint on his tongue that I dream about when I allow myself to miss him. Both hands stay anchored on my cheeks, as if he's scared to let go.

It's scary how right this feels when I know it's so wrong.

Pulling back, he traces my jaw with his finger. The sadness and longing in his eyes are impossible to miss. If I could see my own, I'm sure they'd look the same.

"I'll never recover from you, and I don't ever want to." One last kiss is pressed to my forehead before he steps away. "Good night, Agent Shay."

And as he leaves me alone in my room, he takes my heart with him.

CHAPTER TWENTY-FOUR

 *Shay*

I NEED ONE MINUTE of peace and a bubble bath. Too bad that won't happen anytime soon.

"No, Trevor," I repeat for the tenth time since answering his call. "I'm not going to ask Deshawn's doctor those kinds of questions. If you want answers, you can ask her. My job is to be supportive. Not pushy."

Irritation leaks through the phone. "It *is* your job, Turner. You need to remember you're not his mother."

"I'm not acting like his mother. I—"

"Fine," he interrupts. "His babysitter."

That's ironic considering the only toddler I work with is him. Trevor's refusal to understand that asking Deshawn's doctor to speed up the physical therapy process because of his impending contract renewal is not only unhelpful, but fucking disgusting.

"Deshawn is focusing on recovery. Reminding him about the upcoming season and everything that's at stake won't be helpful. He's already worried that he won't be ready by preseason. I'm not going to add to his stress."

He scoffs. "I hoped after your win with the golden boy, you'd realize this job is about money. Agents who care too much about feelings and emotions never have fruitful careers."

Gritting my teeth, I look up at the sky. "There's nothing wrong with caring about my client."

Shit.

"Your client?" A beat of silence passes before he barks a laugh. "Miller is not *your* client. He's mine. Do you hear me? My clients belong to me. All you do is answer emails and do the work I don't have time for."

If that's true, then he should do it on his own. That would save me six hours a day.

But since I can't afford to get fired, I reluctantly nod. "Got it."

"Good. When you get back to the office, there's a lot I need you to do."

I block out the rest of his rant and start my walk back to Permian. My midday excursion wasn't planned, but the break from the office was needed. After a surprising call from Simon Godfrey, who's very serious about working with me in the future, I sat on hold for over an hour with Clear Lake University for Cade's degree. Annoyingly, no one got back with me. Then Holly and Victoria invited me to brunch to discuss their ongoing soccer season. During brunch, Mom called to say she saw the photos of me with Cade before the All-Star Game's red carpet. With yet another reminder from her that I have no time for anything but work, Deshawn texted and asked if I could make it to physical therapy.

Life has always been busy, but it kicked into overdrive after returning from Atlanta a week ago. More phone calls. More meetings. More endorsement and sponsorship discussions.

Less sleep. Less rest. Less of everything that isn't work.

Sarabeth says my meds can only do so much, and the amount of stress I'm putting my body through isn't doing me or my PCOS any favors. The cystic pimple on my chin, fatigue, sweet cravings, and painful cramps from hell prove that.

For someone who has never taken a day off, I'd kill for one.

"Dogan with the Grizzlies is entering free agency soon. Put out some feelers to see who would be interested in signing him. Need that by the end of the day."

I barely stifle a whimper as a cramp rolls through my abdomen. "Be back in thirty."

He hangs up and leaves me alone to deal with my pain. When I made the decision to walk instead of drive earlier, it seemed like a great idea. Plus, I knew Sarabeth would be proud of my post-meal walk. Feeling the wind in my hair and all that jazz seemed nice, but now I'm dealing with the consequences of my actions.

The snail crawling on the sidewalk beside me is moving faster than I am. Only two miles until I'm—

"Agent Shay?"

Mother. Fucker.

I didn't think it was possible for today to get any worse.

And when did I stop hating that nickname?

The pain in my stomach fades slightly when the lips I kissed a week ago curve into a smile. Like a coward, I've been avoiding Cade, but we both know why. I broke a rule and kissed the man I can't have.

Behind him, an Audi blares its horn, but he pays them no mind. "Need a ride?"

I study the hill in front of me. It's either walk in excruciating pain or get a ride from the one person I shouldn't be alone with. But I'm not in the mood to play with the human body.

"Sure. To the office, please," I say. Cade leans over to manually unlock the passenger door, and I can't help but laugh. "It's been *years.* When are you going to get the locks fixed?"

"If I fix something on Betsy, another thing breaks, so I'm stuck with funky locks." Worry creases his brow. "Are you sure about going to the office? You don't look so good."

"Gee." I click on my seatbelt. "Thanks."

A low laugh slips out as he studies me. "You know that's not what I meant, Shay. As always, you're beautiful." He pauses long enough to make my cheeks heat, but when he continues, I straighten. "You were walking like you were hurting. Let me take you home."

Ignoring the way my pain sharpens at being acknowledged, I point in the direction of Permian. "No. Bad PCOS day. Nothing I can't handle."

The impatient honks shift into unrelenting wails as Cade continues to sit idly in the road. "Have you eaten today? What are you drinking?"

"Yes, and spearmint tea. You need to drive before you get rear-ended."

His brow wrinkles. "I thought you hated tea." As if we're not blocking the road, he turns to search through his backseat. "I don't care about them. I care about *you*. Want some dark chocolate chips?"

Like a dog trained to a bell, my mouth salivates. "You have some?"

A plastic bag drops onto my lap, and once he's buckled, he finally pushes the car into drive and waves politely at the asshole behind him. "I stopped by the grocery store earlier. They're not frozen, but eat as many as you want. I read online that dark chocolate can reduce inflammation in people with PCOS."

My eyes fly to him. Sarabeth loves dark chocolate being part of my daily routine for that reason.

I should ask why he was researching PCOS, but I can't handle hearing his answer.

"Thank you," I whisper. Then, in an unladylike fashion, I shove a handful into my mouth and moan. Manners be damned. "This is what I needed. Now I'm ready to get this damn promotion."

"Promotion? You're up for a promotion?"

Closing the bag, I nod. "An internal one, but yeah. Me against all the other junior agents. All I have to do is submit a letter of intent to my supervisor, along with my personnel file."

"If that's the case, you're definitely going to get it."

His certainty buoys my response. "I hope so. Part of me is scared to apply, which is probably why I haven't started my letter of intent."

Working with athletes is all I want to do, but being a woman in this business is like running through a field of landmines. One wrong step could end my career. Being romantically linked to a player, especially one who's my client, might ruin everything for me. Which is why I have to stay focused.

But my focus goes hazy as our elbows brush on the center console.

You weak woman.

"You know there are a lot of things I love about you, right?" he asks, but he doesn't wait for a response. "Picking a favorite seems impossible, but if I had to, I'd say it's that you always reach for the stars. And no matter what, you find a way to make it there. Every single time."

His words knock the wind right out of me. "Is that really what you think of me?"

"Amongst many other things." The car sputters as he makes a right turn. "Nothing slows you down when you want something. Shayzilla's your nickname for a reason, but even in normal Shay mode, you're driven, passionate, and aren't afraid to do things scared."

When I started my degree plan, I ignored the doubt from my professors and classmates. When I decided to be a multi-sport agent, I refused to listen to Trevor's criticism. When I realized I wanted to be with Cade, I let go of the fear of not being able to control our hearts.

And I did those things while terrified.

I blink fast, willing the sting in my eyes to settle. "Thank you."

"You don't need to thank me. It's just the truth." The veins in his hand pop as his grip tightens around the steering wheel. "I'm guessing all this stress is why we haven't talked since we got back from Atlanta. Or have you been avoiding me because you regret the kiss?"

The sadness in his voice pierces me, and I'm the reason for it. As someone who was so hurt when he didn't communicate his feelings and fears to me, I did the same thing.

"I'm sorry. I should've talked to you." Turning in the seat, I face him. "I'm scared more than anything, but I don't regret it, Cade. I just don't want to ruin our partnership."

His relief is immediate and palpable. "I promise kissing won't."

"*One* kiss," I argue. "We agreed on *one* last kiss."

"Nope. All I said was that I would try my best." Stopping at a red light, he finally looks at me. There's a tiny tremor to his hand as it travels across the center console and hooks a braid behind my ear. "I never believed I could get you out of my system, and that kiss proved it. But I'll follow your lead. I know what this job means to you."

Something snaps inside me at that. It was naïve to think I could get him out of my system.

Finally, we pull into Permian's parking lot. I made it through the entire drive without leaping over the center console and into his lap.

Go me.

The minivan rattles as it bounces over a speed bump, but the choked grunt Cade releases sounds even more painful. It's too low and strained for my liking. I should be more concerned that I'm in his car at my job, but my focus is trained on the way he's gripping his upper thigh.

"What's wrong?" I ask when he maneuvers into a parking spot.

His muttered *nothing* comes out too fast to be true. It only takes a short staredown for him to acquiesce, and he schools his pinched expression. "My hip gets tight sometimes."

Bile rushes up my throat. "I knew it. I knew I noticed a limp."

"When?"

"Our first game as agent and client."

A smile cracks through his grimace. "I hate how well you know me."

"You're going to hate what I have to say even more." I manually unlock the passenger door. "Talk to a trainer soon, okay? I know it's hard, but it's better to miss a few games than ruin the rest of your season. You're more than your job."

Cade's brows scrunch in that stubborn way I'm familiar with. Missing games may feel like the worst thing in the world, but Cade needs to put himself first. Not the golden boy who feels like he needs to perform no matter what.

The clenched fist at his side tells me he won't be saying a word to anyone, so I turn to leave.

"Before you go," he says, stopping me, "I have something for you." He relaxes his hand and digs into his pocket, pulling out my dice.

I smile. "Am I finally getting them back?"

"Never. I need them more than you know." Then he lifts a dainty chain between his large fingers. "When I saw this at the pawnshop, I knew I wanted you to have it. Since you're always on the phone, this wristlet thingy reminded me of you."

Tiny hearts, flowers, and beads in the prettiest shades of pink and orange are pressed against my palm. My clients occasionally surprise me with small tokens of appreciation. Holly fuels my caffeine addiction with mugs. Brett gifts me a stress ball every time we meet to counteract the chaos. Lionel loves personalizing office supplies for me. Victoria buys me books about badass women in sports. Delilah sends postcards from whatever country she's in.

Still, it's hard to accept a gift from the client I kissed last week.

Regretfully, I hand it back. "I can't accept a gift—"

"Don't think of it as a gift." Strong hands carefully fold my fingers around the beads. "Think of it as a reminder to do it scared."

Our eyes meet, and I wonder if he knows how hard I'm struggling to stay in my seat.

Pulling my hand back, I hold on tight to the not-gift and swing open the door. "Thanks for the ride, Cade. And the reminder."

His lips lift into that small smile I've always loved. "Anytime, Agent Shay. And take a breather sometime. In the words of my genius agent, you're more than your job."

That gets a real laugh out of me, and I close the door before he hears.

Our conversation follows me through the parking lot, up the stairs, and into my office. Trevor's demands can wait for a little bit longer.

It's time to write my letter of intent.

Chapter Twenty-Five

THIS PAIN COMES CLOSE to what I felt when things ended with Shay, but nothing will ever touch the anguish of losing her.

Every nerve screams as Isla digs mercilessly into my left hip. The padded pillow under my head is the only thing keeping me from cracking my skull open against the treatment table.

Isla yanks an earbud out, and her attention swings from my hip to my face. "Is something wrong?"

Forcing my scowl into a smile, I shake my head. "No. All good. Sorry."

Apprehensive eyes narrow, but she goes back to work. Isla's the Pilots' assistant athletic trainer. Within two weeks of signing her contract, the infielders claimed her as their own, and she secretly loves it. Being tortured by an elf-like woman with large tortoiseshell glasses and tiny fingers isn't fun, but her stellar reputation for being able to work out any knot is usually worth it.

Telling Shay about my hip yesterday wasn't planned, but I can't bring myself to keep secrets from her anymore.

Learning she doesn't regret our kiss was icing on the cake.

After leaving her alone in her hotel room that night, I couldn't sleep. I checked my phone every few seconds, waiting for an email saying that we could no longer work together, or asking me to come back and finish what we'd started.

I will follow her lead, but being with her is all I want.

As if shocked by lightning, my hips buck off the table and a scream claws its way out before I can stop it. There's no chance I can play it off either, not with Isla and my teammates looking at me like I've lost my mind.

Wisps of agony crawl all the way to my toes as I prop myself up on my elbows.

"I need to go," I rasp out.

Isla adjusts her glasses. "Cade. I think we should talk."

Swinging my legs off the table, I plant my hands on the cushioned top. My breath catches on the edges of pain as my hip flares, white-hot and blinding, but I keep my expression neutral.

"I'm fine, Isla. Thanks though."

With a little wave, I keep my gait steady and rush out of the training room. Once safely in the empty clubhouse, I fall onto the ground in front of my locker.

I almost told Rio the truth this morning, but my opportunity disappeared when Amber from PR rushed into his office with news. People were lined up for tonight's home game before the sun had risen. The first thousand fans to enter the stadium will receive limited-edition T-shirts with Marcus's and my signatures and miniature replica All-Star Game trophies. The stadium even sold out of my jersey.

Clawing my way to the majors was hard. Jon's voice found its way into my head at every turn, always reminding me what was at stake.

"Everyone wants to be golden, but gold is tested in fire."

"Worth equals output. Sometimes, you've got to put up with pain."

"Missing a single game could be the end. Replacing you is easier than you think."

"Golden boys don't break. Even when it hurts. Especially when it hurts."

I corrected my gait, ice bathed until I was numb, slept on heating pads, took over-the-counter meds, and did all the treatment I could find. I pushed and pushed until offseason came, when I could recover and put myself back together, all to restart before spring training.

Tonight's game matters. Everyone's watching. This is the kind of night people will remember. The kind they'll replay in highlight reels.

And if I'm not on the field, then what was the point?

Eyes stinging, I fumble for my phone. A distraction is needed, and the only message on the screen does exactly that.

Agent Shay

Not going to make it to tonight's game but grab me a shirt, please!

And just be Cade

You don't need to prove anything to anyone

I've got you

The screen shuts off, leaving only my reflection. Tired isn't the word for what I see. My eyes are shattered, every line and shadow a testament to how broken I feel.

A single tear slides down my cheek, but I don't look away.

Her words don't make sense. I was built to play through pain. Built to perform. Built to keep quiet and smile. Built to prove myself over and over until there was no reason for anyone to doubt me.

But this message? It makes me question everything.

On autopilot, I haul myself up. Each step down the hall is a fight, but I don't even try to hide the limp I've been concealing almost every day since the season started. I don't care who sees it anymore.

Maybe Shay's right. Maybe I don't have to prove that I'm built to last.

I hook my fingers around the doorframe and step inside the room. Rio's hulking figure slumps in his seat, as if he has been waiting for me to drag my ass down here for weeks and tell him the truth.

"Owens. What can I do for y—"

"My hip's bothering me," I blurt, clinging to the last thread of my confidence before it unravels. "It has been for a long time. I'm sorry for not telling you sooner, and I think it would be best if I skipped tonight's game. I don't think I can—I don't think I should play."

The fluorescent lights above flicker, casting shadows across Rio's perpetually stoic features. A beat of silence stretches long enough for me to take it back, but I don't.

"Oh." Leather squeaks beneath Rio as he stands. "Finally."

I blink hard. "What?"

"After you went off on Scott Butts, I told you to be honest with yourself. It took some time, but here you are finally doing that. Putting yourself first." Rounding the desk, he leans against the edge with his arms crossed. "I didn't think you heard me."

The golden boy wouldn't dare say this, but I do. "Didn't think I was allowed to listen."

A gentle weight lands on my shoulder. "I'm proud of you, rookie. Takes guts to take a step back when your whole life's been about stepping up. I'm not sure who you've been talking to, but thank her for me."

Her.

"Go get checked out by Isla," he continues. "She will make sure you're all fixed up. And when you're ready and completely healthy, your spot will still be here. There's no chance in hell I'm losing you."

Placing my hand on top of his, I wish my throat wasn't so tight. I need to thank him for saying everything I've needed to hear. For not making me feel replaceable. For letting me put myself first for once.

But mainly for proving Jon wrong.

Just like that, I'm walking away from the game, and I don't feel like a failure. Tonight isn't about being the guy who plays through it. Maybe it's about being the guy who finally doesn't have to.

And all I want to do is run to the woman who made this all feel real.

CHAPTER TWENTY-SIX

WHOEVER IS RINGING MY doorbell is about to get their nuts crushed.

I finally take a day off, and this is how the universe rewards me?

Technically, it was a sick day, but it's the first day since starting my internship that I've done very little work. None of my clients had any meltdowns or disasters to take care of. Not once did I have to listen to one of Trevor's tirades. Instead, I took a bubble bath, had an appointment with my dietitian, cooked meals for the week, decorated, took another bath, and fell asleep early.

Rushing through the living room, I kick the paint-splattered tarp aside. In an attempt to make this place home, I'm testing splotches of pastel pink, peach, and cream paint in the living room and foyer.

But I can't get rid of the kitchen's textured floral wallpaper. Mallory loves it too much.

On tiptoe, I squint through the peephole and clutch the baseball bat like a lifeline. "Who is it?" I call out. "I have a weapon!"

The dark blob is unfamiliar. So instead of being a hero, I back away from the door and prepare to call the police, but my body freezes when the intruder's laugh weasels its way through the tiny gap under the door.

"Stand down, Agent Shay. It's me. Can we talk?"

There's only one person who calls me that, and he shouldn't be at my house at midnight.

"Can it wait until the morning?"

Cade sighs. "I'd like to do this now, if that's okay."

"Am I being fired?" I ask. "I'd like to formally request being fired at a normal hour. Preferably after I've eaten so I'm in a better mood and less likely to have a meltdown."

God. There's that laugh again. "I wouldn't dream of losing you again. You can't get rid of me that easily."

I'd open my door for any of my clients at this hour, especially if they sounded as determined as Cade does, so I do. The man who occupies most of my thoughts is leaning against the doorframe, as if being here is the most normal thing in the world. Navy deepens his sun-soaked skin, practically identical to the hue of his eyes in the darkness. His chest doesn't budge, unyielding against the baseball bat jammed against his sternum.

It's a warning to stay back and stay outside.

With his hands raised, he grins. "This is *very* on brand for you."

I step onto the porch and close the door behind me. "What are you doing here, Cade?"

He looks as uncomfortable as I feel, with stiff shoulders and eyes that won't stay on me for more than a second. It could be the fact that I'm in a matching set of sheer pajamas, but it looks more like he's in physical pain.

Mint fills my nose as he exhales. "I'm sorry."

"For waking me up in the middle of the night when I'm sick?"

"Sick?" Discomfort shifts into worry as one hand cups my cheek and the other presses against my forehead. "What's wrong? How long have you been sick? Mallory didn't tell me that. Do you need something?"

"Sleep," I murmur, trying to sound annoyed, but biting down my smile proves to be impossible. "I'm okay, Cade. Still having a rough PCOS flare up, but I listened to some advice from my least favorite client and took a much-needed day off work."

"Least favorite client my ass, but I'm happy to hear that." His hands fall from my face, but he's still smiling. "What would you say if I told you I took a much-needed few days off?"

The good mood vanishes as my eyes snap to his hip.

This is why I don't take days off. I'm supposed to know what's going on with my clients, regardless of what I'm going through. If I hadn't fallen asleep after asking him to get me a shirt, I would've known. I would've already sent Rio an email.

I should have been there for him.

"Rio found out and benched you?" I ask.

His face darkens under my poor excuse for a porch light. "Actually, I benched myself."

If I weren't sure I was wide awake, I'd probably pinch myself. Cade choosing not to play baseball doesn't sound possible. Not after everything I've learned about him and what he's gone through during his baseball career. It doesn't make sense.

My silence must stretch for too long because he says, "Is that okay? Are you upset with—"

I hold up my hand. "Why would I be upset about you prioritizing your health?"

He doesn't have to say a word. The rigid line of his shoulders tells me his answer, and I swallow down the urge to scream.

Fuck Jon Sweeney.

"That's why I apologized. I'm sorry for not coming to you earlier about my hip. I was worried that all agents were the same."

The accusation shatters my heart. "You thought I could be like—"

"Hell no," he spits, leaving no room for discussion. "Not for one second did I think you could be like Jon, Shay. You never would've tried to convince me that pushing through an injury was the only way I'd live up to my name. I know that. I think I always have. Then I saw your text, and it snapped me out of the hypnotic spell I've been stuck in. Jon may have only cared about himself, but you care about *me*. All of your clients. Selfishness isn't who you are."

These are the moments I remember that Cade knows *me*.

As an agent *and* as a person.

"You said I don't have to prove anything to anyone, and I believed you. I *really* believed you, so I walked into Rio's office and told him I couldn't play." A tremor cracks his voice and my resolve simultaneously. "I'm not good at this. Having someone see me when I'm not so golden. When I feel like I could break at any moment. And I know it's midnight, but I had to talk to you. I messed everything up between us once by not being honest, but that was my own fear. You never failed to show me that you were there, and I hate that it took me so long to trust that."

Any residual anger over our breakup fizzles at his words, melting the ice block around my heart faster than an ice cream cone in the middle of baseball season.

"And I do trust you," he continues, as if he hasn't already rocked my whole world. "With my career, my family, my future. My heart too. You're the best agent I could ask for. Hell, you're my best friend, Shay."

Best friend.

I never thought I'd call Cade my friend again after what happened. It was brutal to go from strangers to friends to everything and then back to nothing. Even though every professional bone in my body tries to convince me he's like the rest of my clients, my heart knows the difference.

The Cade I loved then isn't the same man standing in front of me. Old Cade hid behind a smile that boasted everything was okay, when in reality, nothing had been for a long time.

This Cade is real, full of emotion and honesty and confessions as he lets me deeper into his world.

He's on my doorstep in the middle of the night to tell me something he could've hidden forever. If that isn't proof that Cade has changed, then I don't know what is.

And with that knowledge, I feel myself start to fall for him again.

"Can you say something?" he asks.

I blink out of my stupor, catching the shade of red coloring his cheeks. The words I want to say can't be spoken out loud. Not if I want to keep this professional boundary up.

"Thank you for telling me. And for trusting me."

His brows furrow. "That's it?"

My back presses against the front door. "Do you want me to yell?"

"Sorta." He drops his gaze to the ground. "You still haven't been angry with me about how things ended. We both know I deserve it."

I spent a lot of time thinking I'd never get answers from him, and now I've gotten more than I could've ever imagined. If anything, I'm mad at myself. For not trying harder. For leaving him alone. For not saying I knew something was wrong.

In anger's place is something I didn't think I'd ever feel again.

"The only person I'm upset with is me." Opening the front door, I glance at him over my shoulder. "Now, if you'll excuse me, I only have a few more hours until my phone starts ringing again. Get home safely, and take care of that hip."

Closing the door on his smiling face is hard, but I do. On both him and these feelings. I may be falling again, but I have to catch myself before I hit the ground and lose everything.

CHAPTER TWENTY-SEVEN

Cade

WAG USUALLY STANDS FOR wives and girlfriends, but today, the *A* stands for agent.

"I still can't believe you said yes."

Shay's focus stays on the email she's been typing for the last ten minutes. "Why would I pass up an opportunity to play at Pilot City Stadium? I'm not an idiot."

The Pilots' WAG game, consisting of the wives, girlfriends, and partners, is an annual tradition. It used to be held during offseason, but most players use that time off to relax and get away from base-ball. So now, we pick a random day off during the season, open the stadium to the players' families, grill hotdogs and burgers, and watch the partners battle it out on the field while we sit in the stands.

"I get it, but someone may assume you're my stunning girlfriend. What will you do then? I know that's the worst-case scenario for you."

"Easy!" Sparkly eyes narrow, but I soak up her smile. "I'll make it *very* clear that I am your agent. Here for work and a little fun."

It's the billionth reminder that she's my agent and nothing more, but quite frankly, I don't care what she calls it as long as she's here with me.

I lift my hands in surrender as we make it to where Gina, Rio's wife, is standing behind the folding table. She's the friendly chaos to his stoic order.

"Hey, Cade. And Shaylene! So happy you're here. You'll be on Team B with me!" Gina digs through a box before pulling out a navy jersey. "And per Cade's request, I made this!" When she flips it around, Shay gasps at the gold lettering. While the wives and partners have their player's last names on their backs, Shay has something more special.

"Agent Shay," she squeaks.

"Of course. I want to make sure everyone knows who you are." I point at the eight on the back. "But that you're still, you know . . . mine."

"Your *agent*," she corrects, but my knees go weak when she loses the battle and smiles up at me. "Thank you, Cade. I love it."

When she disappears into the ladies' room to change, I take a seat and stretch out my legs. Thankfully, the MRI Isla ordered only showed a minor hip flexor strain and inflammation. After being placed on the injury list, my life has become a revolving door of treatment, physical therapy, daily check-ins, and recovery.

Even Rio took a step backward when Isla's voice went from librarian to gym coach, putting the fear of the athletic training gods in us both.

Today is day seven of being benched.

Day zero was numb, watching my teammates from the dugout. Day two was miserable, avoiding Jon's texts that vowed being benched is the worst thing I could've done to my career. Day three was full of fear that Jon could be right when Rio called up a shortstop from the Triple A league to fill in. Day five was my first counseling appointment with Armin while my teammates played in Tennessee. Day six, I re-entered my worried phase when Rio mentioned keeping the minor league player for a little longer, which is the entire reason Shay is here with me today.

Which makes Gina the best for making Shay's jersey last minute.

"How do I look?" Shay asks, pulling me out of my own head.

My mouth goes dry as I take her in. The deep blue jersey is a cropped version of mine, landing right above her hips. Gold leggings capture the contour of her thighs and calves with a softness that contradicts the hard muscle. But it's her smile, unrestrained and contagious as she spins, that zaps my fears about being benched. It all feels lighter when she's here.

I snap a mental photo and save it in my brain. "Like Agent Shay."

"Swing a little harder, Rosie!" Dawson hollers. "No noodle arms!"

"Yeah! No noodle arms!" Luke parrots, cupping his hands around his mouth like his dad. "Use your muscles, Mama! Hit it!"

Rosie Huber glares at her family from the batter's box. "Don't you think I'm trying? I get worse every year!"

"I'm glad you're seeing how hard I work every single day." The seat creaks as Dawson leans back in his chair with that lovesick look on his face. "Come on, wifey. Make us proud!"

Weston, the Pilots' pitching coach, waits on the pitcher's mound for Rosie to reset her too-wide stance. As a former major league pitcher, Weston's no joke, but he throws another Rosie-appropriate pitch. This time, when she closes her eyes and swings wildly, the bat manages to connect with the ball.

Luke scrambles off his dad's lap and leans over the railing. "Stop dancing and run! They're gonna get you!"

As if suddenly remembering the next step in baseball, Rosie stops shimmying and takes off.

I find Shay in the dugout, cheek to cheek with Gina as they cheer for their teammate. Like I'd hoped, they welcomed Shay into their circle with open arms. I can't help but picture this being our normal. Shay being friends with the Pilots' partners, but not as my agent.

Being here as mine.

"Up next, we've got a different kind of WAG," Rio announces over the speakers. "Shaylene Turner, agent for Cade Owens is here and ready to rock it."

Marcus shivers. "Can't lie. She's scary, but in a hot way."

A ponytail of braids hangs from the hole in the back of her helmet, swaying around her hips. Lines of black war paint are striped under focused eyes. She's called Shayzilla and the Angel Devil for a reason. Her favorite pastime was collecting yellow cards like they were souvenirs. She's here to win.

I've seen her at the batting cages many times. Shay can hit a ball.

"Two hundred bucks the little lady strikes out."

"Little lady has a name," I inform the man behind me. Justin's an outfielder who I've always admired, though he's way too good at poker for my liking, but I don't appreciate the way he's talking about my agent. "Use it next time."

Dawson sighs. "Oh, this is gonna be good."

Justin holds his hands up in surrender. "I meant no disrespect, Cade. I swear." He clears his throat. "Two hundred bucks *Shaylene* strikes out."

All I see is red. "Five hundred she makes it all the way home."

Marcus bumps my shoulder. "Dude."

"Feeling cocky?" A snort leaves Justin's crooked nose. "I know she played soccer in college, but baseball's different. She's not gonna—"

"Two thousand," I interrupt. "Take it or leave it."

Justin hesitates, but like the gambler he is, an eager grin takes up half of his face. "Two grand on a WAG game? You're willing to bet that much on your agent?"

I've never felt more sure. "Yup. Now watch and learn."

In in the batter's box, Shay grips the bat with the same kind of determination she puts into everything she does. From working with her clients, to fighting for the promotion, to loving her friends.

I'd go broke betting on her any day with no regrets.

Weston releases a pitch that's significantly faster than what he's been throwing to the others. Shay digs her toe into the plate but doesn't swing.

"Strike!" the plate umpire calls.

"What?" I leap up. "That was a ball!"

Anytime fans scream that at the umpire, I assumed they were obnoxious because they didn't like the call. Now that I'm on the other side of the fence, it's not fun.

Another quick pitch flies by, but Justin groans this time.

"Ball!"

The stadium holds its breath for the next pitch. Then Rosie speaks from first base and claps. "Breathe, Shay! And knock the ever-living shit out of that ball!"

Static crackles in the air, followed by a signature Rio grunt. "May I remind you all that this is a family-friendly event. Let's keep the cursing to a minimum. I'm talking to you, Mrs. Huber."

When he winds up, I spy a slight tilt to Weston's lips. Maybe he senses Shay's bloodlust. She's desperate to hit the ball, and he wants to see her do it. That's why he's putting some real oomph behind each pitch.

The moment the ball leaves his fingers, the hairs along my arms stand at attention. It's beautiful how her entire body uncoils like a whip—smooth, fast, and precise, like dominos falling in a clear line. The motion starts in her legs, travels through her hips, flows into the torso, and finally bursts out through the hands and into the bat with one clean swing.

Then there's the long-awaited *thwack* of success.

The outfield is a mess, scrambling to grab the ball, which gives Shay all the time in the world to pass first base. Then second. And damn if she doesn't send the whole crowd into hysteria when she makes it to third and races all the way home.

Before I can cheer for her, fingers grip my shoulder.

Justin looks more proud than disappointed. "Props to the little lady named Shaylene. I'll have your money by tomorrow."

Looking down at the field, I make a decision. Shay's here, happy, having the time of her life, and that's more than enough for me.

"Keep it," I say. "I've already won today."

"Your agent is a keeper, Cadey." Rosie swings an arm around Shay's dusty shoulders. "Don't do anything stupid and lose her, okay?"

We step onto the practice field, and I shake my head. "I'm trying my hardest, Ro."

"I don't think you need to worry about that. Cade is never letting her go." Marcus rushes in front of us and turns to walk backward across the lush grass. "You should've seen him. He was like a one-man army up there defending her honor."

With a low chuckle, Dawson readjusts Luke's sleeping body against his chest. "A one-man army that won two grand."

There's a bounce in Shay's step as she leans against her new friend, but all I can see is my number on her jersey.

It looks like it belongs there.

"Can't believe you were going to make so much money off me," she chuckles. "I was out there doing all the work while you sat up there looking pretty."

A thrill runs through me as I fall into step beside her. "You think I'm pretty, Agent Shay?"

Those usually downturned lips tilt. "Oh, shut up."

I'm about to ask if she wants to watch the fireworks with me, but she's whisked away by Rosie to grab snacks. I probably won't see her for the rest of the evening, but I'm going to pretend she's here as more than my agent. Even though I shouldn't.

"You're so fucked, man," Dawson whispers. "*Majorly* fucked."

Claiming a spot on the grass, I drop my bag. "What do you mean?"

He stares like I announced chocolate milk comes from brown cows. "Don't act dense. Betting on her. The constant eyes. The flirting. You like her again, don't you?"

"Again?" My laugh holds no humor. "I never stopped."

Marcus presses a hand to my chest and shoves me, but he's grinning at me like he's known the whole time. "You can't keep information from me! I need to know these things! Is that why you were being all protective and weird when I wanted to ask her out?"

"Nope. I just knew that she wasn't the one for you."

"Fair." Marcus looks at me carefully. "What are you going to do?"

Looking up at the night sky, I sigh. "Not a thing."

"What do you mean? You can't do nothing!"

"I don't have a choice, Marc. She's my agent, and I respect her and her job more than I care about what I need. I'm not going to hurt her by ruining everything she has worked so hard for."

Dawson pats my shoulder like he's conducting a symphony of sympathy. "You're a good guy, but I do hope it works out for you. You're kind of perfect for each other."

Tired of the pity party, I send them on their way to find their people and spread the red-checkered blanket Gina handed me as we walked outside. Shay mentioned needing to head home, but Luke and Marcus are masters of the puppy dog eyes and convinced her to stay for the fireworks show.

At least five times today, I caught her searching for something in my face. Maybe anger or disappointment, but she won't find any.

"Hi," a tired voice says. "Ready for the show?"

She came back.

Looking up at my dream woman, I gesture to my blanket. "Want to watch with me?"

"No, I grabbed all your favorites to eat by myself." The colorful tower of snacks cradled in Shay's arms falls onto the blanket, a multitude of potato chips, pretzels, and sour gummy bears.

I follow her lead and lie down. Our heads are so close that a braid tickles the back of my neck.

"What are the odds you'll fall asleep?" I ask.

She yawns, long and languid. "No need to play because I'm already halfway there. I have no idea how you do this almost every night for nine innings. I played six, and I'm beat."

With her eyes closed, dark lashes frame the almond shapes like delicate strokes of ink. It would be so easy to reach out and trace every plane of her face that glitters under the moonlight.

But I know I can't.

"What are the odds that I get to come to another WAG event?"

A beat passes. Then two. She deserves to know the truth.

"If I had the chance, Shay, you would always be my plus one."

Her shoulder goes rigid against mine. "Well, at least until the day you get a wife or girlfriend." When her eyes flutter open, I catch a flicker of something in the deep color I can't place. "Right?"

The air grows thick as I digest her words. Living without Shay has been my own self-inflicted personal hell, and I haven't been with anyone since her. Couldn't even fathom the idea. I'd rather be alone than spend my life without the only person I want.

Before I can drop a bomb on our partnership, her attention is stolen by a burst of sound and light. Bright red, yellow, and orange fill the sky, but I keep watching her.

There will be no girlfriend or wife unless it's her. That I am sure of.

CHAPTER TWENTY-EIGHT

Cade

WHO KNEW TAKING A break would be somewhat enjoyable?

I may have already missed eleven games, but I'm finally waking up without sharp pain traveling down my leg, I've researched a list of back-up universities with my degree that Shay sent, worked three catering events with Mom, and Kenneth and I hung out like we used to—him puzzling and me playing video games.

And today, I explored Philadelphia.

"How's the pain?" Isla asks as I crawl onto the cushioned table. "On a scale of one to ten?"

It's a relief to not yelp while tugging my sweatpants off. "One, but I wouldn't necessarily call it pain. Let's call it soreness from yesterday's jog and your nimble fingers."

She pops in her earphones and pats my shin. "Good, Cade. Happy to hear that. Now let me work my magic and see if we can get you to a zero by the end of the week."

Just like yesterday, I don't flinch when she digs into my hip. After two years of constant twinges and pinches that left me breathless in pain, I feel fresh. And as ready as I am to get back on the field, I'm looking forward to being completely healthy when I finally do.

My phone vibrates beside me. Since Isla's preoccupied with the heavy-metal blasting in her headphones, I might as well take the call.

"Is there a reason I'm at the ticket office and there are two tickets waiting for me?"

I chuckle. "Hello to you too, Shay." It shouldn't, but her exasperation brings me pleasure. "Are they good tickets at least?"

"They're incredible!" she hisses. "Right behind the visiting team's dugout. How did you—"

"It was easy," I say. I may owe Dawson and Marcus a six-month supply of Mom's famous Oreo treats for their will-call tickets, but it's totally worth it. My single will-call ticket is already reserved, and even though it hasn't been picked up once all season, I won't give it away. "Is your dad excited about the game?"

"Excited? He almost bounced out of his seat when I told him I got us tickets to the Pilots game tonight. Now that we've been upgraded to near the field, I might actually have to sedate him."

Call it kismet, but Shay being in Philly for her clients' soccer match perfectly aligned with our game.

"Good. Did he have fun at the soccer game last night?"

"Dad has fun literally anywhere. I think he liked watching me work, but this will be the highlight of his weekend. We haven't been to a baseball game together since high school. I always told myself I'd take a day or two off from work, but I never have."

The regret in her tone stabs at my heart. "You're the hardest working agent. Just enjoy the game. Tonight is for y'all."

"Yeah," she chuckles. "I've missed spending time with him."

"So, you're not mad at me for upgrading your tickets?" I ask.

"I'm a little less upset than I was earlier. I don't know how you did it with a sold-out game, but it's perfect. Thank you, Cade."

I shift closer to the left side of the table and prepare for Isla to stick needles into my hip. "You're welcome. You deserve some happy."

"Some what?" Her volume rises to shout over the people waiting outside the stadium. "Sorry, I can barely hear you. It's getting crazy out here! I think they're about to open the doors."

There'll be more opportunities to remind her of what she deserves.

My throat tightens, but not from pain. "Do you think your dad would like a tour later tonight? I'd love to meet him and show him around—"

"Yes."

Her answer is so quick but sure, and I find myself smiling. "Good, because you already know my family, and they love you more than they love me. I feel like meeting your dad will be another step forward in our *professional* relationship."

Shay's little snort of laughter wraps me in a hug. "You're making this really har—" She stops abruptly and screams something that sounds a lot like *dad*. "Sorry, Cade. My dad tripped getting off the bus, and oh my god. His jersey. I'll see you soon, okay?"

I swallow hard. "Yeah. Have fun, Agent Shay. See you soon."

I'm pretty sure she doesn't hear me over her excitement, but I listen to her and her dad's muffled identical laughs for a few moments before forcing myself to hang up. When I look up, Isla is watching me from behind those thick tortoiseshell glasses.

"What?" I ask.

She shakes her head. "I'm between songs. Didn't hear a word." The mischief in her eyes gives her away, and all I can do is laugh.

I'm about to meet the father of my almost-ex, current agent, and the woman I'm never going to get over.

Dante Turner is the proudest father.

"We used to come here almost every night to watch games, and now look at us!" He drapes his arm around Marcus's shoulder. "My baby girl has a pro baseball shortstop as a client. She went from soccer star to sports agent for one of the best agencies in North Carolina!"

They don't look alike. Outside of their identical ebony skin, the similarities fall away. Dante's got that *friend to everyone* thing going for him, all easy smiles and open body language.

Shay is the opposite: measured, cautious, and guarded. She goes through life with so much control, careful of what parts of herself she offers to people. Nothing about her shouts for notice, yet she draws it in anyway. It's quiet too, as if asking to be held rather than followed. Chosen, rather than left behind.

That's what has always drawn me in.

"He did this throughout the entire game to the wonderful couple sitting next to us." Shay sighs as she hands me a water bottle. "I'm pretty sure they would have moved if they could."

"And miss an opportunity to sit next to *the* Dante Turner? No way." I spin the top off and take a drink. "He's so proud of you."

"He tells me every single day." Then her eyes trail from my feet to my face. "You're standing up straight today. Good treatment?"

I nod. "Spent some extra time in the hot tub, but I'm ready for the tour when he's done entertaining them. He's the life of the party."

"Always has been." There's a lightness to her voice as she watches her dad chat with Marcus and Dawson. Even Rio broke and grinned when Dante mentioned that Rio's muscle tone hadn't diminished, even though he has been out of the league for a decade.

"And his jersey?" I ask, lifting my eyebrows twice.

"Don't let it go to your head. It has nothing to do with *you*," she argues. "He just likes the number eight."

Leaning backward, I admire the eight on the back of her WAG game jersey. "Looks like you do too."

Ignoring me and my valid point, she waves her dad down.

The former basketball player smiles and turns to face us. Being six-foot-five, there aren't many people who are taller than me, but it's like looking up at Goliath as Dante jogs across the locker room toward us. He's got at least three inches on me.

I brace for a handshake and get a full-on hug instead.

"I hope you're a hugger because I am. I'm Dante. This wonderful woman's father."

"Sure am. Thank my mom for that." Once he releases me, I grin. "It's so nice to meet you. I've heard great things."

"Likewise!" He wraps Shay in a one-armed hug. "Sorry to hear about the hip, but I'm glad you're letting it heal. You've been one of my favorite players since you were at CLU! Did Shay tell you?"

My eyes fall to her. "No, sir. She never mentioned that."

She refuses to make eye contact with me. "It wasn't relevant."

Dante throws his head back like that's the funniest thing he has ever heard. "Ever since she was little, she's liked to keep things close to the vest. Not as open as me, more like her mom."

Rolling her eyes, Shay mutters something under her breath that sounds like *this was a mistake.*

His gasp is half offended and half humorous. "I'm a treasure, and you know it, Shaylene." When he refocuses on me, I'm slightly dizzy from all the back and forth. "I've been watching you all season, Cade. I was a little surprised to find out you benched yourself."

I point at his daughter. "All her. She's the one who reminded me about what's really important."

Dante's chin lifts, and I feel like I passed a test. "Shaylene has always cared about the *person*, not the career. So, when she puts time and energy into something, it usually turns into something good." He pauses, keeping his eyes on me, "Real, too, if it's meant to be."

There's something weird in his tone. It sounds like hope.

A sharp ring cuts through the tense silence, and Shay frowns at the phone in her hands. "Work call," she says. "I need to take this. Be right back."

Dante chuckles when she's far enough away. "That girl. Doesn't know how to turn it off."

"Agreed, but she's good at what she does," I say.

"Most people don't even catch half the things she does. Her mom taught her well. Made sure she knew she would always have to work harder and smarter than everyone else. Especially in a field like this. But you see everything when it comes to her, don't you?" His elbow jabs my side softly. "Look, I'm not trying to make this awkward, but I know you two have some kind of history. I've been around long enough to be able to read a room. Especially a room where my daughter and her heart are involved."

I roll my lips. "There's honestly nothing going on between us."

"Maybe not right now, but I see the way you look at her."

It's tricky to force my attention from her to her dad. "What do you mean? I look at her like she's my agent."

"Lies, but I love how much you respect her career. Makes me like you more, Cade." It's sort of terrifying how his energy has shifted. That easy smile is still there, but there's something more thoughtful about the shape. "About halfway through the game, I noticed she doesn't quite look at you. At first, I thought it was because she doesn't want to. Then I realized it's because she won't let herself. Like I said, she has been like this since childhood. I can't blame her mom for teaching her to protect herself. To lead with her work. To put her heart on the back burner. It keeps everything tidy, so nothing slips out of her control and hurts her."

Our pink sticky note comes to mind. "She likes her rules."

"She does." A heavy hand thuds against my shoulder. "I'm not saying this to scare you off. Actually, the opposite. Whatever happened between you two obviously meant a lot to her, because if it didn't, she wouldn't be standing here with you now. Shay doesn't let people in halfway. It's full throttle or not at all. Do you want more with my daughter?"

"More than anything," I breathe before remembering who I'm talking to. "But I'm sorta agent-zoned these days."

Finally happy with the truth, Dante grins. "Whatever this is, whatever it becomes, just be good to her. That's all I care about."

Our agreement is silent. That if I have another chance, I'll never let her go. That being good to Shay is easy, and if the opportunity arises, I'll be good to her until the day I take my last breath.

"What did I miss?" Shay asks, eyes darting between the two of us.

"Nosy much?" As if a switch flips, Dante moves from protective father to energetic puppy, grabbing one of her braids. "I was just telling him how lucky he is to be working with you. They don't make agents like you anymore."

She narrows her eyes. "Uh-huh."

And I swear, for a brief moment, she knows exactly what was said and is too scared to ask. She isn't ready to hear those words yet. She may never be ready for them, but it doesn't matter because I'll be right here no matter what she chooses.

"So," I say. "How about that tour?"

CHAPTER TWENTY-NINE

THERE'S A SONG FOR every moment, and Mallory is the queen of finding the perfect one.

MalPal

> *Without Me by Eminem*

> Because GUESS WHO'S BACK. BACK AGAIN

> Congrats on being cleared, Cader Tot! ILY

It chimes five more times as I readjust in bed, shifting my computer to rest on my lap. After three practices at full intensity with no pain or tightness, I got the stamp of approval from Isla and Rio to play in tomorrow's game.

"Seems like people are excited about the good news," Armin says from my screen. Self-help and psychology books with worn and cracked spines fill the shelves behind him. There isn't a photo, plant, or personal effect in sight. "How are you feeling today?"

"Much better," I answer, silencing my phone. "Sorry about that."

The first rule of counseling is no phones.

"No need to apologize." As usual, his cadence is unhurried. "I'm sure missing fourteen games wasn't easy. It's nice to see a real smile today."

Within ten minutes of our first session, Armin read me to filth.

"You smiled, but your eyes didn't agree with you. You don't have to wrap hard things in a smile, you know. Want to talk about it?"

Before our first session, Reed warned me about his therapist's unflappable reputation, stating many players consider him to be cold and detached, but Armin is exactly what I needed. From the moment I saw his cream sweater vest and the practical leather watch on his wrist, I knew he was perfect. There's no feigned warmth or performative empathy. No fangirling or flattery.

He's just Armin, and I'm just Cade.

"Let's continue a discussion from our second session." He flips through a small journal, pausing when he finds what he's looking for. "We role-played a session as if the 'golden boy' version of you was in the room with us. Do you remember what you said he looks like?"

Clearly. He was me until about three months ago. "Smiling all the time, even when things suck. Outwardly confident but cracked straight down the middle. Like he's two steps ahead of everyone and ready for whatever gets thrown at him, but it's only because that's the way he has been conditioned to act."

"What does he want from the world? And what's his biggest fear?"

Saying it for a second time hurts even more. "To be exactly what people expect of him, and he fears losing the golden boy title. He believes it'll be the end of him."

"That's a lot for him to carry every day, don't you think?" Green eyes flicker behind thick lenses. "I know your mother gave you the nickname as a child, but when did you start feeling"—he pauses to check his notes—"the invisible weight?"

Grabbing a pillow, I press it against my chest. "I'm not sure, but I remember the day I became aware of it. It was my freshman year of high school at the state championship."

The newspaper clipping Rio keeps in his office flashes in my mind. Every newspaper ran with the nickname, spreading it like wildfire around the baseball world. That's when colleges started reaching out, wanting to talk to the golden boy.

Not Cade. Never Cade.

Clear Lake University was the first team that wanted to speak to *me*, so I signed there.

"Would you say the nickname was always tied to baseball?"

"It didn't start off that way, but after that game, yeah. Then it became a cage. 'The golden boy should worry about baseball rather than try other sports' or 'Why do you care so much about a college diploma? You're going to be a star.' It sucked to know that they looked at me and only saw baseball." My laugh is dry. "Everyone wanted the charming, reliable, and always-okay guy with softened edges, tucking away real emotions."

Armin doesn't press or jump in. The quiet stretches as if it's part of the conversation.

I hate it as much as I need it.

"Not my friends and family," I add. "I'm sure they don't expect the golden boy all the time."

"That's good." His ballpoint pen scratches against the paper. "Does that mean you let them see the sharper edges and the real emotions?"

My prolonged silence is a resounding no. Keeping the people I love from worrying about me has always been my main priority. It's why I didn't tell Kenneth how hurt I was after things ended with Shay, because he would've hopped on a plane to be with me. It's why I hide the cracks from Mallory, because she loves harder than anyone I know and would put her life on pause to be there for me. It's why I never tell Mom how I think about quitting every damn day, because she sacrificed so much to get me to this point, and I can't let her down. It's why I stopped talking to Jimmy, because I didn't want him to see how unhappy I was after years of loving baseball.

"It's easier this way," is all I can say.

"Easy? Sounds exhausting if you ask me." Armin's words reignite the fatigue I've carried for years. "Do you know what a martyr is?"

His question takes me by surprise. "Someone who sacrifices their own needs and desires for others."

"Exactly. The guy who always smiles. The guy seen as perfect and effortlessly happy. The guy with no issues. The guy who's golden." The notebook closes with a quiet thud. "Can you see how those titles could damage an identity? Could cause confusion and doubt?"

I squeeze the pillow in my arms. "Asking the hard-hitting questions today, huh?" Armin's brow arches, waiting for me to continue, so I do. "I can see how it can be damaging, but I have shown one person. My agent. She knows more about my feelings than anybody else."

His neutral expression shifts into one of surprise. "How did she respond when she saw the Cade that nobody else sees?"

"Perfectly."

"Do you feel like it dragged her down and made her life harder by helping you?"

"Not at all."

He leans forward. "And why do you think that?"

"Because she told me so, and I trust her. All I needed to do was tell her what was going on, and she listened. She cares about *me*, not the golden boy." I swallow hard. "Just me."

Shay has always seen me. It's the reason I hid from her.

It's the reason I'll always love her.

"What did it feel like to be seen like that? Like the real Cade?"

My eyes sting as Reed's word comes to mind. "Honestly? I felt free."

A smile, the first one ever, appears as Armin looks straight into the camera. "Then it sounds like you're on the right path to finding yourself without the title and labels, Cade. And surrounding yourself with people who see *you*. That's the best thing you can do."

Why did nobody tell me therapy is emotionally and mentally draining?

I crawl out of bed and nearly trip over my suitcase. The Pilots leave for Washington D.C. bright and early tomorrow, and I'm ready to get back on the field. Marcus and Dawson are equally excited, unrelenting with messages and reminders of what to bring, as if I've been gone for months instead of a little over two weeks.

It's Shay's all-client dinner tonight that has me nervous.

With a stretch session and hot shower on my mind, I open the front door and grab the package that contains my massage gun. But something leaning against my porch railing makes me halt. Then I spot those assessing eyes topped with caterpillar brows, and the air grows thick with history.

History I have no interest in rehashing.

Jon pushes his foot into the gap before I can close the door. "Come on, Cade! Don't do this. You haven't answered my messages, so I had to try the old-fashioned way."

I scoff at the use of my first name. "Get lost."

"Just give me five minutes!" he pleads, slamming his palms together.

There isn't a chance in hell I'm letting him inside for a second.

Pulling my phone from my pocket, I set a timer. "Five minutes."

A relieved sigh rumbles out of him as I free his trapped foot and he bends down to inspect the expensive shoe. "I was hoping things hadn't changed too much, but I guess everything I heard was true. You're not talking to media. You benched yourself. Can't believe it only took three months for you to fuck everything up."

"I fucked everything up?" The words rush out of me. "You're not going to come to my house, demand my time, and then talk to me like this. It's why I fired you, remember?"

Broad shoulders sag. "That's why I'm here. To fix things."

"You're ready to apologize?"

The lines around his eyes tighten, and I try not to laugh. Getting an apology from Jon is as likely as the sun rising in the west. He never believed he was in the wrong. Not when he screamed for hours about my poor game performances or pushed me past my limits. He was always doing what he deemed best for my career.

Which was code for *his* career.

"I've got some potential clients I *need* to sign, Cade, and your silence is loud. Athletes are paying attention to it. ProPact Agency is even starting to question things."

I knew there was an ulterior motive somewhere.

"You're here because you need me to speak to the media?"

"No! I came here to talk," he says quickly. "But I also wanted to ask you to break your silence. A quote would go so far coming from you. And after all I did to get you where you are now, I think it's worth some compassion. You could—"

"You think I owe you a glowing review?"

"Honestly, yeah. You need to grow up, Cade. Stop pouting because I pushed you to be the best. We were a team! Me and you. We could've made it all the way to the top together, but you couldn't handle the pressure. You were supposed to be my shining achievement."

My calm begins to slip. "I'm not a trophy, Jon. Or a title you can use. Managing my career was your job, but you were creating a version of me that made *you* look good."

"And made you successful!" he shouts, revealing the real Jon Sweeney. Not the calm guy he tried to emulate when he stepped onto my porch. "All I did was take the title and image you came to me with and made it better. Stronger. Irreplaceable. The league wanted the golden boy, not Cade Owens, so that's what I gave them!"

"But I lost myself in the process!" I shout before I can stop myself.

In the sleepless nights filled with critiques and stuffing my brain with film and spray charts until I was fuzzy-headed and barely able to function. All because I felt as if my image was nonnegotiable.

"All I did was help you become the best shortstop you could be and the player the league adored. And you got everything you wanted. Didn't you?" He gestures at the house behind me. "The big house back in your home state. The major league contract and salary. When will you realize that *I* did this?"

I am certain Shay would never say that to any of her clients. Taking credit for her athletes' achievements would never cross her mind.

Jon isn't half the agent she is, and he never will be.

"If you got a quote from me, I can promise it wouldn't save you."

The skin under his eye twitches. "And what if I lose everything? What if I don't get these clients I need? What does that say about you?"

"That I have boundaries. And when they get crossed repeatedly, I can hold the line." I flash him a real smile. Nothing like the one I gave him for years. "It's called growth."

He staggers backward. "You're gonna let me fall like this?"

It's weird how the question calms me, anger and betrayal dissipating as I look down at the man standing on my porch. Jon always seemed so powerful back then. He acted larger than life, so I believed he was. Now I know better, and I'm done with the manipulation.

"You're not falling, Jon. This is what we call dealing with the consequences of your own actions." I check my buzzing phone. "Your time is up. Now, if you'll excuse me, I've got a party to go to."

Stepping back into the house, I close the door behind me and don't look back. It's only when I hear a roar of anger that I take a deep breath.

Good riddance.

CHAPTER THIRTY

 *Shay*

"WHAT IF EVERYONE HATES it?" I despise how whiny I sound, but I'm freaking the fuck out.

"Why would a group of athletes hate mini golf and fajitas?" Holly asks. She heaves her body onto the front desk, even though the lone employee has asked her not to four times. "I personally am over the freaking moon about tonight."

GloGolf Gardens looks like an ethereal garden party and a night arcade had a baby. Plants, fake and real, grow from every surface, mushrooms bounce, and fairy lights stretch overhead. Everything is neon green, electric purple, or blacklight blue with random splashes of coral and orange—colors that make Mallory's closet look normal.

All-client dinners aren't the norm, but I wanted one night with them. With Cade being cleared, he'll be traveling tomorrow for a series. Lionel and Brett are starting to prepare for preseason. Holly and Victoria have the night off. The only one missing is Delilah, who's currently in Montreal.

Mini golf was my choice, but now it seems childish.

"I really hate it when you get in your head." Holly grips my face and leans in, giving me a great view of the freckles across her nose. "Since

I met you, you've walked into every room with your head held high. You're not going to start doubting yourself tonight because you're doing something special for your clients."

"I could have at least taken y'all to a real golf course," I say, words warped by the fingers squishing my cheeks.

"Why? Almost everything is better when it's mini!"

Finally, she accomplishes her goal when I laugh. Holly's a little younger than me, which is probably why I see her as a little sister. She will always be my first client.

"Thank you. I needed that."

"Good," she grins. "I was ready to slap some sense into you."

The bell over the door chimes as the first person arrives. Bringing five professional athletes to a popular venue in Charlotte would've been risky, so on my own dime, I reserved the place for the entire evening.

"Shay Shay!" Brett hollers. "Where are *youuuuuuu*?"

"Front desk." I stand, preparing for a look of pure disappointment, but when Brett and Lionel round the corner, their eyes are wide, grinning like two kids with free rein in a candy store.

"Mini golf?" Brett pulls me into a bone-crushing hug. "Hell yeah!"

An adorable dimple appears in Lionel's russet cheeks. "I knew you'd plan something fun. This beats a fancy dinner any day."

I look up at the two mountainous men. "You guys are happy?"

"More than!" Brett's white shirt glows blue under the UV lights. "Think of the most powerful word to describe happiness, and that's me."

"Ecstatic?" Holly offers.

"Better than that. Like frolicsome!" Then like the giant teddy bear he is, he starts skipping around the room until a glowing mushroom captures his attention.

Holly hops off the counter when the door chimes again and flicks her blonde ponytail in my face. "Told you they'd love it."

Victoria's bright white sneakers, neon green dress, and newly turquoise coils match the vibe perfectly. "Now *this* is a fun night out! Y'all better get ready for a smackdown. Not to brag, but you're looking at the mini golf champion of Houston four years in a row."

Feigning a shiver, Holly rubs her arms. "*Ooooo. I'm sooooo* scared."

The teammates bicker before dissolving into giggles about the new drama between their strength coach and head athletic trainer. Apparently one margarita turned into ten and escalated into a very messy one-night stand.

I'm still smiling when Cade enters, looking effortlessly cool. His locs are pulled back, giving everyone a clear look at his sculpted jaw and flawless complexion. Denim shorts hang above his knee, paired with a fitted white tee that hugs his chest and an unbuttoned navy flannel. I didn't want to spoil tonight's activity, so I made sure to tell them all to wear close-toed shoes and dress comfortably.

Cade guessed dodgeball, which would have been fun too.

"Agent Shay." There's something sweet about his professional tone, and my heart soars because he takes my job seriously, even with our history and his confessed feelings.

Before I can respond, Cade is lifted into the air.

"Cade Owens! It's nice to finally meet you! I'm Brett. You and Dawson are the reason I like baseball now," he babbles, sounding more like a fanboy than a fellow professional athlete.

Lionel appears, never too far from his teammate. Once Cade's feet are back on the ground, he extends his hand. "It's nice to meet you. I'm Lionel. This idiot's teammate."

Holly and Victoria swarm him too, overly eager to meet the man who demanded to work with me. But when the bell chimes again, I almost squeal. It can only be one person.

"Deshawn! You made it."

His face brightens as he finds us gathered in the middle of the room. After continuing intense physical therapy, his quad's muscle tone is returning. With him returning to practice soon, he deserved an evening to not worry about basketball or recovery.

"Miller!" Brett shouts. "When did you sign with Shay?"

"He's not—"

Deshawn cuts me off. "As much as I'd like to be part of the team, I'm technically not her client, but she's been a big help lately. And I couldn't miss an opportunity to kick your ass at mini golf."

Cade is too busy putting two and two together to introduce himself. I nod, verifying Deshawn is the client I've been going to physical therapy with. If I would allow myself to look at him for more than a half second at a time, I bet I'd find a look of relief on his face.

It's time to get the night started.

"We're sadly missing Delilah, but thank you all for coming. I know mini golf may seem a little juvenile—"

"Shut up!" all six of them yell.

"Okay! Sorry." I hold my hands up in surrender. "Now, who's ready to get beat?"

It's hard to be a sore loser with a stomach full of fajitas and a heart full of love.

I stand and tap a plastic knife against my red solo cup of lemonade. We're all crammed in a neon-green-and-black picnic table, but nobody seems to mind the closeness. "I know we're all reeling from the loss, but congrats to Holly for destroying us in what was meant to be a lighthearted game."

Across from me, Victoria pouts. "I wasn't warmed up properly."

Holly jabs a finger at her from the head of the table. "Yeah right."

"Which means," I continue, "whatever she wants us to say, we say it."

Holly crawls onto the table and smirks down at us. "Repeat after me, losers! Holly Trent is not only the best mini golfer . . ."

Everyone sighs. "Holly Trent is not only the best mini golfer . . ."

An evil grin twists her lips. "But she's also Shay's favorite client."

Beside her, Brett slams his hands against the table. "In your dreams, Holls! We all know it's me. I make her laugh the most."

"Yeah right," Lionel snickers. "You annoy her too much, B."

Victoria glares at both men. "If you believe it's not me, you're stupid."

To my right, Cade chuckles. "Shay has made it very clear that I'm not her favorite, so fight amongst yourselves."

Everyone's eyes shift to Deshawn, who's silently watching from the end of the table.

He shrugs. "I'm not even a client, but if I were, you'd all be in trouble."

Holly claps three times. "I don't care if you disagree! Say it!"

Even though it's preceded and followed by huffs, everyone recites the final line of Holly's required speech.

She beams. "Even if you all lied, you said it."

Once Brett helps her off the table and she's seated, I stand again. Emotion catches in my throat as I look at the people gathered around the table. Each one is special in their own way to my agent journey. They would've been happy and successful without me, but my life wouldn't be the same without them.

I'm sure of it.

"Thank you for indulging me tonight. An all-client dinner is something I've wanted to do for a while, but with our varying schedules, I never thought it would happen." I pull a pinky sticky note from my back pocket. "Now for a little bit of work. Cade's heading to D.C. tomorrow since being removed from the injury list this morning." They cheer for their new friend while Cade's cheeks flush. "Victoria and Holly, kick some ass at tomorrow's game. And for my basketball boys, rest. Preseason will be here before you know it."

Brett groans. "Don't have to tell me twice."

I laugh and take a seat. "Feel free to stick around and hang out for a bit, but that's all I have for you—"

"I'd like to say something."

My eyes fly to an oddly determined Lionel. "Oh. Sure."

He stands. "I'm a man of few words, but I'd like to kick off the speeches."

"S-speeches?" I stutter.

"Yup." His shy smile appears. "I know we can all speak directly to how amazing you are, but I want to thank you for everything you've done for me in the last year. When my brother got into that car accident, I froze. But you? You jumped into the fire and bought the first flight you could find, promising you'd take care of everything with the Grizzlies. When pushed to come back before I was ready, you fought for me to have extra time with my family. You never stop going to bat for me, and I hope you know I'd do the same for you any day."

"Lionel," I choke out, but Brett raises his cup of lemonade before I can finish my sentence.

"Hear hear!" he sings. "Shay Shay, you make this life so much easier. You're the first person I call with news, genius inventions that'll make us both rich, updates, and tea. Hell, I know I can call you just to talk about nothing because you always answer. I appreciate you every day. You keep me on track, and you keep me sane. I can't wait to annoy you until the day we retire."

My laugh is sudden, and I'm once again cut off before I can respond.

Victoria jumps up. "When I first met you, I thought you reminded me so much of myself. Hardworking. Dedicated. *Hot*. Stubborn in the best way. But within ten minutes of our first conversation, I realized you were a million times better than I'll ever be. I felt a little lost after being traded to North Carolina, but you made it home. Rage Smut Book Club wouldn't be here without you, and neither would I. You're the little sister who acts like the big sister I always needed."

A sob catches in my throat. "This is unfair, guys. You aren't giving me time to tell you how I feel about you."

Lionel chuckles. "You show us how much every single day. This is our chance to tell you how much we care about you."

Beneath the table, something grips my trembling knee. A quick peek reveals Cade's hand on my lavender jeans. It's the supportive touch I need to make it through the speeches everyone seems determined to make.

Deshawn pushes himself up with a soft grunt. "After my injury, I felt lost, but every morning, I woke up to an email from you. You made sure I was getting out of bed, eating breakfast, and taking care of myself. Even when I ignored you. Being an athlete, even with all the fame, can feel lonely, but you make me feel seen. You're the best agent I've ever had." His smile widens. "Adjacent or not."

"Deshawn," I try, but Holly leaps from her seat.

"My professional soccer dreams were practically dead when I met you. I had no team and no future, but in the Permian restroom, you gave me a chance when nobody else would." Teary eyes meet mine, and she presses her hand to her heart. "When I think back on how I got to this point, you're the first thing that comes to mind. When people ask how I did it, I say that I couldn't have done it without my agent. You don't just negotiate. You fight for me and help me get into rooms I never thought I'd see. You're the best agent and friend a girl could ask for."

Tears are already threatening to fall when Cade releases my knee and stands.

"There will never be enough time to tell you how I feel, so I'll keep it short and say it's such an honor to know you and work with you. Every time I hear people talk about your fierce loyalty and determination, I get so happy because you've always been this way. In a world full of bad agents, who only care about themselves or performance, I can say with certainty that you're the best. I don't even think you know how much you have changed our lives." His eyes are more brown than green tonight, and they're full of something only I can read. "Mine especially."

Hooting pulls my gaze from him to their raised glasses.

"And I messaged Delilah," Holly says. "She was so sad to miss this but said you'll be receiving her fifteen-minute speech by voice memo after she finishes practice."

"We love you, Shay Shay," Brett hollers.

My eyes roam the table. I know I do my job well and they're happy with their careers, but everything they said was personal. Things completely separate from their sport. In reality, we're all doing life together. In a professional sense, but also in a personal way that I'll never be able to thank them for enough.

Even though working at Permian feels like hell, I love them too.

That's why I hope the letter of intent I submitted to Trevor this morning gives me that promotion so I can stay with them for a long time.

CHAPTER THIRTY-ONE

Shay

I SHOULD NOT BE here.

Agreeing to meet Cade at his home after the all-client dinner is objectively a bad idea. Last time I was here, it almost ended with me on his lap and our lips sewn together. But I'm a damn good agent, and his vague comment at the third hole about Jon not being an issue anymore won't stop needling at me until I make sure he's okay.

Pacing across the wraparound porch, I weigh my options. There's still time to leave. Sure, he watched me park my car from the window, but I can come up with a good excuse.

Explosive diarrhea? Food poisoning? Bubble guts?

Maybe something less stinky.

"Debating how to let me down?"

I didn't even notice the door had opened. Cade stands in the doorway, leaning casually against the frame. It's hard not to stare, especially now that we're not surrounded by my other clients. He's still wearing his mini golf outfit, but a pair of glasses are perched on his nose. He always hated wearing contacts.

"Sort of," I admit, toe scuffing the ground. "Why did we need to meet at your house for this?"

Cade grins, sparkly like the white walls behind him. "There's something I want to show you in person, but if you prefer, I'll bring them to your office when I get back from D.C. Whatever you want."

"It's okay," I say with false ease. "I'm already here."

Stepping aside, he gives me freedom to roam his space. I didn't have time to take in the house when I delivered the All-Star Game news, but I can now. Floor-to-ceiling windows wash the room in the moon's silvery glow. My pink Converse squeak across the espresso hardwood. Stacks of video games sprawl beneath the biggest television I've ever seen. Framed photos of the people he loves cover the walls.

One of our many unfulfilled goals was to live together if Cade was ever traded to North Carolina, but the universe had other plans. He made himself a home here while I'm still struggling.

The hole deepens in my chest as I follow him into the kitchen.

"So, what did you want to show me?" I ask, taking a seat on a cushy stool at the island table. It's so polished, it could double as a mirror.

Cade opens a taupe cabinet, grabs two glasses, and fills them with water. "Don't you want to know what Jon said?"

Honestly, no. If I hear anything else he did to hurt Cade, I might explode. But I'm starting to realize this conversation isn't for me. *He* needs and wants to talk about it.

My dismay dims slightly at his openness. "Sure. What happened?"

"You've never been a good liar, but thank you." He slides onto the stool beside me. "It was a short conversation. He wanted me to make a statement about our time working together. Apparently, my silence has been keeping him from getting some valuable clients."

"He asked you to lie for him?"

"Basically. He said it was the least I could do after everything he did for me, and that I could help him out."

"Help him?" My fist slams against my table. "That emotionally abusive and manipulative piece of shit! Oh, when I get my hands on him—"

"No, Shay. It's okay. Really."

Cade's voice is too calm and measured when speaking about finally confronting the person who forced him to cling to a title, ignored how unhappy he was, and pushed him through physical pain. Yet the man sitting beside me is composed and kind.

Two things I wouldn't be if I were in his position.

"That sad excuse for an agent didn't do his job. If you decide to break your silence, he should be dragged through the mud. Complaints should be filed, Cade. He should lose everything."

"Maybe, but I don't care anymore. Not about what the media says or what anyone expects of me." A sharp laugh leaves his lips when my jaw drops in disbelief. "Okay, I do care, a lot. And I always will, but I don't want to live life like this anymore. Spending every moment worrying I'll make a mistake and get demoted or traded. Caring about the expectations of others. Staying up too late preparing for games and running on fumes. I want to just be."

Just being started off as nothing more than a phrase that left my lips in an attempt to help, but Cade took those words to heart. A state of *just being* is different for everyone, and for him, it's releasing the weight of the world's expectations.

I've never been more proud of him.

Breaking rule five, I press my bicep against his. "Do you feel better?"

"I do." He shatters rule five and rests his hand on top of mine. "And CLU emailed me this morning. I'll be able to finish my degree in person during offseason, which means you did it."

Finally. After getting no response from them after multiple follow-ups, I started looking at other universities that would take his credits. But I know how much Cade loves Clear Lake University. It's his dream to graduate from there, so I stood in the reception area until someone finally made time to meet with the woman who refused to leave.

"I've always got your back, Cade. In baseball and in life."

"I know you do. It's what made saying goodbye to Jon so easy. *You* showed me what a good agent looks like." My hand goes cold when he lets me go, but he grabs a box and slides it in front of me. "And I want to show you this."

With cautious hands, I peel back the flaps of the box. The penmanship of a physician is scrawled across every inch of yellow paper. At first glance, they look like love letters, but they're anything but kind.

This is your worst game so far. Gotta work on your quickness.

I reach for another, and the rest are equally atrocious.

Do you want to be in the minors forever?

First good stop of the night. Sucks that we're in the eighth inning.

Not good enough for the golden boy. You can do better than this.

"What the fuck?" My voice echoes, ricocheting off the beams in his fancy ceiling. "He wrote you anti-love notes? "

Cade doesn't seem to grasp just how pissed off I am, because he looks downright cheerful as I plunge my hand back into the box. But my curse is cut short when my fingers snag on something daintier.

Screw yellow legal pads. Pink is better. Thanks for being honest

My chest tightens as I continue sifting through the box, finding more pink scattered in the yellow.

Great stop on that rocket from Ulysses! You're a machine tonight

Rookie of the year? I think yes

Just be Cade. That's all that matters

It's kind of annoying how good you are at this

How cool is it to be Cade? Looks pretty fun to me

Stop beating yourself up over one mistake. One mistake doesn't dictate the entire game unless you let it, so don't

By the time I've read every pink sticky note, my vision is a kaleidoscope of light and colors from the tears clouding my vision.

"You kept these?" I ask, wiping my eyes with the back of my hand.

"Every single one."

"Why?" I ask. I need to know.

Cade shakes his head at me like I should know the answer. "Because you wrote them for me. At first, it reminded me of our BYOB nights, and I was happy to have them back in some form. We may not have been breaking down each game side by side, but your feedback was always special to me." With a lazy smile, he hands me a shoe box. "Now open this."

I follow his instructions, and the sight of more pink sticky notes makes me hesitate. These aren't from the last three months. They're faded, crumpled, and ripped, with doodled smiley faces looking up at me.

Appointment with team doc for my hammy. Come by after?

Mally's making spaghetti. Invite Kenneth if he promises to act right

30-minute nap! New record!

I'll be studying at the library tonight for a sports marketing exam, but stop by and keep me company if you have time

My heart stutters as I lift the last note I wrote him. I had mailed it to him a week before things ended between us.

What are the odds you come home right now? I miss you

"This is what I used to counteract Jon's notes." Cade hauls himself from the stool, steps behind me, and brackets me in his arms. "After I ruined things, these notes were the only way I could hear your voice. I always read them in hopes that your words, your love, would outweigh the bad until all I could see and hear was you." A rush of air escapes my lungs as his chest presses against my back. "And if it isn't clear, all I see is you, Shay," he continues, breath dancing across my collarbone. "And you see me. You're the person I want to tell everything to at the end of the day. The good, the bad, and the ugly. I can't change the past, but I can promise there will be no more running away. I want to run to you always."

Each word sinks into my skin like a tattoo of his promise, but it doesn't hurt or sting. And even if it's stupid of me, I know I believe him.

I only get one last moment in his embrace before he backs away. He wasn't lying about letting me take the lead. He's a gentleman to his core.

It's one of my favorite things about him.

Clearing his throat, he opens the pantry. "Want to stay and make s'mores with me? I got chocolate bars with almonds because you like them crunchy."

A quick peek at the clock tells me it's way too late. Dinner went past our reservation, because after the impromptu speeches, Holly challenged everyone to a rematch and won again.

However, I'm not ready to go home yet.

I stand. "I'll stay as long as we burn his notes."

"Have I told you lately that I love your brain?" Tossing me a candy bar, he grins, and it widens when I catch it. "Because I really do."

If I didn't know otherwise, I'd assume Cade had a secret girlfriend because the backyard is too perfect. Flowering garden beds line the tall fence, providing extra privacy. A picnic table sits in the middle of the yard, covered with Jenga blocks. But it's the string lights hanging over us that are making me overthink. They're too golden, and a little too romantic draped between two massive oak trees.

It's as if we're at our own backyard wedding.

"Do you throw a lot of parties?" I ask over the crackling fire. "You've got the perfect house for it."

"No." Tired eyes drift around the massive space. "The family I bought the house from left everything behind. It's not my forever place, but I'm happy here until that day comes."

His words land heavily, like he knows my little red house is where he should be. With me. Like we planned.

Crumpled yellow papers flutter across the gravel, carried by the cool breeze. Halfway through Jon's disgusting notes, I lost it. The paper might as well have been his head, because I crushed each one in my fist.

As Cade loads fluffy marshmallows onto sticks, I ask, "Are you sure you want to do this with me?

"Without a doubt. I started this journey with you years ago, Shay. Way before going pro, it was me and you, filling out sticky notes and spending our days at the batting cages." There's a grounding intensity to him as he looks into my eyes. "So, if I'm closing a chapter, it'll be with you. You're the one I want here."

He reaches for my hand, and I freeze, unsure if I should let him hold it. Instead, he uncurls my balled-up fingers and presses the stick into my palm, forcing me to relax.

"He's no longer my problem. It's time for me to let it go."

Taking a page from his composed playbook, I straighten and hand him the box. "Then let's make it an official ceremony. Do you have anything you want to say first?"

There's no resentment as he studies the cardboard in his lap. Instead, his lips are curved upward in that small smile I know so well.

A real Cade Owens smile.

"Goodbye, Jon. Out of all the things you believed you did for me, I can only think of one to thank you for. Thanks for pushing me back to Shay.

Every moment working with you hurt like hell, but I'm finally back with my favorite person."

Then he tips the box into the fire. The flames greedily attack the paper, roaring to life before they settle, flickering and calm, like even they've had enough. As if they read the notes, the comments, and the doubts and decided there was nothing worth keeping.

And in the silence that follows, something shifts.

It's a subtle kind of loosening, like the knot inside Cade finally lets go, and I can't look away. Broad shoulders drop a fraction, and I realize how high they've been since he walked into Permian. His left hand loosens, fingers uncoiling one by one, no longer preparing to fight. His exhale is slow. Not a sigh, but something deeper and more serene.

Pushing his hand over the armrest, it hangs between our chairs for a moment. And even though I shouldn't, I do the same. It's not a surprise when our pinkies brush, nor is it a surprise when they interlock in a silent promise to always be there for each other.

No matter what.

With his free hand, he holds up a marshmallow. "To the future."

I tip my marshmallow against his. "To the future."

CHAPTER THIRTY-TWO

Shay

"Babysit? Shaylene Turner does not babysit."

The other side of the phone is quiet for a beat too long. Then he laughs. "I did call you, didn't I?"

I roll my eyes. "Lose the sarcasm, Cade. Did Mallory tell you no?"

Out of our little crew, Mallory is the best with children. Then Adri, leaving Jo and me tied for last place. Keeping kids entertained has never been my strong suit, which is why Mallory became the go-to babysitter to Jax and Jules, her favorite twins, and I'm the cool one who feeds them chocolate when she isn't looking.

"Who says I called her first?" He clicks his tongue. "I love my MalPal, but I picked up the phone and dialed you. You've never been an afterthought to me, Agent Shay. First place forever."

Using the yawn he lets out, I catch myself and reset. I can't let his incessant flirting work on me today. It has never been so hard to follow my own rules, especially ones that directly affect my job and future. Rules give me control when nothing else does. Love is unpredictable. People leave. Feelings change. But rules have structure, giving me a sense of safety in a world that often doesn't.

You won't wear me down today, Cade.

"I'm sorry for springing this on you," he continues. "Mom's usual sitter is sick, and we couldn't find another. She tried to cancel, but the event for CLU's Provost is too important. I'll come pick up Violet after my game. Shouldn't be too late."

If Trevor were here, he would say this is what I asked for, considering he believes I babysit my clients. Now look at me. *Literally* babysitting.

I honk at the Jeep merging into my lane without checking their blind spot. "What if I already have plans?"

The line goes quiet. "What if I told you Mom's at your house?"

"You wouldn't." Turning onto my street, I spot the brown Cadillac in my driveway. "You ass! I don't have time to babyproof!"

Or clean. Now that I'm making an effort to make it more of a home than a museum, it seems I forgot how messy a space can get when you actually have stuff. After finishing work last night, I painted the living room pastel pink. Grocery bags litter the kitchen floor from my shopping trip. The half-built dining table I've been putting together for days is still in a heap in the middle of the room.

"Babyproof? Violet's eight. I think she knows not to stick her fingers in electrical sockets." Cade pauses. "Wait. Are you nervous?"

I chew on my bottom lip. "Sort of. What if she thinks I'm boring?"

"Don't worry about that," he assures me. "Violet thinks you're way cooler than me, and the betrayal doesn't sting much because I agree with her. It'll be great."

Somehow, my fears are soothed as I pull into the driveway. "Play well tonight, and don't forget that I'm mad at you for not giving me more than a two-minute warning about babysitting."

It's impossible to feel a smile through the phone, but I do. "As long as you're still talking to me, Shay, I'll survive."

The smug man doesn't deserve a response, so I hang up and park. He better be glad I love the two people standing on my doorstep as much as he does. Becoming friends with Cade freshman year gave me so much more than a potential partner. I became part of the family.

In the driveway, Violet leaps into my arms. "Shay!"

"Hello, sweet girl!" Squeezing her hard, I carry her to the front door, where her mother stands. "Hi, Ms. Billie! Sorry for making you wait."

"How many times do I have to tell you to call me Billie, dear?" If it weren't for the steaming aluminum pan in her hands, I'm sure she would be hugging me, but her sweet voice does that naturally. "And I know Cade didn't ask you before he told me yes, so I'm sorry about my son. He just knew you would come through for him."

Cheeks flaming, I unlock the front door. "Just doing my job."

Violet sprints straight for the pile of stuffed animals on my couch, while Billie follows me into the kitchen. Fresh fruit sits in a bowl beside the stove, a new addition to my protein-and-coffee breakfast before I rush out of the house. Now I understand why Mallory and Sarabeth kept pushing me to eat breakfast.

Even when I get no sleep, I feel so much better.

I take the dish from Billie's hands and place it on the stove. "Can I take Violet to the Carolina Rage game tonight? I have an extra ticket."

The squeal from the living room likely influences Billie's answer, but she looks as excited as her daughter sounds. "Of course!" She slides the steaming tray across the counter. "I had plenty of extra stuffed bell peppers, so these are all yours. Cade told me you hate red ones, so Violet made you a green-only tray. And here's some spearmint tea. Cade said bell peppers help with inflammation and spearmint helps with . . ."

When she trails off, I smile. "Facial hair growth. Acne. Hair loss."

The heavenly smell of ground beef, rice, and cheese makes my stomach flip, along with the reminder of Cade's thoughtfulness. *What Are the Odds* taught us a lot about each other. Our likes and dislikes, our fears and aversions, our comfort zones. Throughout what was meant to be a silly game, we built inside jokes and shared history. Which is how he knows that I despise red bell peppers.

But PCOS research is something he did all on his own.

Billie's hug surprises me, her petite frame packing more strength than I remembered. "Thank you for watching over both of my kids. Puts this woman's heart at ease knowing you're in Cade's corner."

I'll never pass up a motherly hug, so I melt into her embrace. I'm so proud of my mom for girl-bossing it up in Portland, running her sports law office. Many people might call her cold, but I disagree. She made sure I was prepared for the world and could protect myself, and I can't thank her enough. But sometimes, I need a hug.

"Be good for Shay, little one." Billie catches Violet as she dashes through the kitchen and presses kisses to her rounded cheeks. "Don't make a mess, and don't put any forks in electrical sockets."

My eyes fly to the silverware drawer. "She does that?"

At the front door, Billie glances over her shoulder. "No, but Cade texted me to mess with you about it."

As she leaves, I send Cade a mental middle finger.

Maybe babysitting won't be so bad.

Grabbing paper plates and plastic silverware, I turn to Violet. "So, should we eat dinner or make a fort first?"

"Hmm." Violet's eyes, that same striking shade of hazel as Cade's, land on my couch. "Fort and then we eat dinner *in* the fort."

"*Gooooooooooooooooal!*"

Violet, along with everyone in the crowd, spins in wild circles, mimicking Holly's celebratory tornado after her second goal of the night. Holly's on fire tonight, and I thank *Monsters, Inc.* for her tears.

"They're so cool," Violet whispers, watching the dynamic duo, Victoria and Holly, rush down the field.

My chest swells with pride. "The coolest."

I'll always miss playing soccer, but the pain is sharper at times like this. Being a defender was the most fun. I was in charge of protecting my goalie and slowing my opponents' attacks. I miss the lactic acid that burned in my thighs after sprinting across the field. I miss the overwhelming satisfaction that flooded me when I successfully stopped the ball with a slide tackle. More than anything, I miss the camaraderie that soccer brought. From my random roommate assignment with Mallory freshman year to welcoming Adri and Jo into the mix.

Sometimes you have to give up things you love to succeed.

"And you work with them every day?" Violet asks in disbelief.

"Sure do. Most of the time, I'm in the office, but my favorite days are when I get to watch my clients play their sport."

My forehead aches as Victoria heads a ball down the field. Holly's ponytail whips behind her as she darts across the bright green grass. They're so playful and goofy off the field, yet so precise and composed when they play. It's freaky.

"For my summer homework, I have to decide what I want to be when I grow up, and I want to be like you. An agent." Violet shoves a handful of Skittles into her mouth and refocuses on my phone in her lap that's streaming the Pilots game. "You get to watch games and eat candy and hang out with athletes! Plus, C.C. says you're the best agent. I hope he stays with the Pilots forever. I didn't like when he left. He never got to come home, and he was always sad when we talked."

"He told you he was sad?" I ask, trying not to sound too nosy.

"No, but I could tell. Sister powers. But he's not sad anymore. I know that for sure. His smiles look different now." Then Violet lets out a shriek so piercing it could be the referee's whistle. "C.C. got hit!"

I almost laugh. It wouldn't be the first time a bird swooped down onto the field and attacked a player. "Did the pigeons come after him today?"

"No! A ball! He was batting and got hit by the ball!"

Before I realize it, I snatch the phone away. My arm instinctively wraps around Violet's trembling shoulders as I pull her close and use my free hand to rewind the game thirty seconds. I know exactly what's about to happen, but that doesn't stop the sob from spilling out of me.

Cade took a ball to the head at ninety-six miles per hour.

He's still sprawled on the ground, but the sickening crack of ball to helmet has etched itself permanently in my brain. It's even louder than the static in my ears. One second he was upright. The next, his helmet was in the air as he fell into a crumpled heap in the batter's box.

Standing, I hold my hand out to Violet. "Let's go."

CHAPTER THIRTY-THREE

Cade

"Blink once if you're okay and twice if you're in pain."

I bat my eyes twice at Rio, who's looming over me like a guardian angel. The distant roar of the crowd swells and dips, disconnected from the thick tension in the training room. I'm not sure how I got here, and by the look on his face, I won't be leaving anytime soon.

Isla's hands are unsteady as she presses an icepack into my palm. "How are you feeling?"

My fingers go instinctively to the spot where the ball slammed into my helmet, right above my temple. A hot, angry bruise is already blooming beneath my skin. "Like shit."

Nervous energy clings to Rio despite the calm expression he wears. "That's to be expected, kid. You took a fastball to the head."

With one final sweep of the penlight across my eyes, Isla slides it into her pocket. "Tracking is good. Are you dizzy? Nauseous? Having double vision?"

"None," I say, thankful it's the truth. "But my head is killing me."

"As the adrenaline wears off, it may get worse." She squints at me for a moment before the tension eases from between her brows. "Well, the good news is there are no signs of a concussion. Your pupils are normal, and the baseline is good, so no glaring red flags at this moment. You got very lucky, Cade."

Cold from the ice pack seeps into the side of my head. The stubborn ache reminds me how fast a pitch travels.

When I catch sight of my helmet, the piercing pop echoes in my ears once more. A shard of light runs across the earflap, highlighting the jagged line through the carbon fiber.

If the earflap wasn't there, it could've been lights out for me.

As dramatic as it sounds, it's true. Had I taken that ball to the temple without protection, I might've lost my life on the field tonight.

The thought is sobering, but instead of breaking down like my body begs to, I swallow the fear and force a smile onto my face.

"Got cleared a week ago, and now this? I think life is saying to chill."

"And that's exactly what you're going to do." Rio rests a hand on my shoulder. "It could've been so much worse, Owens. But you're here, sitting up straight and talking normally. The win is that you're okay. Nothing else matters."

"Agreed." Isla hands me two pills. "No NSAIDs, okay? Tylenol only. No screens. Not even your phone. Hydrate. And you can't stay by yourself tonight. Sleeping is fine, but someone must be with you all night."

Swallowing the pills dry, I shake my head. "I live alone."

"Doesn't matter," Rio grunts. "Shay's on her way. It took her a while to get in touch with your mom since she's working, but your mother said you'll be staying with her tonight."

"Shay was busy. She didn't need to—"

"I didn't ask her to come," he cuts in. "She was already driving when she called and demanded to know if you were okay."

For the first time since the hit, my heartbeat seems to slow. I want her to be in control of what happens between us because her career is the one that's at risk, but I know the moment I see her, I'm going to want to hug her and never let go.

Now that the adrenaline is lessening, fatigue is creeping in fast. I want nothing more than to let sleep swallow me whole, but I know better. They need me upright and awake for a little longer while we play the game of patience.

And that's okay. Could've been a hell of a lot worse.

"If your re-evaluation tomorrow morning goes well, we'll discuss next steps." A knock at the door distracts Rio. "By the way, before Shay called, we found out that someone picked up a will-call ticket for you tonight. Security went up and got them because we didn't want you to be alone. They're outside if you're ready for a visitor."

Will-call ticket? There's only one person on that list.

When Rio clears his throat, I straighten. "Sure."

Isla walks to the door. "Remember what I said, Cade. No being alone. No screens. No NSAIDs. And drink water like your life depends on it. I'll come watch you if I need to. My husband would love to babysit a pro baseball player."

She leaves the room with Rio on her heels, but my focus is on the man who looks like he hasn't slept in days.

I haven't seen Jimmy since the night Shay sneakily forced us to reunite at the batting cages. Before that, no words had been exchanged since I decided to work with Jon. I've sat outside of Slim Jim Batting for hours, running through the things I wanted to say to him. But every time, I'd go back home without saying a word.

The moment I try to stand, Jimmy hurries over and guides me back into the chair. "Stay seated. Do you have a concussion?"

I shake my head, not trusting myself to speak.

"Good." With a gentle touch, he cups my face in his hands. "I'm so glad you're okay, Cade. I was so damn worried."

The tight coils at his temples are silver under the garish lights. His face looks weathered too. I always believed Jimmy wouldn't age, but a lot has changed since I left for California.

One of my promises to Jimmy when I decided to play professionally was that he would always be my will-call ticket guest. I'd pay for my friends and family to come, but as the coach who changed my life, he deserved the one ticket.

But the ticket had never been used. Not until tonight.

"I hate that the first game you come to is the one where I take a ball to the head."

Jimmy blinks hard. "You think this is the first game I've attended?"

"You've never picked up the ticket for you. Not once."

"Because I buy my own tickets, Cade. Haven't missed a game all season."

My vision goes hazy when my head snaps up. "Then why use the will-call ticket tonight?"

"A silly mistake. I accidentally bought a ticket for the wrong night, but when I showed them my ID, they said there was a ticket waiting for me. I almost went home, but I'm glad I didn't. When they came to get me . . ." Voice trembling, he trails off. "I just needed to make sure you were okay."

He moves to go, but I reach for his wrist and blurt, "I'm sorry, Jimmy. I'm so sorry." That stops him cold, giving me a chance to say the words I haven't been able to say. "I should've listened to you and trusted you when you said Jon was bad for me, but I thought I knew better. I hoped you were wrong. Part of me worried you were trying to keep me from entering the league."

A muscle jumps in his cheek. "After everything we had been through, why would you think that?"

"Stupidity? Fear? Jon made it clear that working with someone less experienced and talented than him would ruin my baseball career, and I believed him."

Jimmy's face flames, giving me a flashback to the coach who ran us ragged after my teammate cursed at our calculus teacher. "That man's a grade A narcissist."

"I know that now, but that doesn't change anything. Everything's already ruined."

Jimmy's lips press into a flat line. He has every right to be upset.

My dad may have left us, but Jimmy always showed up. He's the man who taught me how to tie a tie. Helped me choose my prom tux. Moved all my crap into my college dorm.

And I messed everything up.

Pulling up a chair, he settles beside me. "You didn't ruin anything, Cade. If anything, I did. I shouldn't have snapped at you that night. All I could see was that predatory look in his eye and I freaked out. You always knew what you wanted to be, and Jon didn't care about the guy I adored. Just what you could give him."

Knowing that Jimmy saw the real Jon makes me feel better, but only slightly.

"I don't think I ever knew who I was." My temple throbs as I remove the ice pack from it. "Looking back, everything seems warped."

His question is earnest. "In what way?"

"My whole life, I've been a baseball player. I grew up playing baseball, traveled for baseball, went to college on a baseball scholarship, and didn't finish my degree so I could play baseball. That's all people saw me as, the golden boy, and it's all I saw myself as too."

As if ashamed of coming clean, I look away.

This is why I kept my distance. All I heard in my ear from Jon was that I wasn't doing enough or living up to the title that was created for me, and I didn't want to hear it from Jimmy too. Disappointing him was my biggest fear. I wanted him to be proud of me for making it. Instead, I lost one of the most important people in my life.

Jolting me from my shame spiral, Jimmy bellows a laugh. "Well, I'd like to officially welcome you to the pro-athlete club."

I stare at him, thoroughly confused. "Club?"

His head falls forward. "There's something about the way the sport shifts from fun and competitive to being the thing that not only pays your bills, but also the only thing everybody knows you for. The guy who either messes up all the time or the guy who is constantly smiling, which means the moment he slips up, everybody jumps on it." His hand finds my knee and squeezes. "The reason I didn't use your will-call tickets is because I didn't want you to think I was using you. Watching your games was the only way I could see you, so I watched from afar. I knew we'd talk someday."

A chuckle slips out. "I've never been good at the whole talking thing."

"Nope." He snorts. "But you've gotten better. Any idea why?"

There's no need to think about my answer.

"Three months ago, I got a wakeup call that I desperately needed. Hurt like hell, but I was reminded about who I am outside of baseball."

Jimmy smiles. "Around the time you signed a new agent, huh?"

We both know it.

"It's sad," I say, shaking my head. "I ended things to make life easier on her, and look at us now."

He hums. "Did you ask her if ending things would make things easier for her, or did you just assume it would?" My silence is answer enough, and he takes my hand. "You were drowning and didn't want to take her down with you. It's noble, but Shay has spent every day since you left trying to hide how she felt. Trying to forget you. That's why I was shocked when she became your agent. But seeing you together reminded me why you two worked so well."

We never talked much about Shay, but Jimmy knew how I felt about her. Even before we decided to try for more, he knew I had fallen in love with my best friend's best friend.

"Why?"

"Because that loyal woman was always going to have your back, even when you pushed her away. She's stubborn in the best way."

I'm about to ask him how to get her back when the door opens.

"C.C.!"

Her shriek shatters my heart, and I drop to my knees and open my arms for my little sister. Violet slams into me, and even though my head throbs from the impact, I focus on her tears soaking through my shirt.

"Don't cry, little. Look!" I pull back so she can see my whole face. "I'm barely even hurt. Just a little bruise, but I'm totally fine."

"Don't lie to me!" she snaps. "I watched you get hit!"

I trace a finger over her tear-streaked cheeks. It's clear she cried all the way here, and the worry makes her look far older than eight.

Grabbing her shoulders, I smile. "I promise, Vi. I'm really okay. No concussion. And I get to sleep at the house, so you can watch over me all night. We can have a sleepover in the living room."

After a few minutes of reassurance and promises, Violet takes Jimmy's extended hand so I can talk to the woman with red-rimmed eyes.

Shay studies me as if I'm a ghost as I meet her in the middle of the room. Slowly, she lifts her hand to the side of my face, and I sigh into her touch. Since being carried off the field, my temple has pulsed incessantly, but with her fingers on it, the spot dulls to a minor ache.

"Are you okay?" she whispers. "It's okay if you're not."

Before I can lie, I pause. I've spent my whole life being strong. Hiding behind a smile. Forcing myself to be okay even when I wasn't. But this woman reminds me that having emotions isn't a weakness. I got hit in the head with a baseball. I could've lost my life and everyone I care about.

So I let myself not be okay in front of her.

"No." My voice trembles, cracking under the weight of my honesty, but she doesn't flinch or turn away. Not even as the tears start to fall. "For a moment, I didn't know what was going to happen. I kept going in and out, watching Isla and Rio rush around me. I was just lying there, hoping I would get to talk to my mom and Violet one more time. Tell Mallory and Kenneth how much I love them. Promise Adri and Jo that I'll make their next graduation parties." I shake my head. "I didn't know if I'd ever see you again. I didn't know if I'd ever get the chance to feel this, *feel you,* again, Shay. I thought I had lost you all over again."

Shaky fingers swipe under my eyes. "You didn't lose me. I'm right here, Cade. And I'm not going anywhere. I don't know what I would've done if—" A sob cuts her off, but she doesn't need to finish the sentence.

Professionalism be damned.

I pull her to me, and she doesn't hesitate to throw her arms around my shoulders. It doesn't matter that Violet and Jimmy are watching us hold each other. Or that Rio's now standing by the door. Nothing matters right now except for this.

"You're safe," she breathes into my chest. "You're okay, Cade."

I close my eyes. "I'm much better now."

CHAPTER THIRTY-FOUR

THERE ARE MANY TWO-WORD phrases that irritate me. Low battery. Road closed. Monday morning.

But for some reason, on this random Wednesday evening, I'm up in arms about the annual Permian BBQ flyer Winston sent out. What should be a fun way to celebrate finding out who will receive the promotion has now become my worst nightmare.

Partners allowed.

Winston's wife will be there, according to their enthusiastic RSVP. Andy is bringing Henrietta. Even Trevor is bringing someone. I could always bring one of the girls, but that's not the point.

I slam my laptop closed and push it aside. Being angry about being alone is pointless. In one week, I'll hopefully be leaving the BBQ with a promotion that'll come with a career jump and the respect of my peers. It's what I gave up soccer for. The reason I missed so many girls' nights. The fuel that kept my heart on lockdown. In a battle of work and everything else, work has always won without a fight.

Yet I can't stop thinking about him.

"Hey, Agent Shay."

It's late enough for me to wonder if I'm hallucinating, but the words and the person in my doorway seem too real. I didn't hear anyone enter Slim Jim Batting, but that's what I get for blasting Vivaldi.

I yank my headphones out. "What are you doing here?"

Cade makes no effort to enter the room. "Can we talk?"

The desk is a disaster, covered in paperwork I was working on before receiving the BBQ invitation, but I gesture at the empty plastic chair.

"Is everything okay? How's your head?"

Dark purple blooms across his temple and down to his cheek. After being cleared during re-evaluation, he played in last night's game. Still, every time he stepped onto the field, I chewed my fingers until they were raw. Three days have passed since my heart shattered at the possibility of losing Cade again.

I still hear the sound of the ball hitting his helmet.

His fingers fly to the spot I'm staring at. "Better today. Been icing it off and on." Dropping his eyes, he studies the mess. "Looks like you could use a distraction. How about a penny for your thoughts?"

I'd play, but I don't know where to start. Between work and Cade, I'm a mess.

If I knew my feelings for him would return, I wouldn't have agreed to be his agent. But if I hadn't said yes, who knows if we would be here right now. Him telling me things in confidence, feeling safe enough to show me real emotion, and not being afraid I'll see him exactly as he is.

Being friends with Cade was special. Moving to friends with benefits was exciting. Trying for more was scary.

But this time around, falling for him seems safe.

I dig my elbows into the desk. "How about a penny for *your* thoughts?"

Cade's persistent look sharpens. "It'll take more than a single penny to explain the things in my head right now."

Same here.

"How about we play our game instead?" he asks. "What do you say, rule breaker?"

Rolling my eyes, I agree. "Fine. What are the odds you'll leave so I can finish my work in peace?"

"That's not nice, but if we say it at the same time, I'll leave you alone to drown in paperwork." His smile tilts as he lifts his fist. "On three." *One, two, three.*

"Seven!" I shout at the same time he says "One!"

Rolling my eyes, I lean back in my seat. "You know I never call the number one, so that's practically cheating."

"Is it cheating? Or do I know you better than you wish I did?"

"Both," I say, not even trying to hide my smile. "Your turn."

Cade scans the dreary office as if looking for inspiration. My little spot at Slim Jim Batting isn't as fancy as Permian's building. The desk creaks every time I lean against it, and the chairs are plastic, but it's infinitely more comfortable than Permian has ever been.

His eyes stop roaming. "What are the odds you tell me your first impression of me?"

"That seems like a waste of a turn, but whatever," I say, holding up my fist. "On three."

One, two, three.

The number five coming out of his mouth at the same time it leaves mine is not ideal.

Cade raises his arms. "Yes! I've been waiting five years to hear this."

Taking a deep breath, I think back to the day I met Cade. I remember it like it was yesterday. "You were sitting on the floor in the study room with your back to me. It sucked because I wanted to not like you, but without even seeing your face, you changed my mind. I listened to the way you talked to Mallory and Kenneth. Your patient, brotherly tone told me you had a little sibling. Likely a sister, based on the Hello Kitty Band-Aid on your elbow. Your laugh was light in a way that didn't seem forced or trained. And your shoulders didn't slump. Confident, but not in a prideful way like a lot of the guys on campus." The sparkly wrist chain attached to my phone glitters in the dim light. "My first impression of you, Cade Owens, was awe."

His jaw goes slack. I know I went overboard with my answer, but he has been so honest with me, I thought it was time I returned the favor.

Checking the clock, I start gathering my stuff. "It's getting late. We should call it—"

"What are the odds you want to be with me?"

The file in my hand falls, landing on my foot. "What?"

"Just indulge me for a moment." He's on his feet before I can say no, rounding the desk and dropping onto his knees in front of me. "Answer one question for me."

I stare down at him. "Okay?"

"Are you happy with your life?"

The question slaps me across the face. "What do you mean?"

"I'm asking if you're happy, Shay. Do you feel fulfilled?"

"Why wouldn't I be?" My voice goes thin at the answer I've repeated so many times in my head. "I'm on track to have everything I want in my career."

He chuckles. "That's not what I'm asking you. Do you wake up in the morning and feel like your life couldn't get any better? Do you feel like you're living the life you want? Do you feel like there's anything missing?"

Closing my eyes, I take a deep breath. Achievement is what has driven me through my entire life. Happiness was fleeting, but success was forever. I assumed I'd be happy with success.

Until now.

My system has always worked. I followed the rules, studied hard, and fought for a great position at Permian. I keep things moving. I keep things sharp. I keep things successful. It's kind of my thing.

But as I debate his question, the machine in my head kicks on, and the list begins to form. Every win I've accomplished flashes before my eyes. From this angle, the success looks more like armor rather than joy as I face the endless battle.

None of it sounds like happiness. It sounds like running.

Then I think about Cade and the way his voice softens when he calls me Agent Shay, even though he wants to say Shay baby. About how honored I felt when dropped his impenetrable shield and confided in me for the first time. About the way he held on to me in that tiny training room after being hit by a baseball. About how this whole terrifying, beautiful partnership has split something open in me that I can't tape shut anymore.

"I don't know if I am," I whisper. The words taste raw in my mouth. "I honestly thought happiness was what I've been chasing through career achievements this whole time."

Suddenly, the truth claws up through my ribs, too big to hold anymore. I've known it since the moment he let me in.

"But I know this." My voice breaks. "I've been happier in the last three months than I've been in years. Pretty much since the day you walked into Permian."

There. It's out. Shaky and unvarnished, but real.

"Then let's start there." The chair screeches as he drags it across the floor and presses his chest against my knee. "Tell me about the last three months. Every single part that made you happy."

I'm hit with a wave of memories.

"I've spent more time with the girls in the last three months than I have in over a year." Cade's smile encourages me to continue. "I was so close to skipping my graduation party because Trevor gave me a mountain of work, but I'm so glad I went. Jo taught me how to golf, and I'm going to miss her so much when she leaves for med school. Adri went to a baseball game with me and made sure I kept my head up the entire time. Mallory's my literal soulmate, always picking up every phone call, no matter what time."

"You have great friends," he says, squeezing my knee. "What else?"

"I made a friend at work. My first one ever."

Cade's eyes sparkle. "I've only talked to Andy a few times, but knowing you have someone at work who has your back makes me feel better." His throat bobs as he leans in closer. "Anything else?"

If I'm going to do this, I have to put it all out there right now.

"We fixed things." I pause. "For so long, I tried to push you away, but I can't keep pretending that you don't make me happy. I think we deserve another chance."

With eyes full of desperate hope, his hands find mine. "What does that mean, Agent Shay?"

"That I don't want to be your agent anymore. I want to be yours."

Delicate kisses are pressed to my knuckles. "You trust me?"

"With every piece of me."

Our pinkies entwine, yet he makes no move. "I need to know before I kiss you. This isn't just getting me out of your system, right?"

I laugh. "I don't think I could get you out of my system if I tried."

He leans in until our noses brush. "I can't tell you how long I've waited to hear you say those words, Shay baby."

There's nothing rushed or hurried about the way he kisses me, cupping my face as if he's trying to make sure I'm real. It's the sweetest kind of relief. Maybe it's because we know this won't be like our last kiss, stolen and desperate while pressed against a hotel door.

I choose this.

I choose him.

"Forever," he mumbles against my lips. "You're wondering how long we can do this."

"What are the odds of that?"

"There's no need to play the game because I'm not letting you go. I'll never make that mistake again." He stands and takes a step back. "Now get on the desk and let me show you how much I missed you."

My eyes fly to the door. "Here? At the batting cages?"

Sweet and precious Cade has left the building, his eyes dark and hooded as he steps closer. "Why not?"

Energy thrums through me. I know all too well how proficient Cade's tongue is, so against my better judgement, I swipe everything on my desk aside and press my ass against the edge.

With a hand tangled in my braids and the other guiding me onto the desk, I feel like I'm having a vivid daydream. But when cold air hits my hips and my leggings are eased down, I'm jolted back into the moment.

This is happening.

Deft fingers drag along the edge of my cotton thong, tugging the thin fabric. He hisses as one finger dips beneath the waistband, dangerously close to my clit.

"Fuck. I missed you. I missed *this*," he mumbles against my calf. "Are you sure you're okay with this? Being with me. Telling Trev—"

"Don't you dare say his name while your fingers are so close to me." Sitting up, I grip the front of his shirt and pull his face to mine. "And yes to everything, Cade. I've never been more sure."

"Me either." His lips brush against mine. "Lean back and relax."

I do as he says, but I don't lie all the way back. This is the first time I've seen Cade on his knees in front of me like this in years. I'm going to soak up every second.

Soft kisses trail up my legs, starting at my ankles. By the time he reaches my knees, they've become nips and nibbles, mapping a path to where I need him most. My thighs tremble, desperate to wrap around him, but when he presses his lips against my clit, I sit up and scoot back.

Cade halts instantly. "I'm sorry, Shay. We should stop. There's no need to rush this. Let's just go—"

"No." I shake my head, feeling embarrassed. "That's not it."

How do I tell him I haven't been touched by a single person since him? I'd love to blame it on the fact that I was too busy with work, but that wasn't the problem; it was the fact that I couldn't stop thinking about him. Their laugh wasn't as light. Their heart not as kind.

Bowing my head, I look away. "It's been a long time since I've done this. I haven't been with anyone else."

A groan rips from his throat, wrecked and raw as something breaks inside him. "Look at me, baby. Neither have I." He lifts my chin and places a kiss on each cheek. "Nobody was you. Nobody ever could be. Tell me it was the same for you."

My lips lift. "It's you, Cade. It's got to be you."

"And you for me."

That sets it off like a fire. No more words are needed after a confession like that.

His hands are tender against my face, and it takes no time at all to find our groove. A moan of approval slips from him when his tongue sweeps against mine. His hands are everywhere, my waist, my thighs, my ass. It's as if he can't decide where to touch first, but I'm not going anywhere. We've waited so long for this. And now we can't seem to get close enough.

I spent so long pretending I was happy without him.

Now there's no more pretending.

"I never gave up hope," he whispers, dragging my hips to the edge of the desk. "Of being with you again. Kissing you. Being yours. I'm so glad I didn't stop believing."

Drifting lower, his lips sweep across my throat, nibbling my collarbone, dragging along my stomach over my T-shirt. Each touch feels like a live wire. The string of fabric covering me is off before I can ask him to hurry, tossed across the room, where my leggings lie in a heap.

"You're so goddamn beautiful, Shay." Awe pitches his voice as his gaze rakes over me, hungry and reverent at the same time. My thighs fall open, pressed apart by his hands. His eyes flick up to me one last time. Checking in on me. He has always been good at that.

"I'm great," I pant out. "You've got me?"

"I've always got you," he promises.

And then he's there. The first sweep of his tongue is slow and deliberate, and my hips jolt off the desk without permission as I'm flooded with pleasure and things I had forgotten existed. Nobody and nothing could ever top this, and we both know it. The broken sound that leaves my throat would be embarrassing if it weren't Cade.

This man knows my body better than I do.

"Yeah, baby," Cade groans, his thumb worshipping my clit. "That's it. Let me hear you."

He hums in approval at my throaty gasp, the sound vibrating against my core. The room starts to spin as he takes his time with me. His tongue moves with maddening patience, like he's trying to memorize every reaction. As if he has waited years for this moment and he refuses to not savor every second.

Then he slips a finger inside.

"Yes," I somehow manage to get out. "More. *Please*. I need more."

His smile is all heat and tenderness as he looks up at me. Too damn sweet, considering what he's doing to me with his fingers and tongue.

"For you? I'd do anything."

My nipples harden as another finger slides into me. I reach under my shirt and pinch them between my fingers, and his eyes narrow as he watches me with what looks like jealousy in the almost-black color.

"You want to see?" I ask, but I don't wait for an answer. Lifting my shirt, he gets a perfect view of the fact that there's no bra.

"When I finally get my hands on you, I may not survive." The tightness in his voice pulls at the strings in my belly. "It should be illegal to be this perfect."

The way his voice breaks around the words, I know his control is slipping. That, along with the way his fingers are picking up speed, hitting deeper than before, tells me everything. He's going to break, and I'm right behind him.

"I know, baby. I feel you tightening around me. And while I plan to kiss those lips for the rest of my life, right now, I need you to fall apart on my tongue. Can you do that for me?"

My fingers tangle in his locs as I teeter closer to the edge, gasping his name as he goes back to work. Tongue flicking harder. Fingers thrusting deeper inside me. He knows exactly what I need in order to finish, and with one last lap of his tongue and flick to my clit, I come undone.

Right on his tongue, like he asked.

I don't move. I can't. Cade is lying on top of me as we try to catch our breath.

"That was . . ." I start, trailing off.

"Great? Life-altering? Marriage material?"

A laugh rushes out of me as he stands. "All three."

When he turns around, his smile doesn't quite reach his eyes, and I spot that familiar knot of worry between his brows. "So, you don't regret it?"

I would get up, but my legs are too shaky. Instead, I curl my finger at him until he moves back to me. Gripping his shirt, I pull him into a kiss that's part promise, part surrender. My heart is his.

Always has been.

"Not even a little bit," I say. "Never will."

"That's what I hoped you would say because same here." He pulls me off the desk, and I curl myself into his chest. "Let's get you dressed and go home, baby."

I look up at him. "Yeah. Let's go home."

Not one moment is silent or awkward as Cade leans down to kiss me, gathers my discarded clothes, helps me slip them back on, and pulls me back into his arms once I'm fully dressed. It's as if we can't get enough.

As we step into the night, neither of us says it. We don't need to.

We're already home.

CHAPTER THIRTY-FIVE

"Ho-ly shit, Turner."

If my head weren't already sore from the stress of the last twelve hours, I'd probably bang it against my desk. Instead, I pluck the thick, dark hairs that seemingly appeared on my chin overnight as I came up with a game plan for how to move forward now that I'm officially with Cade.

"Really, Andy? I bare my soul to you, and that's all you have to say?"

Finally, his incessant pacing across my office stops, but he's rubbing his temples like the sides of a genie's bottle. "Sorry, but holy shit. I just found out that you and Cade Owens, your client, were friends in college. You share a best friend. And then after three years of friendship, you were close to dating but he didn't come back during the offseason, leaving you heartbroken. I feel like *holy shit* is the only reasonable response!"

Telling the whole story probably wasn't necessary, but I'd needed to tell someone I trust.

"I never said I was heartbroken," I grumble.

Andy gives me look that calls me a liar in three different languages. "And you had no clue he requested you to be his agent until you heard it in the meeting in front of everyone, but you felt like you had to say yes because Trevor was out for blood."

A text from Delilah chimes on my phone as I say, "That's correct."

"And, now you want to be with him, which means?"

"I have to tell Trevor." I swallow hard. "Today."

"Why?"

My nose wrinkles. "Why what?"

"Why do you have to tell him?" He moves to the tiny window that overlooks the parking lot and presses his fist against it. "It's admirable as hell that you want to, but you know what he's going to say. He's going to be a total dick about it."

"I know, but it's something I have to do. It wasn't a one-night stand, Andy." I'm lost in the memories of last night. The promises. The care. The certainty. "If I want to do this the right way, I need to be upfront and honest. Even if it hurts."

His skepticism doesn't wane. "I get it, but I know how much you care about your job."

"I do." I smile. "I always will. I'll still be an agent, and I'll still have my clients, but I'm doing what makes me happy. Being with Cade makes me happy."

That seems to break through Andy's worry. His shoulders finally fall as he sinks into the plush seat across from me. "Wow. I've never heard you use the h-word in the office before."

Orange and pink beads roll beneath my fingers as I play with the wrist strap from Cade. The happiness I get from success will forever be different from the happiness I get from hanging out with The Quartet, taking a bubble bath, and spending time with Cade. I haven't been this happy in years, even knowing the crap that's going to follow the announcement.

Andy sighs. "I guess I'm just frustrated for you because it's not fair. Men date their clients all the time in sports, music, and television. Hell, Winston married his client, and they have four kids now."

"Women don't get that kind of grace."

"Are you still going to be his agent?"

I shake my head. "I don't want to be his girlfriend and make contract decisions for him. I may not have breached the code of ethics yet, but that totally would."

He snorts. "Once again. Men do it."

He's right, but the decision has already been made, and I have to be okay with the fact that not everybody will be happy. I preach to my clients about prioritizing themselves and their happiness but never take my own advice. Work has dominated my life for long enough; it's time to add some space for the things that bring me joy.

Andy reaches across the desk and pats my hand. We haven't been friends for long, but the moment I walked into my office this morning, I dialed his desk phone.

"Well, I'm glad you're happy, Shay. You deserve that." His smile droops. "But are you willing to pass Cade off to Trevor? I can't imagine he'll be good to him like you are."

"Actually, that's the other thing I want to talk to you about." I reach down into my bag and pull out a manilla folder. Instead of sleeping beside Cade, I worked on this all night. "Trevor won't be Cade's agent. I wouldn't do that to him."

"Damn." His eyes blow wide. "Then who?"

I spread the contents of the folder out. "You."

"Me?" he sputters, eyes flying to the fine print.

"The contract between us can be terminated as long as there's someone who agrees to take over, and I'm choosing you." I wring my hands. When I told Cade my idea, I thought he was going to cry happy tears. I want him to know I'm serious about this. About us. "You've met him before, and out of everyone in the office, he'd pick you. You're the only person I trust with Cade's future."

Misty eyes meet mine. "Even after I was the world's worst coworker?"

"We're friends now, Andy." I laugh. "So, what do you say?"

After a beat, he laughs too. "I say hell yeah! I'd be honored to represent your boyfriend, Turner." His eyes flick to the door. "So, when are you telling Trevor?"

I check the clock and sigh. "Right now."

"What is so important that you had to stop me? Tee time is an hour."

Trevor pouts as he falls into his seat. Although I wish I had been able to catch him in a better mood, he has never been happy with me. And after this meeting, he probably never will.

"I'll keep it short," I promise. "I just need to run something by you."

With a grunt, he waves a hand at me. "Get going then."

Taking a deep breath, I prepare myself for the worst possible outcome. Sure, I may not get fired for this, considering it's not against my contract, but I know things will change once these words are spoken into existence. Agents may not take me seriously, players may think they'll get lucky if they sign with me, partners might not trust me, and any morsel of respect I've gained over the past year and a half might swirl right down the drain.

I'll be tying myself to Cade, but I don't have a single regret.

"I have a personal relationship with Cade Owens. It's brand new, as of yesterday, and I wanted to let you know immediately. I didn't want you finding out from someone else."

As if he's taken ten espresso shots, Trevor's eyes go wide. "What?"

He knows what I said, so I continue. "Starting today, Andy will be Cade's agent." I pull the signed contract from under my arm and slide it across the clutter. "The agent switch request has already been signed by Andy. He'll speak with Cade today—"

"You've got to be kidding me," he seethes.

I grit my teeth. "If there's nothing else to discuss—"

"I fucking knew it!" He bolts out of his chair, sending it skating against the floor behind him. "How dare you? You're going to ruin everything that Permian has worked so hard to build so you can date a client? Don't you ever wonder why you're the only woman here? It's because women can't be trusted around men. Let alone *professional* athletes. That's the only reason a woman would ever work in sports."

My body recoils. "That's like saying the only reason men become gynecologists is to look at women's privates."

He shrugs. "I believe that too."

Fuck, I hate this man.

"You've worked with enough athletes to know this is a bad idea, Turner. He could have any woman he wants, and he's going to choose his *agent*? Please make that make sense!"

I cross my arms. "You don't know Cade."

"I do know the golden b—"

"Stop calling him that!"

Trevor's grin continues to grow. "What happens when he gets traded to another state? Since you're so dedicated to your clients here, you won't follow him. Do you think he won't find someone who's willing to chase him forever?"

This is going even worse than I thought it would.

Before I can find a respectful way to tell him to shut the fuck up, the door opens behind me. When Trevor's smile turns saccharine, I know exactly who is entering the office.

"Everything alright in here?" Winston asks.

I try to figure out a response, but Trevor beats me to the punch.

"Turner's in a romantic relationship with Cade Owens. Andy has been chosen to take over his representation, and the papers were signed without any input from me, their supervisor."

A surprised cough flies out of Winston. "Is that true, Turner?"

There's still time to backtrack. I could act like I don't know what Trevor's talking about and return to my normal *all work, no play* life. Cade would be hurt, but he would be okay. He always is. Trevor's right.

Hold on. Trevor is never right. Never has been. Never will be.

Squaring my shoulders, I infuse myself with confidence. "Yes. It started yesterday, and I immediately contacted Andy to ask him to take over. It's not against my contract to date a client, but I don't want to mix business and relationships. In the spirit of honesty, I came to tell Trevor before he heard from anywhere else."

Winston's eyes bounce between us. After a long beat, they land on me, and I get the surprise of a lifetime. The CEO's lips split into a wide smile as he steps deeper into the office with his arms raised.

"Turner! That's splendid! Oh, look at you!"

Trevor gawks at him. "Splendid? She's dating a client!"

Winston shrugs. "It's not against her contract, *and* he's not her client anymore. Good for Andy! I've been waiting for him to get more clients on his roster. He'll do great with Cade."

"But—"

"But nothing," Winston cuts him off. "Does that mean you're bringing Cade to the company BBQ? I have a feeling he's good at cornhole with that baseball arm."

I nod, dumbfounded. "I'd love to, but is it okay?"

"Why wouldn't it be? Correct me if I'm wrong"—he nudges my shoulder—"but I married my client, and it worked out beautifully. Got the kids, the house, and the life I wanted."

Trevor makes a disgruntled noise, but when Winston looks at him, he reverts back to his fake smile. "Great. Glad everyone's *happy*. I need to get going."

Winston, king of not being able to read a room, wishes him luck at the golf course and leads me out of the office. Even as we march down the hallway, I don't stop feeling the eyes on my back.

CHAPTER THIRTY-SIX

SECOND CHANCES DON'T COME around often, so I'm making sure our do-over is special.

"Damn! Where's the fire, rookie?" Dawson grips my shoulders to stop me from barreling past him and out of the clubhouse. After tonight's win, everyone looks like half-dead zombies. Except for me. I feel like I could run a marathon.

"Sorry. Kind of excited." I fidget with the buttons on my shirt. "Have you seen Shay?"

In a fatherly way, he smooths my collar. "With Rosie and Luke. Ro said she has never met a woman who loves baseball like Shay. Never took her eyes off the field."

Shay has watched me play more times than either of us can count. First as my friend with the potential to be more. Then as my agent, which changed my life for the better. I'm sure this new title, my girlfriend, is the most special though.

"How have things been since she told her boss?" he asks as we head down the hall to the family room.

I wish I had an answer for him. The last four days with Shay have been a dream for me. Pressing a kiss to her forehead before we crawl out of bed in the morning. Brushing our teeth side by side. Waving goodbye as we head to work. Coming home at the end of the day to find her sitting on the couch, working her ass off. Putting together her dining table as she paces across the house on the phone with clients. Drawing her a bath after she finally closes her computer for the night. Her laugh vibrating through me as I drag her away before she can answer one more email.

But I'm not the one in a weird position.

"She's taking it like a professional, but I know it's hurting her," I say.

Trevor was more upset than she expected, but the tense phone call I overheard last night wasn't with him. Shay's mother called in the middle of a movie, and while I couldn't hear her, I heard Shay loud and clear.

I don't know, Mom . . . Impulsive? . . . No, this is what I want . . . I know it goes against . . . I don't know what to say . . .

Outside the family lounge, I peer through the small glass window.

"I hate that she's going to deal with so much stupidity because she's dating me. From her boss. Social media." I sigh. "She's going to bleed for this. I'm not, which isn't fair because we're both in this relationship. I'm happy, the happiest I've ever been, but I know she's just waiting for the other shoe to drop." My heart stutters as I catch a glimpse of pink in the room. "That's what kills me."

After a long look, Dawson bonks the top of my head like a whack-a-mole game. "You're right. It's not fair, but Shay will stand tall like always. And you'll be right beside her."

"I will be," I vow, rubbing my head. "For every damn step."

Whatever comes next, she won't face it alone.

The moment the door swings open, I'm beelining for the woman in pink who has my heart in her hands. I fold myself around her, lips finding her neck, and I bury myself there, wishing I could stay in her jasmine-scented safety forever.

"Well," a chipper voice titters, "can't say I'm surprised."

Pulling my head from her collarbone, I recoil at the sight of the woman in front of me. There's a reporter talking to my Shay while I drape myself all over her.

Way to go, Cade.

I paste on a smile. "Summer. Nice to see you again."

Royal blue eyes shine at being remembered. "Andy Walker seems like a good choice as your new agent, though he'll never be my favorite like this one." She jams a crooked thumb in Shay's direction. "Since the news broke that you two are no longer working together, I was asking Shay if you two were officially a couple or taking it slow."

"And what did she say?" I ask, looking down at Shay.

Espresso-colored eyes roll. "I didn't say anything. I was cut off."

I say I don't want to make her life any harder, then I go and directly throw her into the fire with a reporter. On autopilot, I shift into a more professional stance, but steady fingers catch my elbow and draw me closer until our arms are touching. When our pinkies hook, the tension in my shoulders unravel.

Summer slips her notepad into her tote and smiles. "To be honest, I was rooting for you two the whole time. But no matter what happens, Shay, remember that you've got people on your side. You don't owe *anyone* an apology for being happy."

I feel Shay's gasp more than I hear it. She says the sly comments about her quitting to become a WAG don't bother her, but I don't see how that's possible. Her job is everything to her.

"I know." Shay's voice is soft but strong. "But it's nice to hear after the past few days, so thank you." Then she pulls Summer into a hug.

This conversation has done more than Summer will ever know.

Stepping back, Summer blushes. "I'm planning a series on badass female agents, so I'll be reaching out to you for an interview! Keep kicking ass, Shay! And support my girl, Cade. I'm counting on you!"

With a quick goodbye, Summer leaves the room.

The moment she's gone, I take a half step away from Shay. "Sorry you had to spend the first half of our date watching me play baseball." I swallow hard. "And I'm sorry if being with me is making your life har—"

My words are garbled as she grips the front of my shirt and slams our lips together in the crowded room.

"I made my decision, Cade, and if that means dealing with shitty people, then so be it. I'm not apologizing for being happy." Then she pulls a pink sticky note out of her back pocket and waves it in my face. "Great game, by the way. I wrote you a *really* important message."

Nice ass #8

A laugh bursts out of me. "I see what was important tonight."

"You in baseball pants?" She presses a kiss to her fingertips. "Chef's kiss. Now, about the second half of this date."

Hooking my arm over her shoulders, I lead her to the exit.

Clear Lake University isn't a prime date location, but we're back where it all started.

The lake that runs through campus sparkles like a black mirror, edged in the silver glow of the moon. Considering it's half past eleven, my favorite town is asleep as we sit on a slope of grass. The first week of August has been unreasonably warm, but the breeze is cool against my skin.

Still, I didn't bring us out here to just sit.

Even though we're back together, I'll never forget the reasons we broke the first time. I know what I did. I know what I didn't say. I know what I can't afford to screw up again.

So I came prepared.

"You know I love campus, but please tell me we aren't here to swim."

"No way." I laugh. "We aren't like Mallory and Kenneth. I've got something else planned for us." Reaching behind me, I grab the picnic basket, turn to face her, and place it between us. "Open it whenever you're ready."

She pulls out two bottles of water, a bag of dark chocolate chips, two pens, and two stacks of pink sticky notes.

"Are we having a BYOB night?"

"Sort of." I reach for a pen. "It's still Bring Your Own Breakdown, but not about baseball. Normally, we'd break down the highs and lows of each game, but tonight, we're going to talk about how to not break *us*."

Her body stills. There's no teasing smile. No laugh. She holds the sticky notes in her palm like they're made of glass.

"We're going to break down . . . us?"

"Yeah." I lean forward and brush a loose braid behind her ear. "I want to do it right this time. I can't lose you again, Shay."

If I have one chance to get us on the right track, this is the way to do it. Blending our past and present to make something even better.

"BYOB coming full circle?" She gives a small, sure nod. "It's perfect."

After setting up, I reach into my pocket and grab the rules I wrote on an index card last night once she went to bed. Hours passed before I figured out what I wanted to emphasize and finally narrowed it down to three sections.

"First," I say, tapping the top line, "we list four things we didn't do right last time, and then we break them down."

She places the pen cap between her lips in deep thought, but my answers come easily. They're things I've regretted every single day since things ended. Each sentence feels like a punch to the gut, but I manage to get them all out there.

Never came home

Didn't tell you what was going on in my head

Was afraid to show you I wasn't as golden as I was expected to be

Pulled away because I was struggling and thought it would be easier for you

I take a moment to study Shay as she writes. It's not surprising she found a way to mix pink and navy. A light pink ribbed tank clings to her in all the ways I'm trying not to think about right at this moment, with my ridiculously oversized navy flannel falling off her shoulders.

Just looking at her calms my racing heart better than deep breathing ever has.

Placing the notes facedown between us, she looks nervously at my stack. "Switch?"

When I take her notes, I expect to see she wrote what *I* didn't do right, but these are specifically tailored to *her*. Things she didn't do.

Didn't see that you were struggling

Was too afraid to chase after you because I didn't want to hurt anymore

Didn't fight harder for you or us

Didn't tell you I appreciated every part of you. Not just the golden ones

The ache that fills me is impossible to explain, but breaking it down is part of the process.

"I was scared," I admit, dropping my head. "If I showed you how much I was struggling, I thought it would ruin everything. That you wouldn't be happy if you knew the truth. That you'd either leave because it was too much or stay and regret it."

Shay chews on her bottom lip. "I'm sorry I didn't see it. And I should have always made you feel safe with me."

"You were always safe, baby." My voice breaks on the promise. "I didn't know how to believe it at that point. If you couldn't tell, I was an expert at hiding things."

That stupid yet truthful joke seems to do the trick when she laughs. As she gathers our notes, I prepare for the next prompt.

"Four things that we should have said or done," I say.

Within seconds, four sticky notes sit in front of me with my failures.

I should have come home

I should have told you I wasn't okay the moment I realized you were the one for me, which was way before I left

I should have let you see all of me

I should have trusted you. You never gave me a reason not to

Instead of flipping her notes over, Shay reaches out and takes my hand. Each lingering kiss to my knuckles soothes the burn from the four lines I just wrote.

"This is hard," she chokes out. "Incredibly hard, but I'm happy to do this with you, Cade. It'll only make us better for each other. I'm right here with you, okay?"

Rubbing my finger over her CLU ring, I nod. "Right here with you."

There's a brief moment where I hoped this round would be lighter than the first one, but tears sting my eyes as I focus on what she wrote.

I should have paid more attention. The signs were there

I should have stopped worrying about my fears of being hurt by you and realized you were hurting

I should have made it clear you never had to be anything but Cade

I should have fought harder for us instead of pretending I was okay and trying to forget

"I hated pretending I was okay." A tremor cracks her voice. "Everything about losing you sucked, and not knowing what happened between us hurt. But knowing that you were struggling that entire time and I had no idea? I should have been there."

God. My resolve shatters as I take both her hands in mine.

"I pushed you away, Shay baby. I wasn't thinking of us when I did that. I made myself think I was doing it to make your life easier, but I was too scared to tell you the truth. To let you see the parts I felt I had to keep hidden away. And I'm so sorry."

She shakes out of my grip, and I almost panic until she caresses my face with a featherlight touch. "I've known how sorry you are for months now, and I forgave you right then and there at the batting cages. During the silence, I could've made effort to get answers too. It's not just on you." Shay lets out a little laugh. "It's crazy how simple everything could've been if we talked to each other."

"Yeah, but I like the people we are now. We communicate better. There's trust in the messy and awkward moments. Not two people performing for each other." I cover her hands with mine. "We weren't ready then, but we are now. Which leads me to our last prompt for the night. What we're going to do right this time," I say. "Our second chance."

Steady is the only way to describe Shay at this moment. The look in her eyes, the way her hand glides across the pink pieces of paper, and the way she settles me in this moment. And it leaks into me as I fill out mine.

Tell you when I'm struggling

Always tell you the truth. The good. The bad. The ugly

Fight for you. Even if my brain wants to run and hide

Stay. Always stay with you

The moments are finished, we swap, and her promises feel like air in my lungs. And based on the sharp inhale from her, I think the feeling is mutual.

Fight for you. Even if it means putting my heart on the line
Telling you that I want you. Just you. Always
Ask what you need and tell you the truth. Even if it's scary
Stay. No more running

I pull her onto my lap. "You've got me. All of me."

She looks up at me. "And you've got all of me."

Sticky notes flutter in the breeze around us, pink promises against the dark night that surrounds us. I breathe her in as we watch the lake ripple in the quiet, soaking up every bit of our first date.

With her, I feel everything I always wanted to.

Safe. Wanted. Chosen. Like myself.

And this time, together, we will stay.

Shay tapes the last sticky note to my dashboard as I park in her driveway.

The drive was mostly silent, but with my fingers laced with hers, there was no need for anything to be said. This is more than a do-over. It's a new start for two people who are ready to love each other correctly.

I point at the three shadowy figures watching us through the window. "Looks like you'll be up late for your post-date recap."

Shay yawns but doesn't look disappointed. "With Jo leaving for med school tomorrow, we'll probably be up all night. I've known she would eventually have to leave, but I can't believe it's already time for her to go."

"It's going to be really weird without her," I say, opening my door. "But it sucks that I don't get to stay the night with you. I've gotten used to sleeping beside you again."

A soft, drowsy laugh slips out of her as I swing the passenger door open. "In your dreams. No getting lucky on the first date, Cade."

My brows lift, ready to remind her that I ate her pussy until she came on my tongue a few days ago, but she kisses me to shut me up. After believing for so long that I'd never have this again, I can't stop touching her and kissing her and holding her close. I don't want her to slip through my fingers again, and I'll do everything I can to keep that from happening.

A shriek from her cell phone breaches our little bubble, but I just smile. My woman is a brilliant agent who receives calls at all times.

Our first date is no exception.

"I need to take this," she says. "Go on in. I'll be there in a second."

I press a quick kiss to her temple before heading up the driveway, leaving the sound of her professional voice behind me. The door swings open before I can raise my fist to knock.

"Look, guys! He's blushing!" Adri reaches up and pinches my cheek. If it wasn't red before, it is now.

Mallory swats her hand away. "Did she take any work calls?"

"No." I give her a quick hug. "But Holly texted her a million times."

"That's par for the course," Jo adds. "She loves Shay."

The girls try to pull me inside, but I'm too busy following Shay with my eyes as she paces back and forth with her phone pressed to her ear. Her voice is still bright, but even in the dark, I spot the slight slump to her shoulders. The Quartet must see it too, because they rush onto the porch beside me.

After she hangs up, I run down the steps to Shay. Now that I'm up close, the hairs on the back of my neck rise.

"What's wrong?" I ask. "Are you okay?"

Shay's eyes glisten as she takes a deep breath.

"I didn't get Garrett Blane."

CHAPTER THIRTY-SEVEN

POST-DATE RECAPS ARE SUPPOSED to be filled with tequila, laughs, overly-personal stories, and tea—not the drinking kind.

Not trying to figure out where I went wrong.

And twelve hours later, I'm at the company picnic, where I need to wear my best face and act as if I didn't lose the client I poured my heart and soul into over the last three months.

I knew there was a chance I wouldn't land Garrett Blane, but things had felt so promising—golfing, regular check-ins, and answering every question he threw my way. Maybe it was naïve to be so hopeful. He's not the first client I've lost, but somehow, this one cuts deeper.

The fact that he signed with Jon Sweeney was icing on the shit cake. If the world knew what he did to Cade, nobody would ever work with him again.

A cold mist snaps me out of my thoughts.

When I turn around, Cade's hazels are sorrowful, apologizing for more than surprising me with a blast of sunscreen. He hasn't stopped apologizing since leaving me with the girls last night.

I pull myself a little taller. "Make sure you give my shoulders extra love. Too many Black people assume we don't need it, but we can get skin cancer too."

A real smile breaks through when he laughs, and I turn my gaze to Permian's building across the street. This is my second company BBQ, but the first one couldn't have been more different. Last year, I came alone, too ashamed to ask one of the girls to join me, and spent five hours on the edge of the crowd, watching everyone else have fun.

This time, I'm anything but alone. Cade hasn't left my side for more than thirty seconds. I had to beg him to leave to get me a hot dog.

I take a deep breath and let him sun-proof the rest of my body, but my thoughts snag on the words everyone has been telling me. That losing Garrett Blane isn't the end. That it's a detour. That all my hard work will lead to something better down the road.

I want to believe them. I really do. But I'm struggling.

A hand to my shoulder stops my anxious sway. "You okay?"

"I'm great," I lie automatically. Then I remember the promises we made about doing this right and being honest. Even when it stings. "No, I'm not," I admit. "I'm sad, nervous, and need the promotion."

Something eases in his expression at my honesty. "I know, baby. Thank you for telling me." Sitting in front of me, he grips my waist like an anchor. "That promotion is yours. No one's more qualified than you. Nobody compares to you."

It's exactly what I need to hear, but before I can respond, Andy and Henrietta bound over like golden retrievers who heard the world *walk*.

"Stop sitting around, you two! It's time to have some fun!" Andy grins, but it's stretched wider than normal. Everyone's treating me like I'm made of glass today.

That faint flicker of pity in Henrietta's eyes tells me she knows about Garrett too. "Ignore him. He's just excited." She takes his hand. "He wants to ask if you guys want to warm up for the cornhole tournament with us. I need to practice if we're going to make it past the first round."

After promising them I'll be over soon and convincing Cade that I just need a moment alone, they leave me in the shade.

I've come to the conclusion it's not my pride that's hurt. It's my heart. I gave Garrett everything I had. The phone calls and middle-of-the-night texts, meeting his fiancée, and even learning how to golf. Everything I did was preparing me to be the best agent for him, and he went with Jon motherfucking Sweeney.

Loss is part of the job. I signed up for hard times, long nights, exhausting days, constant noes, never-ending travel, and sexist and misogynistic comments—okay, maybe I didn't sign up for that those—but I *really* wanted this client.

Then Mallory's voice echoes in my head, repeating her favorite line.

"Kick them in the dick and keep your head held high."

That seems to do the trick, and I find myself counting down.

Ten. Nine. Eight.

Garrett not signing with me isn't the worst thing in the world.

Seven. Six. Five.

It doesn't mean I won't have a successful career here. They haven't even announced the promotion yet.

Four. Three. Two.

There is a light at the end of the tunnel.

One.

Cade would be proud of me for that optimistic thought. He's been my rock since I got the call. Even though I went inside with The Quartet for a post-date recap, he had pizza delivered for us as I questioned every interaction Garrett and I had.

Did I slip up? Come off as unprofessional at any point? Was he upset that I beat him at golf?

Could it be the fact that I'm dating Cade?

I give my head a quick shake and banish the thought. Whether it's the truth or not, I can't spend my career wondering if my decision to chase happiness bit me in the ass.

My phone buzzes beneath my leg, and I reach for it.

Holly Trent

Here if you need a laugh

Or a cry

I'm a professional crier <3

I snort, send back a pink heart emoji, and reply to my other clients' messages. After Garrett's public announcement this morning, they rallied around me.

All I can do is focus on the future, which is getting that promotion.

"Turner."

The deep voice is booming but kind. Winston.

"Hi," I say as he sinks into the chair beside me. "Great BBQ you planned for us today."

He points at the stunning redhead throwing a frisbee. "Thank the wife for that. And thank you for planning the cornhole tournament with Andy. She's beyond excited to play." The lovey dovey expression on his face morphs into something more serious as he faces me and removes his sunglasses. "I'm sorry about Garrett Blane. I know you put in a lot of effort to get him on the Permian team."

The sorrow in his eyes is too much, and I have to look away. "Thanks, Winston. I'll be okay."

"Of course you will. You're a tenacious one. When I was in your position, there were more losses than I'd like to admit. It's part of the process, so don't let it get you down for too long, okay?" He stands. "Brighter things are coming for you soon, Turner. I'm sure of it."

As he walks away to join his wife, a tiny spike of hope shoots through me. I feel as if we just shared some secret, and I can't lie. It completely boosts my mood.

Now I'm ready to play some cornhole.

"Come on, Andy!" Henrietta bounces up and down beside me. "Sink the damn thing already!"

I wasn't expecting to go against my only work friend and his girlfriend in the championship, but here we are. Andy stares down the board with an intensity I've only ever seen when charcuterie is involved.

The red beanbag leaves his hand and slaps the board, mere inches from the hole.

Opponents or not, Hen grabs my hand. "Great job, babe!" she cheers.

Cade pats Andy's back proudly before refocusing on the task in front of him. It's unnerving to see him like this. This is exactly how he looks when waiting for a pitch or standing between second and third base, and I love having a front-row seat to his composed demeanor. Being neck-in-neck relaxes him.

"It's not fair," Trevor grumbles behind me. "He's a pro at a game that has to do with throwing balls."

He's only pissed because we took him out in the first round.

Trevor has become unbearable since Cade and I started dating. His passive-aggressive comments are relentless, and it makes me want this promotion even more. I can get out from under his thumb *and* work under Greg, who's better than Trevor.

"Shouldn't have bet against him then, Trev," Winston jokes.

The corner of Cade's lip ticks up, the only hint he hears what's going on behind me. Then he pulls his arm back and throws the blue beanbag high in the air.

It soars for what feels like forever before landing directly in the hole and smacking the grass beneath it.

"Woohoo! Pay up, boys," Iris hollers as Trevor, Kyle, and Jonah slap twenty-dollar bills against her palm. "Winnie! Dinner's on me tonight."

Winston's wife is even better than I could've imagined. The former softball phenom would have probably won the whole tournament if it weren't for her husband, who doesn't have an athletic bone in his body.

I rush across the field to meet Cade, and he hoists me into the air, spinning me in circles.

"Nice game, partner. How are you feeling about that win?"

"Damn good. Might have to keep you around, baseball boy." I laugh against his lips, but my attention is stolen by the hoard of khaki shorts moving toward the pavilion, and Winston's encouragement comes to the front of my mind. "Now it's time for another win."

Once in the shade, I grab a water bottle and ease into Cade's sturdy side as Winston takes his spot at the front.

"Gather around everyone," Winston booms. "I know we all came out here for the free food and beer, but we need to talk about work for a bit. Over the last few months, the intermediate agent position has been open. It has been tough, but the senior agents and myself have worked diligently to choose who will best fill the position Levi left behind."

Trevor boos. "Screw him!"

"Agreed, but it's been nice to dive a bit deeper into the Permian's junior agents. I'm so impressed by everyone who submitted their letters of intent. I wish I had multiple positions because choosing one applicant was difficult."

My hand finds Cade's, and he gives it the perfect squeeze. *I'm here.*

"I'd like to announce Permian's new intermediate agent. When I say the name of the individual, please help me give this phenomenal employee the celebration they deserve."

There are only four junior agents, which means there's a twenty-five percent chance the job is mine, but I don't feel deterred by those odds. I've worked my ass off for this position. I have the most clients out of us, and I've given them and Permian every ounce of my blood, sweat, and tears since the moment I got here.

And today, I'll earn their respect.

"Get on up here and accept your promotion!"

I step forward instinctively, but a tight grip on my hand pulls me back. When I look up to see why Cade stopped me, his eyes are full of a desperate kind of grief.

"I'm sorry, Shay," he whispers. "I'm so sorry."

"For?" I ask, but as the question leaves my mouth, I turn and spot Jonah at the front. He looks as if he won the lottery, and even though I want to be upset, I can't help but think of the joy he must be feeling.

The joy I thought I'd get to feel.

I don't flinch when the celebratory bottles of champagne start to pop. They're mostly drowned out by the roar of blood in my ears.

"Shay," Cade tries, but I don't give him the chance.

"I need to go." I step back. "I'm going to run to the restroom."

"Let me go with you. Please, baby."

No. He can't watch what's about to happen.

"It's okay. I'll be back."

I march away from the pavilion without another word. My pace doesn't slow as I make it to the sidewalk, cross the street, burst through the front doors of Permian, and run up four flights of stairs.

Tears threaten to fall as I step into my office, but they vanish at the sight of my laptop still on, sticky notes with plans scattered around, and papers strewn across my desk. I spent the whole morning before the BBQ crafting a new game plan. I'd add Simon Godfrey to my team and keep building my roster.

I've spent so long dedicating all my time and energy to this job.

To Permian.

Nobody's owed a job, but damn, I worked so hard for it.

Instead of crying, I pack everything into my bag. I'm finally going to use some of that paid time off I've been sitting on. I need to breathe in some air that doesn't flow from a Permian Sports Agency vent.

CHAPTER THIRTY-EIGHT

I FEEL USELESS, WHICH isn't a way I've felt before.

"Shay?" I press my forehead to the bathroom door. "Can I come in?"

There's a splash and then a sigh. "Yeah."

Over the last three days, I've spent more time in this little room than any other in the house. The bathtub has always been her sanctuary, and because she's happiest in here, I've been sitting right beside her.

Her body remains still as I swing open the door. White bubbles cling her torso, dark braids spilling over the edge of the porcelain tub. Even with her eyes closed, they flutter restlessly. It's as if she's playing back every second, desperate to pinpoint the exact moment she went wrong to not get Garrett or the promotion.

"You're back already?" she asks without opening her eyes. "I thought you were helping Billie with a catering order all afternoon."

The tile is damp under my bare feet. "She said she didn't need me."

Disbelief wrinkles Shay's nose. "Impossible. Your mother would never decline the presence of her favorite and only son. So why don't you tell me why you're really not there?"

I can't help but laugh at her all-knowing tone as I set the goodie bag by her head. "Mom and I didn't like that I wasn't with you, so I made a call. MalPal and Kent are filling in so I can be here. But I didn't come back empty handed."

An intrigued eye pops open. "I do love a good Billie treat. How many did you eat on the drive?"

"One." But only because Mom made me promise. "The rest of the dark chocolate chip cookies, with extra chocolate chips, are for you."

"God, I love your mother. She's the definition of an angel. I'll text her when I get out of the bath." Shay's lips lift ever so slightly before they straighten again. "You're hovering."

I know I am. It feels like the only thing I can do right now.

"How long did you take off from work?"

Watery eyes stare up at the ceiling. "Two weeks."

According to Andy, Shay has only taken one day off since they started working at Permian. A single sick day. No vacations. No half days for doctor's appointments. No mental health days. No personal errands. If it were under different circumstances, I'd be happy she's finally taking a break, but it only exacerbates my worry.

"Any fun plans? The Pilots leave for Oklahoma tomorrow, but I'll only be gone for three days. Do you need anything before—"

"I'm fine, Cade." With each frustrated kick of her legs, the water shivers, tiny waves racing away from her. "These are my plans: I'm going to sit here in the bathtub until my fingers are wrinkly and I forget about my complete failures."

Since the two blows of bad news, Shay hasn't cried, but her voice carries a permanent tremor.

"You didn't fail, Shay. I know you didn't get the promotion—"

"Or Garrett."

"Or Garrett," I choke out. "But that doesn't mean you failed."

When Jon said there were clients he *needed* to sign, I never would've thought he was talking about Garrett Blane. I almost want to call Garrett stupid for not seeing the red flags, but neither did I. Not until it was too late. Jon is too skilled at looking like the perfect agent.

Little do people know that he's a nightmare in disguise.

I blocked him after receiving his final message.

Jon Sweeney

Tell your girlfriend better luck next time.

"Cade," she exhales, stretching my name like it's two syllables. "Please don't say it's part of the job or the journey to success or that something better will come. It's not just about that. I believed for so long that I'd eventually gain the respect of my coworkers and move up." The heels of her palms dig into her eyes, less rubbing and more crushing. "I appreciate you so much, but I can't handle optimism right now. Not today. Please."

As the guy who has always been able to fix things and keep people happy, it stings, but I know nothing I say right now will repair this for her.

"I'm sorry, baby."

Her hand appears from under the water, soapy and smelling of lavender, and I take it and bring it to my lips.

"Don't be. I did everything I was supposed to do. I courted him to the best of my ability, buckled down and worked harder than ever, went above and beyond to make sure my clients were happy and taken care of, and it—" She sucks in a sharp breath. "It still wasn't enough. *I* wasn't enough."

There are so many things I want to say, but as a man, my experiences are so much different than women's. Especially one in a male-dominated field working in an office that treats her like an outsider rather than a teammate.

If Shay were a man, not only would she have probably gotten Garrett and the promotion, but nobody would've batted an eye when she started dating a client.

"I didn't want to make your life harder," I breathe against her wrist.

She hesitates, then laughs quietly. "You didn't, Cade. If anything, you make it lighter."

"But what if that's why you didn't get the job? Or the promotion? And that argument with your mom?" When her brows scrunch, I try to jog her memory. "After you told Trevor we were together, we had a movie night and she called you. It didn't sound good."

"Oh, that." Her free hand comes above the surface and she waves. "Mom taught me how to keep myself safe, so when I told her I decided to date my ex-client, I expected a blowup." For the first time in three days, she smiles. "It started off rocky, but it ended up being the best conversation we've had in years. I think that was the first time I've ever heard her say she doesn't care about my job. All she wanted to do was make sure that my heart was okay. That I was safe. My happiness and certainty about you comforted her."

Feeling a sense of relief, I squeeze her hand. I know how important those words from her mother must be.

"I'm still sorry this is happening. But I'll be right by your side."

A full bottom lip pushes into a pout. "Until you leave me for three days." The bath drain gurgles as she readjusts and turns to face me. "Thank you for being here. It's just hard. I knew having it all was a myth, but for some reason I thought I could be the exception. It's clear I can't, and I need to come to terms with that."

"No," I say quickly. "You don't need to come to terms with anything because that's bullshit, Shay. What does 'having it all' mean?"

Foamy bubbles cling to her raised shoulder. "I don't know. I've always seen it as the nice-paying job, the nice house and cars that show how hard you've worked."

"But what does it mean to you? Define what 'it all' is to Shaylene Turner. Nobody else."

"It doesn't matter. It's a dream. A myth."

Fighting her on this may not be the smartest idea, but I can't stop.

"It matters to you, Shay, which means it matters. Tell me."

As if all the fight drains from her, she slumps forward and relents. "To me, having it all means being successful *and* happy. I want to be an agent who treats her clients like human beings. I want to get more than three hours of sleep a night and not feel a pit of dread in my stomach every time I step into the office. I want time with my best friends to be a regular part of my life, not a bimonthly occasion that I spend thinking about work." My stomach takes a nosedive when she sits up and holds my gaze, warm and unhurried. "And I want love. As uncontrollable and scary as it is, I want it. I spent so much time avoiding it because I didn't think it could be part of my 'all.' But now you're here and—"

"I do love you, by the way."

Surprise blooms in her features. "You don't have to say it ju—"

"I'm not saying it just because, Shay baby. I've loved you since before I left for California, and it's only grown since then. You don't understand how hard it's been to not let it slip while eating cereal with you in the morning, or on the couch as you mouth every word to your favorite rom-coms, or when I watch you put your heart and soul into your job." I swallow hard. "If it wouldn't have been utterly insane, I would've said it the moment I walked into Permian and saw you standing there by the window."

I do love her. Always have and I always will.

But maybe this wasn't the time to tell her.

Before she can respond, I shake my head. "I'm sorry. You're drowning your sorrows in a bubble bath, and I'm confessing a long-kept secret. I should've said it over a fancy dinner or after a baseball game. Maybe at Slim Jim's, since it's our place—"

"I love you too, you rambling fool."

Without another word, she pulls me into the bathtub with her. It doesn't matter that my clothes are soaked and there are bubbles in my hair, because this is where I'm meant to be. Shay doesn't love me because I'm good at baseball or the golden boy.

She loves me because I'm a rambling idiot who has been in love with her since college and will be for the rest of my life.

CHAPTER THIRTY-NINE

 *Shay*

"Traitors," I spit, pointing at them. "You're all traitors."

It's only day five of my fourteen-day break, and I'm already spiraling. My time was once filled with constant phone calls and texts, endless emails, and running around town, but now, my days are spent in silence and silencing the silence with running bath water or a rom-com that makes me forget how crappy life is.

"Who else was he supposed to call?" Jo plops down by my feet. Medical school doesn't start for another week, so she delayed her move to Tennessee after hearing I didn't get Garrett. "Do you have another group of friends your boyfriend was supposed to call when you've been horizontal for days?"

I glare at her, not sure if I want to hug her or shove her. "Adri's supposed to be the sassy one. Not you."

Jo clicks on a horror film and smirks. "Since when do we have roles?"

"Since forever." Adri plops onto the rug and starts separating the M&M's from the raisins in my trail mix. "First up, we have our fearless leader, Cap. Mallory's our group mom and resident worrywart."

The neon orange fingernail on Mallory's middle finger illuminates her path to the kitchen. "I have anxiety, asshole."

"Potato, potahto," Adri chirps. "Shay's our black-cat workaholic with a secret soft side. I'm the hot fashionista who despises raisins."

"Hot *mess*," I grumble. "And stop wasting my trail mix."

As expected, she ignores me. "And, Jo, you're *usually* the zen one. Until you get stressed. Then you're our baking queen."

Jo shrugs. "Kinda hard to be zen when you're around."

Up until right now, my home has been peaceful—and borderline depressing—since I didn't get the promotion, but with them here, it's pure chaos. Adri tosses a handful of undesirable raisins at Jo, but most of them hit me in the face.

Instead of stopping them, I hand Jo a pillow so she can retaliate.

"Quit it, you two," Mallory hisses, entering the living room with four water bottles. "We're here to comfort our friend. Not fight."

"Okay, Mommy—I mean Cap." Adri giggles, ignoring the evil glare Mallory shoots her. She loves to antagonize her.

Sitting up, I snatch the remote from the coffee table and rid the scary doll from the screen. "That's what I like to hear. So, everyone get comfortable. It's time to watch *Bridesmaids*."

Honey eyes shift to me. "Cader Tot told Kenneth you watched *Bridesmaids* yesterday."

My boyfriend is a lousy snitch. And so is hers.

"And? It's a classic I would watch on repeat if I could. Now come on. I've got popcorn and plenty of peach rings for Adri—"

"No," Mallory says curtly, grabbing her bag. "You've been cooped up here for days, Shaylene. And yes, the house looks nice with all the paint and decorations, but you need to get up and move around. Feel the sun on your skin and the wind in your face."

It takes a lot of effort, but I pull myself upright and gesture comically at my body. Then I walk over to the window and peel open the curtains. And to seal the deal, I twist the fan around to blast me in the face.

"Done and done." After giving her my best smile, I lie back down on the couch. "Now, if you'll excuse me."

Jo winces. "She's more sarcastic than usual. Is it time for plan B?"

"Plan B?" I ask, but nobody answers me.

"Plan B it is. Take your positions, ladies." Standing dutifully, Adri listens to our group mom and makes her way to the back of the couch. Mallory takes a seat by my head and Jo sits beside my feet. An ice-cold hand slips beneath my T-shirt and yanks my sports bra strap. "The girls have some support, so let's get her out like this, Jo. Adri, grab sneakers and a pair of socks from her room."

"Out?" I watch as Adri sprints to my room. "No! I'm having fun here! Let me watch Maya Rudolph and Melissa McCarthy movies in peace!"

"Hell no. We're getting you out of here," Jo says before nodding at Mallory. "Ready. Lift!"

With ease, they lift me off the couch like a sad sack of potatoes. I'm tempted to writhe until they drop me, but hitting the hard floor isn't ideal. Then I remember I'm still wearing the oversized sweatpants and Pilots T-shirt I stole from Cade. And I smell like I've been rotting in it for the last forty-eight hours.

"I can't go out like this!"

"Well, you can't stay inside anymore either," Adri muses. "I've got her shoes and child lock is on! We're good to go."

Suddenly outside, sunlight hits my face and forearms, setting off a full-on vampire meltdown. I'm pretty sure my skin is sizzling like bacon on a hot grill.

"I swear I'll stop fighting if you put me down! Please!"

The three people who claim to love me more than anything ignore me and continue down the sidewalk. Mallory's car, Flintstone, beeps, and Adri jogs around them to open the back door for me.

"Relax, silly. You're going to enjoy this," she promises.

I snarl at her as they toss me into the car, but I've never been happier to be vertical.

Adri and Jo fall onto the seats beside me and squish me in the middle. The tiny space is almost worse than being dragged out of my house in my comfy clothes with zero idea where I'm going.

Adjusting the rearview mirror, Mallory's eyes meet mine. "You guys look cozy back there. How are you feeling, Shay?"

"Like I'd rather be at home," I say, crossing my arms. But I can't lie, the sun on my skin did feel nice after the initial burn went away. Maybe I did need to go outside. "Where are we going? I deserve to know that at least."

She pulls onto the road. "To let out some of that feminine rage."

And now I feel bad for throwing a fit.

I make my way to where my friends are standing in the industrial warehouse, surrounded by metal walls and a buzz of distant crashes. The air smells like dust with a faint tang of cleaning spray that doesn't quite mask the scent of sweat. Overhead, a yellow sign blinks happily, "LET IT OUT."

We're dressed for mass destruction in our coveralls. Mallory looks like an orange traffic cone in hers, struggling to tuck her coils into the helmet. Adri picked a deep red that matches her lipstick. Jo went with burnt orange, mainly because it was the only one left.

I zip my pink coveralls. "A rage room?"

Using the glass as a mirror, Adri wrangles her waist-length curls into a braid. "How better to release rage than breaking a bunch of stuff?"

They kidnapped me for a good reason.

Mallory taps my clear plastic face shield before I can apologize. "You're allowed to be upset and sad and angry. Baths and comfort food are amazing, but I think you need to break some shit and scream. Nice and calm self-care activities don't always fix everything."

If I try to speak, I'm sure I'll start crying.

"*Thank you*," I mouth. "*I love you big.*"

"*I love you bigger*," she mouths back.

"Woah. You four look ready to destroy some stuff." I turn to find a tattooed woman in a denim jumpsuit sliding behind the counter. "I'm Ellen, and I'll be monitoring your rage experience today in Heavy Hitters. Are we celebrating a divorce or breakup today?"

"Neither." Adri grabs my hand. "We're fighting the patriarchy."

"I like the sound of that." Ellen waves us toward a hallway lined with scuffed floor tape. "I'll add a few extra goodies to your room."

Mallory raises her hand like a perfect student. "Can I play music?"

"Sure can. Hook up your phone and close the box. If you're all ready to go, it's all yours."

Ellen gives my shoulders a little push, so I take the lead and open the metal door. Heavy Hitters looks more like an abandoned workshop than a recreational space. Scarred plywood is painted with scathing graffiti about a man named Carl. The ground is littered with twisted metal and shards of glass. In one corner, a battered fridge leans sideways on a wooden pallet. Next to it, a washer and dryer sit like squat, silent opponents. A gleaming car door stands bolted upright on a steel frame, spray-painted with a black heart.

Ellen's voice crackles over the intercom. "You've got ninety minutes. Choose your weapon. And remember, helmets down *before* you swing."

We all turn toward the steel rack bolted to one wall and gasp.

"Holy shit." Jo's already mild voice is muffled behind her face shield.

Full-size sledgehammers and crowbars hang from the rack, heavy and gleaming. Metal pipes are cold and solid, stacked on the ground. A bucket of mallets and hammers sits off to the side, but my eyes are on the aluminum baseball bats floating horizontally on the wall.

But I burst out laughing when "What The Hell" blasts through the speakers and Adri starts dancing like we're at a bar and not a rage room.

"Did you make a feminine rage playlist for today?" I ask Mallory.

With a wide smile, she closes the box. "You know it. We need good music to get through this. It's like five hours, so I'll share it in the group for you to listen to when you get back to work."

Before I start thinking about returning to work, I need to break stuff.

I cock my head at the washing machine. "So . . . I just hit it?"

"Yup, but this is a talk-and-rage activity. Tell us what's going through your head while you break shit to your heart's content."

The metal bat is heavy in my hand. Standing in front of the machine, I rub my gloved finger over the scuffed paint. The control panel is cracked too, with the door half open, like it's smirking at me.

Winding up, I feel my body tense, but it releases when the bat connects with the washing machine. The metal caves in almost instantly, buckling like tinfoil, but it echoes like a car crash.

"Whatcha thinking about?" Adri asks after I get in three good swings.

Heavy breaths fog my visor. "I'm worried these two losses will dictate the rest of my career. What if I never get another good chance like this?"

"Garrett Blane will not dictate your future." Mallory slams the crowbar on top of the microwave. "He was an opportunity, yes, but that doesn't mean he's the last one you'll ever have! You're too damn good at your job for that to happen."

"And that won't be your last promotion opportunity at Permian," Jo reminds me.

A guttural scream rips out of Adri from her corner of the room, swinging a sledgehammer over her head. "Tell us what you want!"

Swing. "I want to be a good agent!" *Swing.* "The best agent to my clients!" *Swing.* "Never letting them down and making sure they always know I'm in their corners." *Swing.*

"Already accomplished!" The noises from Jo's side of the room are deliberate and surgical, each hammer tap landing with precision as she destroys ceramic tiles. "What do you want when you go back to work?"

"I want more respect from my coworkers. I want to be treated like a fellow agent, rather than some stepsister they wish didn't exist."

Mallory's fist blasts through the drywall. "What else do you want?"

"I want to sign a client who people would never expect to work with me! I want to take up space and not care that they don't like me. I want to speak up for myself. Even if Trevor is my boss, I'm tired of taking his shit, as if I haven't worked just as hard to get here. All because I'm a woman!"

"That's my girl!" Mallory hollers. "Kick them in the dick!"

I fling the bat aside and spot the extra dinner plates Ellen gifted us. With every crash of the glass against the wall, I feel a crack inside me start to repair itself.

Cade knew I needed my best friends today. He knew Mallory, Jo, and Adri would do whatever they needed to do to make sure I was not only taken care of, but that I'd feel better by the end of the day.

Life without Garrett and the promotion is hard, but I can't imagine my life without them.

"I love you guys!" I yell over the racket. "So damn much!"

"We love you more!" they shout in unison.

Static crackles overhead, and we all pause to look up at the speaker.

Then Ellen sighs. "Are you guys taking friendship applications?"

CHAPTER FORTY

I'm a bad bitch. You can't kill me.

These wise words from my favorite Vine are the only reason I haven't taken the closest exit and sped back to Clear Lake yet. There are probably more professional mantras I could repeat to hype myself up, but this resonates most with me.

After raging with the girls, I realized I was hiding, and I do *not* hide.

It's time to go back to work.

My phone has been buzzing nonstop since I let my clients know I was back in the office; a mix of disappointment that I ended my "vacation" a week early and excitement that I'm available again.

I may not have gotten Garrett or the promotion, but I have them.

Ernie, Trevor's assistant, pales when I walk through the glass doors. Technically, he's one of Permian's two receptionists, but Trevor keeps him on a tight leash.

"Turner!" His attention darts to the elevator. "You're back early."

Sliding the two boxes of donuts onto the counter between us, I lift my bag higher on my shoulder. "I needed to come back. Is Trevor free right now? I didn't see anything in his calendar when I checked this morning."

He nods, but his expression warns me to steer clear.

Sadly, that's not something I can do.

Instead of taking the elevator, I head to the stairs in hopes I can work off some of this adrenaline. Demanding respect from men usually goes one of two ways: they either apologize and promise to do better, or they get angry and act even worse.

I can already guess which one Trevor will choose.

Stopping by my office to take a breath would be smart, but the mantra I wrote on a pink sticky note is burning a hole in my pocket.

Demand respect. Sign clients. Be happy.

Right as I'm about to lift my hand to knock, I pause and peer through the tiny crack in the door to find Trevor pacing.

"I still can't believe she took a vacation. It's a surprise she's been able to stay in this field this long if she can't handle hearing the word no. Can't imagine she's going to last much longer."

The pause goes on and on for so long, I assume he's on the phone. But that's when a person out of view speaks.

"I probably would've taken time off too. She got two noes in the span of, like, two days. I can't imagine it'll be easy to get over."

Andy. My friend Andy is talking to Trevor about me.

"I didn't know flaunting around the office in little pink outfits equates to working hard." Trevor's laugh is rough, full of hatred that I've never been able to understand.

"Trev, come on. You know she does a lot for Permian. Doesn't she also do work for your clients?"

He scoffs. "She does scut work. I could do it myself."

"But you don't," I mutter under my breath. Eavesdropping on this conversation isn't right, but my feet are stuck to the ground.

"Please cut her some slack when she gets back next week. You know how it feels to lose a client you've worked your ass off for. Especially when you think they're yours. She's going to need support and—"

"Jesus Christ," Trevor shouts. "When did you become her little body-guard? I know you two are friends now, but I didn't think you'd protect her. You're supposed to be on our side."

"There shouldn't be sides! We're supposed to be a team! I've never understood why you treat her like shit even though all she does is cover for you, me, Jonah, and Kyle on a regular basis without complaint. I think you'd agree that she works harder than anybody here if you weren't so against her."

"Oh, I get it." Goosebumps rise along my arms as Trevor's voice pitches, letting out a low chuckle. "I thought you were smart enough to not fall for it, but it looks like she's got you under her spell. Like she did with the golden boy."

"What the fuck, Trevor? You're going too far."

"Going too far? I'm trying to protect this company and everything we've built. Winston may not see it, but I do. She's not meant for this life, no matter what you or anyone else thinks about her! I think she will last one more year before running off into the sunset after her boyfriend. That's why I didn't submit her letter of intent for the promotion."

My vision goes hazy as I press my back against the wall.

Trevor never submitted my letter of intent.

I wasn't even in the running for the promotion.

"You what?" Andy hisses, taking the words from my mouth. "Why the hell didn't you submit it?"

"Why would I?"

As if an explosion has gone off, Andy erupts. "Because she deserved the promotion! Turner actually cares about her clients. She doesn't look at them like a paycheck. They're real people in her eyes, which is way more than I can say about you. She's the first one here in the morning and is the last to leave. She brings those damn donuts you can't live without every Friday. She does *your* job for a fraction of the pay. She has more clients than any junior agent and *still* chases other athletes. There are multiple reasons you should have submitted her letter of intent! And whether you want to admit it or not, you know she would've gotten it if you had."

"C'mon Andy." The cocky edge in Trevor's voice crumbles as his former minion turns on him. "I did what I thought was best. I knew she wasn't fit for the job long before she slept with the golden boy."

"At least she did the honorable thing! She stepped back the moment things got serious and gave him someone who could work with him professionally. But you? How many clients have you slept with and continue to manage? I remember you bragging about, what? Five?"

He what?

"So?" Trevor's shaky laugh is defeated. "Would you really want some-one like her to be your boss?"

"Yes! I'd love for her to be my boss! Jesus, Trevor! Everything you're saying is discrimination!"

I don't even realize that I pushed open the door and stepped into the office until their eyes swing over to me and their jaws drop in horror.

"You never submitted my letter of intent."

Not a question. It's a statement, and he knows at that moment that I heard everything. I see it in the way his perfectly trained smile cracks.

Trevor straightens. "I never said that."

We both look at Andy, and I hope his boldness will continue for a little while longer. That our friendship means something to him too.

My chest releases when he moves to stand beside me and glares at Trevor. "Yes you did, Trevor. It's time to stop lying." When Andy meets my eye, his face crumples. "I'm so sorry, Turner."

"Don't be," I whisper. "I heard everything. Thank you for standing up for me." I turn back to Trevor, who is shaking in his expensive dress shoes. "All I wanted was to work at Permian under some of the best agents, and one of them was you, but you've spent every single day reminding me that I don't belong here. From the moment I walked in, you made it your mission to not give me a chance."

Trevor shakes his head, but I don't let him speak.

"I have given so much to you and Permian to be seen as equal, but I'm starting to realize I will never win in a system that is against me." As I look down, my eyes catch my badge. Smiley Shay who took this photo on the first day of her internship had no idea this is where we'd end up. "I'm going to be a great agent, but I'm sure it won't be at Permian."

I should feel scared, but as the words slip out of my mouth, I can't help but feel relieved.

"I quit."

"You did what?" Holly shrieks.

I asked myself that question a million times on the drive home.

I have no job.

No income.

No references who can help me get another job.

No idea what I'm doing next.

Turning down the volume on my phone, I curl myself into a ball by the front door and force some false bravado into my voice for my former client. I couldn't even make it to the couch. "I overheard something and decided it was time to leave Permian. For good. It may sound impulsive, but it wasn't. It was—"

"A long time coming?" Holly sighs. "I agree. It's about damn time."

I nearly slam my head against the wall. "What?"

"Don't sound so shocked. You do know that I know you pretty well, right?" Holly pauses, and I nod, though she can't see me. "That office drained your bright pink energy that shined so beautifully when I first met you in the Permian bathroom. You never stopped taking care of your clients, but being there dulled you. I hated seeing you work so hard and be treated so poorly."

If anyone else would've said these words to me, I wouldn't have believed them, but Holly was my first client. Even if I haven't broken our professional boundaries to vent about how much I hated working at Permian, I'm not surprised she noticed. We talked daily, our bond like a professional sisterhood.

The tile chills my calves as I stretch my legs out. "Why didn't you say anything earlier?"

"Because you love us. You would've put up with just about anything if it meant you got to be our agent. It was an honorable sacrifice, but I secretly hated it for you."

Tears threaten to fall. "But now I'm not your agent because I quit."

"And I'm positive the reason is plenty enough," she breathes. "I don't need to know specifics to support your decision and know you did the right thing."

Hugging myself, I sniff. "You don't hate me?"

She sniffs too, and I know she's close to tears. "You're like my favorite person, Shay. I could never hate you."

My eyes start to water as I pull the phone from my ear, place it on speaker, and scroll through the texts that have been popping up since I stormed out of Permian. I didn't even go back to my office to grab anything. I left with my head held high.

Andy

> Trevor is spiraling. Proud of you. Here if you need me

I text back a thumbs-up and a pink heart before opening my group message with The Quartet while Holly swears she will never work with the stuck-up assholes in my office.

GOAL GALS

Menace to Society

> Arson is always an option!

Joelly Bean

> Did you slap him? Please tell me you slapped him

Marshmallory

> Heading to Permian. I've always wanted to whoop a grown man's ass, and it looks like today's the day

Joelly Bean

> Come pick me up! I'll record

Menace to Society

> WORLD STARRRRRRR

Swallowing my laugh, I tune back in to Holly. "Tomorrow, send an email to Winston and say you want to be on Andy Walker's client list moving forward."

She gags into the microphone. "What don't you get about me not wanting to work with any of those bastards?"

"Andy's a good one," I promise.

Not only did Andy have my back when he didn't know I was around, but he stood up to Trevor and verified what I heard through the door. He's a real friend.

"Maybe I can find a way to get out of my contract and follow you—"

"I have no clue what my next steps are, Holls," I choke out the sad reality. "Stay with Permian. I'll always be here for you. To call or cry or chat. Okay?"

"Like a friend?"

I smile. "Like a friend."

"Good, because I've always thought of you as my best friend." She chuckles. "Have you talked to Cade?"

As if summoned, the doorbell rings, and I pull myself up. "About to. Good luck tonight!"

"Thanks! For someone who just quit her job, you sound like a total badass." Her praise keeps me from collapsing, but I can feel my body starting to shut down. "I'm about to watch *Bridge to Terabithia*. I'll shed some tears and play hard for you."

With a quiet goodbye, I open the door, and a wave of floral sweetness hits me. Flowers in every shade of pink, yellow, and orange spill across his broad torso. When I count eight bouquets, I try to smile at the lucky number, but my lips wobble.

"Eight for good luck?" I ask, the strength fading from my voice.

Cade's jaw tightens at the wavering sound, but he follows me into the house and to the kitchen without a word. Before I can put the flowers in water, he engulfs me in the hug I've needed since the moment I stormed out of Trevor's office.

It all comes rushing back to me. Trevor's hatred. My decision.

"I'm so sorry, baby," he whispers. "I'm so sorry."

After somehow managing to hold it together, his words and security shatter my composure. So I finally break and sob into his chest.

CHAPTER FORTY-ONE

Cade

"Want to tell me why you're not on this plane, Owens?"

There's a roughness to Rio's morning voice that reminds me of fingernails across a chalkboard. Dawson and Marcus have been calling nonstop since I didn't show up at the terminal half an hour ago. It's easy to dodge their calls, but Rio isn't a man you can, or should, ignore.

Dropping onto the uncomfortable glass seat, I chuckle. "Well, good morning to you too, Rio."

His growl is menacing. "Nope. I'm not in the mood to play around. We're leaving for California in thirty minutes, and your lanky ass isn't in a seat. Where are you, Cade?"

I start to respond, but the receptionist cuts me off. "Mr. McAllen will be with you soon."

Smiling at the man, I turn back to my conversation. "I'm at Permian."

There's a pause. "Is Shay sick?"

"No."

"Then what's going on? You never miss travel. You'd play through a hurricane if they let you. Is it something with your hip? Isla can—"

"My hip is fine. I swear." The dice in my pocket rattle as I readjust. "Shay quit. There was messed-up stuff happening with her boss."

His tone softens. "Messed up how?"

Sexism. Gross misogyny. There's a laundry list of disgusting things Shay was forced to deal with at work because of her terrible supervisor.

"Discrimination," is all I can get out. I still can't wrap my head around what Shay overheard. "A lot of it, Rio. So fucking much."

It has been one week since Shay left Permian behind, and I've hardly been around because of baseball. It's my job, and we're both aware how busy the season is, but I need to be in North Carolina with her.

"Damn." He exhales. "I'm sorry, Cade. I didn't know."

Nobody did. She doesn't regret her decision to quit, which I'm happy about, but she misses her clients. This morning, as I left her house to meet my team at the terminal, I watched her face crumple when she remembered she had nowhere to go. Still in her pajamas, she donned a brave face to kiss me goodbye. But I heard the way her breath caught the moment the door closed behind me.

It was then that I realized I had to do something.

"I'm not getting on the plane, and I'm not going to California. You can fine me, Rio. I don't care—"

"Good. I'm glad you don't care. If you ask me, *not* missing a series after something like this would've been more surprising. It's nice seeing you make room for things in your life outside of baseball. Although, I was looking forward to showing Cali how much you've grown."

My heart doesn't ache like it should at the prospect of missing tonight's game against my old franchise, the California Hornets. Four months ago, playing against the team that traded me away would have been the most important thing in my life, but as I sit here in this waiting room, I know there's nowhere I'd rather be right now.

"Send the team my love," I say quietly.

Rio chuckles. "I will. Give them hell, and we will too."

I'm blasted with sunshine as I hang up, warmed by Winston's smile. It's as welcoming as it was the day I signed my contract a few months ago.

"Cade! What a nice surprise. I thought you'd be on your way to California with the Pilots. It's going to be a fun series."

"Sitting out this series." I extend my hand. "Thanks for meeting me on such short notice."

To my astonishment, Winston's office is on the first floor. It's not what I expected from a place that screams executive status from the tile to the fresh air in the vents. The interior of his office is grounded too, with framed photos of his family on the bookshelves. There's no ego wall or oversized throne. The view of the parking lot through normal-sized windows makes him feel so much more human.

"Your office is so close to the door."

"Easier to greet everyone when I can pop my head out the door-way." Offering me a room-temperature water bottle, he takes a seat. "I'm guessing this is about your recent contract switch to Andy. Is everything going smoothly?"

My nod is immediate. Andy's as good as Shay promised. His charming demeanor hides a fire that I'm sure will be great when it comes to contract negotiations.

I may not understand salary arbitration, but he does.

"He's great. I'm actually here to talk about Shay."

Genuine sadness fills Winston's eyes. "I was very sorry to hear about her leaving Permian. It was such a surprise. Trevor was pretty upset about the whole thing when he let me know."

Just hearing his name pisses me off. "Did he tell you why she quit?

"Trevor mentioned she took the loss of Garrett Blane hard. I still remember my first big loss. To this day, it still haunts me." He folds his hands on the desk. "How's she doing?"

I force myself not to think about her puffy, red-rimmed eyes. Or the way she longingly looks at her phone that has been unusually quiet. "Not well, and I want to discuss the real reason she quit because it has nothing to do with Garrett."

Winston's brow arches. "Does she know you're here?"

Averting my eyes, I shake my head. "She didn't want me to come."

After showing up on her doorstep with all the flowers I could carry, she fell asleep in my arms, worn out from crying. I had half a mind to drive to Permian and speak to Trevor myself. That desperation only slightly faded when she told me she's at peace about her decision to quit. It may have been impulsive, but she knows it was the right thing to do. Losing her clients is the hardest part.

But I promised not to speak to Trevor, so I'm talking to Winston.

I leap out of the leather seat when the door bursts open behind me and bangs against the wall. Standing in the doorway is Andy, looking frazzled in his wrinkled dress shirt.

"Sorry I'm late," he says, straightening his tie. "I brought backup."

Four familiar faces smile at me from behind him. Holly skips into the spacious office first, with Brett, Lionel, and Victoria behind her. They look like they're ready to go to war as they stand behind me.

I'm not sure what made me call my agent as I sped to Permian to meet with Winston, but he dove into action and reached out to the people who spent the last year and a half with Shay. The people who love her.

Winston's eyes shift nervously between the six of us. "Can someone please explain what's going on?"

Taking a deep breath, I lean into the support of the people around me and dive in.

"We want to discuss the blatant discrimination Trevor Caldwell exhibited during his time working with Shaylene Turner. Starting with how he never submitted her letter of intent for the promotion."

Sizzling bacon is my third favorite sound. The second is the crack of a bat making perfect contact with a baseball. But number one will forever be Shay's laugh, soft and surprised, like it caught her off guard.

Which is exactly what fills my ears when she walks into the kitchen.

The only thing covering her body is the blue button-down I stripped out of when I got back from Permian. It looks way better on her. Partially buttoned, sleeves rolled to the elbow, and falling to the middle of her strong thighs.

"Not that I don't enjoy a nice strip of crispy bacon, but I'm still confused about why you're here when your team is in California for one of the most anticipated series of the season."

Clicking the oven light on, I check on the bacon. "I thought you'd be happier to see me."

Rolling her eyes, she sets her laptop on the counter. "Of course I am, but I know what you're doing."

I shrug. "Making my girlfriend breakfast for dinner before we watch *Legally Blonde* in bed until she falls asleep on my lap? You're right. That's exactly what I'm doing."

The mention of one of her favorite movies slightly distracts her.

"As great as that sounds, you're hovering, Cade."

"I'm not hovering."

"Then why did you miss this series? It's not like you to miss games."

It's not like the golden boy, but the real Cade doesn't care about anything else other than making sure the woman I love is okay. The decision to head to Permian instead of the terminal started off as impulsive, but the longer I drove, the more certain I was about my decision to deal with Rio's wrath and stay in North Carolina.

Stepping behind her, I prop my chin on her shoulder and breathe her in. "Shaylene Turner. You're more important to me than any game. Maybe you don't need me here, but I needed to be with you."

As if I hit the correct button, her spine loosens against my chest. "I love you. I did need you here."

"I love you even more," I say, stealing a glance at her laptop. The brightness is high enough to burn her retinas, and there are way too many tabs open. "Doing some research?"

"Something like that." She pushes the laptop aside, turns around, and hops onto the counter. "I'm job hunting."

Ah. That explains the spreadsheets. "Any luck so far?"

With a dramatic sniffle-sigh combo, she bangs her head against the cabinet behind her. "Nope. Can't find a single opening in North Carolina. It's as if every agency found out I was jobless and closed their listings to avoid having to deal with Shaylene Turner. The disgraced woman who dates her client—"

"Ex-client," I correct her with a scowl.

"Same difference," she grumbles, but she knows it's not. "I don't know what to do. There's a lot of interest from agencies in Florida and Texas, but that would mean I have to leave Clear Lake. Everything and everyone I love is here. My best friends. You."

The thought hurts, so I step back and head to the freezer because I know what will brighten the mood. "Even if you have to take a job in another state, leaving won't change anything. I'm yours no matter how many miles are between us."

"I do know that," she promises. "If I did have to move, I know we would be totally fine. But we just got back together. Being without you, even temporarily, isn't something I want to do."

"But being an agent makes you happy, and if that means you have to go, then you have to do what's best for you and your career." After dropping a few dark chocolate chips onto her open palm, I press my lips to her forehead. "Plus, spending my offseason in Texas doesn't sound like the worst thing in the world. Hot as hell, but I'd deal with it for you." That gets a laugh out of her, and the beautiful sound triggers an idea. "What about striking out on your own? Have you thought about that?"

As if that's the craziest thing I could've said, she tips her head to the side. "Like starting my own practice? No way. I've been an agent for less than two years. That would be insane."

I point at the two diplomas and framed certification exam paperwork hanging on the living room wall. "You're kidding, right?"

"Having degrees doesn't equal being a good agent. Jon went to freaking law school and was still an abusive dickwad. And Trevor said—"

My molars clash. "I don't care what my former agent did or what your misogynistic supervisor said. Never have and never will. So don't even try to use them as an excuse to not do something."

She chews on her bottom lip and lets her head fall forward. "Trevor may have gotten in my head a little bit."

"I know he did, baby. And I'm sorry." Caging her in, I place my hands beside her thighs. "Let's do a BYOB night, but not one where we break things down. Tonight's should stand for 'Be Your Own Boss.'"

Deep-brown eyes assess me like I've sprouted wings. "You're serious?"

"Dead serious. You're free of Permian and Trevor and can do anything. There's nothing stopping you from starting your own practice."

She tries to hop off the counter, but I don't budge. "There are a ton of things stopping me! I'd need to find an office space and build a new client list, which requires money. And a lot of it! I can't jump blindly into this with no plan, Cade."

"Then make one and let me jump with you. I want to help, and if that means covering the costs while you get started—"

"No." The heels of her feet slam against the cabinet. "You don't need to buy my love."

I can't help but smile as I step in between her legs. "Listen to me, Shay. I'm not trying to buy your love. All I want to do is see you succeed, and if that means helping with something I can give you, like money, then so be it. Because I'll also be giving you my time and support and energy. I believe in you as an agent, and I admire your love for your clients." I think of all of them in Winston's office this morning, vocalizing how important and special Shay is. How they can't imagine a career without her. "All you want is to help athletes, so let me help you."

Her voice cracks. "Are you really not trying to buy my love?"

"I don't need to. You're already completely obsessed with me." She shoves my chest, but she's smiling, and that's all that matters. My thumb brushes over her bottom lip, pausing on the small scar that you can only see if you're lucky enough to be this close. "You didn't leave Permian because you couldn't handle it. You left because you outgrew the space they tried to keep you in. So go for it. You don't need their permission anymore, baby."

For a second, she doesn't say a word. Just stares at me like I've given her something like a gift. It's like she's finally realizing she can have whatever she wants in this world.

Watching her pick up the pieces has been hard, but it's moments like this that are so rewarding.

"You think I can do it?" she whispers.

"Think?" I step closer, if that's even possible. "I *know* you can. You deserve the world, and I'm the lucky man who gets to watch you take it."

A shaky hand grips the front of my shirt, twists it tight, and pulls me into a kiss. It starts off sweet, like the chocolate on her tongue, but it doesn't say there long. All heat and honesty as I lift her and wrap her legs around my waist.

Our lips don't part as I carry her out of the kitchen and through the living room. Not as I kick open her bedroom door. Not even as the bedroom door closes behind us.

It's not until I fall on the mattress with her on top of me that I feel the shift. The moment it changes from comfort to hunger.

From *I need to feel safe* to *I need to feel you*.

Shay's hips roll rhythmically against mine, slow and deliberate, and I groan into her mouth at the feeling. No matter how many times we do this, it's still as exciting as the first. Except now, I know the exact sound she makes when I press my lips to that spot just below her ear. How and where she likes to be touched. How to build her up until she's begging for more.

Chilly fingers reach under my shirt and tug at the cotton. In one smooth motion, she pulls it over my head and tosses it to the ground. My hands caress her clothed waist, admiring the curves I could draw blind-folded. When my fingers finally slide under her—my—shirt, goose-bumps bloom across her skin.

"You're still wearing clothes."

"Fix it then," she challenges, lifting her arms.

Gladly.

I don't mean to rip the buttons, but I couldn't care less when I see what she's been hiding underneath. It's criminal how the lacy, lavender bra fits her. I try to take my time exploring the swell of her chest, but she tugs at my locs to lift my head.

"You're stalling," she rasps.

"No." I grin. "I'm appreciating."

My teeth graze her nipple, sending her grinding against my dick. God, I'm so hard, but all I want to do is taste her.

As if she weighs nothing, I flip us and press her back to the mattress. The look in her eye tells me she knows exactly where I'm going.

I kiss down her chest, over her stomach, and give some extra attention to her hips. When I reach the waistband of the matching lavender thong, I snap it against her skin and savor her sharp intake of breath.

"I'm the luckiest man alive." Easing the lavender thong down her thighs, I settle between parted legs. "Fuck, you're so pretty, baby," I murmur, but my eyes are on her face, pinched with ecstasy.

She fists the bedsheets and chokes out, "*Cade.*"

Grinning, I take in my favorite view. "Yes?"

It can't be easy to look upset and aroused at the same time, but she has perfected it. "If you don't touch me in the next five seconds, I'm going to walk out of here and—"

A grateful sob leaves her lips, hands flying to my locs to anchor herself as I work her over slowly. Tongue circling. Fingers teasing.

My girl is so responsive. All it takes is one finger to make her back arch. Two fingers send her hips into the air, and I have to press on her stomach with my free hand to hold her down.

"You're so good to me," she whispers, like it's a secret.

I pull back long enough to take in her flushed cheeks and parted lips.

"You make it easy," I breathe, and it's the truth.

With a moan that curls all the way through me, she comes hard, clenching around my fingers with glassy eyes locked on me.

She reaches for me immediately, and I crawl back up to her.

"You okay?" I whisper.

"More than," she replies against my lips.

Her laugh fills the room as she flips me onto my back and straddles my waist with the quiet kind of confidence that undoes me. The air is knocked from my lungs as I watch her. She's stunning up there, braids flowing around her body that's glittering with sweat in the pale light. Her confidence swells when she catches me watching her, and I know she sees the love in my eyes.

This is the kind of intimacy that only comes from knowing someone's body *and* their heart.

"Ready?" she asks, aligning herself with me.

Not trusting myself to speak, I nod. My fingers sink into her toned thighs as she lowers herself onto me with a satisfied moan. It may have been two years since we did this last, but we still fit perfectly together. We always did, and we always will.

I bring her face down to mine. "I love you."

"And I love you."

The hand I slide between us expertly finds her clit, and she sighs into my mouth. Our movements start to shift to something faster and more erratic, chasing something we can only reach together.

"C-Cade," she stutters.

"I know, baby. Me too."

I match her pace, thrusting up into her as she pushes herself down against me. It's only when our lips meet again that I feel her pussy flutter around my dick, and she has no other choice but to fall apart.

And I'm right there with her.

Limp with exhaustion and completely sated, my body sinks deeper into the plush mattress. I reach out to pull her closer, but she pops up and looks at the bedroom door.

She sniffs once. Then again. "What's that burning smell?"

"Son of a . . ." There's no time, so I leap out of bed. "My bacon!"

The melodious sound of her laugh follows me all the way to the kitchen. "You're never allowed to cook here again! Never!"

CHAPTER FORTY-TWO

Cade

BAJA BREEZE IS WARM in that way only old family places are, with bright yellow tables, hand-painted tiles, and orange vinyl booths that squeak when you shift too much, like I am right now.

Maybe that's why I chose Baja Breeze to finally close this chapter. It has always felt safe. From the owners, Maribel and Eduardo, letting us eat in the private room upstairs after practice, to the constant buzz of happy families.

This is the softest place to release the hard thing I've been carrying.

The door chimes as it opens, and I raise my hand at the woman gliding toward me. It's only seven in the morning, but Summer looks as chipper as the painted sunflowers on the walls.

"Nice dice," she breathes, looking down at the small cubes sitting in front of me for moral support. As she falls into the booth across from me, her hand is already deep inside her bag. The gray recorder is placed between us, but she doesn't turn it on. Instead, she cocks her brow at me. "Andy said you wanted to talk to me about something important. Must be pretty big if you're missing another series."

"It is." I slide a steaming mug of coffee across the table to her. "More important than any game."

She wraps her hands around the white ceramic cup and grins. "Now I'm intrigued." After taking a drink, she still doesn't reach for the recorder. "How's my favorite sports agent doing?"

The thought of Shay brings a smile to my lips. A big part of my decision to meet with Summer is because of her. In two weeks, the life Shay created for herself imploded, and every day since has reminded me why I admire her. She screamed and cried and then got back up. She doesn't regret fighting for her clients because everything she did was done with love. She doesn't regret going for Garrett Blane or the promotion, because she gave it her all. She doesn't regret quitting because she knows it was the right decision.

If she can face the world headfirst, I'll do the same.

"She's Shay," is the best answer I can give.

And thankfully, Summer seems pleased by it. "Tough as hell."

I nod in agreement and gesture at her recorder. "I'm ready when you are."

Swallowing hard, I watch as the red light appears.

For so long, I was ashamed of what happened between Jon and me. I wanted to hide behind the guise of privacy, but I know that the emotional abuse and manipulation I experienced didn't make me weak.

Last night, I told Kenneth, Mallory, and my mom everything. No minced words or diminished feelings. I held nothing back as I explained what I had gone through with Jon, describing my crumbling mental and physical health. After speaking for what felt like hours, I didn't make excuses. All I could do was apologize for keeping it from them for so long. I'm not sure why I expected anger or frustration, but when Kenneth rushed across the room and wrapped his arms around me, followed by Mallory and my mom, I felt whole and human.

I turn my head, spotting tufts of red hair in a booth not far away. Kenneth lifts his mug to his lips, but when he sees me, he gives me a small smile. "*You've got this,*" he mouths.

He's not only my ride home. He's my best friend.

Looking at Summer, I take a deep breath and begin. "Everyone was confused when I fired Jon soon after being traded to the Pilots. Staying quiet seemed easier, but it's time for people to know about the real Jon Sweeney. Not the cool agent he shows the world, but the manipulative man he truly is.

"In two years, I forgot who I was. I forgot why I fell in love with baseball. I forgot how to just be. And I'm certain there are a few athletes on his roster who feel the same way. They're probably wondering how they got to this point, wondering when things went wrong. I know how Jon gets into your head. How he makes you think he's the only one who'll fight for you. Makes you think he's the only person who can make you successful. That without him, you're nothing. And once he's got you, he uses your name, your success, and your loyalty to drain you dry." Outside the window, the sun creeps up higher, casting golden stripes across my arm that remind me something warm came out of the frigid hell I'm revisiting. "Then I had the opportunity to work with an agent who showed me what it truly meant to be cared for as a person. Not another athlete on her roster. I now know that I can't stay quiet about the truth when he's still putting athletes through what I dealt with. Making them hate their sport. Hate themselves."

When I finally stop talking, Summer shifts forward. "Holy shit, Cade. I'm so sorry." She loops her hair into her signature bun and winces. "If you don't mind me asking, why are you coming forward after almost four months?"

For many reasons, but the main one blares loudly.

"Because if he emotionally abused and manipulated me, he'll do it again. And he's likely been doing it for years."

I swallow hard at the thought of Garrett Blane. He, along with all of Jon's other clients, shouldn't have to work with a man who will break them while I sit idly by hiding the truth. My decision to not come forward earlier was selfish, and it's time to rectify that.

"You want to make sure he doesn't get away with it anymore." She inhales slowly, then finally smiles. "I'd love to take him down with you. Are you ready for this? Because I'll make sure every single person in the sports world knows the truth."

There's no need to think about my answer. Hightailing out of this restaurant wouldn't do anything but continue giving him power. As if buoyed by this knowledge, my voice is strengthened by steel.

"I'm ready, Summer. It's time to take down Jon Sweeney."

CHAPTER FORTY-THREE

Shay

BEING BACK AT PERMIAN feels weird.

It's a strange kind of disorientation to return to a place you thought you'd never see again. Especially when your departure was as heartbreaking as mine.

The ground still sparkles as if it's been recently buffed, and the scent of champagne dances in the air. The familiarity almost makes me feel nostalgic, remembering the first time I entered Permian for my interview.

My puffy, pink winter coat stood out against the dark gray walls, but I was ready to wow the internship coordinator. Little did I know, the interviewer, with his booming voice and blinding smile, was also the CEO, Winston McAllen. When I left his office over an hour later, I wanted nothing more than to be on his team.

I loved this place, even if it never loved me back.

The sharp click of my heels echoes throughout the empty lobby until I reach the scanner. I brace for rejection as I press my badge to it, but when the light blinks green and the lock releases, a sigh of relief slips out.

Cade, the girls, and Kenneth offered to clean out my office for me, but I need to do this myself.

Quitting wasn't a mistake, so I won't treat it like one.

A bittersweet smile tugs at my lips as I push open my office door, knowing it'll be the last time I ever walk through it.

The energy drink I sipped on the morning before the company BBQ has sweated out onto the wood, leaving behind a ring that I'll think about for the next ten business days. The little room is more lifeless than I remember, and I'm struck by an odd sense of delight to be leaving. For so long, I wanted this to be my place, but it wasn't meant to be.

I drop the large box onto my desk. "Better get started."

I'm knee-deep in papers and pens, boxing up what seems like a decade of work, when a knock startles me. The light's off and the door's closed, so I hope they assume I'm not here and leave. This was supposed to be my quiet goodbye, but the hinges squeak, and I glance up as the door opens.

"Oh. Hi, Winston."

When he flips the light switch, the easygoing smile I'm accustomed to is missing. This isn't the CEO I enjoyed working under for the last year and a half.

"Turner." He clears his throat. "I saw your car and wanted to see if you had a moment. I won't take much of your time."

Winston has been nothing but kind to me, so I oblige.

I stand to clear the chair across from me that's piled high with colored folders, but he beats me to it. My colleagues preferred digital notes, but I love a good hard copy that I can feel between my fingers and doodle on. Now I get to take home data to refer to in the future.

He lifts them with ease, but pauses and looks down at the blue folder on top. "You were doing work for Deshawn Miller?"

I nod. "He was Trevor's client, but I was his main contact for non-emergent issues after his injury and surgery. The transition was rough for him, so I attended physical therapy with him. Emotional support and all."

Deshawn has texted a few times. After getting cleared to return to basketball, he dove into preparing for preseason, and I've been cheering him on from afar.

His lips pinch. "I wish I would've known that."

I take a seat. "What did you want to talk about, Winston?"

"Yes, sorry. I wanted to reach out earlier, but I needed to take care of some things first." The look in his tired eyes is wild. "There's an ongoing investigation happening, and I need your input before making any final decisions."

"Investigation? About what?"

He bows his head. "About the way you were treated while working at Permian. Trevor's been put on probation."

Everything stops for a moment as Winston and I stare at each other. There's no way those words came out of his mouth.

"Probation." The word feels weird to say.

Come on, Shay. Say something better than that.

I straighten. "It's about fucking time."

There's no point in trying to hide my outburst, but thankfully, Winston laughs. "That's the reaction I was expecting." Before I can join his laughter, he grows serious. "I had quite a few people tell me what went on for the last two years between you two. I knew Trevor wasn't the easiest guy to be around, but he always had a solid handle on teaching newer agents. I should've checked in on you more, and I'm sorry for letting you down."

"I appreciate that," I say. "It's—"

"It's not okay. As the CEO of Permian, my job was to make sure you felt safe. I'm sorry you had to experience that." An exhale cuts through the tension. "I remember when you first walked in here for your interview. By the time you were back in your car, I was already drafting your offer for the internship. If I could've, I would've offered you a full-time position on the spot. On the first day of your internship, I told Trevor there was a full-time position with your name on it. I guess he took that as a threat." Winston places something in front of me. "You've got a lot of good people in your corner who care about you. The discrimination against you was verified by many sources, and it was easy to launch an investigation. Trevor's termination is imminent. He will never work at Permian again. Which is why I'm here."

The manilla folder he slides across the table is thin, and my mouth falls open when I read the first page. "A contract?"

He nods. "I'm in the market for a senior agent and would love to have you, if you're interested."

The typed offer looks too good to be true. "But it requires many more years of experience than I have."

"Sure, but you're the perfect person for the job. I've watched you grow and mature into the agent you are today. When I didn't see your name on the promotion list, I was shocked, but didn't want to give you any special treatment by asking. It's clear I should've, but that's behind us now. Moving forward, there's nobody I'd rather have to fill the position, so I hope you take it into consideration. Of course, I'm sure the world is desperate for their shot at Shaylene Turner."

Maybe, but none of them are in North Carolina.

None are close to Cade.

This position is *here*.

Closing the file, I look up. I've always wanted to work somewhere I'd be respected, have autonomy, and not dread coming to work.

With Trevor gone, that could be my new reality at Permian.

"Would I be able to work closely with clients? Trevor had so many that I managed the day-to-day and more basic tasks, but I like talking to my clients."

"That's why you're good at your job. You care." His smile is thin as his head shakes. "But probably not. It'll be difficult for you to manage every aspect on your own since you'll be overseeing many more clients than your current load allows. A junior agent would handle those things for you."

"Is that normal? To not be able to do everything for them?"

"Sadly, yes. In this field, the bigger you are, the harder it is to do everything. It's part of the growing process. Moving up and forward. But it's worth celebrating."

Winston is standing here, giving me the opportunity to get my clients back, but I might not even be able to represent them the way I want to. What about suit shopping for Brett? Or helping Holly through yet another nightmare of a date. When Lionel locks himself out of his social media once a month, who's going to help him reset his password and save it in a special file folder? Who will answer Victoria's questions about throwing themed parties? Will I be able to answer Delilah's messages about which home decoration to buy at the thrift store?

He chuckles, and I almost think he can see the questions bouncing around in my brain. "Take your time on the decision. I'll be here when you're ready." At the door, he grabs the knob and looks back. "And good on Cade for coming forward about Jon Sweeney. I heard Garrett dropped him the moment the article was released."

My heart swells at the reminder of Cade's bravery. Jon has officially been booted out of Cade's life. The world knows the truth, and Cade can finally rest easy.

I should accept the job offer right now. It's exactly what I want. Right? More pay. More success. More prestige.

So why can't I speak? This is the chance to have it all. Maybe not my version, but the *dream* version. But is it what I want? Having a personal relationship with every client is special to me. It's how I learn about them and can be there for them, and if having thirty of them means I can't do that, will I be happy?

I stand. "I can't take the job. Being with my clients every step of the way is what matters to me. Which means I need to do my own thing."

Cade was right. Over the last week, I played with the idea of opening my own practice, and this solidifies it.

Pride radiates from every single one of Winston's smile lines. "I had a feeling you'd say that. Email me if you ever need a reference. I can't wait to see what you do out there."

CHAPTER FORTY-FOUR

I smile at the business cards. "Do you like it?"

"Like it? I love it." Cade plays with the hot pink card. "It's a little bit of us."

"Yup," I breathe. "It's perfect."

The last three weeks have been a whirlwind. Getting a business up and running isn't for the weak. After leaving Permian for the last time, I dove into creating my dream sports agency. On day one, I chose a name. On day two, I filed for an LLC. On days three and four, I mapped out the business I wanted to create. A comfortable place run by a hands-on agent who sees clients as people while helping them reach their goals with happy bodies and minds.

By the end of the first week, I had an EIN, a business email, social media handles, and a business bank account. During the second week, I finalized my pitch deck that explains who I am, what I do, and why an athlete should work with me. At the beginning of the third week, I realized I had gotten into the routine of eating meals instead of chugging caffeine drinks, sleeping more than three hours a day, and taking my medicine regularly.

My PCOS thanks me for it every day.

"I'll be paying you back," I tell Cade. And replenishing my savings account that is nearly empty these days.

"Whatever you say, Shay baby." He looks over my shoulder at my running list of tasks on the pink sticky notes that I stuck to the dining room wall. "You're getting close. What's next?"

My finger taps a line. *Find an office space.* Flyers of every commercial office for rent in Clear Lake are spread along the dining table, and I slide my favorite toward him. "This one's expensive, but the coffee shop downstairs will keep me sane and caffeinated."

Cade hums at my top choice. He's probably falling in love with the emerald tile of the small office on the second floor like I did. Then he asks my least favorite question.

"Does it fit your business budget?"

I groan. "Nope. At this point, I'll be working from home or in a box on the side of the road."

His hand brushes mine for a reassuring second before an incoming video call pops up. Since leaving Permian, my phone has been too quiet, which is probably why we both jump at the sound.

An assortment of worst-case scenarios run through my mind as I click the green button. "What's going on? Are you okay? How's the knee?"

Deshawn snorts. "Jeez, Shay. I'm healthy. Texting is cool and all, but I haven't heard your voice since everything went down. Can't a guy call to say hi to his old friend?"

Cade waves before walking into the kitchen to give us some privacy. Talking to my former clients is a cacophony of emotions. Andy's doing an amazing job, which is all I could ask for, but I miss taking care of them. I receive daily texts, even from Lionel, with updates and GIFs and unlimited love.

"I'm sorry." I rub the back of my neck. "I'm really glad you called."

Deshawn shifts, revealing an oddly shaped couch behind him. I remember seeing it in a magazine interview he did in his home. "Saw you started an Instagram for your own sports agency. How's that going?"

"Slow," I groan, looking at my list of unfinished tasks. "The good news is that I have the admin stuff done. All I need is a space and some clients."

And to market myself to death. I've got to get my name out there and find people willing to give me a chance.

"How many clients are you planning to take on?"

Propping my phone against a vase of flowers, I grin. "Tough question. I want the agency to focus on quality over quantity. Like at Permian, my main priority will be taking care of my clients and giving them the attention they deserve, so I think a safe number is eight. Got any teammates looking for an agent?"

This time, Deshawn lets out a full-bodied laugh. "Probably, but I'm actually looking for myself."

I pause. "Trevor is your agent."

"*Was*," he corrects me. "I'm free now that the shithead was terminated for discrimination. And to celebrate, I decided it's time to take my business elsewhere. You see, there's an agent who spent a lot of her very limited free time with me at physical therapy. She sat beside me when I was at my lowest, and I don't feel comfortable starting my season without her by my side as my full-time agent. Not agent adjacent."

The air leaves my chest in a very unprofessional wheeze. "You want me to be your agent?"

"I do," Deshawn says. "I meant what I said. I can't imagine getting back on the court without you. So, what do you say, Shay?"

"I . . ." I swallow over a lump of emotion. "Welcome to the Even Odds team, Deshawn."

After scheduling a meeting and a quick goodbye, I hang up before releasing a scream so loud that it shakes the whole house. Cade rushes back into the room and falls to his knees in front of me, gripping my hand so hard, it's the only reason I'm sure I'm not dreaming right now.

"You have a client."

My head lolls backward. "I have a client."

"A professional basketball player. And he wants you beside him."

"He wants *me*," I whisper.

In an instant, Cade pulls me out of the chair and starts spinning us in circles around the room. The pink walls are blurred, but his smile is abundantly clear as I look down at him. Wrapped in his arms, I'm sure this is the kind of happiness people spend their whole lives searching for.

And I'm lucky enough to say I've found it.

When he finally stops, his eyes glitter. "Now let's get to Slim Jim's."

It's been too long since I've seen my friend.

People may find it weird to consider a man in his fifties a friend, but Jimmy was the first friend I made after moving to Clear Lake for college. It didn't matter that all we did was hit baseballs.

When he hugs me, I squeeze him a little tighter than usual.

"How's school going?" I ask, dropping into the seat.

"Either the kids keep getting crazier or I'm getting too old for this." Teaching world history to a bunch of hormonal teenagers can't be easy. It's only the second week of September, but his sigh tells me he's already counting down the days until Thanksgiving break.

It's rare that he's at the batting cages on a Tuesday afternoon, and I couldn't miss my opportunity to see him when he texted me.

"Definitely the former," I say. "Why is the closed sign on the door? Is there a private event happening?"

"Something like that. Congrats on Even Odds. What's next?"

I look down. "An office, but if I'm being honest, I'm thinking about being completely virtual at this point. Most deals are made over the phone anyway, so why should I find a space and spend all that money? I can work from home or in a coffee shop."

"That's definitely cheaper. What do you want out of a space?"

After spending years in an office where I felt suffocated and where I couldn't stand staying for too long, I know what I *don't* want.

"I *need* somewhere comfortable. Where I don't dread coming into work every day. I would love a shorter commute. I know Charlotte is probably the best place to have an office, since it's the heart of so many North Carolina teams, but I'd rather be here in Clear Lake. I think it would be nice to show athletes how special our little town is, you know?"

This place is my home. With a professional athlete family and divorced parents, I was always on the move. For so long I thought that was normal, but now, I've made myself a home and found people who make leaving seem impossible.

"What'll you do if Cade gets traded and leaves North Carolina?"

Thinking of him leaving makes my chest tighten, but a trust we didn't have the first time thrums between us now. "We may have failed at the long-distance thing before, but we won't let that happen again. If staying here is what's best for my business, I will. Cade will always come back."

Opening his arms wide, Jimmy smiles. "So work here at Slim Jim's. That room became your office the moment you claimed it. Couldn't rent it out to anyone because that would mean you'd stop coming by. Nobody loves this place like you do, Shay. And if you're here, I'll be able to keep a close eye on you and make sure you're getting rest. But you'll have to buy new furniture. That stuff in there is junk."

Renting the spare office at Slim Jim Batting never crossed my mind. It may not come with a coffee shop nearby, but it has Jimmy, which makes it my dream location.

"Tell me how much rent is, and I'll start decorating immediately."

Our extended hands shake in agreement. "Wonderful, partner. Now, I think your guy is waiting for you."

I turn to find Cade's cheek pressed against the glass.

After giving him one last hug, Jimmy leaves us alone in the office, and I glare at Cade. "You knew that would happen, didn't you?"

The smug man doesn't even have the decency to look guilty. "I may have had ulterior motives in bringing up a space this morning, yes. But only because I knew you hadn't thought about here yet. Jimmy was waiting for you to bring it up, so I pushed it." His hug is warm and grounding. "You know I'm incredibly proud of you, right?"

I look up at him. "Hmm. Not sure. Maybe you should tell me again."

"I'm so"—a kiss to my forehead—"proud of"—one to my nose—"you," he breathes, before pressing his lips against mine. "Not only are you the best agent, but you're the greatest person I know. I love you so much, Shay baby."

"You better," I whisper. "Because it's you for me."

"And you for me," he finishes.

Our arms brush as we make our way down the hallway to the cages, and for a second, it feels like those first few visits to Slim Jim Batting all over again. Back then, I was a bundle of nerves about being with him without our best friends as a buffer. The first time his hand grazed mine, I told myself it was an accident. Then I found out he had been doing it for weeks, trying to get my attention.

Just before we reach the door to the cages, he tugs on my hand and brings us to an abrupt stop.

"Now don't be mad, but I have a surprise for you."

That alone triggers fear because I hate surprises. But when the cackle I've heard during countless phone calls, voice memos, and voicemails rings out from the cages, I break into a run and push open the heavy door. Hands pull me in before I can make sense of what's happening.

The person closest to me smells like she ate a handful of sour candy and bathed in leftover sugar, and I soak it all in.

"I missed you," Holly chuckles into my neck.

"I missed her more!" Brett hollers. "I need a hug too!"

"Squeeze her extra hard for me, Brett!" Delilah laughs.

My eyes bounce between the six people smiling back at me. Holly, Victoria, Lionel, Brett, Deshawn, and Delilah—who's joining on a video call—are all watching me with the same excited glitter that has been in Cade's eyes since this morning.

He was hiding this all along.

Draping a muscular arm over my shoulder, Victoria laughs. "We couldn't let you open a sports agency without celebrating you!"

Guilt cracks my broken heart. "I didn't want you to think I was trying to replace you guys, but I couldn't go back to—"

"We don't want you to ever go back to Permian," Brett chimes in. "Like ever. Actually, we're here to tell you that we'll all be needing new representation soon."

Hope replaces the guilt. "What?"

"You see," Lionel says, pointing over my head. "Your boyfriend brought a very long pattern of discrimination to light, and we agreed that none of us would be re-signing our contracts when they end."

"What about Andy? You can't—"

"Don't worry about me." The man himself steps through the door with pink tulips in hand. "They've never been mine, Turner. I'm just taking care of them until they can re-sign with you."

I rush to my friend and give him a hug. "What about your job?"

"I'll be fine. Once you get them back, I'll build my clientele."

Holly leaps into the air. "Delilah said she wanted to be first, but absolutely not! Me first! I have to be your first client!"

Pursing my lips, my eyes dart to Deshawn. When I don't smile back, her face pales. "Actually . . ."

"*Please* don't ruin my day, Shaylene. My mascara isn't waterproof."

"Deshawn was my first client. We made it official this morning."

Like a rabid animal, Holly leaps at him. "Judas! You knew we would all be here today to surprise her, and you just wanted to beat me! I expected that from Victoria, but not you."

He takes the beating with a smile, and I know he's going to be a great addition to the team. They already treat him like a brother.

Smoothing her ponytail, Holly collects herself. "I guess second place isn't too bad."

"That's the mindset of a loser," Brett whispers in her ear. "First loser can't feel good, Holls."

I laugh. "Give me a little bit to get settled, and then we can all talk. Go play some baseball. There's plenty of room for everyone!"

For the first time ever, I feel joy at the place where I work. It's full of happiness and people who care for and respect each other. I'm not afraid of negativity around every corner.

This is my dream.

Cade drapes his arm over my shoulders as we watch Brett and Holly fight over the same bat. Lionel, Andy, and Deshawn are by the mural, taking selfies with Cade's face. Victoria applies purple lipstick in the phone's camera, smiling as Delilah gushes about the color.

"So, this is how it feels," I say.

Cade looks down at me. "How what feels?"

I lean against him and smile. "How it feels to have it all."

EPILOGUE

Cade

THREE MONTHS LATER

I HATE MOVING.

Usually, at least. I've moved multiple times in the last two years, but I'm sure this will be the final time I have to pack my belongings, pile them into a moving truck, and unpack them all over again.

Moving in after three months of dating may seem quick to some people, but today is years in the making.

"Why are your bathroom boxes so dang heavy? I thought men only have a toothbrush, toothpaste, and a 5-in-1 body wash that they use for everything from their face to their ass."

With a kiss to Shay's forehead, I scoop the box from her arms. "Blame Lula for that. And ouch. You know my hygiene is better than a teenager's."

This is only the first of four boxes filled with Loc & Key products. Our partnership is thriving, and with Andy still by my side, we extended our contract.

In the bathroom, I place the box on the ground with the others and take in the space. Two towels hang over the door. Two toothbrushes sit beside the double sinks. Two pairs of slippers hide beneath the counter, both fuzzy and pink because that's what she wanted.

There's two of everything because this is now *our* bathroom.

Shay has lovingly reminded me multiple times that this place belongs to us and that I shouldn't worry about taking up too much space. And it's clear she meant it. Pieces of me are woven into every part of the house. My pillows sit to the right of hers, with my alarm clock and glasses on the nightstand. Video games are stacked beside her rom-com DVDs under the television. The beanbag chair I've had since Kenneth gave it to me on my sixteenth birthday sits in the corner. Photos that once lined the walls of my home now line the walls of *our* home, updated with pictures of us over the last three months.

When I walk into the kitchen, Shay is hunched over my lone box of kitchen supplies. We traded my fridge for hers, but other than a few essentials, I'm starting fresh.

"You donated my favorite glass cups but kept the janky toaster?" She glares at the beat-up toaster like it personally offended her.

"She's not *janky*." I pick it up and rub a hand over the toaster protectively. "She has character."

"She has tetanus," Shay rebuffs before snatching it. "It's been years. You need to throw it away already. It literally fell off the back of Kenneth's truck on the highway, shocked you when you tried to unplug it, and Mallory punted it after it burned her waffle."

MalPal punted it twice, but I can't get rid of it.

Shay rolls her eyes, but instead of tossing it into the black trash bag like she wants to, she slides it onto the counter beside her completely functional one.

It may not seem like much, but it's damn near a declaration of love.

To be fair, everything about me moving in has seemed intentional and full of love. She stocked the pantry with my favorite snacks, replaced the batteries in the smoke alarms because she's giving me another chance to cook for her, and made plenty of room for my clothes in the closet.

And not once has she checked her phone.

There was a time when she would've spent the whole day with her phone in hand, sending emails, fielding phone calls, and doing whatever her supervisor wanted, but things are different now. She's her own boss, running Even Odds Sports Agency in a way that makes her happy.

She's lighter now, and it's noticeable as she plops onto the floor in the living room. There's still that busy nature I love, built by ambition and running on caffeine, but there's a calm that allows her to enjoy this moment.

She's fully present and completely mine.

The boxes surrounding us are filled with my childhood baseball memories. Mom didn't want a single piece of memorabilia to be forgotten or lost, so she collected them and boxed them up, hiding them in her attic until I was ready to take them.

Shay pulls out twelve rusted trophies. "If these are just from first grade, I don't think there's going to be enough room on the mantle."

"They can go in storage." I laugh, opening another box that has at least ten more identical trophies. "I guess Mom was happy to get rid of all of my childhood boxes, because she gave me everything she could."

"Or she knew you'd want to fill this space with parts of you." She digs around and pulls out something that makes my heart squeeze. "Like your first baseball glove. This has to stay out."

"Are you sure?" I ask. "I don't want to overrun your house—"

"*Our* house," she corrects me again. "This is our home as of this morning when we left your house empty and you officially started leasing it. I know you've moved around a lot for baseball, and you may get traded and have to leave Clear Lake someday, but this will always be your home, Cade. Your permanent place. Somewhere you can always come back to."

I love the sound of that.

This feels like home.

Shay feels like home.

"Plus," she sings, "it'll fit in with the other stuff. We've got your College World Series rings. And we can't forget about your Rookie of the Year plaque. Anytime someone comes over, they'll see your past and present in baseball."

A month has passed since I received the award, and it still doesn't feel real. Coming back to North Carolina changed my life in ways I'll never forget. The way I saw myself was altered in a matter of three months, and I owe it all to the wrecking ball of an agent sitting in front of me.

Telling the world about Jon wasn't the end of my story with him. Instead, I was approached by more of his old clients who were ready to tell their stories of how Jon pushed them past the brink and into a dangerous spiral of fear. Articles continue to be printed and shared about all the terrible things he did to his clients, like sending one into an early retirement after an injury.

After that, there was no saving his career. We celebrated with champagne when he was no longer listed as an agent on the ProPact website.

And in two semesters, I'll be able to add my Clear Lake University diploma to the wall beside Shay's. Offseason has been full of studying, spending my days with her, and just being.

Baseball is fun again. Life is fun again. Being me is fun again.

When she looks up from the glove, her bottom lip is trembling.

"You okay?" I ask.

She nods, then, quietly says, "It's just real now."

Taking her hand, I pull her up and lead her to the couch. It's littered with boxes, blankets, and picture frames, but I find a space for us and set her onto my lap. With my chin against her collarbone and arms around her waist, she settles into me like it's second nature.

"It was real before," I say. "Moving in together is the next step."

"A big and fun step." She turns in my arms and props her legs across the rolled-up rug. It's a housewarming gift from her mom, who's excited to meet me next month. "Are you sure you're ready for my middle-of-the-night pacing when a client's having a meltdown?"

I smile, thinking of her full client list. Holly, Victoria, Brett, Delilah, and Lionel rejoined her team not long after Even Odds officially opened. Deshawn is healthy and playing like a star. Simon Godfrey, the second baseman who pitched himself to her at the All-Star Game, also joined her team a few weeks ago. And yesterday afternoon, Garrett Blane called and pitched himself to her.

She's a superstar. She wanted eight clients. She secured eight clients.

"As long as you're pacing in our bedroom," I say, "I don't mind at all."

She looks around the house, eyes full of certainty. "Welcome home, Cade. I made space."

I smile. "And I brought the dark chocolate chips."

Her laugh bounces off the walls of our home, where there's dozens of baseball trophies, an endless pile of rom-coms, liters of bubble bath liquid, a busted toaster on the counter, and love in every corner.

"What are the odds we get everything we've ever wanted?" she asks.

Our lips meet, and I savor it.

"Better than even odds. *This* is everything I've ever wanted."

ACKNOWLEDGEMENTS

For a while, I didn't think I'd make it to this point in the book. Shay and Cade, you were a pain in the butt to write, but I love you two more than I ever thought was possible. Thank you for reminding me that just being myself is enough and always will be.

To my mom, I'll always start with you. You cheer so loudly for me that even my doubts can't drown you out. I carry you and your encouragement with me everywhere. I love you, Momma.

To my dad, thank you for championing me and supporting every single thing I do in life. From running, to orchestra, to changing my major, to writing books. Forever your Sweet Pea. I love you. PS: Sorry it's not a PhD dissertation. ;)

To my best friends. Emma, I still credit you for helping me jump into the world of writing my own stories. Thank you for continuing to be in my corner and being the best critique partner and friend. Megan, found family will always remind me of you. Life moves forward and changes, and so do we, but we're always going to be us. Marianne, Elisabeth, and Clarissa, there's no way to thank you enough for over a decade of friendship. The Clear Lake Quartet will always remind me of you three. Tyler and Cheyenne, you've been here since the beginning. Thank you for never giving up on me, even when I blew up your phones. To all of you, you're stuck with me forever.

To Marja and Vai. Be prepared to be in every single book I write until the end. There's not a chance this book would be here if it weren't for our never-ending phone calls and voice memos. I said this in the acknowledgements for Fortunate Misfortune, but it's still valid now that we're here for Even Odds. There are author-friends and friend-friends, and I'm thankful you two are both of those.

To my alpha and beta readers: Erica, Pres, K.C., Elisabeth, Marja, Vai, Dom, Taylor, Jess, Emma, and Dani (my sensitivity reader and a dietitian I admire). Your feedback helped Even Odds grow and evolve into the story it is today. From your hilarious comments, to catching issues my brain couldn't spot, to helping me give Shay and Cade the story the deserve. Thank you from the bottom of my heart.

To Tracy Pope, my wonderful editor. Editing a book I wrote has to be daunting, especially when you have to answer a million questions and panicked texts from me, but you do it with grace and patience. You've helped me grow as a storyteller and human being. Thank you, thank you, thank you.

To Rachel, my phenomenal proofreader. Everything I had heard about you was such high praise, and I'm so lucky to have been able to experience it firsthand. Thank you for catching things I never would've seen and for doing it with a smile. You champion your authors, and I'm so happy to have you on my team.

And lastly to Boone. Even Odds is all about chances. The chances of meeting you at twenty-one and falling in love were low, but look at us now. Years later, and you're still my favorite person. Our life together is pretty chaotic, with school and writing and the dogs, but I wouldn't change a thing. Thank you for answering every baseball question, taking me to games, and taking my "research projects" seriously. You still win the award for "Best Husband" in my book. I love you, honey.

About the Author

Miah Onsha is a romance author and lover of books. She is dedicated to not only crafting stories of real love, but also to filling a gap she keenly felt in her own youth. Through her writing, she endeavors to provide the representation and affirmation that she yearned for as a young reader. As a registered dietitian with a passion for nutrition education, each story she writes holds a piece of that love through the eyes of real characters and real experiences. In each book, you will find healthy relationships, found family, and a whole lot of love.

Miah is based out of Texas and surrounded by her wonderful family, two perfect dogs, and the best friends a woman could ask for.

For inquiries, contact Miah Onsha at hello@authormiahonsha.com.

www.ingramcontent.com/pod-product-compliance
Lightning Source LLC
Chambersburg PA
CBHW020229010826
48973CB00006B/1436